One Summer

Rachel Billington

One Summer

ORION

First published in Great Britain in 2006 by Orion,
an imprint of the Orion Publishing Group Ltd.

1 3 5 7 9 10 8 6 4 2

A CIP catalogue record for this book
is available from the British Library.

ISBN-13 978 0 75286 853 0 (hardback)
ISBN-10 0 75286 853 5 (hardback)

Typeset by Deltatype Ltd, Birkenhead, Merseyside

Printed in Great Britain by Clays Ltd, St Ives plc

The Orion Publishing Group's policy is to use papers that
are natural, renewable and recyclable products and made
from wood grown in sustainable forests. The logging and
manufacturing processes are expected to conform to the
environmental regulations of the country of origin.

The Orion Publishing Group Ltd
Orion House
5 Upper Saint Martin's Lane
London, WC2H 9EA

CHAPTER ONE

2004

The church was small, very English, very charming. I had arrived far too early, driving unerringly through narrow, twisting roads and villages following one after the other with exhausting rapidity: Witley, Wormley, Hambledon. It had been raining when I left London. By the time I reached the tumbled graveyard, protected by two ragged yews, the rain had reduced itself to a fine mist that clung to the air and veiled the distant countryside in which, surprisingly, not one of the many villages I had passed through was visible.

I suppose it was picturesque but my mood was too discordant to admit anything but criticism. It was July. It was raining, so this must be England. I was a fool to be here, a fool to be clothed in morning dress – the coat had belonged to my father and smelt of mothballs – a fool to have drunk half a bottle of Scotch the night before, a fool to be so early.

'Can I help you, sir?'

It was dim at the back of the church where I sat and I hadn't been aware of anyone approaching.

'I'm early.'

The man who stood politely in front of me had a smooth, youngish face but his hair was completely white, like that of someone who has survived a shock. 'Early for what, if I may intrude?'

I straightened up. My thoughts had been so inward that, apart from the rain and the yew trees, I had hardly taken in my surroundings. 'The wedding.'

'I was afraid that might be the case. You didn't notice the lack of flowers?'

I looked round and saw that, apart from a couple of small bunches on a faraway altar, there was a complete lack of floral decoration.

'The wedding's off, sir. I thought there might be the odd guest who slipped through the net.'

'What net?' I was trying hard not to imagine that this cancellation could mean anything. My heart, weakened by the whisky, jumped strangely.

'They assured me everyone had been informed.' His diction was formal, like a thirties butler.

'I've been abroad. Until last night.' I put a bit more vigour into my voice.

'So, what's the story?'

'The bride's father is indisposed. Just a postponement.'

'I suppose you're the churchwarden,' I was chatting to calm myself.

'One of them. The responsible one.' He winked at me. His eyes were pale blue and, with one closed, he had a leering air.

'And has another date been set?' These words were harder to get out.

'Not so far as I know. But, then, I'm not the priest-in-charge, am I?'

'Thank you.' I stood up and walked briskly to the door, meaning to find my car and drive back to my musty flat in London, where I'd lain awake all night torturing myself. But the rain made me hesitate. It was coming down in thick silver sheets. Already a small stream was running swiftly along the sloping path. Above my head a drainpipe gurgled in what sounded like celebration. I pulled out my mobile.

'You'll not find that much use here, sir.'

The churchwarden sounded pleased. I could hardly blame him: it was not often such an obvious loser came to cheer up the day.

'Is there a telephone?'

'Oh, no.' He paused. 'Of course I have one.'

'I suppose you do.' I felt my small surge of energy dissipating. Who had I planned to call? Who would want my call? It was nearly fourteen years since I'd been in England. I had hardly ever called her number anyway.

'You can use mine, if you like.' The churchwarden indicated his home, a stone-built cottage just outside the graveyard.

I hesitated once more, then stepped out into the rain. 'You're very kind.'

We were both soaked in the short journey to the churchwarden's doorstep. His hair, I noticed, had not darkened – as if it had a water-repellent property.

'Mother.' He moved inside motioning me to stay where I was. I huddled obediently under a narrow porch. 'I've a wedding guest to use the telephone.' He was shouting so I could hear perfectly, although not the response. I tried to remember the exact line from the New Testament about the wedding guest but instead recalled the wedding guest who is stopped by the scrawny hand of the Ancient Mariner, determined to recount his tale of woe.

'Come in. The telephone's in the hallway but I like to inform my mother if there's a stranger in the home.' Through the open door I could see a very old lady wearing a plaid dressing-gown. Her eyes were closed, as if she slept. She might as well have been dead.

'Is she asleep?'

'As blind as she's deaf so she feels there's no point in opening her eyes.'

My acute depression opened a crack into a wider world of loss. I wanted to ask why such a person continued to live.

I took up the receiver and dialled what might have been her number. My companion receded tactfully to a room at the end of the hall.

'The number you have dialled requires an additional zero after the first digit. The number you have dialled …' So I had got it very nearly right. Or perhaps it had changed over the years. I replaced the receiver, noticing as I did so that I'd made a small puddle on the carpet, like an untrained puppy.

'Did you get through?'

'I missed a digit. Of course I'll pay you for the call.' I dialled again.

'Yes?' A woman had answered the phone. Not her. What did I think I was up to?

'Yes? Hello! Who is it?' In a moment she would ring off. I could recognise Catherine now. She must be over sixty. Why was age so important? But, then, it always had been. In some people's view the most important thing.

'I'm sorry.' It was too much. I put down the receiver for the second time.

My hands were shaking and my palms were wet, but not from the rain. How had I ever thought I could come to the wedding as a guest? Perhaps they had moved the ceremony to another church because, despite all my efforts, someone had discovered my approach. Thank God. Thank God I had been saved by her father's illness. Until now I had not quite believed it was real, I realised, just a way of stopping the wedding.

'No luck.' I started to leave the hallway.

'Would you like a cup of tea? My mother likes a cup of tea and a biscuit.'

Had I really been planning to visit that house? In the rain? So late in the day? It felt much later than tea-time. I was agitated. My limbs felt as if they were strung on wire like a puppet's, ready to dance. Like a skeleton's. 'Is there a hotel nearby?'

The churchwarden seemed shocked, as if I'd suggested visiting a brothel.

'Don't worry. I think I passed one on the way. You've been very kind.' I was in a hurry to be on my own, away from his stares and suppositions, away from his aged mother. I forced myself to go to the door calmly, to turn, wave and say, 'thank you again,' as he stood silently, watching me with judging eyes. Since that summer's day, any sort of judgement has pushed me into panic.

But I had learnt to control the feeling and walked quietly enough to my car. Once inside, I watched the rain sliding down the windscreen and thought, So she hasn't married today. I allowed this knowledge to seep through me until I understood it was true. At least, it was true for today. I would find a hotel and order champagne.

I drove slowly, getting my bearings after my long absence. My own house had been about ten miles away from the church, over a ridge of hills crowned with pale geometric shapes, houses inadequately disguised by trees. Hers had been only three miles away. The choice of the church for the wedding had already told me her family still lived there, even before I'd heard Catherine's voice.

Without making any conscious decisions, I found myself turning off along a road through thick pinewoods. The afternoon, which was already dark with rain, became darker, the sky almost invisible. After ten minutes, the trees began to thin and a steely glint appeared ahead and to the right. I knew exactly where I was now. I started as a car shot by impatiently. I was hardly moving. On my right was a large expanse of smooth water surrounded to its brink by trees. To my left – I was lingering – just short of it stood a two-storey brick building with a wide forecourt and a sign advertising 'Fresh Ponds Hotel'.

Was this what my wily unconsciousness had been planning all along, even when I was asking the churchwarden if he knew a nearby hotel? Another car flashed by, letting me know with a beep on his horn. I pulled myself together enough to drive on another hundred yards and drew up in the hotel car park. I felt ashamed to be where I was, as guilty as a murderer who revisits the scene of his crime. I couldn't really be planning to stay here, could I?

I got out of my car and walked towards the hotel. It had started raining again but I hardly noticed.

'Yes, sir?'

The reception area meant nothing to me. Perhaps it had been renovated; more probably, I had been too wound up on that other occasion to notice. A man was coming towards me. Tall, thin, almost gaunt, the dark sunburn of his creased face made more startling by thick grey hair, cut short but raggedly. I paused for a second in front of the mirror. I knew I'd lost weight recently but I hadn't been aware quite how much my appearance had changed. Trying to overcome the shock with irony, I thought that at least I hadn't grown a beard, like other runaways.

'May I help you, sir?'

'I'd like a room. On the top floor. At the front.' Oh, what memories! The receptionist, a young woman with bluish stripes in dark hair, stared at me curiously.

'I've been to a wedding. I need a rest.'

'You'll have to book for a full night.'

'Fine.' I gave her my credit card, she gave me a key, but then I found myself unable to go upstairs. 'Where can I get a drink?'

'The bar's to the right.'

It was surprisingly full of people after the spacious emptiness of Reception. I remembered my resolve to order champagne.

'I'd like a bottle of champagne. The best you've got.' My words caused a faint stir around me but the barman was quickly efficient, indicating a table in the corner and asking me whether Piper Heidsieck would be OK. 'It's all we've got chilled.'

'Fine.'

When the bottle arrived, steaming icily from the top, I remembered that I had ordered champagne on that other occasion, even though I knew she hardly drank alcohol. Perhaps I'd needed to be a little drunk.

'You'll never get through all that on your own.' I'd already swigged nearly half the bottle when a man with a waistcoat as red as his face came up to me.

'You're in need, are you?' I think my tone was friendly.

'That's a good one. I'll remember that. In need.' He laughed heartily. 'Yes, I should say so. I haven't seen you here on a Saturday before.'

'Tell you what.' I stood up. 'You drink my health in what's left.' I started towards the door.

'Hey, I didn't mean ...'

I was outside. It was still raining but the alcohol had made me warm and confident. I took off my ridiculous tailcoat and put it on the back seat, before getting into the car. It was half past three. I could be at her house in ten minutes.

Time has a funny way of behaving when things are out of order. The months following that summer's day, before I fled England, seemed like a few days to me. Yet once I had reached Chile, time stretched terrifyingly, each day like a month, an endless ocean of time in which I couldn't decide whether to sink or swim. Of course I never wrote another word.

The moment I re-entered England I was back in the time zone of the tragedy. The evening and the night spent in London after my arrival from Heathrow had passed in a blank of misery. The sterile air of the flat, unused for so many years, pressed heavily around me as I sat or lay unmoving. My hand, lifting my whisky glass or pouring from the bottle, was the only measure of time passing. When I went to the lavatory and flushed it, the noise sounded as loud as a cataract. I glanced at my watch again. In ten minutes I could be at her house. I tried to work out what time it would be in Valparaiso. I live high up in one of the poorest *cerros*. My view over the harbour is splendid but most of my neighbours are insalubrious, if not actually dangerous. In the first few years I was mugged regularly. Now they leave me alone. It was what I had wanted. What I deserved. My greatest hope in those early years was that there'd be a repeat of the 1906 earthquake, and the whole ramshackle place, including me, particularly me, would be wiped out. But the tenacity of the human spirit had caught me out. Or maybe it was something else.

If I sat in the car inactive much longer the effect of the champagne would wear off. I turned on the engine and began to drive. It is remarkable how mechanical capabilities remain even when a man has become a zombie. Our hearts may be dead or numbed, but the hand still moves to the ignition, the feet work the pedals as efficiently as ever, the eye watches for traffic ahead.

The turning to the house had always come as a surprise. It had been marked by a sign, 'Concealed Entrance', but it was so surrounded by shrubs and bushy trees that it gave the impression of being a very half-hearted invitation to visitors. I had driven into the driveway almost every weekday for a long spring and summer but now I missed it altogether. I only noticed this after I'd passed landmarks beyond the house, other entrances, one with new white stone dogs on columns, a garage, more houses visible from the road. Hers had been tucked into the countryside within its own three-acre domain.

I turned the car round and drove back slowly, The 'concealed entrance' was in the past. The shrubs had been cleared and a gravel roadway led into a small estate of four houses, each with its own garage and small garden. I couldn't understand what had happened to her house until I saw a narrow tarmacked drive leading to the right of the estate and guessed it must still be there, hidden behind the new buildings.

It was time to decide whether I was serious about my destination. If I was, I could leave the car more or less where it was. In one way, it would be easier to walk: I would be less conspicuous, able to dive behind any shrubs remaining. Also, it had finally stopped raining and a lemon yellow sun filtered through a streaky sky. This had nothing to do with the aggressive Chilean sun. It was delicate, suggestive of light and colour rather than heat and glare. The sun tempted me out. On the other hand, once I left the car's carapace, I would be vulnerable. If it were necessary to flee, my feet and legs would have to take me away, rather than a 1.8-litre engine.

I was still undecided and might even have driven off when a car came fast out of the driveway. I easily recognised who was at the wheel. Catherine had always driven fast. Besides, her thick grey-blonde hair and regular profile made her distinctive. The moment she had gone, turning left towards the centre of the village, I put my foot on the accelerator and took the route she'd just left. I was too agitated to notice anything about my surroundings, except that there were still trees and greenery.

I stopped short of the house and dared to look up. The main building was a perfect Georgian square with slate roof and large windows. To my left were several outbuildings, stables and a coach-house. My workroom had been in the coach-house. It was through the window of this dim little room that I had watched her.

I had assumed Catherine had left the house empty and I got out of the car bravely enough. But my legs knew better and were trembling after a few steps. The past years had taught me how much more powerful the mind is than the body. I stood in front of that house as weak as a sick child.

At least the sun continued to shine, although the house and the trees on either side – there was a large cedar to the south-east – cast a shadow nearly to where I stood. The question was whether to proceed further (but then what?) or to return, mission accomplished to some extent. I had seen the house where she had lived and possibly still did. I took two dithering steps forward and stopped again. An owl, which should have been asleep catcalled from high up in the cedar.

Could revisiting the past ever give answers for the present?

CHAPTER TWO

2004

I was woken by the sound of a car. I knew Catherine was going back to the hospital and at times of stress she drove faster than ever. She had sent me upstairs to sleep but then she had woken me. I tried not to be irritated, suspecting it was a symptom that, after all these years, I was still not quite better. She has been a wonderful mother to me.

Hardly had she whirled off when I heard another car, this time approaching, and far more tentative. Ever since we'd had to sell the land at the front of the garden, car noises had been audible, but this was definitely near the house although I felt as if it had not come all the way up to it. Then I heard the owl that lives in the cedar. My mother said I had hearing like a bat's and it was true that, since my illness, I can pick up the smallest noise. I think it came about because during that terrible time I listened so hard, although I never knew quite what I was listening for. I mentioned it to my shrink once and she suggested I was 'on guard' and I guess that was about it.

But I wasn't on guard that afternoon. Not for myself, anyway. My father was dying, my wedding had been cancelled: not a happy time certainly but both events, one leading from the other, out of my control. Moreover, I had acquitted myself well, staying beside my father all night at the hospital so that Catherine could sleep. Now it was my turn. My father had been ill for so very long that I could hardly grieve passionately.

Drifting again, I distinctly heard the car drive nearer, take the loop in the front of the house, then drive slowly away. Someone had taken a wrong turning perhaps. Even a few years ago that kind of unresolved situation would have made me nervous, particularly as I was in the house on my own. I turned to lie on my back without my heart changing a beat. But I was fully awake.

It had been raining when I got into bed but now the light was bright through my unlined curtains. The sun must have come out. My curtains hadn't been changed since my childhood and coloured animals sported across a jungle-green background. The sun, acting as a projector, imprinted lions and tigers, parakeets and zebras across the white expanse of my wedding dress, which hung on the outside of the cupboard since it was too big to fit inside. The effect was weird and made me feel uncomfortable enough to get out of bed and pull back the curtains.

I had forgotten about the marquee, and its mammoth whiteness, where I had expected green grass, further disconcerted me. Perhaps my earlier boasts of inner calm had been premature. Breathing carefully in the way I had been taught, I decided to go downstairs to the kitchen, make myself a cup of tea, then ring Oliver. The very name made me feel more composed.

He would be busy, of course. When we had taken the decision two days ago to postpone the ceremony, he immediately cancelled his leave – our two-week honeymoon was booked for Sicily – and went back to work. You can do that if you're a doctor in an over-stretched London hospital. My mother seemed surprised that he wasn't with us here, supporting me as I watched over the death of my father. But she had never understood that part of his attraction was that he didn't hang over me unnecessarily. Certainly, he was the rock to which I had clung thankfully for the last few years. But I didn't demand his physical presence. He was occupied with looking after other people. It was enough to know I came first. In fact, his lack of worry about my living independently in London encouraged my first step to sanity. Not that I was ever properly mad – merely horrified out of my wits. Possibly it came to the same thing.

'Oliver. It's me.' Predictably, I'd reached his answering-machine. 'Ring me when you have a break. The sun's come out so I'm going for a swim. I'll take my mobile. No change at the hospital. My mother's there now. I'll go later. I love you.' And maybe I did.

The water was still warm, despite the rain. The cover had split a few years ago and we'd decided not to replace it. The pool, cracking edges and peeling paint, was a relic from a more prosperous past. In honour of the wedding celebration, four pots newly planted with white geraniums stood at each corner.

I swam up and down slowly and wondered how many million times I'd crossed the same length of water. Today should have been the day I left it for ever and yet here I was, even wearing my old school bathing-suit with its array of round badges sewn across my bosom. Over the years I'd been taught how to look back without panic but I didn't feel strong enough now. Best to enjoy my rhythmic movement and watch the sun, sinking fast now. Soon it would disappear entirely behind the tall row of chestnut trees separating our garden from our neighbour's.

Shivering a little, I climbed out, stripped off my costume, and wrapped myself in a navy blue towel. My father had been so proud of the pool. He gave a party to inaugurate it. I was eight, my sister eighteen, his 'two beauties', as he used to call us. Then we were both fair, blue-eyed, slimly built. It's a very traditionally English look that I thought dull but filled him with pride and joy. He couldn't believe that someone as stocky and dark as he was could have produced such 'princesses' – his other name for us. So, now I was daring to look back. My father was the sort of man, perhaps not many left now – I don't know – who didn't give credit to his wife's genetic contribution. She was blonde, grey now if she leaves the hairdresser too long. I guess she's always felt young because she's ten years younger than her husband. I wonder how she'll feel after his death. It makes me sad for her.

Age differences have played an important part in my life. Maybe there are boundaries that shouldn't be crossed.

I towelled myself vigorously and put on my clothes. The mobile rang. 'Darling!'

'At this moment we should be celebrating our marriage in the smart marquee.'

'Are you trying to make things worse?' I laughed. He invariably cheered me. He had a gift for saying the worst and making it amusing. 'I can see the top of the marquee from here. It looks offended. They're taking it down on Monday.'

'All my colleagues think you've given me the slip.'

'Oh, Oliver.'

'I tried pretending I'd dumped you but anyone who'd seen you for a second knew that couldn't be true. What are you doing?'

'I've just had a swim.'

'So late?'

'I was sleeping. Then a car woke me. My mother's and then a mystery one. It came and went without trying to make contact.'

'A wedding guest?'

'I didn't think of that.' I paused. 'I wonder who.' But I didn't want to wonder. I changed the subject. 'My father's had nothing to eat or drink for four days now.'

'He's a strong man. I'm afraid it could be days more. Darling, I'm so sorry, I've got to go. I'm being bleeped.'

'I'll be at the hospital tonight.'

'So will I. But not with you. Our honeymoon night.' Even he sounded a little bitter, although he tried to make it seem like irony. 'I kiss your left shoulder-blade.'

'Received with gratitude.'

'Over and out.'

Restlessly, I walked round the garden. The marquee was laced up against the rain. It still had damp streaks running down from the two peaks, on which two flags hung looking foolish. Oliver and I had agreed not to try to set another date for the wedding till after my father's funeral but that gave the whole business a sense of unreality. After what had happened that summer, it had become ingrained in me that I could never be married. But in the last year Oliver had convinced me that it was possible, that I didn't have to do penance for ever. Now this mournfully slow dying of my father seemed to be proving him wrong. Perhaps Oliver and I would never be married.

The thought surfaced glibly, with less pain attached to it than I would have expected. It was like falling back into a position that I had never entirely left. The marquee company was fully booked till the end of September. My mother had talked to them, but they insisted we pay the full whack because this was their busiest time of year. She had shouted at them, 'My husband's dying!' But they had remained unmoved. So she had informed me that my 'next' wedding, a strange choice of words, would have to be an altogether simpler affair. I agreed meekly. She loved my father, I liked to presume, even if she'd found it hard to cope with his illness and the money running out. At least she'd stayed with him.

There was another point of ill omen about this wedding that never was. My elder sister, Louise, had lived abroad almost since her marriage to Tom, a banker. First they'd been in New York and for the last few years in Hong Kong. 'Going against the trend', as Tom said. They had three children and the youngest – ten years younger than the others – had epilepsy. Reggie's fits were generally controlled by pills but he'd had one on the day they were supposed to fly to England. Too much excitement, Louise said. She had postponed their departure and then, when the wedding was called off, postponed it further. I supposed she would try to come for my father's funeral.

I was back at the house now but still disinclined to enter its empty dimness. Instead I did something I'd promised myself never to do again: I went round to the stables.

CHAPTER THREE

1990

K dropped Fiona at the station and drove out to the small town's only café. After three weeks it had become a habit. It was not yet eight and it made him only slightly guilty to luxuriate in coffee, toast and bacon, while his wife was sitting on the train on her way to work. Doubtless she was already immersed in her files, boning up on whatever brand she was trying to reinvent. Fiona liked her job and was pleased to be able to support her husband. He was proud of her – and grateful.

After all, he wouldn't stay long in the café. He wiped melted butter from his chin and called for the bill. Writing was an experiment. He'd given himself a year off what even tactful Fiona called 'real work' and he mustn't waste too many minutes. Trying not to feel complacent – the writing muse, he suspected, wouldn't lend itself to the complacent – he walked to his car and drove back the mile to the Laceys' house.

But it was hard not to feel foolishly optimistic. It was a glorious May morning, the green of the trees still fresh and youthful, the air just a little crisp, the sun already gilding the tops of the hedges. He drove slowly up the driveway, with its artfully placed 'Concealed Entrance' sign and, as always, felt a glow of pleasure at the perfection of the house and garden. He had never dared expect to spend time in such surroundings. Even his area, the coach-house, was swept and clean, the red-brick smooth, the woodwork painted a smart ultramarine. Today the horse was peering out of one of the stables. Catherine had introduced him to it, as his nearest neighbour, so in passing he patted the large smooth nose, which made it snort and stamp its feet a little. He passed on quickly to his own door, also painted a shiny blue.

He found the right key and climbed the wooden flight of stairs to his study, his writing room. Visions of Vita Sackville-West's study in the tower at Sissinghurst, which he had once visited, often increased his satisfaction at this point. He knew it was absurd: a forty-year-old advertising copywriter likening himself in 1990 to an aristocratic lady novelist of the thirties but he was serious about his writing. This was real: his passion for words, his determination to shape them into something more than commercial jingles. He remembered reading an interview with Evelyn Waugh in which he stated that words, not character or plot, were the driving force behind his fiction.

While Fiona had been finding her feet in her work, he had been the wage-earner, successful enough to buy their little house in this fold of green just outside London's sprawl. Now it was his turn, his chance.

K looked at his desk with satisfaction. It was simple: ten feet of wood planking, seasoned but not painted, laid across trestles. To his right an Anglepoise lamp, to his left a lap-top (bought second-hand from his previous employers), and in the middle, laid carefully side by side, three piles of white paper. One pile was blank, one was decorated with his own angular handwriting, the other, much smaller, was covered with print. This was the sum of his first three weeks – a challenging blank, impulsive notes, and notes typed into some kind of order. He had given himself a month for such throat-clearing.

Under the desk, in a wire tray, was a high pile of lined yellow paper, also covered with jottings, some printed, the fruit of the years before. An older colleague, also keen to be a novelist, had once shown him a filing cabinet in which, over thirty years, he'd meticulously stowed away all the felicitous phrases and sentences that he planned to incorporate eventually into his great work. Since he was nearly at retirement age and no great work had ensued, K had seen it as a warning: notes for a month, then get started. He had recently given up yellow pads as too affected. Copywriting might not have been his cup of tea for ever but at least it had given him a workmanlike approach to writing.

K took off his jacket, draped it on a hanger attached to a nail knocked in for that purpose and briefly allowed his eye to run along the books on the small shelf: *Roget's Thesaurus*, *The Oxford Dictionary of Quotations*, *The Shorter Oxford Dictionary* in two volumes, Palgrave's

Golden Treasury, the Bible, *The Times Maps of the World*. He had once copied out this list as indispensable to writers and, in all modesty, had not thought to better it, although at the last minute he had added, for inspiration, the two novels he considered nearest perfection, *Bleak House* and *Vanity Fair*, with *The End of the Affair* for good measure. Then, somewhat appalled at the old-fashioned nature of his library, he had grabbed off his shelves the latest William Boyd, Martin Amis and Ian McEwan. He was planning to write a psychological thriller.

K sat down on his chair. On the other hand, it was important not to clutter your imagination with too much from other writers. For a similar reason he had decided not to go on a creative-writing course – although that decision had been hastened when he was turned down for a place on the University of East Anglia's famously successful course. He was too old for such things, he had consoled himself, his life experiences already crowded round him demanding to be transformed into art. As a copywriter, words had been his business for nearly twenty years. Dickens hadn't needed a creative-writing course.

The light was beautiful on the garden in front of him. The sun shone from behind, casting long shadows on the lawn below. In the summer, Catherine had told him, they turned this lawn into a tennis court, rolling the ground, cutting short the grass, putting up nets around it and marking out white lines. He supposed it would be a distraction. Perhaps he would turn his desk at right angles to the window in the more conventional way. He didn't think he could ever bring himself to face a blank wall, as some writers preferred. After years in a London office, with neon lighting, air-conditioning and hardly any natural light, it would be sinful to turn his back on so much gentle beauty.

K picked out a pen from a jar standing beside the paper. Sighing, but not with sorrow, he wrote, 'Death is not necessarily the opposite to life.' Smiling wryly, he started a new line: 'Life is not necessarily the opposite to death.' After more thought, he pulled a sheet of paper towards him, scanned a list of names written on it and added 'Roland'. He put an asterisk beside it and sat back for a moment, then picked out a yellow highlighter from the pot and ran it over 'Clio', four lines above 'Roland'. Names had already taken up much of his writing time. Each one seemed to have its own characteristics – red hair, big ears, long nose, pale skin, fat legs, they seemed to be obvious from the name, which, of course, made it important to get it right. Dickens was a genius at the game but, then, he hadn't had to struggle with the modern penchant for realism. 'Diana' might do for the heroine, he thought, the huntress, tall, fearless, beautiful. He wrote it down, then saw it was already at the top of the page, his first thought. Well, at least he was consistent. He feared his preoccupation with names was a way of avoiding a nasty tangle in the plotting, which he'd failed to unravel last week. If only he knew more about long-haul lorry drivers' habits. Successful writers paid researchers for that sort of thing, he told himself, before admitting, with self-mockery, that he was a mere beginner, a humble acolyte at the altar of writing.

At eleven on the dot, K went back down the stairs to make himself a cup of coffee. The lower room contained a pool table and a small kitchen unit. He found Catherine there boiling the kettle.

'I thought I wouldn't bother to go back to the house,' she said. She was wearing jodhpurs, which gave her a rather 'Diana' look, with her tall slimness and flying fair hair. She certainly didn't seem nearly fifty, which she probably was, given that her older daughter was married and had a child or, at least, a baby.

'Are you off riding?'

'I'm back. Claudie's horse is much too fresh. I've got to find someone to exercise him. You don't ride, do you?'

'No such luck,' admitted K, reluctantly dismissing an image of himself flying over the turf. 'I've spent too many years in suits.'

'That's why you appreciate the countryside so much.' She laughed, throwing her head back and opening her mouth wide. It was rather sexy, a little shocking.

'I do. I'm so grateful—'

'No. No,' she interrupted. 'Douglas and I love having you here, our resident writer. How's it going? Or shouldn't I ask?'

K found he was putting his head down and mumbling, just like a novelist tussling with problems he couldn't be expected to describe to the layman.

'I shouldn't ask.' She laughed again, although this time with rather more restraint.

K poured water into both of their mugs to cover an awkward pause.

Was updating her on his novel's progress part of the deal? It could be a daunting proposition. But nothing ventured, nothing gained. 'You don't know a long-distance lorry driver by any chance?'

Catherine looked at him consideringly. 'They're not exactly my cocktail-party companions. On the other hand . . .' She paused. 'It's for your book, is it?'

'Yes, just a bit of background research.' He certainly wasn't going to tell her how seriously he was stuck.

'You might do worse than talk to Alan.'

'Alan?'

'Our gardener, odd-job man, groom, whatever. You must have seen him around. He drove lorries for a while. Although Douglas swears he's a gypsy. But, then, he's never trusted the man.'

'That's amazing!' It did seem to him amazing that life should be so kind to him, that, through the offices of this goddess Diana, it should help him make sense of those insoluble patterns of ideas waiting for him on his desk.

So, after they'd finished their coffee, K followed his huntress and was introduced to Alan, who was making a half-hearted stab at weeding the vegetable patch and very ready to be interrupted.

It was after twelve when K returned to his desk but his conversation with Alan had taught him some useful facts - for example some drivers routinely urinate into a bottle so that they didn't have to leave their cab. (Apparently they shared this habit with prisoners who, locked up in vans are given no alternative.) He must try to avoid the simplistic and probably lazy sense that only the act of putting words on to paper indicated progress on the novel.

K looked at his list of names. With belated clarity, he recognised that the name 'Diana' was far too closely associated with the Princess to be used in a thriller. Indeed, he admitted to himself, with a worrying awareness of the paucity of his imagination, that his fictional Diana, tall, fair and brave, bore a close resemblance to the public image of the charismatic princess. Decisively, he put a line through 'Diana'. He would try 'Clio'.

There was no excuse now to avoid working on the weak link in his plot – although, with any luck, it would be easier after another conversation with Alan. Perhaps he should make a list of questions.

K drew a fresh piece of paper and, frowning, stared out of the window.

It was sunny all day. Catherine had said that K could eat his sandwiches anywhere in the garden if it was fine. But he felt constrained by the need to protect himself and her with proper boundaries. He restricted himself to sitting on a bench near the cedar tree at the front of the house, which had a more public feel to it. Sometimes he didn't bring sandwiches but walked back to his breakfast café. It was a long day before picking up Fiona at six thirty and it did his brain good to stretch his legs.

On that Monday he was packing up the remains of his lunch, having decided to walk to the shops anyway, when he saw Catherine approaching him across the driveway. She had changed out of her jodhpurs and wore shorts and a halter top. Over her arm, she carried a bathing-suit and a towel. 'I meant to say earlier that you're welcome to swim if you need a break.'

K felt immediately embarrassed, enough to be conscious of a warmth in his cheeks. Her invitation felt like an overture from a woman to a man, not the casual kindness of a hostess to her tenant. He paid for his office, although hardly more than a token sum.

'That's very kind.' On the other hand, maybe he was influenced by the knowledge that Catherine's husband, a man he'd seen only briefly because he commuted daily to the City, looked many years older than his wife.

'Just a thought,' called Catherine gaily, then disappeared back into the house.

K wondered if his reaction had been crass. He'd run it past Fiona that evening. It would be unfortunate if anything came to spoil such a perfect working arrangements. Fiona had initiated it after she had made friends with Catherine at some local charity event. She would either rebuke him for overreacting or teach him to steer a steady course.

K put his sandwich wrapper into his pocket and set out, briskly despite the heat, for the shops.

Fiona was tired. K had prepared a cold supper and carried it out to their small garden. He called, 'It's all ready.'

Just at that moment their neighbour started up his lawnmower but neither of them felt like being inside their stuffy house.

'Country sounds,' commented K, as he often had before. Fiona smiled back at him. They didn't want to tackle the neighbour, who was helpful with such things as packages left in their absence.

Fiona was ready for bed after the nine o'clock news. 'Are you coming up?' she asked. K knew he was slow to read her signals, although it had been going on for two years now. The early bedtime indicated that tonight was an appropriate point on her ovulation chart, or something similar – he was guiltily aware that he had not taken the trouble to understand it properly – for them to make love. It was her lassitude, he decided, that disguised her wish for sex. A woman requiring a man's attention should be more obviously alluring – well, sexy. She, on the contrary, had given the appearance of a woman who needed a cup of camomile tea and an uninterrupted night's asleep.

This was unfair. She probably was tired, but unwilling to give up her quest for motherhood. It was part of their deal. After his year off – year writing, that was – and, assuming the charts were unsuccessful, they would move on to phase three: IVF.

K went up the stairs slowly, not exactly unwillingly because sex with Fiona was simple, serving the needs of both parties, but without the spring of excitement. Of love he did not think. He and Fiona were inextricably bound together. He could not imagine life without her and had no wish to try.

Later, K lay awake in their small double bed. Everything had proceeded as planned, carefully, kindly, even sweetly. She had fallen asleep at once, forgetting even to remove the cushion from under her bottom. Or perhaps it was a new development, to keep herself propped up receptively for the duration of the night.

He glanced at her. It was a bright moonlit night and the curtains were thin. He noted, with something like surprise, her regular features, the smooth pale skin and straight dark hair. She was better-looking than he remembered when they were apart, but so self-contained. Even in sleep.

K turned away from her restlessly. He knew he should be thinking about his book. That would make staying awake worthwhile — as it made everything worthwhile, he reminded himself. Maybe, even with research, he was out of his depth with the lorry driver. And yet he was the major red herring in the book, the perfect murderer, in the eyes of the world, who turned out to be the opposite. This was a central theme to the novel — that black is white and white is black. Could it be a cliché? Of course it was, because everything worth saying had been written a million times. But that didn't mean it had lost its importance. The lorry driver, at present called Lenny, had taken on the features of Alan, Catherine's handyman. It worried him that his visual imagination hooked so quickly on to the real. Look at the fiasco of his bold, blonde Diana, who had turned out to be a carbon-copy of the princess — every man's fantasy.

When he'd been writing advertising copy, no one was interested in his visual imagination: he had been employed as a wordsmith. That was the reason, he supposed, that as the visual element of commercials had begun to dominate, he had become less successful. And yet he cared very much about what he saw around him. That was why Meadowlands was such a good place to work. Just looking out at the smooth lawn from his window calmed his psyche. Surely you had to have a calm psyche to create? Or perhaps you didn't.

K got out of bed and went to the bathroom. He knew that Fiona, hugging his seed, wouldn't stir till morning. He went downstairs and then out to the garden where he sat in the same chair as he had at supper. It was not late, only just after eleven, but there was complete silence, apart from the occasional car in the road beyond their house. He tipped back his chair and gazed up at the sky, massing above his head in waves of blackness, softened by gatherings of stars and a high, steady moon. Even the reflection from the city, the towns and villages below, did no more than smudge the outlines. It was a beautiful balmy night.

Where was everyone else on a night like this? thought K. Making love, perhaps, as he had already, his limbs still naked under his robe? Eating late, like the Spanish? Listening to music? Dancing? Reading? Or, like him now, just sitting quietly at the end of the day?

But was that really what he was doing? An enormous sadness, coming out of nowhere, as if the sky had suddenly descended with all the stars and moon submerged into its darkness, overwhelmed him. He felt utterly incapacitated, pinned to his seat, brain almost numbed but retaining just enough life to ask the unanswerable: why am I here? What's the meaning? What's the point?

Taken aback by the ferocity and unexpectedness of the attack, K tried to smile, to tell himself that this was a ridiculously teenage *angst*, post-coital and probably encouraged by the solitary self-questioning of the novelist. It went with the territory, he tried to tell himself. But his lips refused to smile and the sense of a huge weight pressing on him didn't diminish. Marrying Fiona had been supposed to guard him from such experiences.

He had no option but to give in, shut his eyes and wait for it to pass.

At two in the morning, K stumbled up to bed. Despair, depression or whatever it was – in the past he had known at least one reason – had finally given in to exhaustion. At least he could move. Perhaps he could sleep. He eased himself into his place beside Fiona and, managing to dispel an image of two persons stone-carved on a tomb, fell thankfully into sleep.

CHAPTER FOUR

1990

Claudia felt as if she were ten again. The release from school for the summer holidays always had this effect. It was not that she actively disliked living with five hundred other girls – although it often struck her as a strange preparation for life – but she did love being alone.

She stood on the station, surrounded by her bags, tall and slender, her ragged-edged jeans barely disguising the silver bracelet round her ankle, her face raised to the sky.

'Sorry, darling! Sorry I'm late.'

Claudia watched her mother arriving at the station. People often commented on how alike they were, so she looked for clues to her own appearance.

'I wanted to mark out the court as a surprise. After all, the weather has to break ...'

As she hugged her mother, Claudia noted that she couldn't *feel* less like her mother. Which wasn't a criticism. On the contrary, she admired her mother's outgoing nature, her wish to be 'Catherine' rather than 'Mummy', her apparent belief that all action was good. Claudia knew her own nature to be much more secretive. Sometimes she felt an uncomfortable split between her girlish self, who hung out with her friends and tackled ten GCSEs without complaint, and the self who found an empty space to read poetry or, more often, held a book of poetry and let her mind drift with no particular subject. One afternoon when, by chance, she'd spotted the chaplain walking across the school's grounds, she'd approached him impulsively. But when he'd stopped, his rather protuberant eyes kindly above his greying beard, she'd felt incapable of explaining herself. Instead she'd asked for the time of a service, which meant she'd had to attend it. That hadn't helped either.

As Catherine bustled them off the station carrying rather more of Claudia's belongings than she was herself, Claudia, holding her viola case to her chest, decided that it was only when she played music that her two sides came together. There was a piece she'd just started to learn that wiped out all the mumblings in her head.

K's desk still faced the window. He had become addicted to the bright square of the world outside his rather dark room. It felt like looking at a stage, although until now there'd been few actors. Occasionally Alan passed by, pushing a wheelbarrow laden with tools. On warm days, of which there'd been many recently, he'd glimpsed Catherine, sometimes with a friend, making her way to the swimming-pool.

This morning had been different. Both Alan and Catherine had appeared together on the lawn in front of him. Alan had been pushing an antiquated machine, like a very small wheelbarrow, and Catherine carried various pots and equipment. As they moved up and down the grass, K gradually gathered that they were attempting to mark out a tennis court by most old-fashioned, Heath Robinson means. It struck him as at odds with the bright efficiency of the house and grounds.

When he came down to make his coffee, they'd got no further than laying out netting and putting in corner markers.

'You must think me crazy.' Catherine had come in, as she often did, with her open-mouthed laugh. 'And now I've got to rush off and Alan won't do a thing on his own. Can't say I blame him.'

K had thought of offering to help – sitting inside through so many beautiful days had become a kind of low-key torture – but suspected this would be the thin edge of the wedge. He still had enough self-control to refuse Catherine's offers of a swim. (How could he explain swimming breaks to Fiona – shut up all day in trains and offices?)

Catherine drank her coffee quickly and left. Back at his window again, K watched Alan behave as predicted: tinkering with the machine, shaking a large tin of what looked like white paint, then sloping off to another, hidden part of the garden, perhaps into the shed where he often seemed to disappear in Catherine's absence.

K pulled the laptop towards him. He was trying a rather more free-flowing approach to his novel in which he put aside notes and typed up a few pages without stopping. He'd decided that his commercial work predisposed him to soundbites, buzz-words and snappy dialogue, that he was completely inexperienced in one of the defining characteristics of a novel: *flow*. By which he didn't mean anything remotely like a *roman fleuve* but just something that ran to around a hundred thousand words, the target specified by the agent who'd taken him on, although in a rather conditional way. She was waiting for fifty pages to follow the proposal he'd already submitted.

K didn't admit to losing heart over his writing but, after nearly two month's work out of his year's sabbatical – two months that felt, because of the long hours he had spent alone at his desk, much longer – he would have welcomed even a small breakthrough. Hence the determined tapping at his laptop.

K scrolled back to see what he'd written and, after a quick scan, deleted it all. No point in wasting paper and ink on that lot. He stood up, glanced at his watch, then reached for *The Oxford Companion to English Literature*. It opened at *The Mill on the Floss* and he found himself staring at the name 'Maggie Tulliver'. It struck him that it was the girl's character, the young woman who became the victim, that was holding up progress in his own novel.

He and Fiona came from small families, while work and their home situation outside London had left them with fewer friends than most. Those they had were very like them, fortyish, working and, of course, many with the time-consuming addition of young children. Apart from the receptionist in his ex-office and the temps who came and went like leaves in the wind, he knew no women of around the nineteen to twenty mark as he saw the victim – most recently named Lorna.

K sat down again, pushed away the laptop and substituted a blank sheet of paper. He wrote, 'Lorna', underlined it, and added, 'fresh, naïve, hopeful, inexperienced, outgoing, friendly, optimistic, bright, clear-headed, narrow-minded, clever, sweet, affectionate, fair, blue-eyed, slim, tall'.

He put down his pen and frowned at the last entry. It was a stream-of-consciousness method of finding a character, picked up from a creative-writing book but the list hardly seemed convincing. More like an ad-man's dream of a teen pop star.

Thoughtfully, he wrote, 'Drinks too much, smokes too much, self-conscious, obsessed with appearance, silly, only moves in a group, competitive but only about the unimportant, shallow, cold, lazy, indulgent, selfish, sweaty, bites nails, wears too much makeup, uninformed, unambitious, wears headphones continually, stupid.'

This was going too far the other way but nevertheless had a ring of truth. Or maybe this list, too, was the product of an ad-man's imagination, this time from a jaundiced adult viewpoint.

K pushed away the paper and reached for his laptop. Possibly, brevity would serve him best. His potential agent, after suggesting 80 – 100,000 words, had added, 'Although, of course, a short book can be effective.' She had paused again, a large, formidable woman, staring intently across her desk at him as if struck by a new idea that depended on the shape of his face. 'Fifty-five thousand words, large print, shocking cover. It can be effective. But an enormous risk for a new writer ...'

It had seemed far too big a risk, particularly after she'd remarked while smoothing her left eyebrow, that it would have to be priced low, but now he wondered. Perhaps she had spotted his strength: not flow but constriction.

K tapped in two very short sentences. Then he wrote two more. And two more. They contained neither adjectives nor adverbs, and at last he felt the thrill of creation. They looked good, they felt good, they *were* good. He would print them out at once.

As the printer was on the floor, he was crouching when he heard a noise at the door. It was a surprise. No one disturbed his solitary struggles.

'I'm sorry. I didn't realise ...' The voice faded away as if its owner was embarrassed.

K looked up and saw the long jeans-clad legs of a young girl. Her face was shadowy. He stood up. Behind him, the printer clicked out his six beautiful sentences. He smiled. 'I'm the writer-in-residence.'

The girl laughed nervously. 'I'm Claudia. I just got back.'

'Of course. You're Catherine's daughter. Holiday time, is it?'

'Yes.' She backed away.

In the distance her mother's voice was calling, 'Claudie! Claudie!'

As she turned, a streak of bright light edged into the window and lit her profile. Exhilarated already by the six sentences, K was struck by the purity of the high brow, straight nose and rounded chin. In a second she had gone, but this image remained with him, impressed on his retinas.

'I'm coming!' he heard her call, as he watched dust particles play in the sun where she had stood.

K picked up the paper from the printer and sat back at his desk. In front of him lay the lists of adjectives for his murder victim. Every one seemed lifeless and ridiculous. He was tempted to start again: 'Clean, young, strong, beautiful. No, not quite beautiful.'

Instead he returned to his laptop and managed to write some more punchy sentences. After an hour or so of concentration he decided that at long last he had written an acceptable opening to the novel. The clue had been to make the girl the centre of attention at the outset while before he had always perceived her at a distance, no more than a walk-on part. Now he saw that her death, wherever it occurred in the book, gave her a starring role. To place her on the first page could be a stroke of genius. Well, not quite genius but a fellow had to keep his spirits up.

Claudia liked her bedroom. The windows were big, the furnishing was light and simple (despite her mother's longing for frills and furry rugs), the white bookcase filled with old friends. Even the childhood curtains, with their silly parade of animals, pleased her. She would unpack her trunk slowly and savour being at home with eight weeks of relative peace ahead. Moving in luxurious slow motion, Claudia went over to her bags, opened her viola case, and took out the bow first, then the instrument. She held it under her chin but only for the pleasure of feeling it next to her skin. Later she would play. There would be time to play every day. Brahms deserved no less. She smiled in anticipation.

'Lunchtime, Claudie! Are you upstairs? Lunchtime, darling!'

Catherine had laid out salad and cold ham on the terrace outside the kitchen. The sun was blazing at them so they both wore hats although Catherine grumbled, 'If only they'd never discovered about skin cancer. I can't tell you how I long to stick my face in the sun. After all, most of the time this country's so bloody *grey*.'

Claudia liked her hat, with its wide shady brim. If she'd had her way, they'd have sat under the big trees at the end of the garden. Heat made her skin prickly and her brains stew.

'So, now you're free of exams. No work. Just plenty of time to enjoy yourself.'

'Yes. It's wonderful. I feel wonderful.' She feared her mother would like something more confiding.

'I don't want you to be bored. Is Bella coming to stay? We'll get the tennis court going and then we can invite people over ...'

Claudia tried to hide her sighs as her mother planned away her holidays. Her elder sister, who lived in New York at the moment with her banker husband Tom and two small children, had once explained that Catherine was a thwarted career woman. First she, Louise, had been born and then just when Catherine had persuaded their old-fashioned and older father that she should look for a job, she'd become pregnant with Claudia. By the time Claudia had grown up, Catherine had lost heart. Not that she was ever obviously down-hearted. Quite the reverse, in fact.

'It's been dry for nearly a week so I think we'll get a really good bounce for once ...'

Douglas Lacey had never agreed to his wife's request for a hard court, which annoyed Catherine – as Claudia knew well. Catherine got her own back by the ostentatious use of ridiculously old-fashioned means of marking out the grass court. It had started when Louise was a teenager and both sisters became aware of a subtext: their mother's energetic youth contrasted with their father's old-man stiffness, including an arthritic knee (for which he refused an operation) supported now and again with a stick. Yet he was generous in other ways – with the pool, her horse.

'Vinegar's not properly exercised, I'm afraid ...' Catherine had moved to riding now.

Claudia sighed guiltily. Up to a year ago she had enjoyed riding, although never with as much fervour as Louise, who had gone to Pony club camp and won rosettes at the local gymkhana. She had liked pottering round the lanes and bridleways. But quite suddenly, at the end of last summer, she had found herself utterly without interest. It was as if a tap had been switched off – gone, finished. If only she were not so feeble she'd have told her mother months ago. She had visited Vinegar as soon as she got back and fed him a mint but that was only a matter of habit. She'd felt no welling of emotion as she looked into his wide eyes. 'Who's the man in the stables? I heard a noise and went up.'

28

'You mean our writer-in-residence.' Catherine's proud tones suggested ownership of an endangered species.

'That's what he said. What's he writing?'

'His wife's on the Save the Children fund-raising committee. She commutes to London. A very busy woman. She told me her husband was desperate for somewhere to write. They have a tiny house, I believe. So, I thought, Why not clear out the coach-house loft? He works terribly hard. All day long, five days a week. Hardly comes up for air till he picks up his wife from the station. Would you like some cheese, darling?'

Claudia felt too hot for cheese. She helped her mother clear the table, then wandered back to her room. On her way she saw, through the open front door, the writer sitting on a bench under the yew tree, eating sandwiches. She thought he was pleased to be solitary and wondered, vaguely, what interesting ideas were buzzing around in his head. She had kept a diary on and off for the last five years but her life was so predictable it was hardly worth recording. Recently this conviction had become overwhelming and she'd put it away.

As Claudia reached her bedroom she thought that Catherine had never told her the subject of the 'writer-in-residence's' labours, or even his name.

The room was deliciously cool but she drew the curtains so that the hard afternoon sunshine was further filtered. Then she took out her viola and found a piece of music, which she propped on the bookcase. After a moment or two's hesitation while she settled a piece of cloth against her cheek, then took it away again, she began to play.

It was a piece she'd learnt for her grade eight exam earlier in the year so she could easily play it by heart but she liked having the notes in front of her eyes. It made her feel linked to the composer while she listened carefully to the sounds made by her bow. She needed a fresh day for the Brahms sonata. Even though the first movement was marked *allegro amabile*, which sounded simple enough, it required all her concentration. If only she had someone to play the piano part, but that was hopeless wishful thinking. Their piano was just another piece of furniture.

K felt certain this was the best day's writing yet. In fact the only day in which he'd produced anything worth keeping. It was six o'clock, and for the last hour he'd been vaguely aware of activity outside his window. Now he sat back and paid more attention.

Alan was still there – much later than usual. He had stripped to an unbecoming singlet and his face and shoulders, elaborately tattooed, looked beefily red. He was hammering in pegs with a wooden mallet. Catherine, dressed in shorts and T-shirt, was clearly in charge, shouting instructions while dashing between Alan and her daughter. The daughter, K recalled her name as the unusual 'Claudia', was dressed in the jeans she'd worn earlier but her feet were bare and her hair was pulled tightly back. From his vantage-point above her, she seemed smaller and younger than the Valkyrie figure who had stood in his doorway. She was pushing the strange white-coated machine and marking out not very straight lines on the grass. She was managing to do it, he noted, as if she were not quite there: her face, when she turned to come down towards him, was expressionless as if masking the real subject of her thoughts.

Catherine seemed to sense this because she kept dashing over to her and clutching her arm or the handle of the machine. Eventually she took over altogether and sent Claudia to attach the centre net to the posts, which had already been erected. The shadows were lengthening on the grass so that Claudia became elongated again, her shadow unfurling towards K.

For good reasons, K usually kept the window shut: the dim room was cool enough, he didn't want a breeze to disturb his papers and he liked the protection glass gave him from the world outside. But now he leant across the desk and, with some difficulty, unlatched the window and pushed it up.

Immediately the smells and sounds, of grass and birdsong, the sweetness of a glorious summer evening enveloped him. He found himself widening his eyes and breathing in deeply as if it would make him more part of it. An overwhelming sense of satisfaction at his place in this scenario filled him with well-being.

'Do you want any help?' he called from the window.

CHAPTER FIVE

2004

I cancelled the room in the Fresh Ponds Hotel and started to drive back to London. My visit to Meadowlands, brief and tentative as it was, had been too shocking.

I tried to concentrate on driving and not think too much, but the beauties of the summer evening, swept clean after the rain, gave me such a painful sense of nostalgia that my heart and stomach felt squeezed as if by an iron band. Eventually the pain became insupportable and I pulled into a lay-by, thinking a walk might ease things a little. By chance, although some might believe otherwise, I had stopped a hundred yards from a large church whose tall spire dominated the crest of the hill.

I began to walk towards it.

The light was dimming now, the sun far below the horizon, although a flare of red, tapering into orange still fought off the invading night. I was reminded of those illuminated manuscripts where hell is depicted in a cauldron of flames. I rested my eyes on the coolness of the spire. As I watched, a first star appeared in the darkness above it.

My pace was slow but now I stopped altogether, bent double, like an old man, on the pavement. This time it was not physical pain: the enormity of anguish, rising beyond what seemed possible, turned itself into tears that washed crazily down my face. I muttered some-thing, I don't know what – encouragement to myself, I suppose, then allowed myself to sink down to the ground. It was a moment of grace, of unselfish sorrow (a Christian would say penitence), that I wanted to savour. Such moments had come to me infrequently over the past fourteen years. The last occasion, about two years ago, was when I rescued a small child, almost a baby, lost on the vagabond streets of Valparaiso, and returned him to his parents. We all cried together. The father recited a line of poetry – doubtless Neruda – and I left. Next time when I saw them, I walked by. My heart cannot stand much emotion.

As I sat weeping on the pavement, I became aware of footsteps coming towards me, not a single step but many. I also heard music, but at a distance.

'Are you all right?' Those oh-so-English words of concern, implying goodwill and a strong desire that you should be all right and therefore cause no trouble.

But of course I was all right. The tears had cleansed the black coagulations of my thought and given me a few hours of freedom.

I stumbled to my feet and attempted to reassure the couple who had stopped by me. They were elderly, arm in arm. 'Yes, I'm sorry.' I liked the sound of the apology. Sometimes I could be sorry for nothing. They smiled at me, the woman more widely than her husband, and passed on. It was obvious that they and the others coming by me had left the church and that the music, also, was coming from there.

More to convey that I wasn't threatening than with any purpose, I started walking in the direction of the church. There was still a small crowd gathered in the forecourt, gradually diminishing as they moved towards their cars and drove away. I read on a board that I had reached the Catholic church of St Mary and All the Angels.

I have lived for years in a country where Catholicism permeates to the roots of its existence but I have never, even in my lowest moments when my life hung by a thread, been remotely tempted to enter a Catholic church. Now I found myself in one by chance, perhaps, on a road into London. It was ironic.

The building was very warm, retaining the atmosphere of a place filled with people, of burning candles, but no incense. I regretted the incense. The organist had stopped playing.

I supposed I was there to recover the strength to carry on so I sat at the back, staring ahead rather vacantly, but not too unhappily. After a few moments of this, I saw a man approaching from a door to the right of the altar. I was immediately thrown back to my church visit earlier in the day. I hadn't made the connection before because the experience was totally different. Then I had been held fast on the torture of self-pity. It seemed an exceptionally long time ago.

'I'm afraid we must shut the church.' I saw now that he was a priest – he was wearing a dog-collar.

'You must.' Something about me must have struck him because he paused to look into my face. 'Were you at Mass?'

'No, I'm not a Catholic.' He was middle-aged, English, pudgy but neat, more like a bank clerk than a priest. Not my sort of man.

'I'm just going to have something to eat.'

It was an invitation. But not a pressing one. He locked the main doors, then I followed him back up the aisle. At the altar, he genuflected and crossed himself. Naturally I did nothing.

He led me through various dim-lit corridors until we entered what seemed to be a fair-sized house. In the kitchen, an old woman was preparing to leave. 'It's in the oven, Father.' She hardly looked at me, as if visitors were absolutely normal, which heartened me a little.

'Thank you, Theresa.'

We sat on either side of the table. He had divided the pie meticulously into three, explaining that Bill, his fellow priest, would be back later. The pie was big enough so I didn't feel too guilty. I found I was very hungry.

We ate in silence for a while. Then the priest looked across at me. 'So, how can I help you?'

The simple directness both comforted and frightened me. I had resisted any offers of help immediately after the tragedy, then fled to where no help would be forthcoming.

'Something dreadful happened fourteen years ago...' As I began my story I watched him take up the listening position I had seen in films of a priest in the confessional. I tried to speak without emotion but as I continued, my voice broke and, in the pause, he filled my glass from a water jug between us. I drank.

Now and again, he nodded, but mostly, when I looked up, he was expressionless, eyes half closed.

When I had finished – it must have taken the best part of an hour because I wanted him to see the thing from all points of view as fairly as possible – he said nothing for a while but I saw that his lips were moving slightly. I guessed, without rancour, that he was praying.

In fact, I had asked him no question nor, I had made this clear, was I looking for forgiveness – from whatever quarter. I had felt the urge to speak to another human being, that was all.

I was considering standing up, preparatory to leaving, when he spoke quite loudly – or perhaps it was that I had been murmuring. 'And now you're planning to visit the woman involved?'

I'd forgotten I had told him that – that I'd brought the story up to date as it were. It was the past that had compelled me to speak. 'Maybe. I'm not sure.'

'But that was your purpose in coming to England?'

'Yes. I suppose so. I'm not sure now. I'm on my way back to London.'

'I see.'

He seemed to find it unnecessary to say more, but I wanted to know what he had meant by the question. 'Do you think I shouldn't see her?'

'I don't know. You haven't told me why you want to see her.'

I wanted to scream, 'Surely it's obvious why I should want to see her!' But his calm made me stop to think. I deliberated saying, 'I have loved her since I first saw her,' but I didn't know how he would view such a love, with all that had followed from it. I presumed that priests did not rate my sort of love very highly. 'I have no intention of upsetting her,' I said instead, sounding feeble even to my own ears.

'No. No. So, you do consider what she might want?'

This was what he had been getting at from the beginning. He thought me utterly selfish. Again I wanted to scream, 'Can't you see? The story isn't finished. As long as my love for her continues, there is no ending!' Instead I posed a question myself. 'Do you think I should ask her permission?'

'I don't know.'

'Or not try to see her?' This time he remained silent, which I took as assent. There seemed no reason to stay any longer. 'I should go. You've been very kind.'

He took me to the front door of the house. A man was arriving on a motorcycle in the driveway. He took off his helmet and I saw the dog-collar. He was black-haired and burly, like a rugby player. I wondered if my priest, I had not even found out his name, would pass on my story. Did priests gossip about the poor crippled remnants who turned to them?

'Thank you,' I said.

After a pause, he said, 'God bless you.'

I couldn't decide whether to be offended or pleased.

My father had only a few more hours to live, or so the doctor told me – he turned up just after I arrived and my mother left. I rang her as soon as I estimated she'd be home, but she didn't react as I'd expected. 'Claudie, darling, how can they be sure? He's been dying for so long, so very, very long. This is just another stage, isn't it? If I don't get a few hours' kip, I won't be able to cope at all. I'll come in at six. I'm sure nothing will happen before then.' She went into a whole number about how selfish Louise was not to have come over. It was hardly worth pointing out that she was caring for her sick son. It seemed my mother was right about herself: she needed a rest. On reflection, she had sounded near to tears throughout our conversation.

So, I found myself watching over my father's last hours. They had pushed his bed into a side ward and unhooked him from everything but the oxygen mask and the morphine. I held his hand, which was apparently lifeless, in case that might soothe him a little. His breathing was the only sound in the room, a spasmodic, effortful gasping for air, which sometimes stopped for a heart-wrenching moment or two, then resumed its laboured pace.

It was a surprise to find myself in this position. My father had said he would never forgive me for what I did, and he never had. He treated me with a kind of honourable fairness, which precluded love. He talked to me but as if I were a stranger. During the worst time of my illness, when I was in hospital more or less continually, he had visited every other Saturday and paid, of course, for my care. No NHS for his 'princess', however far she'd fallen. When I returned to the house, and after his retirement and ever-increasing ill-health, he scarcely addressed a word to me.

My shrink once asked me whether his behaviour had contributed to my sense of worthlessness. I suppose she was expecting the obvious answer and then we would have gone on to try to work out how best to deal with it. But my answer was 'No – or at least no more than usual.'

The truth was that my father's view of me as his perfect little princess had long undermined in me any belief in his judgement.

He saw me in the distorting mirror of his own needs, which were far removed from reality. I had been an ordinary schoolgirl, not even particularly pretty. There was one unfortunate phase not so many years ago when I had the habit of sneaking into my mother's room and poring over the old photograph albums. She had kept none since that summer. I think I was trying to see if I could spot any indication of what was to come. But, of course, I could not. All I saw was a tallish, fairish, slimmish teenager, with straight hair, a long nose and a high forehead, which I tried to hide with an ineffectual half-fringe. Yet surely there must have been something different about me or I wouldn't have done what I did.

'Why don't you get yourself a cup of tea?' One of the nice nurses had come in. They were a bit shocked, I think, that my mother hadn't returned when the doctor had been so definite. But my father had been ill at home for years, then for months in and out of the hospital or nursing-home. Somehow we had lost sight of the possibility of his actual death. That was why we had felt able to set the date for the wedding. Even my dearest Doctor Oliver had not demurred. Of course, he was not exactly objective.

'Yes. Tea would be good.' I took my bag and walked through the quiet corridors towards the exit. It was not like a London hospital, whose restless energy is never extinguished even in the middle of the night. This was a country place where the patients respected the hours.

I stood outside the doors in a curious tranquillity. The air was still mild and a half-formed moon rode a chariot of stars. It was very beautiful. I think I was hoping my father would die while I was away, take that chariot to some painless, easeful place.

I took out my mobile. It was cruel to ring Oliver. Either he would be snatching some much-needed rest or he would be involved in an emergency of his own from which he wouldn't be able to extricate himself. I still had the invalid's instinctive selfishness. With an effort of will, I abandoned the call.

I picked up a cup of tea from a machine on my way back to my father and found he hadn't died.

'Warm and wet,' commented the nurse. 'Nothing tastes as good as a cup of tea at four in the morning.'

It was true. 'Shall I get you one?'

'I'm off duty at six. I'll wait till then.'

She leant over my father to check his morphine dispenser and oxygen mask. I guessed she was wondering if he'd last till she left.

Death had played such a sudden and violent role in my life that I was almost bewildered by this gradual sliding. Without comment, the nurse unhooked the mask and took it away with her. As she passed, she patted my hand. 'Back in a mo.'

I jumped up nervously. But he was still breathing, although his breaths were shallower, with no gasping or shuddering. I took his hand again and gripped it fiercely. It wasn't his fault how things had turned out. He was just another foolish, doting father. Too old, perhaps, but you could hardly blame him for that. My shrink had once asked me if I had been looking for a father figure when I met K and I had answered, 'No.' I was always aware that I had a father, even if he was unsympathetic to my nature. Although in a way I had hero-worshipped K, it was not as a father.

I stared at my father's bony, bloodless face and found I had tears in my eyes, which was both a surprise and a consolation. I wanted to feel love.

Love had not been a friend to me, some would say. But it had released me from sterile, inward-looking childishness. It was the passion that had been too much. It had exalted me beyond everything so that I even lost sight of the love. When it was all smashed in a few minutes, the passion turned into the blackest hatred of myself. 'Guilt' is far too weak a word. Three times I tried to kill myself, and each time they dragged me back. Then I gave up. Perhaps the passion left me. Perhaps the love. I don't know. I don't talk to anyone about it. I do not feel the same for Oliver.

My visit to the priest, our talk over the cottage pie, made me undecided about my return to London and the flat. He had questioned my wish to see again 'the woman involved' after so long. I could tell he suspected my motives. He had only just stopped short of warning me off.

I thought again of what might be his attitude to my sort of love. By definition not a worldly man, he might nevertheless echo the judgement of society: I had been infatuated – worse, clung to a high-flown sexual passion to help me through a difficult patch in my life. I had been near the age when men need reassurance about their sexual prowess and the younger the girl willing to co-operate the better. I knew of the crude gossip that had been about at the time but it had meant so much less than the cruel reality. Besides, if it had been merely an infatuation, its ending had had no meaning, made no sense.

The flat where I'd drunk myself into a stupor the night previously had belonged to Fiona. She had put down a mortgage on it in secret that summer. She had used her maiden name, Fiona Banks, but it was to be a present for both of us so that I could visit London and she wouldn't have to commute every day. Somehow I had never found the strength to sell it.

I wanted somewhere to think, but that flat felt like the worst possible place. Besides, I was exhausted.

I returned to the Fresh Ponds Hotel.

The night porter handed me a key without comment, except to direct me up a flight of stairs to a room, thankfully at the back. She and I had been high up at the front, overlooking the water. Without putting on a light – enough came through the window – or undressing, I lay down on the bed.

It is extraordinary how ruthlessly the mind diverts when there's a need for thought. Despite my best attempts to consider my situation and my next course of action, my mind became flooded with images of Valparaiso. It is true that the city, in its most visual and superficial self, had become my lifeline.

Over the last ten years I had turned myself into a painter. I have painted literally thousands of pictures – on newspaper, cardboard and recently on wood panels or canvas – every one of the city. I even painted on its walls, the fabric of its being. The city has a tradition of elaborate graffiti. My paintings were at first abstract. All I knew was how to lay colour on a surface and even that I had to learn. For two years I played with stripes, yellow against green, turquoise against purple. Gradually the stripes became lozenges and then they became houses. Valpo's houses are painted every colour under the sun – or under the *neblina*, the grey mist that enfolds the city on so many summer mornings.

Of course, there was no way I could continue writing after what had happened. It was the writing that had created the particular circumstances. Yet I had always thought of myself as unvisual. I was like a madman who daubs for therapy. Valparaiso had turned it into something more important.

The city is built on canyons or *cerros,* forty-five of them, so steep that, if I possessed a car, which I don't, I'd be afraid to drive it up them, although people do. This is all the more daring because Chile is on a fault-line and is regularly shaken by earthquakes. Quite often, I'm woken by the rattle of my brushes in their jar or sometimes my furniture creaking like the beams of a ship in a gale.

In 1906, at the same time as San Francisco was split apart, the houses of Valparaiso were tossed out of their uneasy moorings. Little, except the prison and the sturdiest buildings, survived. It was not the first time. And yet soon the city was back, tin shacks clawing their way up the cliffs, finding a rock or a plateau and clinging to it for dear life. In the rainy season the corrugated-iron roof of my shack resounds like gunfire. Trite as it may sound, I identified with Valparaiso. Knowing no one, wishing to know no one, as far from my home as I could be, I took on the city's identity and, looking around me, picked up a brush. I, too, am a survivor.

I sat up and, in search of water, went into the bathroom. Once again I was presented with my face, the hooded eyes, the seamed and weathered skin, the ragged hair made greyer by the darkness of the face. Would she even recognise me? The thought flashed into my head with a confidence that forced me to admit I was still counting on seeing her. I had translated the priest's questioning into 'why?' but had not accepted 'whether?'.

All the same, I could wait. There was no rush. After fourteen years there was no rush. I drank my water and lay down again.

My father waited for my mother. We held hands at the end, the three of us connected in a circuit, and I felt that family unity, apparently so fatally destroyed, had been restored a little. I don't think it was just that he had gone, taking his anger and misery with him: it felt more positive than that.

My mother sent me home. It was still only eight o'clock, a Sunday morning so peaceful that I found my nervous breathing slowing in reflection.

As I drove, I watched the heavy mists still lying on low fields, surrounding tree trunks to about head height.

There was almost no one around, but at one point I saw a man sitting beside the road on a bench. He caught my attention because he wore a white shirt and I felt a faint sense of solidarity with his intensely solitary pose. I wondered why he was there. Not a death, surely.

By the time I reached home, everything was bright and sharp again – too sharp. I went to my room and lay down, then remembered I was supposed to ring Louise in Hong Kong, which reminded me that I should tell Oliver the news. I went downstairs.

I tried to throw off the languor of a sleepless night, the draining emotion of my father's death. It was an effort: my body and mind were exhausted, but the effort produced a slow surge of adrenaline.

'Louise, it's me. Claudia.' My voice was lively, as if telling good news. She guessed at once so I only needed to tell the time and describe our father's departure as 'peaceful'. As I spoke that word, ascribed so often to deaths of the old and infirm, I had a mercifully brief but horrible reprise of the events of that summer morning. It left me shaking and unable to hear, let alone respond to, Louise's words – consoling, probably.

'Are you still there?' she asked eventually.

I managed to pull myself together. 'Yes. It was more emotional than I expected.' Would that one episode control my life for ever, wiping out everything good that came before and blackening everything afterwards?

'Of course you're in shock. However much expected, however peaceful, death is always a shock.'

I was amazed she could say those words, in a comforting, big-sister voice, without remembering.

We talked a little more about our mother, about Reggie, who was enough improved that she planned to fly over for the funeral. Then we said goodbye, and I put down the receiver.

Behaving sensibly, I would have rung Oliver. Instead, I went back to my bedroom. My thoughts returned to fourteen years ago and revolved round the question that had dominated my life for so long and which I had never resolved. My therapist had encouraged me to all sorts of answers and, when that hadn't worked, had taught me ways of dealing with the unanswerable. 'Acceptance' was one of the words she used most often. She made it sound near to forgiveness.

It wasn't what I was after, but it helped a little, and then a little more as time passed, with the inevitable blurring of memory.

So it was only occasionally, like now, that I returned to gnaw and rough up the bone of our love. That was all that remained: a bone – hard and indigestible. Our love, which had seemed so natural and so profound, had it always been cursed by the wickedness of circumstances?

CHAPTER SIX

1990

That evening in the garden was so long, the longest evening Claudia had ever known. Later she told K that. After he had come down to help with Catherine's absurd tennis court, she had said, time slowed, the birds twittered less fast and the breeze, which seemed to live in the topmost branches of the tall chestnuts, went away. Not that they were sitting around: Catherine saw to that. K stood at one side of the court and Claudia the other. They heaved and pulled on the thick wire, dragged to the grass, despite all their efforts, by the heavy net.

Eventually Catherine explained, laughing at K with open mouth, that the secret was to attach the wire to the revolving wheel at the top of the posts first, then use the handle to raise the net. As she demonstrated the technique, Claudia watched, leaning meditatively on the other post.

'Right! I'll go back to my netting now and leave you to it.' The netting to enclose the court had been dumped by Alan in a great bundle on the lawn, and Catherine was attempting to untangle it.

'You look like a fisherman's wife on a Greek beach!' called K.

Catherine didn't respond but K could see she was pleased with the image.

At seven, they heard Douglas Lacey's car come up the driveway.

K, who had never been around for his arrival before, suddenly took in the time. He sprinted up to his office, grabbed his mobile, a new acquisition of which he was proud, and rang Fiona. 'I'm so sorry. I—

'Calm down. Calm down.' She was speaking through his stuttered apologies. 'I'm still in London. In fact, I'm planning to stay the night with Katy. I've left at least three messages.'

K calmed down and looked out of the window while Fiona instructed him about his supper – she was endearingly thorough about things like that. 'I'm just a bit tired tonight,' she ended, and K, eyes on the lawn, now half covered by a deep purple shadow, agreed that it was better she stayed where she was. He guessed that her decision had something to do with her pregnancy plans. Perhaps she thought she was travelling too much.

K returned to the garden. The air was now delicately moist as if someone had spritzed with a giant hand. The grass, too, was shiny and slightly slippery. Douglas Lacey had not come out, but Catherine and her daughter were still there, draping the netting over a skeleton of steel poles. 'Would you like help? I've got a free evening,' he asked.

Catherine dropped her end of the net. 'Oh, yes. Thank you. I need to cook and Douglas is feeling a bit ropy.' She went quickly.

Claudia stood watching her. K was struck by her stillness, not at all what he would have expected in a teenage girl. He decided this was research for his novel, and the slight sense of guilt that he was not going home to heat the lasagne, according to Fiona's instructions, lessened. 'What are we doing?' he asked.

Claudia demonstrated. She seemed very tall as she stretched up to fling a net over a pole, then twist a tie to hold it.

'Not very modern.'

'No.' Her legs, in their flared, ragged jeans, were extraordinarily long.

They began to work together, throwing, draping and tying with a fair amount of efficiency. 'It must be great to be at the start of your holidays.'

Claudia looked at him. She pulled her hair loose from the band that held it back as if to disguise her flushed face. 'I still don't know your name,' she said.

He laughed. Around him the trill of wood-pigeons became fainter. 'I told you, I'm the writer-in-residence.'

'But you must have a name?' She seemed confused by his resistance.

'You can call me K.' Why had he said that? Later he remembered K was the lover in Graham Greene's *The End of the Affair*. Much later, he recalled that K was also the subject of Kafka's *The Trial*. He had given himself a tortured literary precedence. Yet at the time it was no more than a joke.

'K? The letter, you mean?'

'But don't assume I'm called Keith or Kenneth or even Kevin because I'm not.' The seriousness of her expression made him smile.

'OK.' They went back to work. They moved more slowly now, Claudia handing K a tie, then waiting quietly until he wanted another.

When she lifted her arms the red bangle she wore looked as if it would slide all the way up over her elbow. But it never did. The shadow was right across the lawn now. The top branches of the trees were still silhouetted against a blueness tinged with orange, but at trunk level it was black as night.

'Do you think we'll finish before dark?' K paused.

Claudia's face, previously rosy with the flush of youth, now looked as pale as ivory. 'I'm surprised Catherine hasn't called me in for supper.'

'You call your mother by her name?'

'She prefers it. Sometimes I forget and say "Mummy".'

Even in the dimness, K thought her face took on a special expression as she pronounced the childish world. 'What would you prefer?'

'I don't mind.' She walked further away as if to curtail the conversation. Her views were private, it seemed.

They'd circled round most of the court, caging themselves into a rectangle of lawn.

'We're a bit of netting short,' called K, his voice suddenly loud.

'Typical.' Claudia came a little way towards him. 'Anyway, I'd better go in.'

K resisted an urge to take hold of her arm. He remembered his research purpose. 'Was it you I heard playing the violin earlier?'

'Viola.' She corrected him without apparent emotion but she took two steps away.

Sensing her unease, K added, 'I could hardly hear, of course. Unfortunately. But you sounded very good.'

'Just average. A school-orchestra player. I really must go.'

He saw that she didn't know how to leave, that saying goodbye and crossing the garden to the house had become awkward.

'Well, we've done a good job.' He left then, not turning to follow her progress but going briskly to the stable and up to his office, where he collected his things.

Soon he was driving along the road to his house. It was after eight and nearly dark. His headlights, going ahead of him, seemed to be taking him in the wrong direction.

Catherine and Douglas had already eaten when Claudia came into the house. The brightness hurt her eyes; went to stand next to the Aga. For added warmth, she lifted the lid and curved herself over it.

'How odd you look!' Catherine watched her daughter. 'There's meat and two veg in the bottom oven.'

'I'm not hungry.'

'Nor was your father. Not too well either. He's gone to bed now. He did wave from the window, to welcome you home, but you were too involved. Did you finish it?'

'There was a net missing.'

'Oh, shit! Sorry, darling.'

Waiting for her mother to go, Claudia got out the plate and began to pick at peas and potatoes.

'I think I'll watch the news.'

The moment the door had closed, Claudia went to the cupboard and poured herself a huge bowl of cereal. She added milk and several spoonfuls of sugar. The cooked food looked reproachful, so she tipped it into the bin and rinsed the plate, wincing at the gluey grease. Then she returned to her bowl and began to eat. All the time, her mind felt curiously distant from these actions, as if it were occupied somewhere else, processing, decoding, recording.

It had been a long day altogether; getting up early at school, the final assembly, parting from her friends, the train journey, arriving home with her mother. But nothing had seemed so long as the evening in the garden. She tried to make herself understand why but she could hardly come near it. There had been her mother and then the writer, who called himself K. She wondered how well her mother knew this 'writer-in-residence'. She guessed he must be in his late thirties or perhaps even as old as forty. She didn't understand him at all. But there was nothing unusual in that. She seldom felt able to understand anyone, except, perhaps, some of her friends,

45

although even they were capable of behaving outside the character she'd established for them. For example, Bella once boasted of snogging a boy for two hours when only three days previously she'd labelled him 'categorically disgusting'. It was no wonder that adults were even harder to understand. That was why she enjoyed reading so much. In a novel, the author took the trouble to explain motivation. She was very good at understanding characters in books. In fact, she was predicted an A* for her GCSE English literature. At this moment she was half-way through *Anna Karenina,* which, of course, was not on the A Level syllabus but recommended by her teacher. She had been reading it on the train and nearly missed her station.

It was peaceful in the kitchen, although she could hear the news faintly from the next room and the Aga spluttered periodically. From the front of the house, the owl that lived in the yew called loudly. Claudia pictured the man, K as he called himself – a bit pretentious really, although he'd smiled as he said it - sitting on the bench eating his sandwiches. Why had he chosen that spot? she wondered. And he'd said he'd heard her playing. That both embarrassed and pleased her. She had lied about her standard. She was the best strings player in the school, even if it was on a viola.

She'd make sure he wasn't around when she practised tomorrow. Presumably he spent most of the day in that murky little room above the stables. When she was young, Louise used to pretend to her there was a ghost up there. She'd said it was a stable boy who'd killed his master's favourite horse, Black Beauty, by letting him drink a bucket of cold water when he was still hot. The boy fell sick and died, but returned to haunt the place where he'd caused the tragedy. Later Claudia found out where Louise had got the idea, but at the time she'd believed in his ghostly presence and screamed with terror when her sister tried to make her climb up there.

Claudia washed the bowl carefully and went up to her bedroom, calling goodnight to her mother on the way. She picked up *Anna Karenina* from the bedside table and clasped it to her.

CHAPTER SEVEN

1990

Fiona was working in the garden while K sat in a deck-chair reading the newspaper. She said she'd taken too little exercise during the week but K felt uncomfortable all the same.

He stood up to go inside – it was an unattractive day, overcast and windless. Fiona looked up as he went through the doors. 'Don't forget I'm going to ask how you're getting on.'

K felt his skin prickle with irritation. Did she really expect him to give her progress reports, like a child to a teacher? Perhaps she would mark him – 'Trying, but could do better'. His irritation was increased by the knowledge that he was being unfair. All Fiona wanted was to show positive encouragement. She was far too busy to pry and peer. Besides, it wasn't in her nature. More than that, she had total confidence that he would succeed, otherwise, as an eminently practical woman, she would never have agreed to his year's sabbatical.

Contradictorily, it was Fiona's confidence in him that was most annoying. As the weeks passed, he uncovered more and more areas of his inadequacy as a writer. His characters remained stereotypical and lifeless, his descriptions inanimate backcloths. His dialogue occasionally showed a spark of talent but too often degenerated into a striving after wit for its own sake – an ad-man's failing. Worst of all, his subject matter, 'a psychological drama of death and regeneration', as he'd billed it to his (potential) agent, utterly failed to grip him, so how could it possibly grip anyone else?

K went to the kitchen and made a cup of tea for Fiona – as a penance for his mean-mindedness – and poured himself a glass of wine. An immediate gulp had the right effect. 'I'm just not used to so much effing self-analysis,' he said aloud.

'What?' Fiona came in behind him.

'I've made you a cup of tea.'

Fiona sat down at the table. 'So, how are you getting on?'

K took a deep breath and forced an unconvincing laugh. 'Half-term report?'

'It's just about three months.'

'It goes so fast.' A guilty twinge told him that the last two weeks had gone particularly fast. He avoided mentioning Claudia's name even to himself. But he *owed* Fiona. 'I've been rather distracted lately.' Isn't the truth (or near-truth) supposed to be releasing? 'The daughter's home from school. She has friends over. They play tennis right in front of my window.'

'That is awkward,' Fiona agreed sympathetically. 'Can you rearrange where you sit? Move your desk round, I mean.'

'I could try.' If I wanted to. K pictured the scene from his window. In fact, Claudia seldom had friends over. Nor did she play very much. When she did, she played most often with her mother who shouted instructions; 'Hold your racket UP, Claudie!'

He had got into the habit of watching out for her appearances around the garden. Sometimes she walked across the lawn, either skirting the tennis court or going through it, bending to lift the net over her head. When she came back, her hair was wet and sleek. Other times he could see her wandering off with a rug over her arm to the big chestnuts at the end of the garden. She'd spread it out and lie down for hours with a book. On those occasions he felt more able to concentrate on his writing. She was there, fixed in his view, but too far away to see very well or make any contact. Or she came round to the stables to talk to her horse and, two or three times, saddled him and went off for a ride. Not for very long, he noticed. Twice she took him to a field down the road, where she left him to graze for a few days. Then she walked back, swinging her helmet in her hand.

If it was his coffee-break time, he felt justified in coming down and having a word. After all, she was still research material although he was gradually recognising that she was far too reticent for there to be any resemblance between her and the sparky nineteen-year-old he had imagined as his victim. She blushed quite often, not in a blotchy down-the-neck way but in an increased rosiness on her cheeks. It touched him as a sign of her youth. He was touched, too, by the way she seldom looked him in the face, as if there were something about him that was too much for her. He felt flattered by this: it was a little boost for his sinking ego. Gradually, he allowed himself to feel that they shared something in common, the outsider's sensitivity, the artist's secrecy.

He liked it less when Catherine was there too, in her usual restless, laughing mode, which had begun to grate on him. Perhaps his favourite moments were when he sat under the yew with his lunch and Claudia played to him – it amused him to think she did but he knew it wasn't so. After their first meeting, she had not played at around twelve thirty, when he took his place on the bench, for nearly a week. But in the last days she had played every day, always the same piece, a wonderfully romantic melody.

One morning at the stable he had complimented her, as he had on the first day, and although she blushed her pleasure was obvious.

'I'm practising a new piece,' she had explained. 'A Brahms sonata in E flat, just the opening *allegro*.'

'Good. I'll be there from the beginning to the performance.'

She had remained serious. 'I need a pianist for a performance.'

'Can't help you there.' He had felt real disappointment at his lack of musical talent.

'A penny for your thoughts?'

K stopped thinking of Claudia long enough to see Fiona was smiling at him enquiringly. How long had he had been silent? He took another gulp of wine.

'You've started early.' There was the merest hint of criticism.

K shrugged. Mindful of his father's history, she kept an eye on his drinking. He didn't blame her. Yet if he had a tendency to obsession, it was not in the direction of alcohol. He doubted if the child of an alcoholic ever felt comfortable losing control in that direction. His problem was lack of nerve, as if the physical world was sliding off his radar. Soon after he'd met Fiona, he'd spotted that her managing qualities went some way to keeping the mists of invisibility from rising. Besides, she had chased him with single-minded determination.

She touched his shoulder lightly. 'Why don't you try working here for a bit if it's so difficult at Meadowlands?'

'I'll see how I go.' He managed to transform a grimace of annoyance into a friendly smile.

*

Claudia picked up *The Mill on the Floss* from her bedside table, then a book of Seamus Heaney's poetry. Finally she got out an A4 refill pad and a pen. Downstairs, she collected an apple and her favourite rug – woven in soft heather colours, pink and mauve. Then she wandered out to the garden. Everywhere, house and garden, was more peaceful on the afternoons when her mother worked at the Save the Children shop: Monday, Wednesday and Friday, two thirty to four thirty, which meant she was away from two until five.

Claudia lingered on the terrace in front of the house. Some tall white lilies growing in round tubs were just opening and already spreading their heavy scent. She wondered how much she liked it – so many perfumes were cloying and fake but, of course, this was the real thing. Her mother wore Chanel No 5 which she liked to say her mother had worn before her. Claudia had never met her grandmother, who'd died before she was born.

She gave the lilies a look of approval, then went slowly towards her habitual place under the chestnut trees. There was little sun and it was not particularly hot but she was still drawn to the trees, with their bulging trunks and large, ornate leaves. She felt protected and even secret. When she lay down, a cluster of yellow flowers became huge in her eye-line and as bright as any sun.

She spread out her rug neatly and lay down. Today was a sleepy day. She read a poem but its words didn't stay with her. She opened *The Mill on the Floss,* but the same thing happened. She felt shockingly unmoved by the trials of poor Maggie Tulliver. There remained her pad, which contained the start of a new attempt at a diary and a few lines of poetry she had felt moved to copy out:

> *How vainly men themselves amaze*
> *To win the palm, the oak, or bays . . .*

It was by Andrew Marvell, called 'The Garden.' At least she wasn't fool enough to try writing poetry herself.

Inevitably the writer-in-residence, K, entered her thoughts. In his presence, her usual reactions seemed to change, giving her the strange sensation of being a little blind, a little deaf. This hindered her understanding. And yet there was nothing odd about him or his situation: a middle-aged man finding peace to write a novel. It didn't seem odd to Catherine. So why did he have this effect on her, as if he sucked away the air from around her so it was difficult to breathe? It was a mystery and perhaps she'd try to avoid him. But the odd thing was, she'd got into the habit of playing for him when he sat eating his lunch. She didn't admit it to him but it gave her pleasure to think of him listening, enjoying the music she created with her viola.

Everyone thought English was her strong subject but she knew her *heart* was in music. On the other hand she had found GCSE Music difficult and, much more worrying, she feared her playing lacked some essential *motor*. She'd seen that in certain players at whatever age. They were dynamos of energy.

Claudia began to think of herself more and more critically. By comparison with her mother, who never stopped 'doing' things, and Louise who, admittedly ten years older, had already got married, had two babies *and* lived in New York, she was a flaccid, supine creature. Even her father, although not well recently, went off absolutely every weekday at eight fifteen and did not return till seven. A boy she'd rather liked had advised her recently to 'lighten up', but she felt too light already, hardly in existence at all.

Moodily, Claudia rolled on to her stomach, and cradled her head in her arms. She had never been seriously in love either, although she pretended now and again. And the two boys who most attracted her were attached to two of her friends, who would kill her if she even admitted to liking them, let alone acted on it. Being so tall with such long feet didn't help. Doubtless Anna Karenina had had tiny feet – not that her fate was exactly cheerful. Two nights earlier, Claudia had cried real tears at the end of the book.

A rustle above her head signalled the arrival of a bird, who'd obviously decided that the large prone object presented no threat. He launched into a virtuoso performance of trills and long-held notes. Claudia listened carefully. He might be a song-thrush, she decided. If she'd had perfect pitch, she would have been able to recognise the notes: B flat, C, at the top end of the register anyway. Perhaps it was just a question of concentration. She would shut her eyes and try.

K's morning had gone rather better than usual. He had added a characteristic to the murderer that seemed to give him a peculiarity and took him away from the generic 'murderer' towards becoming a real human being: he was now a passionate music lover. Unsurprisingly, Claudia's playing had given him the idea. He had never felt himself capable of appreciating music fully, his ear was too uneducated, but listening to Claudia's viola day after day had made him imagine how a music buff might feel.

As a result of this small breakthrough, he returned to his desk after lunch with an unexpected sense of self-satisfaction. Fleetingly, he decided that he would report a little of this – imprecisely – to Fiona that evening, and she would understand that he didn't need to turn to their house. He was doing OK.

At two thirty, soon after Catherine had driven off at her habitual breakneck speed for Save the Children, he saw Claudia crossing the lawn. She was wearing a floppy straw hat, floral skirt almost to her ankles and her feet were bare. A long cardigan dangled to her hips and she hugged books and a rug. Normally, he would have looked down again once she had settled under the tree but his good humour made him more lenient with himself. He watched her lying first one way and then another but always with what he described to himself as 'graceful angularity' – a phrase he might be able to use in his novel. He noted she was restless, unlike her usual bookworm concentration, and might not mind being disturbed. He *deserved* a break.

By the time he reached the lawn, Claudia was lying face down. Her hat lay beside her. He hesitated in case she was asleep, but as he took another couple of steps, a bird flew away from a branch just above her and she sat up. Or maybe she'd heard his tread.

'Hi.' K suddenly felt embarrassed, as if he was intruding on private space. It was the expression on her face, more shock than surprise. The pink flush appeared in her cheeks.

'Hi.' She drew her legs under her so that she was almost kneeling. The soles of her narrow feet were quite dirty, he saw. She often went barefoot for much of the day.

'I hope I'm not disturbing you.'

'I was listening to the bird. It has such a range. Much greater than I guessed at first. ' Her voice was earnest. 'Do you know anything about birds?'

'A bit.' K still felt awkward standing there above her, even though she had introduced a subject of conversation. In fact, he knew quite a lot about birds. But usually he didn't like to remind himself. His father had taught him as a child, leading him on day-long expeditions that always broke for lunch at a pub, which seemed to arise out of the landscape at just the right moment. They had been wonderful days. Until the pub stops became longer and more frequent. 'Can I sit down?'

Claudia didn't answer but she tucked her legs further under her so there was space on the rug. K joined her, lying on one elbow so that his long legs stretched on to the grass. He began to talk about birds. 'That was a song-thrush. You have blackbirds here too, don't you?'

'I don't know. I think so.'

'It's unusual for birds of different species to share the same space. But your song-thrush eats earthworms and slugs while the blackbirds stick to berries and fruit so they tolerate each other's presence. The song-thrush is an inventive bird. It's learnt to crack a snail shell by knocking it repeatedly against a stone. You'll often hear the hammering...'

Claudia listened attentively, her eyes sometimes cast down, sometimes gazing across the garden, but never on his face. When he stopped talking, she shifted so that she was sitting cross-legged. He admired the ease of it and noticed that her feet had disappeared under her skirt. 'How are you getting on?' she asked.

How was it that the same question asked by Fiona threw him into a rage but with Claudia he felt flattered, encouraged? It came with no baggage, of course. 'I had a good morning for once.'

'I would like to be able to write.' She sighed a little.

Again, in anyone else, he would have been irritated and found it difficult to avoid pointing out, probably scornfully, that it wasn't a question of 'liking to write' or 'liking to be able' but a question of doing it. A decision implemented. 'You've got a pad there?'

'Yes. A diary. I haven't written anything for weeks. At school I'm afraid people will read it, and at home there's nothing worth recording.'

K felt his *amour propre* absurdly punctured by this remark. He was part of her life at home, even if only in a minor role – surely not 'nothing'. 'They say a diary is the best training for a writer.'

'Did you keep a diary?'

'I wrote commercials for a living.' He wondered if she would be impressed if he quoted from some of his well-known campaigns. But it hardly seemed to fit in with *The Mill on the Floss*, which he

53

could see near her right knee, even less with Seamus Heaney, whose poems lay near the left.

'Then you haven't been a real writer for long?' The ineptness of 'real' seemed to strike her because the flush which had almost subsided, rose again.

'No, I've taken a year off from my *real* work.' He emphasised the word, smiling, he hoped, reassuringly. 'But if I succeed, I would like to become a *real* writer.'

It seemed to work because Claudia gave him a tentative smile. Yet he could still sense the tension.

'Tomorrow my friend Bella's coming to stay.' The words sounded like a kind of defence.

K had never imagined that a friend would appear to disturb the serenity of their days. Claudia had seemed to him self-contained, with no need of outside contact. At first, it was true, he had found it a little strange and had overheard Catherine trying to cajole her into invitations, even to a local tennis tournament. But then, as the weeks had passed, unchanging, he had accepted it as the status quo, a reflection of her nature. It had made him feel closer to her.

'Tomorrow, you say?' His voice had an edge.

'She's my best friend. She always comes to stay. And then I go to stay with her.' Claudia's voice rose, as if she had picked up his disapproval.

K felt himself full of hatred for this Bella (a ridiculous name) and the very idea of 'best friends'. How childish! But, then, Claudia was a child. He took a grip and tried to convince himself that his spurt of spleen had been prompted by the threat of noisy interruption to his working day. 'That's nice for you, then.'

'Yes.' There was a pause. Claudia looked as if she wanted to leave, yet she crouched there, still gazing up at him – with some kind of appeal?

'I should get back to work.' Now he was going, she unwound her legs restlessly.

'I might have a swim.'

K was surprised. It wasn't the weather for a swim. But the announcement of Bella's imminent arrival had taken the peace out of the afternoon. 'I'll help you take off the cover.'

He gave her no choice. She got up quickly and started, almost springing, across the lawn. He followed her.

The pool was rectangular and not large but there was an elegant little changing hut.

K knew she expected him to leave. In fact, she had probably muttered 'goodbye'. But ever since she had told him about Bella, he had felt perverse. Why shouldn't he stay – sit on the patio and watch her flash up and down? (He had no doubt she was a graceful swimmer.) Or maybe he'd borrow a pair of trunks and swim too. Catherine had asked him often enough. He had done an excellent morning's work, he reminded himself – its excellence was increasing in his memory – and at this moment his dreary room held no delights for him.

Claudia had changed with a schoolgirl's speed into her swimsuit; the glass at the front of the hut was one way so she could look out and see K but he couldn't see her until she appeared at the doorway. She hesitated a moment. Then, seeming to make up her mind, she pushed open the door and, looking neither to right nor left, ran down the steps and dived into the pool.

K, hovering on the far side, caught her meteoric progress in his mind's eye. If she had thought to evade him she'd failed. He had seen her perfectly, the long, slender legs, the narrow torso flowering into surprisingly full breasts. She was a woman as well as a child.

Immediately ashamed of this kind of voyeurism, K walked away briskly, and, after making himself a cup to tea, returned to his desk. He determined not to watch for Claudia's return to the house. He put his elbows on the desk and his head into his hands. The flash of her half-naked body had made him admit to himself for the first time that his interest in her was neither the casual attitude of a nearly middle-aged man towards a friendly (actually, shy) schoolgirl, nor the objective attitude of a writer looking for research. Sitting alone in his darkish room, with the pile of paper in front of him, his sense of shame grew.

It was with relief that, after a while, he recalled the imminent arrival of the friend, Bella. That would shift his focus.

Returning to the house and her room, Claudia thought that her resolution to throw herself into her music over the holidays would be spoiled by Bella's visit. Bella didn't appreciate her playing, or any music other than pop. Worst of all, she liked to bang out 'Chopsticks' on the piano. In fact, they were opposites in most ways. Just consciously, she pictured K and herself sitting on the rug under the tree. She forgot that she had become uneasy in his presence and wanted him to leave, and the moment lodged in her mind as an image of perfection. Bella would break all that. Slowly, and without much conviction, she opened the case and took out her viola.

After a few bars, she found that her wet hair was in danger of dripping into the instrument. She went to the bathroom, wound a blue towel turban round her head and resumed playing.

Half an hour later Catherine, passing by the open bedroom door, stopped for a moment to watch her daughter, so tall and straight, with that funny turban – quite incongruous with the viola. She tried to remember if Louise had been so intense at that age. Of course, she'd been involved with her riding friends. Claudia hadn't ridden more than two or three times this holidays. If it went on like this, she'd better see about selling her horse. Their money was not infinite, as Douglas was beginning to make clear.

The strains of the viola followed Catherine downstairs but she was not musical enough to know how good the playing was. It just sounded sad. She was sure Louise never willingly spent a day on her own. Thank God for Bella.

CHAPTER EIGHT

1990

Bella's presence changed the atmosphere in the house. She was a bright, outspoken girl, good with people, good at tennis, good at enjoying life. Physically, she was not unlike Claudia to look at, fair and above average height; their similarity was accentuated because they swapped clothes with each other, sometimes three or four times a day.

K watched them crossing the lawn to swim or playing on the newly mown tennis court, and told himself that a weight had been lifted from him. Claudia, on her own, had seemed out of the ordinary. As one of a pair, he could see her for what she was: a gawky, introspective middle-class schoolgirl. All the same he found himself listening for her voice. Before Bella's coming, she had spoken very little and he hadn't had much idea of the tone, but Bella and she talked a lot and he heard that Claudia's voice was deeper than her friend's. It should have belonged to an older woman.

On the Wednesday of Bella's arrival, they received their GCSE results, Bella over the telephone from her mother. K saw them whooping across the lawn, Claudia waving a bit of paper. Clearly they had both done well. He opened his window to shout congratulations and hear, perhaps, the extent of their success, but they didn't respond to his call and sped past on their way for a swim.

On the Thursday of Bella's stay the two girls went riding, Claudia on a bicycle. Apparently, they planned to take turns on the horse. On Friday, they set off during K's coffee-break so it seemed natural to go down and introduce himself.

Claudia did it for him, 'This is our writer-in-residence. I don't know his real name so I call him K.' Both girls laughed.

They were dressed identically, in jodhpurs, T-shirts and black hard hats. The horse, very big to K who had never even sat on one, stamped about impatiently.

'Where are you going?'

'You'd be surprised at the number of bridleways.' Claudia smiled at him so brilliantly that he almost took a step back – what had she meant by it?

Claudia swung herself agilely on to her horse. Bella mounted the bicycle.

'You only need a dog,' called K.

'We had one till last Christmas when the poor old thing keeled over.' Claudia had twisted round to speak, her palm resting on the horse's rump.

K found himself ridiculously piqued that he hadn't known a dog had been part of the household so recently.

Catherine appeared at the door to give them some instructions. K watched them go. They seemed to be part of a privileged class that had nothing to do with him. Or with Fiona. He went back upstairs to tidy his desk and thought positively about the weekend ahead. It would give him time to recover, he decided, although he wasn't prepared to identify too exactly from what he needed to recover.

Claudia was enjoying the unusual sensation of overflowing vitality. Perhaps she had caught it from Bella or perhaps it was the eager horse between her legs, or the cloudy sunshine of a summer afternoon, or K's admiration. She was prepared to admit that now, on horseback. She hadn't minding him staring and she had even dared to smile.

'Who *is* that man?' hissed Bella, the moment they were out of the driveway.

'I'll tell you. But not now. This bit's single file.'

'He's gorgeous!' Bella called, as she fell back.

Claudia knew she had no intention of telling Bella about K. For one thing she didn't have anything much to tell. He was writing a novel. That was all there was to it.

K and Fiona spent a particularly happy weekend. When K taxed Fiona with her cheerfulness, she mentioned, without elaborating, a new project, which he assumed had something to do with her work, a part of her life on which she seldom enlarged. Much later, he realised she had been in the process of buying the London flat, to be a surprise for him.

On Saturday, a blustery day with squally showers, they put on their similar lightweight anoraks (it wasn't cold) and went for a brisk two-hour walk on the common. Spirits raised, they drove on to an auction in town where K bid unsuccessfully for a hideous soup tureen with a dozen hideous bowls – they laughed afterwards about their narrow escape. On the way home, they dropped in at a local pub where they met various acquaintances, mostly single but including a couple they knew slightly. Over gin and tonic, life took on a merry glow and K felt a secure rightness in his place beside Fiona. He felt proud of them as a team, of their fifteen years of marriage. This view was encouraged by the couple in the pub who bickered whenever they talked to each other. He and Fiona respected each other too much for that.

'Time to go,' announced Fiona, after an hour or so, and K followed willingly.

'Calling time, is she?' asked Craig, a burly man who always bought more rounds than most. He was in the wine importing business so perhaps he had a personal interest.

'A wife's prerogative,' smiled Fiona, and K agreed.

'Saturdays should always be like this,' he said later, as Fiona placed a plate of salad between them on the kitchen table. 'How about I open a bottle of wine?'

'There's no point in stopping now.'

Whether it was their alcohol consumption or a reflection of the harmonious day, their love-making had a blithe sweetness about it that flattered both of them. Waking later in the night, K noted that the two things most on their minds – her desire for a baby and his trials with the novel – had not been mentioned all day. He thought it strange that this had led to so much relaxed good humour as if they couldn't share what was most important.

CHAPTER NINE

2004

I woke up early to find my face bathed in tears. I lay still, letting them dry naturally in the cool morning air. What should I do? The question was filled with anguish. When I had left Valpo I was certainly expecting to see Claudia, but at her wedding, on the arm of the man she had chosen to look after her for the rest of her life. But everything had turned out differently. She was not married, not yet.

Shakily, I rose from my bed and went to the kettle. It already had water in it and I didn't have the energy to get fresh. I pressed the switch and stood staring stupidly at the red light.

Six months after that never-to-be-erased summer morning, an English acquaintance of mine, a bachelor called Craig, came to Chile, a rare destination then for foreign travellers. Craig had a wine-importing business and had spotted a new source of supply. In 1991 Chilean wine was not recognised as it is now. We met entirely by chance. He had taken a day off from the vineyards to visit Valparaiso, and I was drinking a *pisco* sour on the terrace of the Hotel Weymouth. I had not yet found my shack. In fact, this meeting spurred me on to it.

It was winter in England but summer in Chile, a hot February evening when I had felt myself safely muffled in darkness. I was still half-crazed with guilt and shame.

To be fair, he was quite tactful. Of course he knew my story – it had been widely reported in the papers – but he didn't show undue surprise at discovering me in my hideout. There were no prurient questions: we talked mostly about his wine-import plans. He even advised me to put money into his firm, as if I were a normal person.

He did ask why I had come to Valparaiso when it was 'so very far

60

away', and I was amazed that he hadn't immediately understood that its remoteness was the reason I was there. But I told him I'd always liked Neruda's poems, which was true enough, and I think he got the idea that there was some plan to my new life, rather than the reality of a random escape. I had happened to see a travel brochure about Chile, which included a photo of Valparaiso, on the day I decided to leave England.

Yet it was I who couldn't resist, as we parted, asking him a question: 'How is she?'

He didn't pretend not to understand, although I hadn't brought myself to say her name.

'Not good,' he said. 'Still in and out of hospital.'

'But she's all right?' I said stupidly, meaning, I suppose, that she was alive.

'Just about.'

That was all either of us could bear. I assumed he must despise me, or worse. He had been kind and honest when I deserved neither.

Nearly fourteen years later it was Craig who told me about Claudia's wedding. This time we didn't meet by chance. He sought me out, asked around for the tall *señor ingles*. It was winter this time and we'd sat in my grubby room, which was filled with canvases. Both our lives had changed. He had become successful – he pointed out that if I'd taken his advice and invested in his company I'd be a rich man. I had become a painter.

'They're not bad,' he commented. But he didn't offer to buy one. I presume friendship only went so far for someone like me. Yet he told me about Claudia's wedding. I didn't ask him this time. He told me. 'She's marrying a doctor,' he said. That was all. Then he added, 'A very bright man.' Perhaps he was warning me off. I'm sure he didn't expect his information to bring me to England. Quite possibly, he'd have been horrified to know it had.

'A doctor'. 'A very bright man'. Perhaps I had come to see him, not her. But I don't think so. After so long, I could hardly be jealous.

The kettle had been bubbling for some time so I emptied a sachet of coffee into a mug and poured in the water. I took it back to bed with me as the most comfortable place.

During the sixteen-hour flight from Santiago (including a break in Madrid) I had allowed myself to picture Claudia in her wedding gown. I imagined her long fair hair twisted up into a crown on which the veil floated lightly. Her dress, I felt sure, would be traditional, perhaps cream satin, tight-fitting at the waist with a sculptured bodice and long sleeves. I decided she would wear pearls round her neck, maybe given to her by the groom. Her shoes would be satin too, showing off her elegant feet.

I had more trouble with her face. It was disguised, of course, by the veil as she entered the church on her father's arm. But at some point she would throw it back. At the very point, in fact, where my imagination failed and she was married to her nice doctor.

In sudden agitation, I found I'd splashed the last of my coffee over the duvet. Brown stains spread quickly. I leapt out of bed, dragged it to the bathroom, ran cold water lavishly over it.

I looked at my watch and saw it was now seven. It seemed doubtful that the hotel would serve breakfast so early on a Sunday. I went over to the window and, seeing it wasn't raining but misty with the promise of a bright day, decided to go for a walk.

I had no alternative but to continue in my dress-suit trousers and white shirt of the day before. Luckily, the hotel had provided a razor. I shaved, trying to avoid seeing my face too clearly. Even though I'd left Chile in the winter, the sunburn seemed ingrained now, not a healthy bronzing but a cast of darkness.

The lake, the 'Fresh Ponds' of the hotel name, was hidden in a thick swathe of mist. The trees rose black to half their height when the rising sun, already quite high, illuminated the rich greens of their topmost boughs. But I was at mist level, striding out briskly, trying, with exercise, to speed up my sluggish blood and clear my heavy head. It was cool as the road left the shore of the lake and wound between tall pinewoods. I thought momentarily of returning for my jacket then remembered that the only item of clothing I had with me of that description was my father's tailcoat. There was no point in making myself unnecessarily ridiculous. Besides, I soon came out onto a less shaded, wider road where the sun could reach and there were only patches of mist lying in the fields at either side. I slowed a little. I was beginning to feel hungry, having had nothing but the priest's pie the evening before and nothing at all on the day before that. I was even a little dizzy and when I saw a wooden bench, set back a few yards from the road, I took the opportunity to rest.

The sun was directly in my eyes but I rather enjoyed that. The occasional car passed, rare enough to make me look up as it went by. Inevitably, my thoughts returned to Claudia. It struck me that the reason I couldn't picture her face when the veil was thrown back was because she was fourteen years older than when I last saw her. Then she had been a youthful sixteen, now she was a mature woman of thirty. I repeated the numbers to myself as if to make them real. She might be quite altered, short brown hair (it often changed colour with age), a heavy face, thick-set body or, alternatively, gaunt, spiky, with none of the grace I'd loved so much. I couldn't picture her face beneath the veil because I had no idea what it would be like.

I could understand why I hadn't allowed myself to admit it before. It made even less likely any remaining link between us. It made my presence in England, on this bench, even more ludicrously superfluous.

Cast into despondency, I stared vacantly ahead. I became aware of a car coming rather slowly towards me, from the right, on my side of the road. I watched it, more as a distraction than anything else. The sun was still in my eyes but, as it came closer, I could see that it was driven by a woman with fair, shoulder-length hair. I continued watching. The face, in profile as the car came level with me and passed, was intent, very still, self-absorbed, but just for a moment I felt her gaze take in my presence on the bench.

It was only after the car had gone by that the woman's physiognomy – the high brow, straight nose, flat planes of the cheeks, set mouth and curved chin – registered. I felt a wave of sickness. After my previous thoughts, it seemed a grotesque mockery that Fate should present me with a Claudia lookalike. My Claudia had not been old enough to drive a car, but that woman, her features and even her aura – to use a pretentious word – was as like her as it was possible to be and not be her.

Because, of course, it couldn't have been her. Life was not like that. The sun and my empty dizziness had produced an image from the past. I must go back to the hotel, eat a substantial breakfast and swap ghosts for the comforting banality of a Sunday paper. Despite these resolutions, it was a long time before I found the strength to get to my feet.

*

Oliver appeared at midday. I had not expected it. He crept into my bedroom and I only became aware of him as a dark shadow across the bright curtains. Perhaps he was looking at the marquee. Not that Oliver is dark in any sense. He has fairish, almost ginger hair, grey, rather luminous eyes, and the sort of soft, pale skin that goes with his colouring. This almost childish freshness makes him look much younger than his age, thirty-six, and also less strong: he is very strong and determined. An only child, his mother died when he was eight and he was brought up by his father, one of those pot-bellied Irish men you see laying pavement slabs – at least, according to Oliver. So Oliver became a doctor without the usual advantages. Nothing was too difficult for him. Not even me.

'Good morning.' He had seen me stir.

'Darling, when did you sleep?' I sat up. I knew he wouldn't answer. He had told me when I went days without sleeping (and had gone weeks before) that sleep was a luxury, not a necessity. 'But I need rest from my thoughts!' I would cry.

'Ah,' he would answer solemnly, 'that's another thing altogether. Don't confuse it with sleep. Sleep is a chemical operation of the body which does not necessarily result in rest from one's thoughts. You must find rest from them elsewhere and then, perhaps, sleep.'

He came to my bed and held me. I wanted to tell him about the good end of my father, the way my mother and I had formed a circuit with him between us, but I also wanted to be quiet in his arms. Oliver always had that effect. I had told him more than anyone, including my shrink, but he never probed.

'I'm famished.' He got up.

'Wait. I'll cook you a huge breakfast.'

'Catherine's still at the hospital?'

'I expect so. I've been lying here…' I paused '…drifting.' It was a positive word between us. 'Now I'm ready to go.'

The door to my father's bedroom was closed, as it had been whenever he was in a nursing-home or hospital. Even before that. He and my mother hadn't shared a room for years. After I had ruined his life, he became almost completely reclusive. Not that he had ever been sociable, as Oliver had once pointed out from my description of our family life. In fact, he had only just stopped short of suggesting that my father had used the summer's events, at least in part, as an excuse to behave in a way that suited him. Of course, I felt far too guilty to accept this version but it was true that he had been unfit for years and that it had usually been my mother who attended school events or took me to London for the theatre. But that had been in another world.

The kitchen was filled with sun, almost too much so. I got out from the fridge bacon, sausages, tomatoes, mushrooms.

'Who cares about cholesterol anyway?' exclaimed Oliver, appreciatively.

'Prepare for an olfactory orgy.' I could feel his loving attention following me wherever I went. I had put on an apron, tying it tightly round my waist. As I leant over the Aga, prodding the sausages now and again, he came over and put his hands round my waist and his face in my neck. I knew he wanted to take me back to the bedroom so that we could make love and be joined even closer together. Even on the morning of my father's death. Particularly on the morning of my father's death.

One part of me wanted it too. The part that wanted to loosen the strings of the past, that looked to a bright future.

'Oh, Oliver.' He knew that meant no. I was too tightly bound. The best I could manage was fried sausages and tomatoes.

'So where's the egg?' His breath tickled my ear.

'You're just greedy.' I turned to face him and we kissed, a gentle, undemanding kiss.

After breakfast – brunch, really – we sat in the drawing room, waiting for Catherine. She had telephoned. There were things to discuss.

In years past the room had been gaily coloured, with too many clashing chintzes and patterned cushions, but they were faded now, worn through in places, and the effect was pleasantly unfocused, almost elegant. Lack of money can bring benefits.

We began to discuss our plans. Oliver wanted to forget any kind of public wedding and get to a register office as soon as it felt right to me. Feeling about as unfocussed as the chintz, I agreed that sounded best. 'Maybe October,' he suggested.

'Yes, October.' We were as good as married already. Many of my things were already at Oliver's flat, although I hadn't got rid of my own place yet.

'I suppose your mother will sell this house quickly.'

'She has to. The mortgage repayment and the money she's borrowed from the bank won't leave her with that much anyway. I've told you. We've just been clinging on.' I smiled at him. 'She wanted to give me a grand wedding.'

We both fell silent, struck dumb, perhaps, by too many arrangements. We weren't sitting together. Oliver had taken the sofa but I'd wanted to avoid the white mountain of the marquee and was in a chair facing across the lawn, which led to the swimming-pool and used to be part tennis court. The netting was still slumped in the shed tacked on to the back of the stables. Once, when I was looking for Catherine's secateurs, I had spotted it with some emotion. 'I expect the new owner of the house would build a hard tennis court,' I said, and noted Oliver's expression of surprise at such an irrelevance.

Even at this time, my mother drove fast up the drive. 'My sister's come down from Shrewsbury,' she announced, when she found us in the drawing room, 'and James will pop by later.' James was an old family friend, a lugubrious divorcé who admired her. 'So you won't be too overloaded, Claudie, dear.' She took in Oliver's presence, seemingly for the first time. 'The flying doctor, too.'

'I'm so sorry, Catherine,' Oliver had stood up when she came in and was waiting for her to notice him.

'Yes. Thank you. But it was a release. We must remember that.' She sagged into a chair and ran a hand over her face. 'I'm knackered.'

I looked at her wonderingly – not long enough for her to notice – then went off to make a pot of tea. It felt like the first time I'd heard her admit to being human.

The knock seemed unnaturally and unnecessarily loud. I had eaten a large hotel breakfast, beginning with porridge and ending with grapefruit segments, then returned to lie on my bed. 'Who is it?'

'The management requests hotel guests to vacate their rooms by midday at the latest.' The voice, male like the knock, was bullying.

'Even for guests who are staying a second night?' This was an off-the-cuff riposte but at once seemed the right decision. I could never return to Fiona's flat. I would sell it as quickly as possible, keep a little to finance my narrow life in Chile –I didn't want to end up a charity case – and find a deserving recipient for the rest. What was that line? 'The poor are always with us.' Why not benefit my poor neighbours in Valparaiso? There're enough priests holding out their hands. 'What?'

'I was saying that the management hadn't informed me you were staying another night, sir.' The tone was less hectoring.

'That's because the management has not yet been informed. You may be the one to do so.'

'Yes, sir.' Steps retreated down the passageway. Since they had taken my credit-card number at Reception, I felt disinclined to help him further.

It was clear that I could no longer consider England my home, in however vague or long-term a way. I had left voluntarily, exiled myself as the nearest thing to punishment. And yet it has suited me too, and, gradually, I have made a life for myself. Admittedly, that life doesn't include people, except those I have to deal with as a painter on a minimal business level. I have endured life under Pinochet and life without him and it has made no difference to me. I still feel unfit for human company. The reaction of my (few) English friends and acquaintances confirmed this view. Craig was the only one who had made any attempt to contact me, and if others had, my hiding-place had eluded them. But I didn't believe they had tried. I was beyond the pale and had rightly taken up residence there.

What, after all, would I come back for? Why were people attached to this idea of home? My only occupation depended on the ragged vibrancy of my adopted city. I would give the money from the flat to the little stubby priest whom I sometimes saw straining up the *cerros*. Suddenly I felt swept up in a surge of homesickness for Valpo, for my misty view of the harbour, which my imagination filled with great fleets, like the 1866 Whistler painting I'd found, to my delight, in one of my art books. In other moods I smiled at the fat battle-ships of the Chilean navy, which were actually there, in front of my eyes. I missed the white oleander that grew up through the railings of my balcony, tangling with the ostentatious purplish pink of the bougainvillaea and an almond tree that grew more or less through my neighbour's roof. I missed the chorus of dogs, whose uncon-trolled barking used to mock my sleepless nights, and now kept me company whether I was awake or in my dreams. I missed the spires of the Anglican and Unitarian churches, below me, which had once pointed a finger to heaven at my shame but have now accepted me into the jungle of weak humanity. I am grateful to the very slope of the land, which makes walking a heroic effort, and for the flutter of deep-down earthquakes that remind me of my human vulnerability. I love the blue, red and yellow *ascensores* that crawl bravely up the ravines. I am besotted by the sky, particularly where it meets the sea, and at sunset when the colour changes in two halves like a moving abstract; if I cast my eyes to the right, I can include a third colour where the crescent of land encompassing the bay turns from pale ochre to the darkest Prussian blue. This is my world now. It had been madness to come back.

Yet even as I lay on my bare bed – the duvet was still in the bathroom – thinking such thoughts, one part of my mind held on to the determination to find Claudia.

In the afternoon Oliver and I made love. I never liked to disappoint him for too long: love was simple to him – you loved, you made love and then you married. He had loved and made love several times before he met me but, in the course of his long training to be a doctor, he'd not found time for marriage. I was lucky.

What I never quite knew (or wanted to know) was how far he understood the difference between us. Love was anything but simple to me. An outsider or, indeed, my shrink on occasion might suggest that my first experience had distorted my perspective so thoroughly that it could never be smoothed. But I think my own nature made me and makes me what I am. Right from the very beginning, even as an inexperienced child. Any other explanation makes me seem so passive as to be almost without will. It was the disparity of our ages that encouraged people to jump to the conclusion that I was the led, never the leader. Yet why shouldn't a young person be as strong-willed as the old? I wanted K as much as he wanted me. Not at first, when I was uncertain and afraid, but my love made me grow up fast. Then I wanted him as fiercely as anyone could, of any age. More fiercely.

CHAPTER TEN

1990

Bella's visit had become painful to K. He might have been consoled if he'd known that Claudia herself was beginning to find her friend irksome. They were quarrelling, over silly, childish things, in which music usually figured. Bella had brought a selection of CDs, which she liked to play, if possible, non-stop and loudly. Even when Claudia was practising her viola, she could hear the beat in her head. Bella had also brought with her half a dozen films on videotape, which she suggested they watched after Catherine had gone to bed. If Claudia said she was too tired, she said, quite sharply, 'It's not as if you have anything to get up for, is it?'

Bella made it clear that she felt bored, trapped and out of sympathy with her dreamy friend. Claudia wasn't even interested in discussing the local talent (i.e. boys) who lived near Bella, and seemed to know none on her own patch. In Bella's view, Claudia was immature and no fun. Then Bella had toothache. Claudia stole glasses of sherry for her and plied her sympathetically with paracetamol, but it did little good. Now Bella was not only bored but in pain. 'A blocked wisdom tooth is equivalent to third-degree torture,' she told Claudia, imprecisely. On the Wednesday, a week after her arrival, she spent the morning in bed reading the latest Jilly Cooper.

Struggling as usual with his novel, K saw Claudia cross the lawn on her own to the swimming-pool. When Bella didn't follow her, he couldn't control a surge of hope. Perhaps she had left the evening before, after he'd gone home. It was already a beautiful day, the shadows pale across the grass, the sky a shroud of perfect blue, but now it became even more lovely. He would swim at lunchtime, he told himself, eyeing the bag in which he'd brought trunks and a towel. The cool water would clear his mind the way nothing else could. Inevitably, he pictured Claudia flashing past him and diving into the pool.

The moment Bella left, he felt sure everything would return to normal and he would be able to savour again the particular aura that was Claudia's, a subtle mixture of self-possession and secrecy, a tentative looking outwards with a real delight in the things around her, the garden, its flowers and birds, her music, her books, the pool. He didn't need to talk to her, he told himself, it would be enough to see her restored to her real self, not squeezed into being one of two.

Claudia was feeling much the same about herself. For an hour or so she was free to behave as she wanted. She could swim, dream beside the pool or try without interruption to finish *The Mill on the Floss*. The garden, which had, through Bella's eyes, begun to seem dull, was filled with delights once more. Wrapped in a towel, she wandered round, head high. The thought crossed her mind, 'perhaps Bella's tooth is so bad she won't want to stay.

Meanwhile Bella had used her own independent time to nip downstairs and ring her mother. 'My tooth's agony, Mum. I must see a dentist ...'

Claudia and Bella had been best friends for so long that this splitting up was more important than it seemed. It was a recognition that they were growing up to be different people, although Bella thought it was about her growing up and Claudia staying behind. Over lunch she explained that her mother would be picking her up in the morning to take her to the dentist. Somehow, without any words, it became clear that Claudia would not be going as usual to stay with her.

Catherine, in a hurry to depart for her Save the Children afternoon, commented, 'Only a year more and you'll be able to drive yourselves. What a difference that will make.' Claudia, who had been picking at a cheese salad, suddenly found herself filled with the joy of a released prisoner. Her face, however, showed none of this. 'Poor Bella,' she said. 'I do hope the dentist sorts it out.' As she said it she felt hypocritical.

*

As this was decided, K was ploughing up and down the pool. He hadn't swum since the previous year when he and Fiona had taken a week's holiday at Camaiore on the Italian coast. His joints felt stiff but loosened gradually as the water flowed round him. He would swim each day, he decided, allow his mind to idle a little and, with any luck, untangle a few of the conundrums the book presented. He had begun to think of his novel as a complicated cat's cradle, which he was striving to smooth into a shapely whole before it turned on him and strangled him in its torturous threads.

After swimming, he sunbathed for a while, almost falling asleep. He had olive skin, which darkened easily without burning. When he heard Catherine's car leaving, he got up, dressed slowly and returned to his room.

Half an hour later, the girls came out with tennis racquets and balls. They had decided to part with good humour. K watched them in dismay. 'Go on, Claudie, run. Run!' shouted Bella, sounding eerily like Catherine. When they had finished, they flung themselves on to the grass with cries about how exhausted they were.

K decided to go home early. He would prepare supper. He knew there was rice, cold chicken, tomatoes and peppers, enough ingredients for a curry.

K measured out the rice with some satisfaction. He had always liked cooking now and again. Perhaps this was the time to take it more seriously. He opened the jar of curry paste and began to chop the chicken, peppers and tomatoes. He remembered with pleasure that cookbook phrase 'combine the ingredients'. He was sure he'd seen some onions.

Making the curry filled over an hour but there was still another before he needed to leave to pick up Fiona.

He sat in the garden with a book. It was the third travel book written by a contemporary of his, who'd briefly tried his hand in the advertising agency where K had worked. The earlier two books had been bestsellers. For this one, the author, whom K remembered as a jaunty little man with a taste for flamboyant bow-ties, had journeyed through the equatorial jungles of south west Africa, surviving malaria, the aggressive attentions of diamond smugglers and a flood while searching for a lost tribe. Or possibly a lost city. This book wasn't holding his attention, although that might have been due to envy. He put it down, then picked it up again. He read the first line: 'The customs officer looked at me and I looked at him. He had just removed a packet of heroin from my suitcase. Was my journey to end before it began?' That was three lines.

He looked at the final line on the final page. It was a Latin quotation. K had never been taught Latin but he guessed at some of the words. He suspected it was to do with the fruitlessness of man's endeavours. There had been a particularly startling bow-tie, he remembered, which the bestselling author had worn at important meetings: crimson spots against a turquoise background. Perhaps this peacock brilliance was to protect himself from the despair he purveyed in his writing. It surprised him that people wanted to read this sort of thing in such large numbers. He would have assumed they'd enjoy something more upbeat, more in reflection of their own aims and ambitions.

He closed the book. His own novel was a murder story, a thriller, but it was not a story of hopelessness, of cynical despair or failure. He could never revel in shadowlands or abandon his belief in the possibility of happiness, of self-fulfilment. Of course he couldn't. He *strove* for it. It was, most probably, an inheritance from his father.

CHAPTER ELEVEN

1990

Claudia and Bella clung together before they parted. Their slim bodies were clasped round each other as if at a dreaded separation rather than a longed-for release.

Catherine hovered around, even more than usually active. She had forgotten when agreeing to this plan that she, too, was leaving that morning. It was Douglas's firm's annual dinner-dance. She was already dressed in a smart suit with broad shoulders, and her case, with its sequined blue dress, was packed and waiting in the car.

After Bella and her mother had left, Catherine tried once more to persuade Claudia to accompany her to London. 'I'm sure we can find you a room in the hotel, darling.'

Claudia cried out, with more passion than usual, 'I'm sixteen, remember – perfectly capable of looking after myself for one night!'

K, on coffee-break, had watched some of this from the stables, and Claudia's shouted affirmation of her independence reached him. It caused the strangest sensation of inward breathlessness as if something momentous had occurred. Overcome by this feeling, which he did not wish to analyse, he was about to withdraw to his office fastness when Catherine caught sight of him. She called him over, in rather peremptory style. 'You'll keep an eye on Claudie, won't you? I've got to go to London. I'll be back at teatime tomorrow.'

K thought her appeal to him was a kind of joke. She knew he left in the evening. It seemed easiest to agree, however. Claudia, he thought, was looking at him coldly – or, rather, looking anywhere but at him. 'Must get back to work.' He walked away briskly enough, but as he heard the car drive off, his heart turned over and he felt a strange urge to yawn. He climbed the steps to his room as quickly as possible and slumped at his desk. But in a few minutes he stood up again. His face was burning, although the day was cloudy and the air in his room seemed cloudy too. He returned to his desk and stared out of the window.

It was impossible to disguise from himself the expectation that he would see Claudia. However remote or uncaring of his presence, at some point she would appear in his eye-line, unfettered by friend or mother. Instead he found himself looking at Alan, only a few yards from his window, intent on doing something to the lawn but finding time to glance up and wave cheerily: 'Need any more advice, guv'nor?'

Feeling like a marksman who finds an extraneous person between his sight-line and his victim, K waved back and returned to his computer. He had forgotten that this was one of Alan's days. But what difference did it make? He must stick to a routine, under which heading he now included a lunchtime swim.

Claudia felt like dancing when, first, Bella left and then Catherine. Indeed, she whirled about the driveway a bit, before running into the house and whirling about there too. The question was, how to use every moment of this precious time. It was now just about midday. Half an hour's practising, a swim before a snack lunch, then a long afternoon under the trees, another swim, a little more practising, maybe a walk – but then she ran the risk of meeting other people … I am luxuriating in being alone, thought Claudia, and only the merest shadow of another agenda crossed her mind.

K was still swimming when Claudia approached the pool. She was already in her swimsuit and wrapped in a turquoise sarong. She hesitated. He hadn't seen her and it would be easy to retreat. But this was her free-spirit day and the lightness carried her forward. She let her sarong float from her, ran and dived into the water.

K, on his twentieth length – he was counting for something to do – felt his world heave and surge around him. A little breathless, he dropped his feet and touched the security of the floor. He was at the shallow end and when he stood up, the water came only to his waist. He shivered a little, for the air was cooler than the water.

Claudia swam as if water was her element. Like a fishy angel or an angelic fish, hair flowing behind her, she flashed up and down, droplets glittering like stars around her head and hands. Looking up, K saw the sun had come from behind the clouds. Humbled by the glory of Claudia's youth, he climbed out of the pool and went into the changing hut. In the greenish darkness – plants grew over the side windows – he changed back into shorts and T-shirt and tried to compose himself.

Her arrival from above, like a meteor descending to earth – or, at least, to water – had confused him. What did she mean by it? Or did she mean nothing? Was it merely youthful high spirits? Perhaps she had scarcely noticed, or anyway discounted, his presence.

But it had not felt like that. It had felt like an advance, an overture, almost an invitation.

By the time K came out of the hut, Claudia was out of the pool and lying stretched out on the turquoise sarong. Her skin was perfectly smooth, pale golden on her arms and lower legs, pale silver on her upper thighs. Her wet hair, splayed out round her head, darkened the turquoise to blue. Her eyes were shut.

'I didn't know what had hit me!' K approached. His voice, he hoped, was jokey, 'avuncular', even. Yet what an ugly word, and there was a lump in his throat.

'I didn't hit you.' She spoke without opening her eyes.

K came and sat on the grass about a yard from her. He noticed the sheen on the still wet parts of her body and the bracelet round her slim ankle. He had an almost unbearable urge to touch some part of her, to smooth the downy hairs on her arms, to stroke her as you would pay homage to an object of great beauty. But, however beautiful, she wasn't a statue and he could see the deepening rose in her cheeks and the movement of each breath from her slightly parted mouth.

K knew he must take himself away but felt mesmerised, fixed to the spot. Desire, usually such an ordinary mechanical response, rose like a reflection of the sun, the sky, the water. He loved her. He was aflame with love, panting, roaring. Meanwhile, he sat absolutely still and silent, aware that only inaction made this love possible. Minutes passed. K felt the pulse of his body weakening his strength of will.

'Are you still there?'

K groaned. Or thought he groaned, but maybe it didn't get out into the air. 'Why are you keeping your eyes shut?' Her voice was a release. She stopped being only a body. If she opened her eyes, she would become Claudia again, shy, reclusive, sensitive, not this glorious houri laid out for his temptation.

'It's so bright.' She moved one leg fractionally so that her thighs relaxed a little, soft flesh parting from soft flesh.

Now was the time to jump up and run. Vaguely, K heard an engine start up at the far side of the garden. Again, he felt a lessening of tension. 'There's Alan with the mower.' His voice sounded strange to his ears.

'Yes.' Her voice was drowsy as if she was about to fall asleep.

K, trying not to look at her lips, said nothing. More minutes passed, during which, more in command of himself, he allowed the feelings of love to return. There was nothing but good in them, he told himself and it was natural that he, a virile male, should be moved by a partially clothed, beautiful young woman. Call it lust or love – how could one be separated from the other?

'What are you thinking about?' The question, delivered in the same languid, half-awake tone, touched K immeasurably. It had the naïve innocence of youth, of a girl asking her friend, from one bed to another.

'I am thinking of you.' The truth was out before he could stop it.

'Oh.' She said no more. He didn't know if she was startled or pleased.

Another silence followed in which K could hear the mower coming nearer.

Claudia's eyes fluttered. She put up a hand to her face. She wanted this time to go on for ever. She had never felt like this before. K's presence was so strong that she could almost feel his hands reaching out to touch her. She was so ready for him, so eager. But if she opened her eyes, it would be spoilt. She would be Claudia, a silly teenage girl again, and he would be the unknowable writer-in-residence.

It was a moment of stasis. The sun had become blazingly hot, fixing them both in the heat of passion, but still apart.

'I love you,' said K.

'Yes,' murmured Claudia, after a pause. Her agreement meant recognition and assent.

Yet still he didn't touch her.

Claudia felt her skin burning, and the sensation pressing through her eyelids to her eyes. She sat up slowly and looked at K. She smiled at him, a smile filled with trust, love, admiration and, in the simplest way, desire. He moved across the short space that separated them and took her in his arms. He hugged her as if she were a child, except that Claudia felt sure her naked skin scalded through his clothing. The smell of chlorine rose from her hair.

Suddenly the sound of the mower was very near. They broke apart. Claudia was immediately distressed, almost distraught. She muttered, 'I'm sorry,' and tugged her hair to the back of her head.

K looked at her steadily. 'There is no reason to be sorry.'

Vague thoughts fluttered through Claudia's head, making her even more agitated. He had said he loved her. He was married, she thought, but perhaps she was wrong. He never talked of a wife. She had caught the sun. She must be red, scarlet. Then her thoughts calmed. She was happy! She gave K a dazzling smile.

'Disturbing you, am I?' Alan had brought the mower right up to the entrance to the pool enclosure which was surrounded by a hedge.

'We've finished,' said K. He put out a hand as if to pull up Claudia, then dropped it again.

'Hot now,' suggested Alan. He nodded towards Claudia, 'You'll burn if you're not careful.'

She gave him a muted version of her smile to K. 'I'm going to change now.' She got up at once and went into the hut. She didn't look at K or speak to him because there was no need. He had told her he loved her and so he did. She didn't want to question what it meant but just allow the knowledge to fill her with joy.

K walked slowly past Alan and climbed even more slowly up to his room. His face wore an expression of dazed happiness.

At about five, after Alan had left for the day, Claudia made herself a glass of lemonade filled with ice and set off with the books to her favourite spot under the trees. Although she didn't admit it to herself, she knew there was only an hour before K would leave.

Already the thought of not seeing him until the following day made her feel desperate.

K caught up with her half-way across the lawn. She seemed to shiver.

'That looks cooling.' He indicated the glass.

'Would you like some? It's so hot now.'

'I'd love some.' That word. She put down her books and turned back to the house. He followed her. It was odd, she thought, that he had never been inside the house before. She saw he felt uneasy and might retreat.

'I've got a jug in the fridge. I just made it, with fresh lemons.'

They went together into the kitchen, almost too warm from the Aga. Claudia had changed into shorts and a T-shirt as skimpy as a vest. She wore blue beads and her hair was in a pony-tail.

Murmuring something like 'Just once,' K took her into his arms and kissed her. At first he was gentle.

They broke apart, trembling. Claudia immediately opened the fridge and bent down until she was half inside it. K walked to the far side of the room. 'I'll wait for you in the garden.' He went out, and when Claudia looked round she saw that one of his hands was touching the wall as if for support.

She put the jug of lemonade on the table and sat in front of it. Her heart beat so fast that she thought she might explode. She had been kissed before but it had never felt remotely like that. How could she carry out the jug as if nothing had happened? On the other hand, he would be gone soon enough and she would be on her own. She'd just let her heart-rate settle a bit.

K, sitting under the trees, watched her approach. She held a tray high, like a waiter. He started speaking before she reached him. 'We're going to read some of your poetry,' he said. 'I used to read poetry a lot but since…' he paused. He had been going to say, 'since I got married'. 'Now I seldom do.'

Claudia, failing to disguise her shaking hands, poured a glass of lemonade and K began to read. She had brought out a collection of the metaphysical poets again so he began with the same poem by Marvell she'd been reading before.

Fair Quiet, have I found thee here,
And Innocence, thy Sister dear!

His voice was rich, with a low-timbre. He saw that Claudia's hands had stopped shaking. The bright sun spotted through the trees making a kind of crazy pavement on the grass. He started on a second poem,

'... But at my back I always hear
Time's winged chariot hurrying near; ...'

and above their heads the same song-thrush began to tune up before launching into a cascade of arpeggios and trills. Claudia hugged her knees and half closed her eyes.

After several poems, K glanced at his watch and saw it was six o'clock. He took Claudia's hand and pressed his lips to the back like a stamp of possession. He stood up. 'I've got to go.' He didn't say, 'I've got to go and pick up my wife.' Without even considering it, Fiona had become unmentionable in front of Claudia.

Claudia didn't get up or even watch him very far as he went away. Yet his departure felt like a draining of herself. With a self-conscious effort at overcoming the feeling, she picked up the book he'd been reading from and read aloud one poem after another. The words meant nothing to her but the rhythm gave her courage. After a while she heard a persistent tapping behind the trees. Craning round, she saw the thrush with a snail in its beak. He was beating it on a stone to get at the snail inside, just as K had described. She would tell him about it in the morning.

Claudia stayed there for a long time, until only the wood-pigeons were softly calling and damp was coming up through the grass. Then she went inside the empty house where she wandered from room to room, sitting for a while in each, before moving on. Everything, the chintzes in the drawing room, the polished stair-rail, the rather bumpy walls of the kitchen, made a peculiar impression on her as if she'd never seen them before. She ran her hands over them, tested the texture, checked the colour. Several times she came face to face with herself in the large gilt-framed mirror in the drawing room, the smaller one in the hallway. She stared at herself as she had at the chintzes, with a wish to understand and appreciate. Her eyes stared back, extraordinarily blue and fixed like those of someone in shock. Eventually, unable to feel any interest in eating or drinking, she went upstairs and prepared for bed. Her pinkness from the midday sun was more obvious in the bathroom lights. She found some aftersun lotion in the bathroom cupboard and smoothed it over her skin.

It began to be late and, although she knew she wouldn't sleep, she went to her bedroom and got into bed. The night would pass, however slowly, and then it would be morning and *he* would come again.

K lay in bed with Fiona asleep in his arms. They had made love several hours earlier after she had indicated that it was an appropriate time. In his heart he was shocked, but his body had performed efficiently enough. In fact, if he wished to be honest with himself, he would have to admit that he had been more aroused than usual. Now he lay awake in the dark, guilt mixing with a sense of a duty performed until, at last, the night was black enough and deep enough for him to enter the powerful realms of romance. He thought and dreamt of Claudia. He told himself that he loved her with reverence, hope, delicacy, inspiration, passion – of course, passion. But, more than that: when he was with her or even pictured her, he felt filled with goodness, with virtue. His love expanded to the world around him. He felt tolerant, charitable, capable of anything.

It was obvious that he wouldn't sleep that night, not only because his imagination was flying like a boat in high seas, but because he was so impatient to begin a new day. Of course he could never, would never, impose himself on Claudia. At this moment (with his wife sleeping quietly in his arms and perhaps even germinating his seed within her womb) it was enough that he was fired up with love. If her feelings were less strong than his – she was young (he didn't acknowledge how young) – his love was great enough for two.

CHAPTER TWELVE

1990

At first light K was up, making tea, bringing a cup up for Fiona, kissing her warm cheek, pulling back the curtains.

'Isn't it early?' She reached out a hand for her watch.

It was. Far too early. Embarrassed, K drew the curtains again. 'I'm sorry. I was thinking about the book. I've decided to call it *One Summer*.' It was true that, in the last hour of his wakefulness, he had found himself honing in on various problems hanging over his book. And one by one they had fallen at the hands of his new clarity.

K crept out of the bedroom and went down into the garden. He wrapped himself in a winter overcoat and sat with his head tipped back against the deck-chair. He supposed the sun was up somewhere but he couldn't see it. The world was muted to a soft grey, which exactly accorded with his tender sensibilities.

He remembered that night not so long ago when he had sat in the chair and gazed up at the night sky. Then he had been filled with the desolation of his heart's emptiness. He had felt the true negative anguish of despair. His feelings for Claudia seemed like a miracle, as if a benign star had decided to redirect his fate.

Gradually, the greyness began to break up, and the harsher sounds of working life came with the sharper light: cars, aeroplanes and lorries. He was turned away from the house but, behind him, he heard Fiona draw back the bedroom curtains.

Rousing himself, he went in to make breakfast.

K and Claudia did not rush together that Friday morning, even though they had both lain awake all night thinking of each other and they both knew Catherine would be back at teatime. They had too much trust in what they felt to want to rush or grab. They were happy to be aware of their presence within the same boundaries.

The sun had come up brightly, but as the morning progressed, a wide muffling of cloud rose from the horizon. They worked till eleven o'clock, writing and making music, hearing Alan hurrying to finish the mowing before he was rained off.

At eleven o'clock, K made two mugs of coffee and went to the bench under the cedar where he usually ate his lunch. Claudia met him there a minute for two later. She was smiling as she walked towards him. K felt her smile offered him everything he'd ever wanted.

'Thank you.' She took the coffee and sat close beside him.

I'm afraid it's beginning to rain.' K turned to her tenderly.

'This tree is like a roof.' Claudia stared upwards. Her throat was pure white, except for a very small mole at its base. 'When I was younger we had a tree-house in its branches. If you look, you can see part of the floor still there.'

K imagined Claudia as a little girl. 'I think of you as more of a bookworm than a tomboy.'

'I think I've quietened down a bit. Catherine would say too much.'

K saw she was nervous. Her face was shiny and her shoulders pink from yesterday's sun. 'You have an older sister, don't you?' He didn't want Catherine's view of Claudia, but he did want to know everything else.

'Ten years older. She's living in New York with her husband. He's a real high-flyer but it's sad because I hardly ever see her.' Obediently, under K's questioning, Claudia told him the story of her life. It didn't take long and he noticed she became most animated when she talked about her viola, as if it were a living presence. But although he tried to take in what she was saying, hesitantly and with pauses, he knew that her closeness on the bench beside him was knocking out a good part of his brain.

He put down his empty mug and picked up her hand. It was much warmer than his. He made an effort to speak. 'Will you play for me some time? I mean out of your room. In the garden?'

Claudia looked away from their two hands clasped together. 'I might.' She frowned as if he had presented her with a mystery. 'Did you write this morning?'

'A bit. Not too bad, actually.' He leant across and, with his free hand, stroked her face. She stayed very upright, eyes cast down. 'You have the smoothest skin.'

'I got quite sunburnt yesterday.' A blush rose up her cheek.

'Yes. I can see.'

They both became silent. K stood. 'You've never seen my den, have you?'

'No.'

'Would you like to?'

Claudia stood too and they walked to the stable. The rain, from which the cedar had protected them, spattered down in large, sparse drops. On the other side of the garden, Alan was driving the mower into its shed.

K was thinking, One kiss, that's all I ask. Not so much in today's world. Then he thought, She's the only person in the world to whom I would want to show my work in progress, which proves her importance in my life. This reassured him.

Claudia stopped to talk to her poor, abandoned horse. She stroked his silky neck and kissed his nose.

K put his hand on her shoulder. He could feel her quivering. Together they went up the dark staircase and into K's workroom. The rain was heavier and a wind blew it against the window. On the desk, the laptop glowed a brilliant green.

Claudia went over and peered at it as if it had a message for her. 'No words?' she said, looking back at K so her face caught a greenish reflection.

'I saved them on to a disk before I came out.'

'That's wise.' Claudia nodded approvingly as if she were a computer adviser. 'I'm looking for ghosts.' But K knew she was nervous for other reasons. To stop her fleeing, he took her in his arms.

Outside, Alan tooted his horn as he drove his car away from the house.

K staggered away from her. He glimpsed her surprise at how their kiss had affected him. He sat down in the chair in front of the computer. 'You'd better leave now.' His voice was muffled and unsteady.

'Yes.' Claudia put her arms over his shoulders and her cheek against his. It was very hot. 'I'm going,' she said obediently. She pulled back from him and left the room.

K slumped further over the desk, and heard her footsteps receding against the pumping of his heart. What could he do now? What should he do now? The second question was easy enough to answer. He tried to mock himself: he was behaving as if he were in the worst type of melodrama. It didn't have any effect. What was clear was that he must remove himself entirely from any chance of seeing Claudia – at least until her mother returned. He must go now. This instant. Drive away. Go anywhere.

Picking up his bag and mobile, but failing to turn off the computer, K hurried downstairs and started towards his car. The rain poured down unnoticed. It was the surprised and innocent look she had given him after they'd kissed that had saved him – saved her, he thought wildly. Quick. Quick. He must drive away before he remembered that smile.

Claudia wandered round in the garden, enjoying the rain cooling her flushed skin. She didn't hear K's car departing. By then she was far away under the chestnut trees. The rain was loud on the leaves. She couldn't imagine what would happen next but she hugged to herself the extraordinary expression on K's face after they'd kissed. She had no idea she could move someone so profoundly, and someone so much wiser, cleverer, more attractive than her oh-so-ordinary self. He was a writer, probably more than twenty years older than her; she was a dull schoolgirl with nothing more than a taste for music and Eng. lit. She remembered suddenly how Bella had exclaimed at his attractiveness. What were her words? 'He's gorgeous!' Bella would find it impossible to believe what had happened. Impossible! Of course, thought Claudia, moving out from under the trees, she could never tell her or anyone else. Now, half-heartedly, she considered the idea that he was married. That he had a wife. But the idea had little reality. She had never seen a wife, K had never talked of her. Perhaps they were separated, or had an arrangement, she thought vaguely. He didn't *feel* married. Besides, that was his business, not hers.

Throwing off a sense of disquiet, she walked across the lawn, wondering if K was watching her. She would go for a swim now, before the rain stopped. Of course she believed he would join her.

84

CHAPTER THIRTEEN

2004

The longer I stayed in my small room in the Fresh Ponds Hotel, the less I felt inclined to move. The proximity to Claudia's home – it was only a few miles down the road – made me feel that the next step was within my grasp. The miserable exhaustion that had gripped me almost since I left Chile was exchanged for a taut vibrancy. I had seldom felt more alive. And yet I lay on my bed, unable to take action.

One of the things that held me back – or, at least, muddled any clear decision – was the sense that I had been in this situation before, that it was a replay of a previous time in my life.

It was when I went to the bathroom and glimpsed the look in my narrowed, elderly eyes that I remembered. The weekend when I had run from Claudia, and spent the time quietly with Fiona, I had felt like this. She had noticed something strange about me. As now, I had felt filled with energy yet incapable of movement. I had stayed in bed late. I lay on the sofa in our living room – I had tried to be outside on the deck-chair, but it rained. Whenever Fiona suggested going out, a simple trip to the shops, to friends, the cinema, a pub, I declined without producing any reason. At length she had decided I was ill and given up. So I had been left to my terrifying lethargy, to the need to make a decision. I even hoped I would become ill so that it would be taken from me. Yet now, looking back, I think I knew all along that I was not strong enough to resist. It had felt like a choice between life and death.

And was that still the same now? Was it possible I could have carried all that emotion for fourteen years, despite the guilt I bore for its outcome? Dreams and delusion. Why could I not admit that the only reason I hung on to my great love, like a drowning man to a branch, was that otherwise I had no excuse to live and should have thrown up my hands in despair long ago?

The priest's face came to me: sympathetic, tired, calm. He had been trained not to believe in my sort of love. He understood its dangers but he could never understand its beauty. It had been years since I thought of Claudia's smile but I did now. Its extraordinary power came from a fusion of the spiritual and the carnal, the soul and the body – I truly believed that. Even a priest might have understood.

I found my thoughts had at last spurred me out of bed and I was standing upright in the middle of the room. I went out at once, taking the stairs almost at a run.

The hotel surprised me by being full. It was early afternoon on Sunday, their busiest time. I could smell alcohol on the breath of a man who asked me the way to the toilets. Outside on the terrace, people gathered round tables, enjoying the warm sunshine, some with plates of food. Beyond them and on the other side of the road, the lake sparkled. I could see leaves from the trees reflected in its ripples.

I walked quickly to my car. I had not locked it the night before and saw at once that someone had been in there. My father's tailcoat, which had been laid across the seat, was now crumpled in a corner. Perhaps it had been used as a blanket by young lovers. The idea pleased me rather than otherwise. Two or three empty beer cans by the door made it a likely scenario.

I got in and began to drive for the second time towards Meadowlands.

Oliver was on duty again that night. Just as he was leaving, I had a passionate urge to go with him. It was a kind of panic attack. I hung round his neck – we were still in my bedroom – and behaved in the kind of hysterical way I hadn't for years.

He was concerned, of course. 'What is it, darling? You've been so good, so steady. Don't lose it now when we're nearly there. By tomorrow we'll know when the funeral is. Everything will be more settled.'

I allowed him to comfort me. He had Wednesday and Thursday

off so I would go to London for one of those days. I went down-stairs and waved as he drove away.

Avoiding my mother, her friend, James, and my aunt who had arrived in the afternoon, I returned to my bedroom. I straightened the bed where Oliver and I had lain together, he with love and me with loving gratitude. It was to be expected, I told myself, that I would feel disturbed on the day of my father's death. His long illness had been, after all, only a partial preparation. Perhaps the doctor in Oliver, used to facing death almost daily, had underestimated the effect on me.

Tomorrow the marquee would be taken down. Thoughtfully, I drew the curtains against its whiteness and walked over to one of the cupboards. They were deeply recessed into the wall and held all kinds of junk from my past that I'd never found the courage to clear. I needed to pull out several boxes of old textbooks and essays before I found what I was looking for. Then I brought it over, laid it on the bed and stood over it as if it were a bomb.

Fourteen years had made it seem smaller and grubbier. I undid the clasp and opened it. My heart clamoured and banged in my chest, making its own music of fear and distress. Yet I persevered, lifting out the viola, which, in its dust-free zone, was as shiny and pristine as the day I had put it there – for ever, I'd felt convinced, my first and major penance. It was like a sleeping princess, I thought fancifully, roused from her velvet bed. I placed it under my chin, feeling the cool, smooth curve like a caress. I knew it would be so wildly out of tune that there was no point in attempting to play it. I held it for several seconds until my mother called from downstairs: 'Claudie! Claudie! We need you.' I'd never managed to train her to call me 'Claudia'.

Guiltily, or at least secretly, I replaced the instrument, shut the case and put it back into the cupboard, although this time not so far in, not so buried. It was extraordinary to think that Oliver had no idea I had believed my viola-playing to be central to my existence.

'Claudie!'

'Coming.'

CHAPTER FOURTEEN

1990

Claudia realised K had left when her mother drove up to the house. She was full of gossip about her father's colleagues at the dinner-dance and complaints about London's traffic and parking, interspersed with pleasure at the shopping she'd done that morning.

Claudia, standing in the drive, listened to her with a more than usually stupid expression on her face – or so she imagined. K's car was not there. He had gone without saying goodbye. After her lovely swim in the rain, she had gone back to the house, eaten an apple and played her viola, but she had never imagined he was not around somewhere. She had assumed him to be writing or thinking, creating.

When Catherine said, quite casually, 'Our writer-in-residence bunked off early then,' Claudia felt sick. She also felt like hitting her mother, who was so excited by ordinary events and yet had put the boot in to her daughter – worse still, without knowing she was doing it.

'You were all right on your own, then?'

'Fine.' There was no other way to answer the question, particularly now when the extraordinary events of yesterday and even this morning seemed to have been nullified by K's disappearance. Must she pretend it had never happened? That he had never told her he loved her? That their kisses meant nothing?

Claudia helped carry her mother's case and bags into the house but her arms and legs felt weak and her head spun. 'I'm feeling a bit funny.' She needed to go to her room and be alone.

'Funny? How funny?' Catherine liked illness, Claudia remembered – too late. It gave her a busy role with thermometers, pills, hot-water bottles and cool drinks.

'Nothing. I'm just a bit tired. I didn't sleep too well ...' But that was a mistake too.

'So you *were* nervous on your own. I said to your father—'

Claudia tried to cut her off. 'No. I listened to the Proms. I was fine. I just had a headache. My period.' She stopped herself. That was the silliest of lies. Catherine always seemed to know when her daughter's period came. Luckily, she was still fixed on the guilt of leaving her on her own and had stopped listening. Claudia let her worry on, then slipped away. At least she hadn't cried in front of her mother. But how would she survive till Monday? She was overcome by sheer astonishment that K should behave like that, so churlishly, so ignobly. He had said he *loved* her! The word clamoured to be shouted round the house, no longer in pride but in despair. No, not despair, anger. If she could feel anger, her blood would run again and she could take action. What action she had no idea. But she knew she wasn't a flaccid heroine to be played with and discarded. 'Dallied'. The word, old-fashioned, like most of her novel-reading, came to her with a sort of ferocious pleasure. Maybe he had been *dallying* with her.

Claudia felt herself growing up with every second. This was an adult problem and she would face it in an adult way. Certainly she was introspective and shy, but she was not foolish. On Monday she would be direct with K. She would say to him, 'Why did you leave on Friday without saying goodbye to me? It was really weird of you.' And perhaps he would have an answer. But here Claudia's mix of sense and sensibility, which was giving her some justifiable confidence in her ability to manage the occasion, swerved a little. The most obvious reason for K's speedy retreat was an emergency in connection with his wife. But Claudia had written his wife out of their drama – or, rather, not written her into it – so there was no way she could be used as an excuse.

Even when Claudia decided that the worst aspect of K's defection was that she must wait two whole days to discover the reason, she didn't try to imagine how he would spend this time apart from her. Her growing up – if growing up is an ability to separate fact from fantasy – had not progressed as far as that. She could only picture K as he appeared to her, in her life. Beyond that was *terra incognita*.

*

89

The weekend passed. Claudia felt herself suspended, like a high-wire performer whose partner had left her aloft with no means of descent. For two nights, she hardly slept and passed the days in a dream so that Catherine, unknowingly coming to the same conclusion as Fiona had with K, assumed she was suffering from a summer bug. She was at a vulnerable age. Claudia agreed that this was probably the case.

On Monday morning K drove Fiona as usual to the station. Up to the very last minute, he thought he would take some sort of pre-emptive action. He'd examined all the options exhaustively. He could return to Meadowlands and tell Claudia face to face that he was sorry, that it had all been an absurd mistake, probably a mid-life crisis, and that his *love* was reserved for his wife. This was the cruellest yet most honourable course of action, and the one he most disliked. He could tell Fiona that there were too many distractions at Meadowlands (irony indeed) and he must return to working at home. This was cowardly but would, presumably, be effective on the lines of 'What the eye doesn't see, the heart doesn't grieve over.' He could plead illness all round and spend a week at home, allowing things to cool down. But even he could see this option was both cowardly and probably ineffective. He could tell Fiona everything that had happened, thus destroying his own romantic dreams and encouraging Fiona to police his movements and feelings. But even as he thought this he knew he could never do it. Besides, he reassured himself, there was no reason to hurt Fiona unnecessarily. Finally there was the option he seemed to be taking: do nothing and trust to Fate. He *loved* Claudia. How could he ever hurt her? Besides, all they had done was exchange a kiss. Well, two. He mustn't get things out of proportion. It was a glorious summer fantasy, he pretended to himself. That was the biggest lie of all.

On Monday morning Claudia had the frantic energy that is fuelled by adrenaline and sleeplessness. Her sunburn had faded and her face was sallow and drawn. Unaware of the time, she began to play her viola even before her father had left for London.

He opened her bedroom door and stood watching her for a

moment or two. His face reflected his surprised admiration. Eventually she saw him and stopped.

'I didn't know you were so competent.'

A tight, obstinate look came over Claudia's face. Her father had vetoed any idea of going to a music school. Her teacher had recommended her for a famously good one in Manchester but he wouldn't even consider it. It was not for him to tell her she was competent. Anyway, she was more than that.

'I'm sorry. I woke earlier than usual.' Or, rather, never slept.

'I'd like to hear you play some time.'

'OK.'

He looked as if he wanted to kiss her but was overawed by her taut pose, the viola still held in one hand.

'Have a nice day.'

'Thanks.'

Claudia stopped thinking about her father as soon as he'd passed the doorway, but his presence had interrupted her concentration and she put the viola back into its case. An image of K gave her a sick feeling. In fact, beyond his height, thick hair and greenish eyes, she couldn't have described him. It was the *feeling* he gave her that made her try to recover with gulps of air.

She found her watch on her bedside table and saw it was seven forty-five. Perhaps she should try to eat or drink something while her mother was at the station. Her queasiness might be due partly to hunger. Braced by this good sense approach, she hurried downstairs, although she was shaky enough to need the banister as support. Her legs felt positively spaghetti-like. She tried to smile at the idea and, in that second, remembered her anger on Friday evening when she'd discovered K's sudden departure. Where was that anger now that she needed it?

Claudia flung up the Aga hood, dragged the heavy kettle on to the hotplate and tried to instil some guts into her wilting body.

She was still sitting at the table over a plate of uneaten toast (there was no point in puking) when Catherine returned in her usual whirlwind way. 'Guess who I saw outside the station? Our writer-in-residence. He usually drops her off for an earlier train, then goes and has breakfast at that horrid greasy-spoon café before coming on here. It's an unusual arrangement, the wife being the breadwinner. Although, I suppose, if his book's a success the roles can be reversed again or made more equal. It certainly wouldn't appeal to your father. I think he's quite shocked at the idea. But, then, Fiona's a stronger character than I am.' Catherine laughed, her morning lightened by this chance meeting.

Claudia bowed lower over the table. She felt her mother's loud and cheerful words like hammer blows on her head. They immediately induced a violent headache. She screwed her eyes tight shut. She would not let the name 'Fiona' settle in her memory. With all the selfish determination of youth, she resisted her mother's information.

'You're up early.' Catherine glanced at her daughter. 'Feeling better?'

'Yes.' Claudia fled. Music would blot out greasy-spoon cafés and unequal marriages.

She played for over two hours, until she was too exhausted to bow another note and the pads of her fingers hurt. Then she put away her viola and thought, By now K will have arrived. Maybe he will have heard my playing and understand my feelings. Perhaps he is thinking of me at this very moment. The warmth of loving exhilaration overwhelmed her and she found herself smiling broadly. She sat on the bed, better to enjoy the moment. All the miseries of the last two days were wiped out by the supremacy of love. He had told her he loved her. He would not lie. And she loved him.

K sat in his room above the stables. He could feel a kind of inward shakiness that made it impossible to work or even think clearly. The only thing achieved by his premature departure on Friday and the next two days of soul-searching, was a heightening of his feelings for Claudia. His whole being seemed turned towards her. His trembling was a mixture of anticipatory delight and sheer terror.

Claudia looked out of her window and saw that the world was cloaked in a dove-coloured veil of fine rain. Behind it the summer brightness burnt steadily. When the veil lifted, it would be another warm day. She dressed carefully in a pale pink T-shirt and her long skirt. She wanted to be graceful. She looked forward to the sensation of wet grass under her bare feet.

At ten thirty, Catherine called up to her: 'I'm going in to Witley.

Want to come?' Claudia didn't bother to answer. She was engaged in monitoring the minute-by-minute progress of time. She had decided to have coffee with K at eleven. Her attention had narrowed to the small disc of her watch. The face had an interchangeable surround, which today was lemon yellow. In half an hour she would go downstairs, out of the front door, along the driveway till she reached the stables. The hands of the watch jerked a little with each passing minute.

K descended the wooden staircase earlier than usual. For the first time he noticed that the balustrade had only two supporting posts but each was carved with a star at the head. In the room below, a beam running along the far end was covered with rosettes, pinned up in rows of red, blue, yellow, green. The sun came in through the clear window-panes and made the coloured ribbons shine. How had he failed to see them before?

K filled the kettle and plugged it in. As it began to boil, the noise was very loud. His face was reflected and distorted in its gleaming sides. He'd cut himself shaving that morning and put up his hand to the nick, a slightly raised ridge now. He imagined Claudia's fingers touching it, or her mouth. He walked to the door restlessly, letting the kettle boil and turn itself off behind him.

Claudia was coming towards the stables. He was standing in the shadow of the lintel so she couldn't see him. She was wearing flip-flops to cross the gravel and the crunch of stone against stone seemed exceptionally noisy.

K thought there was something heroic, almost soldierly about her approach. Her youthfulness was always obvious but this morning she seemed less vulnerable. His heart was jumping.

Four paces away Claudia stopped. Obviously she had caught sight of him. He stepped out. 'Good morning.' He wanted to sing and dance like a madman, but that was all he said.

Claudia stared at him soberly. 'Where did you go on Friday?' Her voice broke a little but the words were brave enough.

'Oh, Friday.' K had forgotten about Friday. That was another life. Now that they were together again, it was unimportant.

'You just went.' Flushed and unsteady, but clinging to her sternness, Claudia looked as if she wanted to say more.

'I'm sorry. I should have said goodbye.' He paused, certain she wouldn't walk away. But he wanted more than that: he wanted her smile. 'I've been thinking of you all weekend. The least you can do is have a cup of coffee with me.'

Claudia hesitated. She seemed to be testing the meaning of his words. Then he saw a softening in her expression.

K went to her and took her arm. As his fingers reached out, he thought he couldn't do even this if Catherine were there. But he disowned the thought as quickly as it had come.

Claudia walked with him into the coach-house. K dropped her arm, and saw how she let it hang loosely by her side.

'I only just noticed these.' He waved at the rosettes. 'What a lot of winning!'

Claudia took a step back as if he were shouting. Probably he was shouting. She turned to the rosettes, so bright and gay. 'Far more belong to Louise. At least ninety per cent of the red.'

'Is the red first prize?'

Claudia looked at him wonderingly. 'Yes. Red is first, blue second, yellow third and green fourth and white highly commended, although it can vary. But red is always first. I specialised in yellow.'

K laughed. It was odd but delightful to have this beautiful girl in her long pale skirt instructing him in gymkhana lore. 'Shall I make you coffee?'

'Coffee?' She reached up till her fingertips touched the dangling ribbons.

K thought it was one of the most beautiful sights he'd ever seen: her upraised arms, straight back and slim waist. He took three steps and clasped her in a close embrace. Somewhere in his mind he pictured a Victorian painting of the strong male claiming his young bride.

'I love you,' he whispered, into Claudia's ear. He felt her body stiffen, then relax as she dropped her arms and faced him.

'I love you, too.' It was the first time she'd said the words and she seemed astonished by them.

What could he do but kiss her, then?

A breeze, entering through the open door, fluttered the tails of the rosettes.

*

At a quarter to one, Catherine drove up to the front of the house. She called through the door, 'Claudie! Come and help me carry the bags in!'

Claudia appeared quite quickly. She hadn't bothered to put on her flip-flops and curled her long toes against the sharp stones of the driveway. She felt like a sleep-walker. The half-hour she'd spent with K – he'd sent her away after that – had changed everything. They had both declared their love. They were lovers, even though they had done nothing but kiss. There was no going back.

'You look better.' Catherine dumped the last bag in the kitchen and glanced at her daughter.

Claudia smiled – the first smile her mother had seen for three days. 'I am better. I've put some soup on for our lunch.'

'So you've got your appetite back too.'

'I went for a swim.' She had done that too. On her own. Happily.

'I'm so glad, darling.'

After lunch Bella phoned. She talked about dentists and boyfriends in such an intermingled way that Claudia could hardly follow. Was it the dentist or Ed who'd said she made the sun come out? She'd also got a job two nights a week stacking shelves at the local supermarket. 'Well, we can't live off our poor old parents for ever, can we?'

Claudia had not thought about Bella since she left and was amazed to remember that, up to last Thursday, she'd felt closer to her than anyone in the world. Now it was a struggle even to listen to her news. 'Is your tooth less painful?'

'Pulled out. Dug out with a shovel. I was in agony. I just told you, you idiot.'

'Sorry.'

'What have you been doing? Clubbing nightly?' Bella's laughter made it clear she didn't expect an answer.

'Nothing, as per usual,' said Claudia, but she thought, I've been falling in love, and, already forgetting the anguish of the weekend, felt an almost smug certainty that Bella would never know anything like her feelings for K. He was so far above the gangly youths that attracted Bella's attention that they seemed like a different species.

To put Bella off the scent, she introduced a new subject: 'I'm thinking of reading music at uni.'

Bella was only mildly interested. 'Someone told me it's seriously hard work. But what do you think about me getting a job? Bit of a turn-round, wouldn't you say?'

In her turn, Claudia couldn't bring herself to concentrate on her friend's newly discovered conscience about money. She herself still took for granted that her parents were happy to pay for her with no contribution. They seldom talked about money, and although she saw how hard her father worked and knew his health was not perfect, she put the first down to choice and the second to old age – sixty seemed very old to her and he was older than her friends' fathers. She knew he worked in London, in the City, but beyond that she was vague about his employment – something to do with money, probably, but she was never interested enough to question him. In fact, she guessed, if she had wanted to stack supermarket shelves, her father would have forbidden it. He was not a modern father.

Despite Claudia's lack of concentration on her friend's preoc-cupations, their conversation rambled on for half an hour, Bella apparently noticing no lack of interest. She always did most of the talking anyway.

By the time Claudia put down the receiver, she found herself gripped by impatience. At first she thought it was just to be alone and silent, then admitted that it was about K. She wanted, she *needed* to see him again. But at their parting, an hour and a half earlier, he had made no mention of further meetings and she had been far too full of their kisses to think of anything.

Soon it would be lunchtime. Would he come out and sit with his sandwiches under the tree? Or might he go for a swim? It was certainly hot enough. Out of her bedroom window she could see the sharpness of the line dividing the shadow under the chestnuts and the brightness of the sunny lawn. If he did swim, should she join him? But she'd swum once already. What did he want? Or expect? She had gone to him at eleven but perhaps she couldn't do that again. Suddenly the certainty that she'd felt at eleven thirty deserted her and she found herself sliding back into the miasma of the weekend. What should she *do*?

Undecided, she wandered down to the kitchen.

'There you are, darling.' Catherine was washing lettuce. 'I've taken pity on our writer and asked him to join us for lunch. Just a picnic. Look in the fridge, would you, for the pâté I bought in town?'

K consulted his watch. Catherine had said one thirty and it was now one o'clock. Perhaps there was time for a swim. Perhaps Claudia would come. He was uneasily aware he should have said no to the lunch invitation, but Catherine had been so pressing that he couldn't think of any excuse. And if he was honest with himself, the prospect of lunching with the admiring mother and the daughter he'd been kissing so passionately was not without its own shameful appeal.

Even in his dim room, he could feel the heat of the day. He made up his mind quickly, grabbed his swimming trunks and clattered down the stairs.

Floating on his back, K stared up at the blue sky with its puff of white clouds. In a few moments he would see Claudia again, in the sun, with, perhaps, a glass of wine in his hand. What greater delight could life hold?

The table was laid on the terrace. Catherine had taken more trouble than usual, adding pretty napkins and wine goblets. Claudia watched and carried as requested in a kind of daze.

When K came striding across the lawn, his long legs in faded jeans, his thick hair still wet from his swim, her mood changed. It seemed his presence was enough to give her confidence.

'Sun or shade?' asked Catherine. 'Silly question, you've just been swimming.'

'I always love the sun,' K smiled at Claudia.

'And yet you work in that dark room?'

'It doesn't do to be too comfortable when writing.'

Claudia understood that her mother and K would carry on the conversation. Seeing them close together round the table, she couldn't help noticing, although she repressed the thought speedily, that they were far closer in age than she was to K – drinking wine while she stuck with coke. Their colour and their voices rose while hers remained the same.

'How far along with the book are you?' she asked, in order not to be altogether silent.

'That's an unanswerable question. What if I decide that everything I've written so far is a load of rubbish?' He played with this idea for a while, wittily enlarging on a one-step-forward, two-steps-back theory until he had emerged for a year's work with minus half a book.

Catherine laughed in her full-throated way and Claudia found herself watching K's mouth. It was redder than most men's, she thought, wide but not thick. She remembered the heat and urgency of his lips against hers.

Now her mother had raised the subject of advertising. If she had been able to pursue a career, that was the direction she'd have tried. This was news to Claudia.

'I've kept a diary for the pleasure of writing since I was fourteen,' Catherine went on.

This was also news to Claudia. What could her mother find to write about in the regularity of her marriage and day-to-day life?

K began to explain that although he'd found copy-writing fairly easy he'd stopped enjoying it years ago, with the result that his work had suffered. He couldn't bring himself to care enough about increasing the sales of a brand of dog biscuit or soap – and they were the useful items.

'So you upped and left,' said Catherine, admiringly.

Claudia was struck by a chill presentiment of where – or, rather, to whom – the conversation might lead. She got up precipitately, under the pretext of bringing out water. In the kitchen, she looked round the room she'd known all her life, at the familiar decorative china plates, the row of cooking tools above the Aga, the potted plant on the window-ledge. Today she noted them with a kind of coldness. They were no comfort to her any more. She was on a new waveband.

She found a jug, filled it with water, then walked slowly back to the terrace. She stood by the french windows, listening to the conversation. They were talking about a contemporary novel they had read recently.

Claudia set the jug on the table, then announced she was a bit hot and would go for another swim. It had struck her that she did not have to sit through such an emotionally charged lunch like a good little girl. She was surprised, however, that Catherine didn't even pretend to object. 'Fine, darling. I'll follow you later.'

K watched Claudia's departure, but without much concentration.

The sun, the wine and Catherine's flattering attention had put up a barrier between him and the man who had made such delicate love to Claudia. In a befuddled way, he felt almost resentful of her purity. She was right to leave. Regretfully, he saw that the bottle of wine was empty.

Claudia swam slowly up and down. In hardly more than half a day, she had been through greater extremes of emotion than in all her previous life. She still felt the joy of her meeting with K at eleven, she still believed in their feelings for each other, but the lunchtime experience had taken her another notch up into adult awareness.

As she'd crossed the lawn towards the pool, she'd glanced back and seen K and her mother across the table from him, glass in hand, talking energetically. The picture stayed with her, its meaning not quite comprehensible but disturbing all the same.

'Claudie! Claudie!' Claudia heard Catherine's voice – she would ask her mother to use her full name in future.

'You're still swimming! Mind you don't turn into a prune.' Catherine stood at the entrance to the pool. Even from a distance, Claudia could see that her cheeks were pinker than usual, her eyes brighter. She swung her swimsuit from her arm. 'What a lovely day! I'll join you in a minute.'

'I'm getting out.' Claudia swam to the side and, water whisking round her, pulled herself out. She bent to smooth the trickles off her slim legs and arms, then picked up a towel. She couldn't decide whether to stay or leave. 'I'm going for a ride,' she announced, as her mother opened the hut door.

'It'll be dreadfully hot. And the flies! Why don't you go later?'

'You're always trying to make me ride, but when I suggest it, you …' she tailed – Catherine had gone into the changing hut.

Claudia saw that her fingers were wrinkled just as her mother had suggested. The pads were still a little sore from the morning's long session at the viola. The flies *would* be fiendish. She'd walk instead. Perhaps she would go by the really long route she hadn't taken yet this year. It passed behind a cricket pitch, across a piece of semi wasteland and eventually, after crossing a road or two, entered the woods. It would be cool there. She imagined the medicinal smell of pine and the thin spattering of light.

It had been a mistake to drink at lunch. K felt liverish and old. Swimming might have cured it but he had seen Claudia and her mother head that way. The lunch had been a mistake. Not just the wine. K tried to recapture the elevation of his feelings for Claudia, declared only a few hours ago, but her mother's face, her voice, her laugh, got in the way. Work was the answer. K turned on the computer determinedly. The screen came to life with a smirk.

Claudia returned from her walk around six. It had taken her nearly three hours to complete the circuit and she felt a sense of satisfaction. Although she had had no real sleep over several days, her body had performed nobly, and the further she went the greater sense of ease she attained. The muddle and nastiness, the ridiculous, meaningless lunch fell away, and were replaced by her quiet, secure self, in which she could enjoy her love for K. It was a blessing that had been given to her. As she looked up to the heads of the tall, dark pine trees with their broken areole of blue, she spread her love further to include the natural world around her. Not usually religious, she found herself fervently admitting the presence of a greater being who had given everything, including her ability to love and be loved.

In this light-headed mood, she turned into the driveway and narrowly missed being run over by her mother.

Catherine called out of the car window, 'Your father's feeling a bit grotty. I'm picking him up early.'

Claudia continued towards the house and, however strong and pure her feelings, couldn't help noting that her mother was absent and K – she could see his car – was still there. She sat on the steps of the house to untie her trainers and release her hot feet.

K came out of the stables. Earlier, he had fallen asleep in his chair, which had successfully counteracted the effects of the lunch. Then he had made himself a strong coffee and got down to work properly.

He stood at the doorway breathing in the sweet coolness of the evening air. He was thinking of his book. The victim, the young woman, had undergone another transformation. She was called Natasha now, dark and small, with a sharp, worldly manner. Very unlike Claudia.

*

Claudia wondered if he would see her before he got into his car. She made no move to catch his attention. She was happy to be near him in this moment of beauty. The cedar was almost black at its topmost branches but enough light found its way over the house and stables to cast stripes of luminous green across the lawn.

In a few minutes, her parents would be back. Claudia spread her toes on the stone and wished, like a child in a fairy story, that time would stand still.

K spotted Claudia as he strolled towards his car. He went over to her.

'I've been walking,' she said, looking up at him. 'For three hours. On the heath. In the woods.'

'I wish I'd been with you.' He meant it, although he couldn't repress an image of Fiona and him on one of their Saturday walks. Nothing could be more wonderful than treading the soft bed of pine needles with Claudia at his side. 'I'm sorry about lunch. You were upset, weren't you?'

'Not any more. Not since my walk.' She was evasive, unwilling, he saw, to admit he could hurt her. He admired her for it and tried not to think it let him off the hook. 'Let's take a walk together some time.' She smiled calmly at him and he thought she looked somehow older.

'That's a date.' Her calmness suggested that time stretched ahead of them. He was not so confident or so patient. He was disturbed by her presence, by the need to touch her. He took her hand and tried to pull her up into his arms. She came reluctantly. 'Catherine will be back in a moment.'

'I love you, Claudia.' Why did he feel the need to say it again? Because it was such an astonishing truth? Or to assuage the anxiety that came with it?

Claudia gazed into his face confidently but she didn't tell him she loved him. Instead, she smiled.

He would have kissed her then but Catherine's car, flinging gravel from the tyres, separated them.

'Just off, are you?' Catherine spoke over her shoulder as she bent to help her husband out. Dressed in a well-cut City suit, he was a heavy-set man; his shoulders hunched forward uncomfortably and his face was closed.

K had never met him before and waited distractedly to be introduced. The emotions of the last few moments couldn't be so easily cut off. Claudia retreated to the doorway.

The two men shook hands. Douglas Lacey's was a little loose and clammy. K thanked him profusely for the hospitality of his stables and had his thanks briefly acknowledged before the older man turned away. K felt himself relegated to the position of charity case and didn't like it. He decided he didn't like the man either. A cold fish, even making allowance for his present disability, whatever that might be. As far as he knew it was only a touch of arthritis, no reason to make such a fuss.

As she reached the steps Catherine turned again, her arm still in her husband's. 'Why don't you and Fiona come for a drink before lunch on Sunday? We've been meaning to ask some friends over for ages.'

She seemed to assume the answer would be yes because she turned back at once. K looked for Claudia, but she had vanished from her post at the doorway. He decided to assume she had left before her mother issued the invitation. He went quickly to his car.

Inside the house Claudia, who had heard Catherine's words, hugged herself nervously while whispering under her breath, 'I love him! I love him! I love him!' For some reason she hadn't wanted to say it to him in the driveway. In the wood, on the heath, beside the cricket pitch, every step she had taken had expressed her love.

CHAPTER FIFTEEN

2004

I parked in the road outside Meadowlands and its new little estate. I couldn't bring myself to leave the car immediately.

The most carefree time with Claudia had been just before the drinks party Catherine had insisted on giving. I would not revisit that. But the week before – more precisely, the four days, Tuesday, Wednesday, Thursday, Friday – had been filled with happiness.

Claudia and I were lovers in everything but the physical act. We drank coffee, we swam, we read poetry, she played to me, and twice, when Catherine was out for the afternoon, we went for a walk. Once we took her horse who butted me in the back and made her laugh. I told her we needed a dog to make life perfect and she said I would have hated Bingo, who smelt awful and attacked strangers. 'But I'm not a stranger,' I'd protested.

Our kisses, mostly snatched secretly, were filled with innocence and joy. We didn't think of the future. Neither of us mentioned Fiona and I was just glad that she, too, seemed happier than usual. I determined not to feel too much relief when she stayed in London on Wednesday night and I could be on my own.

Even my novel was going well and the sun shone almost continuously. Those days would never be darkened in my memory.

Eventually I got out of the car, locked it, and started walking towards the Meadowlands driveway.

Once again, I was walking past the estate, then through the bordering shrubs up the driveway. Although no gardener, I noticed that they had expanded their girth considerably and their outlines were ragged and unkempt. The gravelled surface of the drive was thinner and in places moss or earth showed through. I moved slowly, determined to take note of everything because this might be my last visit. Or maybe I was merely putting off my arrival at the house.

The great cedar remained, minus a gigantic branch that lay, like a fallen and decomposing colossus, on the ground. I couldn't see if the bench I had sat on while I ate my lunch was still there. If it had been squashed by the fall, that would be absurdly apposite. Once, Claudia had pointed out the remains of a tree-house she and her sister had played in as children but I couldn't see that either.

Behind the tree, and therefore still at a little distance from the house, I paused a minute, lurking like a burglar casing the joint. Anyone looking out of the window could have spotted me easily enough. But no one did. There were three parked cars, one in front of the house and two in the direction of the stables. Of course I didn't recognise them, yet the sight jolted me. Had it not been for them, I might have thought the house uninhabited. Although there were no obvious signs of disuse – tubs on either side of the stone steps leading up to the front door had been planted with flowers – there was a more general air of neglect. The paint round the windows was much less bright than I remembered and the front door, once so shining white, was yellowish and dull. I wondered what I would do if it sprang open and someone came out, if *she* came out. Why should I think of running? It was she I had come to see.

I continued even more cautiously towards the stables. There was no horse's head peering out of the box. That, at least, was no surprise: Claudia had seldom ridden during our summer together. Again, the paint was old and peeling in places, the same blue I remembered from the past, but dimmer now. Despite the strong sunshine, I had a curious feeling that everything was just out of focus, blurred, a little removed. Perhaps the change was as much in my eyes as in what I was looking at.

Naturally I was heading for the old coach-house where I had had my workroom. The door was open so I entered quickly and shut it behind me. Clearly it had not been used for some time. Dust, thick and sticky, cobwebs, clotted with flies and small debris filled every corner and ran up the balustrade of the stairway. It was almost too painful to look at the rosettes that had once been so fresh and gay, a backdrop to our kisses. Every sad sight deepened in me the realisation of how long it was since Claudia and I had loved. And it had been for such a short time. But that I would not recognise. Love has no time tag attached to it.

Sickened by the smell of mustiness and decay, I left the building without going upstairs. Instead, I slid round the front of the stables, the back way to the swimming-pool. It didn't cross my mind to imagine anyone would be there and no one was. The pool cover was wound back off its rollers, the plastic split in half for a foot or two. But there were four tubs at each corner, freshly planted with white flowers, as at the front door. The grass, too, had been recently mown, leaving me with the impression of a cosmetic exercise. I didn't consider an explanation. Eventually I turned from the water, which was blue enough, to look across the lawn to the house.

In shock I took a step backwards. On the west lawn, between the house and the row of three large chestnuts, a huge whiteness filled the gap, mounting towards the sky in what was both a blankness and an aggressive presence. I was so disoriented that it was several seconds before I grasped that it was simply a marquee, put up, of course, to entertain the guests at Claudia's wedding. Rather wildly, I wondered why quite such a large space was needed when the little church I'd visited the day before could hardly have contained more than a hundred people. Yet it brought home to me, as nothing had before, that Claudia had decided to marry and to celebrate the event under the eyes of the world. I was amazed by the confidence it suggested. Had she thrown off the past so completely?

Scarcely aware of my actions, I sat down on the steps leading up to the changing hut. If Claudia were so thoroughly rehabilitated, so cleansed of guilt, then the priest had been right: her erstwhile lover and companion in crime had no place in her life. The connection was severed and I had no right to force myself into the picture. The contrast between us had become too great.

Here I crouched, an elderly, skulking interloper, broken by events, with only a few canvases and the tenacity of a far distant city between me and eternity. There was she, a bride to be, loved and lauded, crowned by a veil of virtue, taking up her place in her own society, which welcomed her graciously. There would be music and singing, speeches and laughter. As in the parable of the prodigal son, the celebration would be all the greater because of her earlier fall from grace.

No! I could not, must not, break into this. I stood, about to start my retreat.

The day your father dies is sure to be a long one. We sat, my mother, her friend James, her sister, and tried to talk sensibly. So many decisions had already been made over the long period of my father's illness. The house would be sold. For some time now, I had felt we were merely camping there, clinging on while my father clung to life although both of us with a shared lack of enthusiasm. My wedding was to have been the swansong for Meadowlands, a jolly thrash. Then there would be a new start for all of us. But the timing of my father's death had put the kibosh on all that.

We sat together in the chintzy drawing room with a gap where the piano, sold several years ago, had once stood, while outside the estate agents circled. I wished the house had been sold fourteen years ago.

'Has Louise been in touch about her arrival?'

'Not yet.' Catherine fiddled with a jade amulet round her neck. She had bought it on a visit to Hong Kong. Sometimes I believed that if Louise hadn't married young and left the country, everything would have turned out differently. The ten-year age gap between us made her seem to me like a second mother, but calmer and more sympathetic to my nature. She was the only one who had understood about my music. My parents were never interested and I was feeble. I only ever struck out for one thing.

'I suppose I'd better go.' James stood up. He was always reluctant to leave Catherine. I think he lived off her vitality, although I liked him well enough. Putting off the moment, he walked across to the window, the one that overlooked the lawn. He gave a small exclamation. The room was quiet and we all glanced up at him. 'Nothing.' He turned back to us. 'I thought for a moment there was someone out there for a moment, a man, but there was nothing.'

My aunt and I didn't comment. But my mother laughed. 'Don't talk about ghosts now, James dear, I couldn't take it.'

'Sorry.' She walked him to the door then, but I was curious enough to take his position at the window. As I stared out across the grass I, too, saw a ghost. But that had happened many times before.

CHAPTER SIXTEEN

1990

Catherine's Sunday drinks party was never discussed between Claudia and K, although they saw more of each other in the four days before it than they ever had or would in the future. On Thursday, when Douglas Lacey had returned to work and Catherine was spending the day with a friend, K took the afternoon off and accompanied Claudia on the long walk she had described, past the cricket pitch, over the heathland and through the woods.

The pine needles felt like a soft bed beneath their feet but they didn't consider sinking on to it. Instead, as if time stretched before them, they talked. K told her about his father, how he had taken him walking as a boy. How he had loved and admired him and how long it had taken him to admit his drunkenness, his faithlessness, his inevitable road to self-destruction. 'We lived in a small house in north London and my father's behaviour made it impossible for me to bring back friends. My mother and I huddled together as if we were harbouring a force of nature outside our control. When he left on his final downward spiral, I slept through the night for the first time in my life.

'I sometimes think,' K added, in a dark grove of tall pines, 'that men only have two modes: strong and weak. And when they are strong, they live in fear of becoming weak, which, of course, makes it much more likely to happen. My father worked for a small engineering firm but he thought he was a poet of the countryside. He was set in the belief that he was strong and brave so he needed the booze to boost the illusion.'

K said this with a smile but Claudia answered seriously: 'I know so few men' – with this she discounted all the boys of her acquaintance

– 'but it certainly fits my father. He's so strong he can hardly speak to ordinary mortals. And, of course, he wants his family to be strong too.'

K didn't want to talk about Claudia's family so he began to walk again. After a while, he told her the sad tale of the last years of his father's life, the misery he had caused his mother by taking up with another woman who drank with him glass by glass, his eventual death, after he had left them, of throat cancer.

'And did your mother go on loving him?'

'I believe she did. You can't stop loving a force of nature. And he could be charming.'

'Some people make such a mess of their lives!' exclaimed Claudia, as if it was the first time she had thought of such a thing K could have cried at her innocent wonderment. He took her hand.

Thus linked, they strolled, like Adam and Eve, through Paradise.

Now and again Catherine decided to go to church, behaving as if everyone should have guessed that was her intention and be prepared to accompany her. Claudia usually did to avoid a row. It wasn't important to her. At school she went every Sunday as a matter of rule. Some of the hymns moved her, 'Sing to God with gladness of all my heart ...', but the message of Christianity hadn't reached her heart.

'I go to church when I'm anxious,' Catherine announced, as they drove down the main road, the late-afternoon sun in their eyes. They were going to evensong on Saturday evening. 'I'm anxious about your father's health. He's not so young and he works too hard. I've told him he must take a proper holiday. Not later, but now. I'm looking into last-minute bookings. It will do us all good. When we get back I'll force him to go for a proper check-up. Why are men so obstinate about getting medical help?' She sighed.

'What do you mean "a proper holiday"?' Claudia was hardly attending. Her thoughts were on the drinks party to come. Should she be there? Could she avoid it? Catherine had invited the children of friends too. How could she resist the opportunity of seeing K? But who would accompany him? Did he really have a *wife*?

'I'll try Tuscany first – that would be good for your history of art A level – then the Dordogne, or anywhere we can find a bit of sun and comfort.'

'But we have sun and comfort here!' Claudia cried. Was she to be removed from the only meaningful experience of her life, like an extra suitcase?

Catherine seemed surprised but unfazed by her daughter's horror. 'I thought you'd be thrilled. You can bring a friend, if you like. Anyway, let's see if it happens first.'

Claudia knew it would. It seemed to her that Catherine's great talent was to make things happen. Now the circle of worry in her head extended from the drinks party to the future. She had only three weeks left of her holidays. Was she to spend the principal part of them sitting under some desolate olive tree?

One result of Catherine's holiday plans was that Claudia decided she would attend the party. Desperate times require desperate acts. She and K loved each other. They must not be separated, whatever the circumstances.

Catherine was up early to organise her party. Claudia could hear her outside her bedroom window, pulling tables and chairs around on the terrace. Eventually she got out of bed. It was not so early after all. She drew the curtains and there was her mother, still in her dressing-gown, dragging around heavy pots of lilies. Claudia moved back from the window before she was spotted.

The party had grown in size. Despite Claudia's determination to be deaf and blind until the moment she came face to face with K, who would then block out everyone and everything else, she couldn't help becoming aware of the guest list. There would now be twelve people. The additions were Catherine's closest friends, James and Annie, their son, Mark, and two newer friends, Richard and Penny, with their son Charles and daughter Daisy. The children, of course, were invited for Claudia. Charles was fifteen, Daisy fourteen and Mark eighteen – just the right age for Claudia, as Catherine had informed Douglas to stop him grumbling about the numbers. 'We don't want her to turn into a recluse like you,' she added blithely. Her confidence in this plan was perhaps surprising: the two families had been close for years but neither Mark nor Claudia had every shown any interest in each other. To the contrary: on a shared family holiday in Cornwall, they had achieved what might have seemed impossible – they had not spoken to each other, apart from 'Pass the salt, please', during the entire week.

Claudia debated whether to go back to bed or wash her hair, which wasn't dirty. But she had a new colour-lightening shampoo.

Catherine heard her daughter in the bathroom and felt glad that at least she cared about her appearance. Born so long after Louise, Claudia was in effect an only child, sure to be a little slow in making relationships. She returned to placing dabs of smoked salmon on small squares of bread.

At twelve o'clock, with the sound of a car coming up the drive, Claudia had a panic attack. She felt her skin flush red and tears started in her eyes. Then she turned icy white and sweat bubbled over her body. Her vision blurred and there was a booming sound in her ears. She'd been in the process of tying a sweater round her waist because the weather had turned cool and cloudy (Catherine was in despair) but now she dropped to the floor as if she wanted to crawl under the bed.

Yet despite the craven collapse of her body, her mind remained strong. She blocked out the cause of all this and held on to her confidence in the love she and K shared. Slowly normal life was resumed, and she remembered similar, if not so intense, feelings before playing her viola on stage. It was performance nerves, that was all. She got up and retied her sweater, listening to voices going through the hall to the terrace. Her mother called, 'Claudia! Mark's here.'

Claudia looked at herself in the mirror. Her face was a normal colour again, although her eyes were very bright and her hands were still a little sweaty. She was wearing a white top and she liked the effect against her tanned skin. She had put tiny yellow studs into her ears. She liked that too. She was bold. She was brave. She was in love. She had nothing to be ashamed off. She had absolutely nothing in common with Mark.

'How dashing, darling!'

K had put on his pink seersucker jacket. He'd bought it on a trip to New York about ten years ago but had only worn it occasionally.

'Perhaps I look silly,' he smiled at Fiona. 'Not enough sun about.'

'You're so handsome – I'm proud of you.' Fiona tucked her arm into his.

K felt her possessiveness like a reproach, although he knew it was the opposite. This drinks party was a disaster. He should never have accepted the invitation. Somewhere a sneaky voice whispered that this unlooked-for event might be the catalyst for dramatic change – to what outcome the voice did not tell him. 'Who's the duty driver?'

'Definitely me. I don't feel much like drinking anyway.'

K, who had already had a nip of sherry, thought he needed a bucketful. But as they got into the car his mind, which had been racing wildly with imprecision, suddenly slowed. He was filled with the beauty of his feelings for Claudia, which outreached anything else in his life. His love for her made him a better person, more able to write his book, more able to love Fiona and make her happy. How could it be anything but right to be on his way to see her, with his wife comfortably at his side? The sneaky voice remained silent.

'My darling.' He laid his hand on Fiona's knee and smiled.

Claudia was talking gaily to Mark, who looked dazed, as well he might. Catherine, glancing their way with satisfaction, noted that although Mark was two years older than Claudia, he was an inch or two shorter and still didn't seem fully mature. His open shirt, worn over T-shirt and jeans, flapped across his rather concave chest. An unfortunately late puberty, she thought, but at least he's male and Claudie's chatting him up.

'No, I've missed the Proms so far … I'm ashamed of myself … Just chilled out here all summer … Actually, I sometimes prefer listening on the radio … Yes, there's no boring people around …'

K, coming through the hallway behind Fiona and Douglas, heard Claudia's voice, even though she was standing on the far edge of the terrace. It seemed like an omen, proof that they were inextricably linked. He stood docilely, being introduced to James and Annie,

Penny and Richard, but he listened to Claudia's voice, easily discounting the male murmurings that replied to her. He felt he was leaning in her direction like a tree seeking light.

Fiona was competent in social settings. K assumed that her working days spent with colleagues or clients gave her the confidence to deal with strangers. In fact, her public persona was in contrast to a private vulnerability, which K sensed only occasionally because she wouldn't show it even to him.

'We love it round here,' she was telling James. 'Even though I work in London, the weekends give us a chance to get out and about. We're both keen walkers.'

Unconsciously, K heard the 'we' and 'us' as discordant notes. How soon could he move towards Claudia? Why should he wait?

Claudia heard her voice trilling like a recording of someone in a play. She was immediately aware of K's entrance on to the terrace and her body responded with a shiver, quickly repressed, and a flush, not so easily banished. His presence, only a few yards away, was both terrifying and joyous. She was amazed she could carry on speaking to the shadowy figure in front of her but her voice continued brightly, disconnected from her feelings. Now the two other young guests, Daisy and Charles, joined them, so that she was in a circle of youth. Charles looked older than Mark, although he was only fifteen, and was extremely keen to play tennis.

'I'm terrible at tennis,' contributed Mark.

'Charles loves smashing balls all over the place.' Daisy, the youngest and smallest, had red hair and appeared capable of dealing with her brother's excesses.

'Daisy's in her school team,' said Charles.

Claudia and Mark exchanged a look, becoming in that moment allies against the other two. Claudia noticed for the first time that he had a sympathetic face, dark eyes, clouded with self-doubt. Poor thing, he'd obviously been dragged unwillingly to this adult idea of fun.

'Why don't you two play?' she suggested to Charles.

*

K, carrying on a conversation with Penny about rose manure (a subject in which she outshone him effortlessly), watched the gathering
of the young. He didn't want to see it like that, he only wanted to
see Claudia, his beloved, and as his beloved, ageless. But they so
obviously formed a group, just as the four pairs of adults formed a
group, that she seemed submerged, if not barricaded against him. It
would have seemed odd to go across and talk to her.

Then Claudia broke away and, tin of Coke in hand, was approaching. For a moment, as K took in her beauty, the pale golden skin
against white, the high brow and graceful neck, he thought she was
coming towards him. But she was going to her mother.

'Charlie and Daisy are going to play tennis. Mark and I don't feel
like it so I'm going to show him the garden.'

K heard these innocuous words above Penny's information that
the secret of healthy roses was the same as for healthy children,
plenty of feeding but no spraying – 'or, for children, antibiotics'.
Since it was her two children who were longing to dash about the
tennis court, she was doubtless right.

'Yours look very healthy,' said K, eyes fixed on Claudia. Behind
her the skinny, shambolic boy hovered nervously. Was she really
going to take him round the garden without acknowledging his own
presence, without even attempting a polite 'hello'?

The narrowing of the space between herself and K had made Claudia's
adrenaline surge. She couldn't believe she had just announced to
Catherine that she was leaving the party, before she and K had even
a chance to say hello. She felt suddenly helpless and stood for a
second, staring at her mother.

'Don't rush away, darling!' cried Catherine, who seemed even
more frenetic than usual. 'I haven't introduced you to half the people
here.'

Too late, Claudia admitted that was why she was running away (or
leading Mark round the garden): it had been to avoid this moment.

'Of course you know our writer-in-residence and James and
Annie, but you haven't met Penny and Richard or Fiona.' For a second Claudia hoped she wouldn't have to distinguish between the two
women, Penny and Fiona, who both wore flowery skirts and pastel
tops, but the name Fiona rang a leaden bell.

'Hello,' said Claudia, shaking hands with a pale, dark-haired woman, who had wide-spaced brown eyes and regular features.

At least she could turn away now to Penny but that meant meeting K. She felt tears in her eyes, the adrenaline only just holding her together.

'You're abandoning us, are you?' said K, in a jovial, avuncular voice. He wanted to say how lovely she looked, how happy it made him to be in her presence, even under the difficult circumstances – although he was so exhilarated by seeing her that he hardly found them difficult at all. He was only sad, almost piqued, that she was leaving him, that she was taking this boy round the garden.

'We might swim,' said Claudia.

'Swim!' K looked shocked.

'It's rather cold for that,' said Penny, 'although I bet Charles and Daisy will jump in after their game.'

K hadn't been thinking of the weather, which had remained cool, with a spot or two of rain. He had been thinking of Claudia's beautiful body exposed to this callow youth's eyes. (Mark was still hovering uncertainly.)

'Darling, can you remember the first name of ...'

The voice that interrupted K's thoughts so startled him that he literally jumped round to face her. Fiona, who had come to ask an innocent question about the man who serviced their boiler – Catherine had fallen out with hers – stared with surprise at her husband's expression.

By the time he'd answered, or failed to know the correct answer, Claudia had gone from their circle. He couldn't think what he was doing there, and noticed, vaguely, how something was going on between Catherine and James. They seemed to avoid each other, then come together with extra vitality. Why would either of them bother with that sort of pathetic flirtation? he thought sourly.

Claudia walked with Mark past the tennis court, where Charles was adjusting the net with much shouting of instructions to Daisy, who stood in the middle measuring the correct height by balancing one tennis racquet on top of the other. 'You're such a *girl!*' shouted Charles, in exasperation, which caused Mark to smile for the first time that afternoon.

He looked at Claudia, who seemed not to have noticed the scene and they strolled on towards the swimming-pool. Mark decided Claudia was a bearable companion. Most importantly, she didn't tease him with semi-flirtatious questions, which he never knew how to answer. If he tried, he provoked either laughter or stony silence. In fact Claudia had hardly said a word, which suited him fine.

'The swimming-pool,' suggested Claudia. 'Do you want to swim?'

'It's raining,' pointed out Mark.

'Only spots.'

By silent but mutual consent, they sat down on two deck-chairs placed side by side. Claudia watched the few drops of rain hit the surface of the pool and make three or four wide circles. Then the water smoothed. Charles and Daisy's shouts accompanied the soft thump of the tennis balls. Beyond, the adult cocktail-party chatter was just discernible.

So K had a wife, who was pretty and lived with him in his house, and accompanied him to parties where she called him 'darling', as if that were normal. Claudia found she was trying to think of the situation objectively, as she might analyse the structure and characterisation of *Tess of the d'Urbervilles*, as if there was a coherent way of looking at things, even a 'right' way, for which she would be awarded an A or even an A*.

'I wouldn't mind another Coke,' said Mark.

'A Coke?' Claudia stared at him. Finding him another Coke would entail returning to the terrace, unless they sneaked into the kitchen via the front door, but that would seem too odd. She hadn't con-sidered returning to the terrace. She was still trying to assimilate the earlier scene there, and now she was being drawn back.

'It doesn't matter,' muttered Mark.

'Of course you can have another Coke!' Claudia jumped up. 'We'll see if Charles and Daisy want some too.'

Suddenly, Claudia was a whirlwind of activity, dashing across the lawn, applauding a winning serve by Charles and arriving once more at the terrace, with a panting Mark in her wake.

There she paused. The scene had shifted. Everybody was seated, and the animated chatter had slowed to a more relaxed conversation.

Her father was wearing his Panama which she thought affected. It had stopped raining and the sun had come out, although Claudia hadn't noticed until now. It lit up K's pink jacket and Penny's red hair. They were bending close together and the colours made Claudia's eyes swim. Catherine sat on K's other side, one hand dangling near his. Her diamond ring sparkled. Claudia blinked. She didn't have to say anything, merely pass by on her way to the drinks table at the other end of the terrace. So why did she crouch down like some eastern slave?

'Any orders for drinks?'

Catherine looked at her daughter with surprise. 'How sweet of you, darling.'

K leant forward till his face was only a few inches from Claudia's. So that was why she had taken up this position, she thought. To claim him as her own. He was so close that she could see the golden flecks in his irises and read there his hot love for her. 'I'll have a glass of red wine,' he said. Her attention moved to his lips.

'White for me,' smiled Penny.

Claudia stood up. She was aware of her height and slimness directly in front of K. She knew it was a provocation and walked away slowly. She felt the bracelet round her ankle, which had ridden up a little, fall gently back into place.

'I'll help,' said Mark.

'You should have a beer,' suggested Claudia, magnanimously. 'Or wine, if you prefer.'

Collecting orders as they went, they reached the drinks table. 'I've never met a girl like you.' Mark picked up a corkscrew, then stopped to stare at her.

Claudia took it as her rightful homage. She thought, In this instant he has fallen in love with me. It happens like that. She felt sorry for him. 'I don't expect you wanted to come today.'

'No. I usually hate this sort of thing. It all seems so pointless.'

'Yes.' Claudia thought they were talking honestly, as equals. Yet she had this huge secret. Nothing was pointless to her. A few weeks ago she would have felt just the same as Mark. She recognised a crazy wish to tell him she was in love.

'Let's have some wine. Let's take a bottle and go and sit at the other end of the garden.'

'We'd better get them their drinks first.'

Claudia had lost interest in being an eastern slave. Now she wanted Mark as *her* slave, sitting on a rug under the chestnuts. Evidently Mark wanted it too, because it didn't take them long to deliver their orders and slope off across the lawn with a bottle of white wine not exactly hidden in the crook of Mark's arm. Claudia, who had removed her sandals, was half draped in a rug and carried a glass in either hand.

Catherine watched them indulgently. 'They've known each other since they were children,' she told Penny and K, then gave one of her special laughs. 'Although I can't say they showed much interest in each other then.'

Penny responded with a meaningful laugh and K, fearing they would expect a response from him, took such a large gulp of wine that he nearly did the nose trick. He felt he was being made a fool of and knew that that made him a fool. All the delicacy of his love for Claudia was mocked by these cackling women and, worse still, by Claudia's blithely receding back with her chosen companion, attentive, if lank. Was she doing it on purpose? He hadn't thought such conniving in her nature. But how well did he know her?

Reluctantly, K refocused on Catherine, who had taken his arm. 'I expect you'll be relieved to be on your own for a couple of weeks.'

'I'm sorry?'

Catherine expanded further on her great good luck in having taken up a cancellation on a villa in Umbria, 'So helpful for Claudia's history of art A-level,' she added.

Of course, K knew that the holidays had to end and Claudia return to school, but that had seemed distant enough to discount. But Catherine was talking about Tuesday, *in three days' time*. And Claudia, who must have known, had said nothing to him. Even now she was sitting on her rug quaffing wine. He had been right to feel a fool.

'You're going on your own, then?' asked Penny.

'Not necessarily. It depends on Claudia and who's around. Fancy a trip?'

'If pigs could fly ...'

As Catherine and Penny embarked on a detailed review of flights, holiday villas, companions, tourism and staff, K got to his feet. His head spun – he'd drunk more than he'd thought. He determined to summon Fiona and return home. But Fiona was having a good time. K could see at once that she wouldn't be easily removed from Douglas's side – he was laughing at something she'd said. Since Douglas's face, below its pompous panama, wore the lugubrious folds of someone with whom laughter was a low priority, this was obviously a triumph. That was the thing about Fiona: she almost never failed in anything she set out to achieve. He found himself thinking that that was why she would get her baby. And why she had got him, if it came to that.

'Come and join us!' invited Douglas, his rather short legs (Claudia certainly hadn't inherited them) stretched out in front of him. On his other side a not very happy James wasn't talking to anyone.

'Left something behind in my room,' mumbled K. 'Need to pick it up.'

The corollary to this unplanned manoeuvre was that K found himself walking across the lawn to Claudia on his way (although it was in the opposite direction) to his room.

Claudia, lolling, a glass of wine at her lips, apparently only saw him at the last minute when Mark, also lolling, sat up abruptly.

'Hello, sir.'

Recovering from this knife wound, K smiled, more piranha-like than pleasantly. 'You look comfortable.'

'We've only got two glasses,' said Mark, not, after all, so supine.

For a moment Claudia said nothing. Then she looked up at K, blinked a little. 'Mark plays the piano so he can accompany me on my piece.'

Mark seemed surprised at this but agreed that he would *love* to accompany her. 'I didn't know you'd remembered.'

'Oh, yes,' said Claudia, earnestly. 'There was a piano in that hotel in Cornwall. I saw you there one morning when you thought we were at the beach.'

'Well, have fun,' said K. There was no need to prolong his humiliation. She hadn't even bothered to look at him properly, except for that once.

He walked away, across the lawn, into the driveway and round to the stables. He would make sure he couldn't hear them playing.

*

Claudia took another sip of wine. He had come to her. He loved her. She thought K so far superior to herself that she hardly thought she was capable of upsetting him. He could upset her, of course, as he had that Friday when he'd left without saying goodbye.

'Who is that man?' asked Mark, his wits sharpened by love. Claudia had been right.

'Nobody,' replied Claudia, smiling into her glass. She rolled on to her back. 'Sometimes when I lie here, a bird comes and sings just above my head. Do you know about birds?'

'Not a thing. I'm too blind to see them, I think.'

'What a pity. I adore birdsong. Shall we go in and play now?'

'You enjoyed yourself!' K hadn't meant it to come out like an accusation. Or perhaps he had.

Fiona, who was driving them both home, smiled agreeably. 'Without a drop of alcohol.'

'Amazing.'

'I like Douglas. He's got his own style.'

'Like, half dead.'

'Didn't *you* enjoy it?' Fiona glanced at K, his red, dissatisfied face.

'They're just the sort of people I don't need in my life. Complacent, boring, narrow-minded!' This came out more explosively than K had expected.

'Are we so much better? Not so rich, certainly.'

'Rich! So that's why you liked him. For his money. Well, I'm sorry I can't do more for you.'

'I'd no idea you felt like that.' Fiona seemed genuinely concerned. 'And you've been going there every day for weeks – months.'

'I hardly see them when I'm working.' K felt irritated by the inexorable logic of Fiona's mind.

'They love having you there.'

'I'm a trophy,' said K.

'Is it the class thing, then? I must admit they were all almost anachronistically middle class.' K knew Fiona always preferred to mollify him if she could do it rationally.

'You know I don't believe in class.' K saw that Fiona, in her good humour, was trying not to laugh. Of course it was an absurd statement. 'I mean the importance of class.'

'Of course, it hardly exists except in places like this, neither fish nor fowl, neither London nor the country.'

' Sometimes I wonder whether we didn't make a stupid mistake deciding to live here.'

'Maybe you're right.' Fiona appeared to have decided to concentrate on driving.

K stared out of the window grimly. Fiona was right (although she hadn't said anything of the sort): Claudia was a spoilt middle-class brat. It had all been a ludicrous mistake. Now he must grow up and get on with his writing. Thank God they were going to Italy and he could have a bit of peace and quiet.

'Sorry I acted like a moron.' K took Fiona's hand as they entered the house. 'Too much booze and not enough food.'

'Whatever time is it?' Fiona glanced at her watch. 'Two thirty! The sort of time any unfed man turns into a brute.'

K wasn't sure about the brute, but he let it pass. The lethargy of depression stopped him helping Fiona prepare the lunch. With a mixture of admiration and irritation, he watched her bustle about.

'Outside or in?' She paused.

'Oh, in.'

He noted, as they closed in to the table, that her unaltered cheerfulness had an anticipatory note in it. What could she be looking forward to? It wasn't her fault that Claudia had come into his life and changed everything. Now that some time had passed since the dreadful party, he was inclined to feel a little more sanguine, a little more optimistic. How had he expected Claudia to behave? She could hardly have thrown herself into his arms – not that she did that sort of thing anyway. Nor could she be blamed for her mother arranging a holiday. If they were serious about each other, they could survive a two-week separation. Although he was vague about school terms, perhaps not liking to label her a schoolgirl, he assumed there must be some more time at Meadowlands after her return from Italy.

'Are you sitting comfortably?'

K realised Fiona had been waiting to speak. His mind on Claudia, he had no premonition of what she would say.

'I took a couple of hours off work yesterday,' she began.

'That's not like you,' he said, although he had little idea of how she spent her days in London, where or with whom she had lunch, who were her special mates. He had no wish to pry but if she did tell him something, he liked to believe he listened attentively.

'I've had some good news.' Her dark eyes were bright and fixed on him expectantly as if she needed him to guess. 'The thing I've most wanted in the world…'

' Do you mean…?'

'We're going to have a baby!'

At this moment of Fiona's greatest triumph and joy, he found himself concentrating on that idiotic 'we'. Women had babies. Men merely took part in kicking it off, in a subservient, if enjoyable role. He pulled himself together. 'That's wonderful! I can hardly believe it! How do you feel? It's incredible!' Aware that he was in danger of overdoing it, K stopped and looked at her.

Her usually pale face was flushed and her eyes were fixed on him. She was radiant – there was no other word for it. Now he took in the glory of the news. She was going to have a baby. Even, *they* were going to have a baby.

'My darling.' He went to her, kissed her, hugged her, told her how clever she was, how happy he was. Yet at the same time a little voice was saying, T*his has nothing to do with what really matters to me,* and, W*ill this separate me from Claudia*? So dizzying were the contradictions in his head that tears welled in his eyes.

'Oh, darling.' Fiona put a comforting arm round his shoulders. 'I never thought you'd feel so emotional about it. It's always been my dream, not yours.'

'We can both dream,' murmured K, and put his hand over his eyes.

Claudia had secretly despised moody girls, girls who shrieked with happiness or misery so you could hardly tell the difference or, worse still, became overtly despairing by refusing to speak and hiding in the kind of places where they'd be easily found. Claudia had been the confidante to many such drama queens, remaining calm, kind and confident of their ultimate recovery – which was not always exactly what was wanted.

But now she found herself on an emotional roller-coaster. The scene under the chestnut tree had raised her high, not excluding Mark's attempt to kiss her, which had only emphasised the depth of her feeling for K. 'Don't be stupid, Mark,' she'd cried. 'You know

I don't feel like that about you.' But it seemed right that he should want to. She was desirable, desired by all.

But now – and unaware of the ultimately depressing effect of sharing an entire bottle of wine – she fell into slothful gloom. She was sitting in the deck-chair by the pool that she had occupied when she was with Mark, who had, incidentally, dropped out of her consciousness. The sun had remained strong and she knew she should move to find a hat or sun cream or, better, *do something useful.*

To her horror, tears trickled down her cheeks. She felt cut off from everything that had previously seemed important. Only one thing could bring her back to life: the appearance of K, strong and confident, walking towards her. But that was impossible, at least until Monday.

Inexorably her gloom, which had been negative and vague, the bitter *angst* of youth, even if linked to her love for K, began to change. She no longer had the strength to keep out the spectre of his wife. As Fiona's name entered her mind, Claudia felt a fierce wave of hatred, followed by rage. By what right did this woman claim K? Obviously he felt nothing for her or he wouldn't have come to her, Claudia. She was the one he loved. His marriage (the word made an ugly clunking sound) had all been a ghastly mistake. Some time he would explain it to her. Perhaps he had been forced into it in some way she couldn't imagine. The fact that there were no children made it clear it wasn't a 'real' marriage – just low-grade companionship.

By the time Claudia had thought all this through to her reasonable satisfaction her tears had dried and she felt capable of movement. She stripped off her sticky clothes and dived into the cool waters of the pool.

CHAPTER SEVENTEEN

1990

They met by the pool. It was still early. Nine thirty in the morning. K had seen Claudia cross the lawn with her swimsuit.

'Claudia!' He had opened his window and called softly. The afternoon of loving celebration with Fiona, the agony of contradictory loyalties, had been banished by the merest glimpse of Claudia. She squinted into the morning sun, said nothing but waved the swimsuit. He took this as an invitation. He picked up his trunks but he didn't mean to swim.

At the pool, they clung to each other, strove to become one and wipe out the terrible Sunday.

'I love you,' he whispered, into her ear.

'I love you too.'

Now he had held her, K could move away. He took several deep breaths and laughed. He felt he could write a million brilliant novels. 'I should work.' His love was not greedy – it was better than himself. He could feel Claudia's eyes on him, staring.

'Yes. You must.' She nodded but her face was a little anxious.

'We'll see each other later.'

'Oh, yes!'

'We must live in the present,' he said suddenly, just before he turned away. The present always seemed to make sense while thoughts of the past or the future presented far greater difficulties. It struck him, as he took the side route back to his den, that this concept had a real relevance to his story. The collision of aggressor and victim was a result of the aggressor's refusal to let go of the past and the victim's determined picture of the future. It was an idea worth pursuing. He quickened his stride, pleasingly conscious both of the creative buzz in his head and the loving presence behind him.

Claudia stood where he had left her. She hadn't wanted him to go away. She wanted him closer. She wanted them to go together into the changing hut and kiss. At least. But she had been too shy to say so.

If they had spent time together she would have added that her father, who had not gone to work, was to accompany her mother, rather surprisingly, for holiday shopping. But even that had seemed too forward. Besides, she didn't feel like mentioning the holiday. She was happy, of course, but unsure of her next move. She reminded herself of her resolution to take her music more seriously but she had come to a difficult passage in the Brahms – although Mark had been admiring the day before – and she knew her concentration wouldn't be good enough to tackle it.

Perhaps she would go and look out clothes for the holiday. A small part of her wanted to punish K for leaving her, for putting his work first.

At ten thirty Catherine came along to the stables. K had not yet come down for his coffee so she went up the wooden stairs and knocked at his door.

K opened it with a welcoming expression of joy that surprised her. He had assumed she was her daughter.

'I'm so sorry to disturb you.'

'That's fine. Don't worry.' K recovered himself. 'It was great fun yesterday. Thank you.'

'I was glad to introduce you to some new friends.' She paused to look round the room. It was very neat, orderly, workmanlike, but she was startled by the effect of the window on the lawn. From where he sat, it must be like sitting in a darkened auditorium with a brightly lit stage in front of him. She continued, 'You know we're off to Italy for two weeks tomorrow and Douglas wondered if you might be willing to house-sit for us.'

As Catherine elaborated – Douglas had a thing about burglars – K became acutely uncomfortable. He knew he didn't want the job and that Fiona's pregnancy would make it equally unwelcome to her.

'I'd have to consult Fiona,' he said.

'Of course. I'm sorry to throw it at you like this.'

After Catherine had left, K went down to make his coffee. He heard the Laceys' car drive away and, half-consciously, awaited Claudia's arrival.

He became aware that it was raining slightly, the drops spattering on to the driveway. He took his coffee to the open door and stood there, staring a little vacantly. He thought how dark the greens of grass and shrubs and trees had become. The yew seemed almost black, although that was unchanging, he told himself, no indication of the deepening of summer, merely a matter of light. He thought how right the poets were to emphasise the beauties of spring and, by a process of natural links, whether Fiona and he weren't too old to become parents.

'Darling.' Claudia had swept up to him so quickly that he hardly had time to change his attitude before her arms were round him and her mouth on his.

This outgoing love, this *darling*, was quite different from any of their previous engagements. It surprised him, even shocked him a little, but excited him too. He began to kiss her back, with all the emotion of the last few days.

Eventually he broke away. 'What about Alan?'

'He's not here.'

K moved further into the coach-house. He needed to recover himself. Claudia followed him. He knew she wanted more but her youth and sweetness were suddenly distressing him. He leant against the wall, then put his forehead against the rough bricks. He pictured Fiona's radiant face.

Evidently Claudia didn't understand this theatrical gesture. 'Are you all right?'

How could he say, No if she didn't see it? 'I love you,' he whispered.

She came over to him. 'I know.' But he didn't want her near him. It had become clear to him: it wasn't a case of love *and* desire, it was love pitted against desire. If he loved her enough, he wouldn't touch her. She was a child. At last he had admitted it to himself. She couldn't know what was happening or imagine the consequences. She was a romantic child who believed *amor vincit omnia*, as Chaucer had made the venal old Wife of Bath quote. Rather wildly now, he tried to see a way forward. He couldn't deny his love, not to himself or to her – it was the strongest, most *real* emotion he'd ever felt in his life – but he must not act on it.

Yet he was weak, so weak. Until this moment he had never known how weak he was.

'Please. Tell me what's the matter?'

She sounded upset. He felt as if he were seeing her charming, virginal face for the first time. That was it. He must objectify her, strip her of the aura of love, return her to her simple schoolgirl self. As K pronounced words like 'virginal' and 'schoolgirl' to himself, they caused him pain but, also, he thought, made him a little stronger.

'I love you,' he repeated, edging a little further from her. Couldn't she understand without him telling her?

But apparently Claudia – usually so sensitive – saw only his misery and wanted to make him feel better. She stepped up to him and put her hand on his cheek.

At her touch, K shuddered. 'I'm so sorry,' she said. 'Whatever it is. I'm so sorry. I watched you standing there. You looked so sad.'

Her voice gave K the chance to break free. 'Your mother has asked me to house-sit while you're away.'

His words, half mumbled, explained nothing but anything was better than silence. He spoke more, sentences jumbled as if he were drunk.

Claudia looked bewildered. 'It's not for ever,' she said. Then, after a pause – they were now standing several feel apart from each other, 'Shall we go for a walk? My parents are staying out over lunch.'

The innocent look she gave him with this invitation struck K's heart and allowed him a glimmer of hope. What *could* be more innocent than a walk? They had taken others, hand in hand.

'Yes. Yes.' He was almost feverish. 'Shall we go where we went before? Through the pines? Let's go now so we're not rushed.'

'What about your work?'

'I'll have two weeks for that. Two weeks without you.'

Oblivious of the rain, they set off down the driveway.

CHAPTER EIGHTEEN

2004

I had no expectation of finding anyone more corporeal than James's non-existent ghost. I walked towards the swimming-pool. It was more for something to do, a reason to leave the house with its burden of death and memories.

I reached the pool and, hardly bothering to look around, sat on the steps to the changing hut. I was thinking, however vaguely, about the importance of a regular occupation in my life, how I would never have stood the strain of life as a musician. I would tuck the viola further back into its cupboard. My present job, which I had held for the last three years, suited me perfectly. I worked for a Non-Governmental Agency that specialised in aid to projects in southern India. I was office-based, between nine thirty and five thirty, with little real responsibility, but gradually the work was restoring my confidence. I would carry on after my marriage, whenever that might be. Was it possible that I was more like my father than I'd ever believed? All during my childhood and growing-up, he'd worked like an automaton, day in, day out, only dragged away by Catherine for two weeks' holiday each year. And the moment he stopped, he fell apart. Of course it was his illness, but not only that, I believed. People can live pretty good lives with chronic myelomas, or so my mother had quoted his doctor. Nor was it entirely my fault, I reminded myself, as my shrink had taught me to do. My father had been a closet romantic, expressed only in his adoration of his daughters, and romantics are almost, by definition, incapable of rolling with the punches.

At a movement, I turned a little, but casually. It was probably a cheeky squirrel – they'd increased in numbers over the last few years as if guessing no one had the energy to worry them. But the sound was coming from the hut. I supposed, half-heartedly, that I should investigate.

When I saw Claudia approaching the hut and realised I was trapped, I panicked. My head throbbed as if it couldn't cope with the shock and a band of steel settled across my forehead. I could hardly believe it was her, although she'd changed far less than I'd expected. Her hair was still long and fair, the shape of her face unchanged, perhaps a little more defined. In a flash I guessed she had been the driver of the car I'd seen earlier. In a sense she'd been with me all day, aware – why not? – of the stalker's presence. What was I but an old man, preparing to bring new horror into her life? I pictured the face of the priest who'd more or less advised me to stay away, and begged him to save me with whatever spiritual power was in his grasp. In one more second she'd turn the door handle, in another she'd be with me in this damp-smelling little room – much damper and dirtier than it used to be. I imagined her screaming, and screaming as she had that morning fourteen years ago.

The band round my head tightened. Perhaps I could break through the glass panels, pretend to be a burglar, run away so that she never saw my face. But then the police would be called. There would be a man-hunt, resulting in my ignominious capture.

One can have so many thoughts in two seconds. My head felt as if it was bulging with terrifyingly possibilities. There was even time for one more as the handle turned, the most frightening of all: perhaps she would look at me, recognise me and, far from screaming in horror, turn away indifferently.

CHAPTER NINETEEN

1990

Springing past the empty cricket pitch, in her sawn-off jeans and trainers, Claudia confided in K that she had always felt herself different from her peers. 'Maybe it started with my father being older than my friends' dads and kind of *uninvolved*, but truthfully I think it's more about my nature. If he'd let me study music seriously, go off to Cheetham's School in Manchester, I think I might have fitted in. Or, at least, I'd have known music wasn't the problem. As it is, I've always felt sort of alien.' She laughed, tossing her head, for the first time reminding K of her mother. 'I don't mean an alien with funny ears and things, but different, remote.'

By now they were entering the heath, scrubby ground with unexpected tufts and holes, even when they were following the path. K, in baggy loafers, was wary of turning his ankle. Although the rain had stopped, the ground was wet and the sky overcast. Clouds of flies were following them, although too high up to be a real nuisance. He knew what Claudia was trying to say: until they met, she had felt unconnected to her fellows, groundless, floating. He understood it because he felt the same.

'Of course, you wouldn't feel like me,' she continued, 'because you've got your writing. You've got a reason for living.'

She was so grand in her statements, so sweepingly certain, thought K. Should he tell her that his writing was an artifice to keep him alive while his love for her was the best part of his life? But he wouldn't. He couldn't. She thought him special. She admired him. She looked up to him.

'I love you,' he said. It had become a defence, even a disguise. He could explain his growing disillusionment with his work in advertising, although he played down his inadequacies and up his moral disapproval. She listened eagerly. Jobs and work were still outside her experience. It became clear that she didn't even know how her father earned the money that kept his family in a large house and sent her to a private school.

She was humble about this and embarrassed, so K forgave her easily. It was her father's pride, he thought, picturing the lounging man on the terrace, with his dark face and Panama. He wanted his daughter unsullied by the world.

By the time they reached the woods, it had started to rain. The water filtered down the pine trunks, filling the warm air with their aromatic scent. At first K and Claudia were hardly wet, then it came down more heavily, soaking their hair into their eyes, plastering their clothes to their bodies. The air, which had seemed so comfortably at skin temperature, was now dank and cold. K glanced at his watch. It was one o'clock. 'I don't know about you but I'm hungry. Starving actually.'

Claudia looked surprised but pleased too, as she did at everything he said. 'Don't tell me you know a local burger joint.' She stopped walking and stared up to the black rods of trees with their burst of bushy branches at the top. Rain ran into her eyes and mouth, as if she was standing in a shower. 'Aren't these called *umbrella* pines?'

K answered her first question. 'As a matter of fact, I do. Or I think I do. There's a restaurant I've been to once, in a hotel. I'm sure it's nearby.'

'But we can't go in like this!' Claudia laughed. 'We're dripping. Just think of their carpets.' She was in high spirits, apparently carefree.

'You're like a dryad.' K caught her arm, hugged her wetness close to him. She was like a puppy, too, her secrecy and shyness momentarily dissolved. 'Hotels are used to rude people dripping on their carpets. That's what they're paid for.' He whispered this into her ear but he didn't feel lascivious or insinuating. He wanted to take her to a warm place where he would buy her lunch. There was innocence in this, a loving purity of intention.

'Is that thunder?' She whispered too, and he thought it might have been the joint roll of their heartbeat. But then it increased in volume, followed after only a short pause by a hard flash of lightning.

'It's come so close so quickly.' She seemed frightened, jumping away from him. 'Let's go!'

Perhaps she expected one of the tall trees to be struck and transformed into a flaming torch. The dark canopy above their heads had disguised the approaching storm so that its suddenness made it seem all the more dramatic. He took her hand. 'Let's run.'

Their journey through the wood took on the quality of a dream. There was not much undergrowth so tree trunks were the main impediment, sometimes like the heavy bars of a great cage, sometimes glistening from the lightning above.

Soon they stopped running but continued briskly in the direction K thought the hotel stood. 'We're not being chased,' he panted at one point.

Then, like the shimmer of an oasis in the desert, they were out of the wood and at the edge of a wide lake, its surface tossed askew by the pelting rain.

'There!' K pointed beyond the water.

'So there really is a hotel.' She glanced up, scarcely out of breath, as lightning broke open the sky. But it was a small crack, and the thunder was insignificant. 'The storm's going.'

'We're still wet and hungry.' He didn't know what she was thinking. Maybe she was worried about being seen with him in public. But her eyes were clear and untroubled.

'Just for a quick bite.'

If K had been a religious man, which he wasn't, he might have imagined the devil's whip in their precipitate race out of the woods towards the apparent nirvana of the hotel. There was no real reason for them to stop there. K's sandwich waited for him back at Meadowlands, the rain was easing and their thin clothes would dry quickly enough on the walk back. Besides, there was a risk in delaying their return that her parents would be back before them. But the hotel, which K had only visited once for a wedding reception, had become as irresistible a magnet as if a two-horned creature with cloven hoofs sat on the roof and crooked a welcoming finger.

In reality, the hotel was a grey, flat-topped modern building, whose only claim to distinction was a wide terrace overlooking the lake.

They arrived hand in hand. They crossed the deserted terrace without pausing and entered the hotel reception as strangers in a strange land. That, too, was empty, without anyone behind the desk.

'Monday's always slow,' said K.

'Perhaps it's closed,' suggested Claudia.

Until this moment, she hadn't imagined how strange it would seem to be with K outside her home. Aside from their walks, she had only seen him in the context of Meadowlands, where his appearance had dominated the landscape. But this hotel – she read on the plaque above reception it was called 'Fresh Ponds Hotel' – made her look at K anew. Far from diminishing her feelings of breathless and bewildered love, it seemed more remarkable that such a tall, distinguished man, so handsome and clever, should care for such a dull, ordinary, only half-grown-up girl as herself. A door banged, making her start.

A small plump woman hurried forward. 'The restaurant's shut,' she announced, before she'd properly arrived.

Claudia turned to leave but K caught her arm. 'Don't you have any guests?'

Claudia was surprised at the immediate belligerence of his tone.

'Yes. We have a few.' The woman held an apron in her left hand. Clearly on Mondays staff had to double up.

'Don't you have to feed them?'

'That's room service, isn't it?'

'You tell me.'

'If you don't mind ...'

'I do mind.' K took two steps towards her. 'We'd like a room, a bottle of champagne and two rounds of sandwiches. We're not choosy about the filling. Ham or cheese and tomato.'

The woman seemed confounded by his effrontery. Claudia was nearly as surprised. She watched the woman go to the desk with an obedient, scurrying air, as if to say that the sooner she dealt with this madman and got back to the real business of the day the better. K produced a credit card from his back pocket, the receptionist produced a key and the transaction was complete. She hadn't looked at Claudia, who was beginning to feel invisible.

'They'll be ham sandwiches,' announced the woman, then hurried away down the corridor from which she'd appeared.

At last K seemed to remember Claudia. He turned to her questioningly. 'Is that all right with you? It's one thirty now, so we'll make sure we're out as near two as possible.'

Since he had taken the trouble to arrange this, Claudia felt that it was impossible for her to demur. Nor did she want to. Her heart was

132

beating fast and irregularly as they took the staircase up two flights. He went ahead. He was almost bounding.

She caught up with him along a windowless corridor. He was struggling to open the door to number thirty-two. He pushed it inwards eventually, saying over his shoulder, 'It'll probably be grim but we won't be here long enough to notice.'

The room was small and stuffy, filled with objects: a television, a table, a Teasmade, a chair and two narrow beds. The ceiling was low.

Claudia ran across to the window, which jutted out as if it was under an eave. She undid the lock and swung it open. 'There's a view of the lake,' she cried.

But K had gone into the bathroom. So now they were as far away from each other as they could get in the available space.

When he came out they stared at each other. The divide was enormous. There was a knock at the door. K opened it to a boy who looked about fourteen and held a tray with a bottle of champagne in an ice bucket and two glasses. He kept his head down while he placed it on the table, then scuttled out.

Claudia guessed he had been embarrassed and a pang of dread held her rigid at the window. K opened the champagne quickly and efficiently. He poured two glasses and lifted one in Claudia's direction. She didn't move. The situation had become too strange, too threatening. The room was hideous, her wet clothes clung to her and K was a grimacing stranger. She wanted to be away, on the other side of the lake, under the pine trees, under her chestnut trees, in her bedroom, anywhere but in this dingy, vulgar, horrid place.

K put down the glass and came over to her. He put his arms round her and hugged her so that she felt the length of his body against hers. She realised he understood what she was feeling. Gradually the warmth grew between them and she began to relax.

'We'll go now if you like,' he whispered.

She said nothing. A moment ago all she had wanted was to leave but now she couldn't bear the thought of separation from him. An inch of space between them was too much.

K broke away. He drank some champagne, then some more. He indicated her glass. 'You don't want any, do you?'

'I'll have a sip.'

They came together again. This time they kissed. Claudia had the oddest sensation that her brain had grown wings and was floating out of her body, leaving it to look after itself. Even the tiny amount of champagne she'd had combined with K's kisses to make her feel utterly drunk.

'I love you,' K said. 'Even when you're soaking I love you.'

'I love you too.'

He led her to the nearest bed.

Claudia came back to herself with a strong sense of light and sound. She heard a bird just outside the window and, before she opened her eyes, she knew that the sun was entering the room. They were both naked. K's heavy body, so much darker than hers, was lying half across her. He was asleep, breathing deeply, not quite snoring. She lay as quietly as she could, treasuring, hoarding, these minutes of perfect love.

They were lovers. They loved each other. They had made love. She became almost gleeful. She would have laughed, but she didn't want to wake him. She watched as the sun, slanting across his shoulder, moved nearer his face.

'Darling Claudia.' Eyes closed, K put his arm across her chest, just above her breasts. Claudia was astounded by the intimacy of the gesture. Even though they had just performed the most intimate act, she hadn't lost her awe of him.

'We'll have to go.' He still spoke with his eyes closed and his body splayed across her and the bed. She could tell that he didn't want to move, which pleased her.

His eyes opened. 'Thank you. I can't tell you how happy you've made me.'

Claudia wasn't sure about this. Surely she should be thanking him. Or they should be equal in thanks as they were equal in love. Except that this was not quite right either. He had given her far more than she could ever give him. He had started up her life. 'I don't want you to thank me,' she murmured. She felt a fluttering as if her brain was descending again, intervening in her few moments of perfect happiness. But it was too late, far too late. She was welded to him now. Nothing could prise them apart.

'I thank you because you are more important to me than anything in the world. If I believed in God, I would thank him.' Gently K drew Claudia towards him and held her in his arms. He caressed her face and neck and the length of her body as if he wanted to turn the passion of his love-making into something calmer. Claudia felt it was an even better moment than when she'd first woken because then she'd been on her own and now they were as close as they could be. She felt her body soft and pliable, moulded into his.

K reached for his watch on the bedside table. He did it clumsily, uncoordinated by sleep and love, and it fell to the floor. Claudia bent over to retrieve it. She felt the supple gracefulness of her waist, and her hair, the dry surface of it, floating round her face.

'You're so beautiful.'

Claudia smiled at the gruffness in K's voice. She was beautiful. Vaguely, she remembered the stories of Bella's sexual encounters. She felt as if she inhabited another world. She handed the watch to K.

'Not good.'

'What's wrong?'

Time was what was wrong. Claudia watched as K left the bed and began to collect his damp, crumpled clothes lying with hers on the second bed. She tried to make herself feel it mattered, but her parents seemed impossibly remote. How could K care so much?

He saw she hadn't moved and seemed to understand why. He sat down beside her and took her hand. 'I love you. I will always love you. But it will be better if we're back,' he hesitated, 'before your parents arrive.'

She stared into his face and believed him. 'I love you too.'

'Look.' He smoothed the sheet behind her. There was a red mark – her blood. 'We're blood brothers. Now we can never be parted.' He smiled and kissed her. In a moment she began to dress.

When K opened the door to leave the bedroom, they nearly tripped over a plate of sandwiches placed outside. K crouched down and picked up a sandwich in either hand. He smiled at Claudia. 'Can't waste these.' He handed one to her and took a huge bite of his.

Claudia felt her joy – dented by the hurried dressing and leaving – return with a fizz of triumph. They were lovers. She, too, bit into a sandwich.

Munching, half running, they left the hotel. The speed of their exit whirled Claudia into a further exhilaration.

'If we go back along the road,' said K, 'we'll do it in ten minutes.'

It was true; the road was a much more direct route. Claudia, young, if not athletic, felt her long legs bounding obediently. If she could have chosen, she would have lain naked with K for ever. She would have asked him to stroke her and enter her again so that it would all seem more believable, even more final, but the crazy running and jogging and sometimes walking, panting, holding hands, had a crazy appeal. None of this day would be ordinary. She would remember every moment for ever.

K's sense of love, panic and despair was lessened by the physical pain of the wild running. He couldn't think and run at the same time. He was not particularly fit and he was sweating heavily. The storm had swept the sky clear of clouds and his clothes, which had dried in the first few minutes, became damp again. He could hear Claudia's feet, and her panting, sweet and short like a child's.

'Let's have a break.' He stopped so suddenly that she cannoned into him. It was an excuse to kiss her, even on the pavement of the fairly busy road. Claudia's face looked calmly blissful, encouraging his heartbeat to slow a little.

'It's not far now.'

'No,' agreed Claudia, pointing to her right. 'We can cut across Mr Wynott's field.'

He remembered that this was more her home territory than his.

'You're hot.' She ran a finger over his face.

'And you look fresh as a daisy.'

'I'm not. I'm puffed out.'

'Nonsense!' They stared at each other. K wanted to kiss her again, to take her into the field and lie with her among the buttercups. 'I adore you.'

'Here's the stile.' Obviously she had followed this route before. 'I adore you too.' She turned to him at the top, smiling triumphantly.

K saw that it was three fifteen. A sense of fatalism took hold of him. Either Catherine and Douglas would be back or they wouldn't. Either he would think of a plausible excuse for his walk with Claudia or he wouldn't. Either they would be discovered or they wouldn't.

The field was grassed and a small herd of cows grazed in one corner, more cowpats than buttercups. It sloped gently upwards. They walked slowly hand in hand. Claudia said, 'Usually I don't like this time of year. The green is so dull, the trees so dreary, as if they're waiting for autumn.'

'But you like it now?'

'Oh, yes!' She didn't have to add anything else. It was clear that everything had changed for her, as for him. He would not think further. What had happened had happened. It was the oldest story in the world. Who was he to change the script?

Once they had crossed the field and come to the next road, they arrived surprisingly quickly at the driveway to Meadowlands.

K let go of Claudia's hand. 'Here we are, darling. I love you.' He thought, with a kind of pride, that he had never said the words so often in his entire life.

'Yes, we do.' She was so serious. It cut his heart. He squeezed her hand once more and let it fall again. It occurred to him that it would be sensible for them to arrive separately. He tried to say to her, 'You go first,' but the words stuck in his throat.

'I think I'll go ahead,' said Claudia, her voice tentative, as if the idea might displease him. 'It'll be easier if they're back.'

'Yes. I'm sorry.'

'Don't be sorry. Please, don't be sorry.'

'I won't be, then.' He managed to smile.

They parted. She walked without a backward glance and with a purposeful tread. K thought she looked like a girl who'd been out for a run and got caught in the rain.

He waited for what seemed like a long time but was probably no more than ten minutes, then crept, by way of the shrubs and bushes, to the stable-block. His heart beat a little faster as he spotted the Laceys' car in front of the house but he recovered quickly. He thought he would skulk for ever if it meant he could see Claudia again and hold her.

His legs were shaking as he climbed up the stairs to his room. He sat at his desk but without even the intention of working. How could he play with words after what he had just experienced? Ten minutes or so later, he stood up and took down from the shelf the first volume of *The Shorter Oxford Dictionary*. He laid it on his desk and turned the pages till he found 'love'. He read aloud the first definition: *'"That state of feeling with regard to a person which arises from recognition of attractive qualities, from sympathy, or from natural ties, and manifests itself in warm affection and attachment."'*

K began to laugh. He had never come across such an understatement in his life. He imagined the author, surely a dry old stick, weighing each word as he wrote it. He stopped laughing before he became hysterical and read it through again, this time to himself. After all, it was true as far as it went – he did feel warm affection for and attachment to Claudia – but what about passion? He'd need a poet for that. Rather feverishly, he began to tug at *The Oxford Book of Quotations*. Dust flew into the air, reminding him that the book had been untouched since his arrival.

He flung it onto his desk and turned the pages of the index to 'love'. There were eleven columns. Eleven columns! He was beginning to feel absurd, and worse, that he was losing his sense of Claudia. But he persevered all the same. Someone must have felt as he did and put it into words.

But the eleven columns wouldn't settle in front of his eyes – *if it be l. indeed...if l. were what the rose is...if my l. were in my arms...if of herself she will not l.... if this be not l., it is madness... if thou dost l. pronounce it... if I know what true l. is...*

So many 'ifs'. Abruptly, K closed the book and stood up. What were all those people to him? Nothing. Only Claudia meant anything.

CHAPTER TWENTY

1990

Claudia lay on her bed, heart beating fast. Her mother had called to her as she came in but she would not, could not, go down to speak to her. When Catherine called again, 'Claudie! Claudie!' her voice filled with excitement – their shopping trip had obviously been a success – Claudia got off the bed and went to her viola. The process of unclasping the case and taking out first the bow, then the instrument gave her a special feeling, as if she was doing it for the first time but with the reassurance of meeting an old friend.

She pulled the stand towards the open window, placed music on it and raised the viola to her chin. As she played, she remembered the day she had chosen to abandon the violin for the viola. She'd been ten, and had already studied for several years on the violin. For the past six months she'd shared her lessons with another girl, Sally, who was a couple of years older than her. Her teacher had explained to Catherine, who had passed it on, rather vaguely, to Claudia, that Sally would be a good influence on Claudia's playing. While Claudia was content to be quietly proficient and listened to the music with a kind of attention seldom found in pupils her age, Sally had fire and brio, which often made for the better performance, even when her technique was lacking. So the two girls learnt together, played for each other, and soon, with quite the opposite effect to the one intended by the teacher, Claudia grew to hate Sally's style. She wanted to stop her ears against Sally's confident swoops and trills. To her they sounded sloppy and meretricious – although she couldn't have used those terms – and had nothing to do with the music she wanted to make or listen to.

One afternoon during their lesson she noticed a viola on the teacher's piano. She asked to hold it, feeling its greater weight as a proud mother might cradle a plump baby. She was about to ask whether she could try playing it when Sally, who'd just finished performing her piece and who still shone from the experience, launched into an attack on what she called 'a second-rate violin' with none of its range or dash. Her voice held all the scorn of a clever twelve-year-old.

The teacher had listened, smiling, and when she'd finished, remarked mildly, 'You'll find in every violin player there's a closet violist.' Claudia hadn't understood at the time but discovered that the viola had been her teacher's first instrument. The woman had played a few bars for her, then laid it aside. The sound was enough for Claudia to make her decision. 'I want to play it,' she'd said, cheeks flushed. And when Sally had laughed she'd felt even more certain, 'Please, may I change over? Please!'

K had opened his window and could hear the viola loudly enough to recognise the tune Claudia had been practising all summer. Brahms. He wished he understood more about music since it was so important to her. Next time they met he'd ask all kinds of questions.

But tomorrow she'd be gone to Italy. It seemed impossible, grotesque. He grimaced and rubbed his face. He must see her as soon as possible. They had been apart for two long hours.

Claudia went down to the kitchen. Her mother was alone there, sorting through piles of clothes on the table. Some, judging by the labels, had been bought that day.

'Oh, darling.' Catherine looked up. 'I've been calling you for ages. You'll be so pleased. I've bought you two really pretty T-shirts.'

Claudia was astounded at her ignorance. Where was the maternal instinct? Surely she could sense the difference in her. She hadn't even washed. Her whole body was filled and scented with K. 'You know I don't want to come.'

'Of course, it would be more fun for you if you brought a friend or if Louise didn't live so far away,' began Catherine, then paused as if she had, in fact, heard something new in Claudia's voice. She continued, in a placatory tone, unusual for her. 'The holiday's for your father mostly. So that he cuts off, does nothing. We had a good talk about it all today.' She hesitated. 'Well, I won't tell you now,' she continued, more cheerfully, 'and you and I will do the sightseeing. I haven't been to Italy for twenty years.'

Claudia considered this appeal. At least her wants were being taken seriously. 'I wish you'd asked me first,' she said to emphasise the point.

'Yes. I'm sorry.' Catherine returned to the piles of clothes but Claudia saw that the zest had left her. It was the first time she'd been aware that she could affect her mother's mood. Through the veil of her extreme self-absorption, she grasped that her mother was saying she would be lonely without her.

'Daddy will take his chess-set and play against an imaginary partner, or read the new Freddie Forsyth or Wilbur Smith.'

'I wish it were just a week.' A week would be bearable, even good, Claudia thought. She needed at least a week to come to terms with what had happened. A week of Italian cities, paintings, churches, perhaps concerts. She would bring back her experiences and lay them at K's feet.

'What's the matter, darling?'

Her mother was looking at her without her normal blindness, Claudia realised. How surprised she'd have been with the true answer. Nothing's the matter: I'm in love with your writer-in-residence. We've just made love in a scrubby room in a scrubby hotel. She tried hard not to smile crazily. 'It's my music,' she answered slowly, the lie becoming almost true as she spoke it. 'I hate not practising for so long.'

'But of course you can practise.' Catherine sighed with relief. 'The villa's not very big and the garden's shared but everyone loves the sound of a violin – even when it's a viola.'

'It's just that I'm hoping to play this Brahms sonata in the Christmas concert which may sound far away–'

'I quite understand!' Catherine broke in, her confident gaiety restored, as if this musical explanation had re-created the equilibrium.

Claudia saw this and understood for the first time what a huge secret she had to hide. Yet the guarding of it had caused her to be more honest with her mother than ever before. She'd never told her about her ambitions to be a soloist in the school concert. Even that she'd kept secret. 'Maybe,' she said innocently, 'I could come back a bit early.' She looked down and away. 'I could get Bella to stay over if you're worried about me being on my own.'

'I'll never be able to swap your flight, darling.'

'Perhaps you could try.' Three or four days alone with K! Her parents in Italy and unable to check whether Bella was here or not. 'If it's not so long I'd be much happier when we're out there.' This was a threat and she'd never threatened her mother before. Shamelessness made her smile too brightly.

Catherine handed her the two T-shirts, which were indeed pretty, striped pink and yellow. 'I'll talk to your father.'

K saw Claudia walking in the garden. The wood-pigeons were gathering in the trees, a signal that his day at Meadowlands had nearly ended. He had been trying to convince himself that he and Claudia had made their farewells in the best possible way but now he was desperate to hold her. His screen, growing brighter in the dimming light, displayed the two sentences he'd managed to write that afternoon. 'Hugo stared grimly at the message scrawled in red paint on his door. Had anyone else seen it?'

He felt in danger of succumbing to the kind of muddled panic he hadn't felt for years – not since he married Fiona. He tried to repress that thought. As a young man, he'd been so lacking in confidence because of his father's descent into alcoholism, his mother's and his own inability to deal with it. At the same time he'd been filled with ambition, knowing he could succeed, given the chance. How hard he'd worked to pay his way through a journalist's course! How hard he'd worked to get into advertising! He felt worn out, yet also tough and battle-hardened when he contemplated the energy he'd used to get where he was. But it was never enough. Nothing was enough.

K stood up and went closer to the window. Claudia was walking under the shadowy trees. She'd changed into one of her long, flowing skirts, which trailed on the grass. She might have been a medieval lady in a Book of Hours, reading her breviary. Indeed, she had a book in her hands, although it was closed. Surely she should be packing, preparing herself for the holiday.

Or was she still waiting for her lover? A knight in silver armour, or velvet doublet with lace at the neck and sleeves. But she had chosen him, a battered foot-soldier, a horny-handed man of the soil, a worker, hardened and scarred in his not very successful life. They were ill-matched. All the same, he had to go and find her.

K was about to dash down when, out of the corner of his eye, he saw Catherine cross the lawn to join her daughter. Soon they were talking intently. K was struck by a change in their attitudes. Usually Catherine talked and Claudia listened – or half listened – but this time their stance was more equal. They were engaged with each other.

I shall go out to them anyway, thought K, brushing back his hair in an unconscious gesture of preparation. He needed to talk about the house, keys, lighting, other organisational matters. He'd already told Catherine that he and Fiona wouldn't stay there.

Claudia saw K walking towards her. She thought how often over the last weeks they had crossed and recrossed the lawn towards each other. She imagined a pattern of their passionate trajectories deco-rating the garden like a flaming cat's cradle.

'Oh, good!' Catherine welcomed him. 'Now we can talk.'

So they did. Claudia could watch K and remember holding her breath then letting go in a gulp, what they had been doing only a few hours earlier. She felt herself flush and was amazed that the three of them could stand together like this. Tears threatened, not of anguish but of sheer emotion. Most of all she wanted him to hold her. As the minutes passed – it seemed very long to her – the deprivation forced a contradiction of joy and sadness that was quite new.

'... and Claudia will be back a little earlier than us.'

Catching these words, she responded with an irrepressible smile to K. She saw him dazzled. Her own sadness was forgotten. Soon they would have three whole days together! She wanted him to celebrate with her but his dazzled face was also a little bewildered, almost stern. Was that for her mother? If only they could have a moment alone together.

Now Catherine was leading K towards the house, talking about keys and window locks. Claudia wandered away in the direction of the pool.

*

143

K and Catherine had reached the kitchen. 'Here you are. Four altogether.'

K was aware of his fingers touching Catherine's as she handed him the keys. He felt a distinct physical reaction from her. It was as if sex with the daughter had made a link with the mother. Were humans so close to animals?

'Don't worry about a thing,' he said, forcing an obliging smile. He tried to continue with reassuring platitudes, but other words, which would have been monstrous to her and maybe were monstrous in themselves, blocked his speech. *Don't worry about a thing. I've only fucked your little daughter this afternoon.*

Catherine was smiling winningly, handing him written instructions. Of course it hadn't been fucking, it had been love. *Don't worry about a thing, I'm in love with Claudia.*

'Don't worry about a thing, I'll be here every day.'

'You're so kind. Douglas is very grateful. He's not too well and there are problems at work. Not serious …'

He didn't want to hear any of this. He was not a family friend. He was a big cuckoo in the nest and cuckoos shouldn't be trusted. At last he broke free and, clutching a bottle of champagne that Catherine had pressed on him, returned to his room. He'd noticed the direction of Claudia's departure but couldn't face following her. He needed a moment of peace.

Already it was nearly six. There wasn't much time before he must pick up Fiona. The thought filled him with dread, yet also brought a faint echo of the comfort he felt in her company. She was his best friend. She understood him better than anyone, his aspirations and failings. But that, too, was not to be thought of.

'Oh, my God. Oh, my God.' K found that as he stepped down the wooden stairs, he was whispering this incantation like a soldier keeping up his strength. It would be cruel and cowardly not to say goodbye to Claudia, his beloved.

He found her sitting on the steps of the changing hut, apparently studying her feet. She didn't look up as he approached and sat beside her, although not too close. 'I'm sorry about that. Your mother, I mean.'

'Yes. It's strange.' She turned to him then, as if waiting for his explanation of how it was strange. Having nothing to offer, K took her hand. It was cool, almost cold. He had got used to her childlike warmth and felt disconcerted by the change. He was afraid she might cry, that she might refer to things that were better left alone. He knew so little about her.

'Shall we swim? I've still got half an hour.' His voice was tentative. 'Or shall we just sit here?'

Claudia heard his uncertainty. It made her uncertain too. She wanted only to look forward to the three or four days when they would be alone together. The ten days between seemed far less important.

'Shall we go to your room?' She sensed immediately he didn't want that: he had almost flinched as she spoke. Did he think she'd jump on him like a silly schoolgirl with a crush? But she did want to kiss him, make it real again and counteract the disturbing spell of her mother.

'No. We'll be too sad.'

Was that it? Why didn't he understand she was never sad when she was with him? She tried to show him. 'I'll be so cultivated when we next meet. I'll be able to lecture you on Piero della Francesca and Tuscan architecture.'

'I want you just as you are. I couldn't love you more.'

They were both silent but Claudia was filled with happiness. Suddenly it struck her that he might not have taken in their approaching days of togetherness. But he must have. Her mother had said she was coming back early. It seemed crass to remind him, as if she were trying to pin him down. Her love wasn't like that, she told herself. It didn't need to ask for anything because it had everything already.

'I love you too.'

So they sat together, neither speaking and, eventually, K kissed her gently and walked away.

CHAPTER TWENTY-ONE

2004

As the door handle turned I moved back into the corner of the hut. Even so, I could see the expression on her face changing quite suddenly. Instead of the unfocused, inattentive look of someone alone, thinking her own thoughts, it became decisive. She took her hand off the handle as if it had become hot and turned her back on me.

She could not have seen me. I knew from the past that the glass was treated so that those inside could see out but not vice versa. Yet her eyes, blind like a sibyl's, had seen something, if not me, something she wanted nothing to do with. She walked away slowly, but with no hesitation or looking back.

I sank into a crouch. I was as absurd as a monkey in a cage who both fears and wishes for a visit from his keeper. Gradually, above the continuous throbbing in my head, a huge disappointment overwhelmed all other feelings. Once again I felt tears in my eyes. I was as miserable as if she had seen and spurned me. This was the time to move out but I found it utterly impossible to take any kind of action. Darkness seemed to be closing in on me, like the blackest depth of sleep. I shut my eyes and abandoned myself to the hot torture of grief.

I could not be certain. The hut was dark, climbers and shrubs blanking out the windows at either side. Ivy had even wound itself inside, creeping through cracks, then hanging negligently as if hoping to be mistaken for decoration. It hadn't been used for years. Not since some boys had come in and flung stones through the windows. We mended it reluctantly, regretting the cost but it had looked so ugly. Of course we had put in cheap glass, ordinary clear glass.

If it was K, he wouldn't have known that. But a tramp, a man of the road, would have assumed I could see him. I like that description, man of the road. It suggests a freedom that I've never come near to in my own life. Not that the man in there looked free. He might have been tall – as tall as *him* – but he was so huddled and hunched that it was hard to tell. He was thin too. I could tell that by the spiky angles of him, a Quentin Blake drawing against the walls.

I had turned away decisively but I didn't feel decisive. It was more an instinctive retreat from something I didn't know how to deal with. I walked half-way back to the house, then stopped. What should I do? Ring the police immediately, talk urgently of an intruder? Whoever it was, he was an intruder. Or should I talk to my mother, admit my fear of his identity, defuse the situation with openness. That was the lesson from my shrink: never encourage the black magic of secrecy.

But I knew I wouldn't do that. Despite the poor woman's efforts, my nature hadn't changed. I would say nothing. Probably do nothing.

I returned to the house and to my bedroom. It was only then I admitted to myself that the most obvious course was to ring Oliver. It was as if the shocking apparition, following so quickly on the death of my father, had cast me back into childhood habits. I should ring Oliver, who, by now, would have reached London.

Yet I didn't. I looked out at the great white marquee now taking on a bluish tinge as the evening progressed, and thought about K. I had, of course, thought of him a great deal over the fourteen years since his exit from my life. During my years of crisis – the worst time lasted for about three years during which I had no will to live or expectation that I would – his image was a blurred mass of horror, shame, misery and despair in which nothing positive had a chance of survival. Self-hatred was the dominating force, which only lessened very gradually. I did not therefore allow K to share the blame for what happened. I felt fully responsible and fully guilty.

Perhaps this is a normal reaction when you've caused something so cataclysmically dreadful. I was trying to make my guilty penance equal to the crime. I used the word 'crime' then, in an attempt, maybe, to simplify my situation, although it wasn't at all an accurate description of what had occurred.

It was only when my shrink insisted on going back over old ground – it took her years with me resisting all the way – that I allowed K to re-enter the scene in a more realistic fashion. I believe now I was protecting our love from too close analysis. I didn't want to tear apart those summer days when I'd felt, in that cliché of the passage from child to adulthood, that I had woken up to a bright new world. Looking back, it seems extraordinary how fearless I was. I admire that still. I suppose K provided a way out of what truly seemed to be a dead-end. His only rival was music, but I had never been allowed to take that seriously. How different things might have been.

Pointless speculation. Very probably, I wasn't good enough anyway. So K came and swept me off my feet and I swept him off his and we were happy and I didn't want to hear my shrink's sensible words: K was a muddled, disappointed, weak man. They hurt me even now. Or it hurts my pride to wonder how, if they were true, I could have given myself entirely to such a man. I refused to accept the description.

So then she'd said that the sexual urge was at its strongest in a sixteen-year-old and I remembered that I was just finishing reading *Anna Karenina* when I met K. I wouldn't let her turn our love into a crude mechanical exercise. That is what I do with Oliver. Our bodies join with affection but not the passionate fusion of lovemaking I had with K. So much is written about love yet no one has managed to explain to me what makes two almost random people raise each other to the level of gods.

A priest came to visit me when I was in hospital. He didn't come by invitation and sometimes I suspected he thought I was someone else. I suppose I could have stopped him, but in my catatonic, drug-laden state, it seemed too much like hard work. Anyway, I grew to like him. He sat in the chair, not too close although close enough for me to see he was sweating heavily. It was always very hot in my room.

He looked at his watch as he arrived, timing his visit exactly, as I gradually realised, to twenty minutes. Since I never spoke, it was up to him to make any conversation, which he usually did, except once or twice when he must have been tired because he pulled out a book – of prayers, I supposed – and read quietly to himself. He never looked at me, even when he blessed me as he left, which is why I concluded that to him I could have been anyone.

Which is probably why I let him come. To him, I was anonymous, a pitiful, tormented soul. His conversation, when I began to listen, invariably circled round the same theme: God was all merciful and all consoling. I only had to hand over my life to him and my suffering, whatever the cause, would be eased. It was a tempting message. I used to imagine my suffering, a hard, miserable little brown thing, floating upwards, expanding as it went, burning perhaps a pale blue or pink, until it came to rest comfortably on the expansive shoulders of God.

I never knew the name of the priest – he had a gentle Irish accent – but he did help me for the twenty minutes he sat in the chair. It never lasted. I was too mired in my guilt to believe in his message. It was just a lovely fairy-tale. I was grateful to him all the same, and sad when he stopped coming.

Now I come to think of it, he did once deviate from his theme to explain that human love was a vain seeking after the Almighty. So perhaps he did know my story. Of course, I was even less inclined to take that seriously. Maybe I said something. Maybe that was why he stopped coming. I can't remember now.

The Almighty didn't get much of a look-in with my shrink. She took a sensible approach. She told me I was very young, meaning I would get over it. The only problem was that, to me, it sounded like a life sentence. Yet she was helpful too, giving me practical ways to deal with my depression. They worked, up to a point, so that the beak and claws of the black vulture tore less cruelly and less often at my head. I had a moment or two of lightness when I felt able to think, move and speak almost normally.

Now and again, recently, I've wondered whether my recovery would have been easier – well, quicker, at least – if K hadn't vanished so completely from my world. After that terrible morning, I never saw him again. He might as well have been dead too. In fact, the vanishing act was worse than death. It lent an air of unreality to the summer, as if I had conceived a dream that, of course, had turned into a nightmare. And the nightmare truly was so dreadful as to be unbelievable.

Maybe if K had stayed in the picture, I'd have been able to make some sense of it, or at least start earlier on the road to forgiving myself.

Ironically, perhaps, the hardest thing of all was that nobody blamed me. They saw it as the story of a young girl seduced by a much older man. Twenty-four years older. He must take all the blame. So he disappeared and I blamed myself and didn't know how to think of him at all – except that he wasn't the wicked seducer they presumed. I was confused. And, if I'm honest, I still am – about him anyway.

I turned away from my window, unable to deal with even the possibility that the skinny, wild-looking man with the tufty hair (I had taken in more than I had at first allowed) was K returning to my life. Yet if the man was a potential burglar, I should tell someone. I thought about this. I looked at my watch. It was nearly eight o'clock and the light outside was failing. I supposed we'd get something to eat soon. Surely any burglar or tramp would have scarpered after he'd seen me peering in at the window. Anyway, there was little of value left in the house.

Over the last few years, Catherine had randomly sold silver, pictures and even furniture, the piano, for example. She said it wasn't so much for the money, although we were borrowing massively from the bank, but because she wanted to start afresh when we eventually sold the house. She meant, of course, on my father's death. She said she wasn't too old to do a real job for the first time in her life and that she would buy a small flat in London and discover who she really was. I suppose it was aggressive stuff, but I didn't blame her and my father was past caring – in fact, quite out of it for the last year. Recently I'd thought none of this would happen and she would marry the divorced and admiring James. But, then, I'm cynical about how much people can change. People tell me I'm a changed person but inside I know I'm exactly the same. I've just learnt to mask the wide-eyed look.

'Claudie! Claudie!' Long after this house is sold and lived in by some happier family, I shall hear Catherine's voice calling me down from my bedroom. Each time I appeared in front of her I disappointed her. Even as a child I knew I couldn't provide her with what she needed. Louise once told me she had felt exactly the same. It didn't exactly propel her into an early marriage but she clocked a huge sense of relief.

As I went down the stairs, I decided to say nothing about the man in the changing hut. For the time being.

CHAPTER TWENTY-TWO

1990

It surprised Claudia how easily she became the dutiful daughter on holiday with her parents in Tuscany. The joy of her secret love overspilled in the direction of her parents. In her absence from K, Claudia had never felt closer to him. Each minute of the day and night were filled with romantic memories. She thought of him constantly, and effortlessy suppressed any fears for the future.

One evening she sat between her parents, listening to a chamber concert in a church in Siena. The church was warm, painted a soft amber and perfumed by the lingering scent of incense. The orchestra was playing a programme of seventeenth and eighteenth century Italian works, Corelli, Scarlatti, Torelli and Vivaldi, many of them Claudia's favourites. She tried to listen to the music as a whole but she found herself constantly returning to one of the violas, identifying with the sounds and the player. He was dark and young – it was a student orchestra – and played with a smile on his lips, as if there was no greater pleasure than to be exactly where he was. Claudia noted with amusement that his hair, which had been elegantly wavy at the beginning of the concert, was fast forming lustrous corkscrew curls.

She had already been in Italy for a week. Each day she and her mother had made an expedition – to the Uffizi in Florence, the Piero della Francescas in Arezzo and the Giottos in Assisi, where Douglas was persuaded to accompany them and spend a night. As Catherine had predicted, he stayed mostly in the villa in the hills outside Siena. There were four small houses, a swimming-pool and a tennis court but the other families were German and knew each other already so they didn't mix much.

On their trips, Claudia discovered a new sort of mother. Catherine didn't push her to do anything she didn't want or make plans without consulting her. In fact, they had fun. For the first time Claudia understood and sympathised with her motherly frustrations. Inevitably she blamed her father, the lugubrious presence to whom they returned in the evening.

One morning as they climbed to the little chapel that housed della Francesca's sublime pregnant madonna, Catherine explained that Douglas was ill. It was not just overwork. Without telling her, he had seen doctors in London and been diagnosed with myeloma, in his case not a killer as long as it was managed properly, but debilitating. He also had a minor heart problem. He might live for twenty years, or he might not.

Claudia's attitude to him modified at once and she became more tolerant and obliging. In return she noted her father actually listened with apparent interest when she explained that Haydn had played the viola and that the piece she'd been playing all summer had originally been written for the clarinet.

So, on that evening in the pretty Sienese church, with great vases of white lilies on either side of the players, she identified a burst of happiness. She was a good daughter and in four days she would be released back to K. Her *lover*. She pronounced the word caressingly to herself.

At the interval the audience were invited to a glass of wine in a courtyard adjoining the church, but it soon became filled and Claudia stood with her parents on the narrow street. The stone flagging and buildings retained the heat of the day, lightened only by the starlit strip of sky above their heads. Claudia moved away a little to enjoy the moment quietly and found herself next to a young man, smoking. She recognised him as the violist.

'*Ciao*!' He acknowledged her presence, smiling.

She smiled back at him. She wanted to tell him how much she was enjoying the music but her few words of Italian failed to rise to the occasion. '*Ciao*.'

'You like the music?'

'Oh, yes. Yes! *Superbo! Magnifico!*' He laughed at her absurdity and she noticed, even in the dim light, he had remarkable eyes, black and lustrous with very long lashes. He was even younger than she had thought when she had seen him on the stage, not more than seventeen or eighteen.

He stubbed out his cigarette on the wall, letting it fall to the ground. 'Now, I return. Part two. Later we meet. Yes?'

Claudia looked at him for a moment, uncomprehending. Then she found herself, ridiculously, blushing. 'I'm with my parents.'

'Ah. *Mamma y Papa.*' He shrugged expressively, presumably to indicate how she could get rid of her parents.

Claudia felt childish, feeble, and could think of nothing more to say.

'*Ecco.* We *studenti.* We meet in the Campo Santo. *Caro, certo,* but tonight is big night.'

Claudia saw he wasn't suggesting a one-to-one date but that she should join a gang of students, musicians. 'I'll try.'

'*Bene.* If tonight *non è possibile,* tomorrow at the Caffè Svengali – I am Raffaello. Your name?'

'Claudia.'

'*Bella* Claudia.' He pronounced it 'Cloudia', '*Andiamo.* '

'What a handsome young man!' Catherine commented approvingly, as Claudia returned to her.

'He's asked me to have a drink in the piazza after the concert.'

'It might be fun.'

'I wouldn't know anyone.'

'That's true.'

They went back into the church together, and Claudia wondered if everyone's mother would hand over her daughter so easily to a random Italian. But the invitation had confirmed her happiness. Would K be jealous if she told him? She could offer it to him as a conquest, although it was hardly that. He would be unsurprised, of course, because he adored her. Perhaps he *would* be jealous. She tried and failed to imagine him with black looks, and smiled as the violist turned his languorous eyes her way. Clearly he thought the smile was for him.

'Of course, I won't show for weeks and weeks yet.'

Watching Fiona, naked but for a pair of briefs, preen in front of the bedroom mirror, K was amazed at the change in her. Although she had a well-proportioned, compact body, she seldom showed it off unclothed. K had never missed it particularly – she was naked when he wanted it, in bed. He had put down her attitude vaguely to old-fashioned middle-class modesty, something he knew little about. But now it was as if someone had told her she was beautiful, giving her a new confidence, encouraging her even to flaunt. Contradictorily, this new daring made her seem more vulnerable.

'You look beautiful, darling,' said K, still lying in bed, although only for another few minutes. It was after seven, another day pushing him forward.

It was not just Fiona's confidence in her looks that had increased. As K drove her to the station, he reflected that since the news of her pregnancy she had become more relaxed about all kinds of things; her work, his work, both previously areas of tension and anxiety, could be dealt with smilingly now. At that very moment, she was telling a story about a colleague who had nearly got himself sacked by asking out to dinner his boss, who happened to be a married woman. 'He thought he was doing her a favour,' laughed Fiona, 'and she declared it harassment.'

'One woman's harassment is another man's job loss,' agreed K. He glanced at Fiona. 'You look well.'

'I feel very well.'

Just for a second, K wondered whether this sparkling good health was altogether normal. Surely pregnant women started the day head bent over a basin? Perhaps that was old-fashioned nonsense. One thing was certain: her wish to start a family had not been exaggerated. It was based, he knew, though she hardly ever referred to it, in her own background. She had been adopted as a baby by a relatively elderly, childless couple and had never found her own mother or father. Creating her own family had gradually become an obsession. It was strange when, to an outsider, she appeared so eminently balanced and straightforward.

For some reason K accompanied Fiona on to the platform and watched her train leave. There was not a scrap of blue in the sky. White clouds piled on top of each other like pillows on a bed. Deciding he needed a walk, K left his car at the station and set off along the road for Meadowlands.

Since Claudia's departure the previous week, K had found the days impossibly long. He hardly managed to concentrate on his writing for more than a couple of hours and then there was still interminable time ahead. Alan gave up coming as soon as the Laceys were down the drive so the house and garden were completely silent, apart from the birds and a couple of cheeky squirrels who had descended from the trees and fought noisily on the lawn.

This Monday K had to force himself to walk up the driveway. He noted that the house looked secure, the shutters in place, but he couldn't bring himself to check further by going inside. On the day after they had left, he had opened the door boldly and, thinking only of his love for Claudia, had investigated every room, including what he guessed was her bedroom. He stayed no longer there than anywhere else, finding the childish décor a little disturbing, although he hardly admitted it to himself. His main impression was of the size of the house. He hadn't realised there would be so many rooms, with so many windows and so much furniture, the ceilings so high. Douglas Lacey had earned this and owned it. The contrast with his own home was too great for comfort. By the time he left, once more by the front door, locking it carefully, some of his lover's swagger had drained away. Thereafter, he confined himself to the quick peek of a bored security guard. This was not his life. His life was in the dreary room above the coach-house, a servant's place for one who had risen furthest up the ranks in a profession he had disliked and from which he'd walked away. Although these feelings were only half defined in his mind, they left a moody residue. Even Claudia's image was a little dimmed, although at the same time a little more radiant, like that of a star that has moved deeper into the sky. His feelings hadn't changed, but he was less inclined to dwell on happy images.

On that cloudy Monday morning, K stared intently at his screen. On Friday he had discovered, to his surprise, that he had written twenty thousand words. Despite the many weeks of agonising, he had never quite believed a book would result. But there it was on his word check: 20,511 – almost a round number, perhaps a good omen. On Monday, he had resolved, he would print it out, read it through and, if he were satisfied, revise some, or even all of it, to send to his agent – rather, his potential agent.

But this *was* Monday and instead of printing off the pages he found himself scrolling aimlessly backwards and forwards. Here was the beginning of a flashback scene in which Natasha, the vivacious murder victim, scorned the advances of a friend. How extraordinary to think he'd once believed association with Claudia could teach him something about this crude young woman's behaviour. Here was the moment when the lorry driver suspect admitted to the police that he had a lover in Cleethorpes. Or the tender moment (supposedly) when Ned (another suspect) stroked his new baby's cheek. Scene after scene passed in front of his watchful eyes, was checked through his critical mind, and all were drivel – total drivel.

K got up and walked agitatedly about the room. How could he possibly have given up a proper – as in paid – job to produce this *drivel?*. It was not even as if he was aspiring high. If the theme of all novels was supposedly the meaning of life, then his was the exception. Working himself into even greater misery, he wondered what was the *point* of it all. He supposed, although he was no longer certain, that there was a point in great fiction, but he knew only too well he would never aspire to even the second-rate. Drivel. Drivel! K started towards the door. He would look for a job, highly paid, and buy a house like Meadowlands. He would emulate Douglas Lacey, instead of despising him. He would earn his place in the world and forget these self-indulgent ramblings. The purveyor of words who pretends to be God and is actually a cheap charlatan, a counterfeit god!

K was half-way down the stairs before he turned. He might as well print out the revolting stuff and then, like bad food, chuck it out or burn it. He put in the paper, pressed the various buttons, then went off, feeling trapped and despairing, to walk about the garden. When he had disposed of the book – the non-book – it would all be over, this garden, this house, Claudia. It was a mirage. He would return to what he was, a clever boy from a dysfunctional working-class family who had been saved by a good woman. He had aspired too high. Now was the time to admit it. It was torture to sit under the chestnut trees where he and Claudia had been together, but he did it all the same.

Some time around midday, K's stomach began to rumble. He felt ravenously hungry, but his sandwiches were in the room where the machine would be spewing out the nauseating pages. Or perhaps it had finished and the pages lay there, like an unwanted, worse, diseased, prostitute.

Before he'd met Fiona, K had had a two- or three-year period when he'd visited prostitutes regularly. He had never told Fiona, although he'd been open about his various short-lived love affairs. He didn't despise prostitutes – on the contrary, they had served his needs well – which made it odd that he should liken those pages to them. But, of course, that was the point: he was on their side. He felt sorry for the diseased tart, sorry for the book that didn't come up to scratch. The rush of despair had passed and he felt more disposed to be kindly towards those words that now existed independently of him.

He would return to his room, eat one of his two sandwiches to give him strength, then pick up the pages. He had an afternoon to fill. Nothing could change immediately.

On the morning after the concert Claudia and Catherine drove back to Siena. Douglas was resting but advised them in some detail about the paintings and frescos they shouldn't miss. Obviously they would spend time in the Palazzo Pubblico in the Campo Santo and with the jewel-like Duccios in the gallery of the Duomo ... but he had never forgotten a fresco in which winged cherubs were just like little boys pretending to be aeroplanes, arms outstretched. It had made him laugh so much as a young man, he had said, surprising Claudia, who had assumed her father had been born without a sense of humour. He couldn't remember the name of the church whose wall it decorated but drew a route from the Campo Santo.

They had set out early and on the drive in Catherine had confided in Claudia that she planned to have her hair done. 'It will please your father,' she had said, 'He likes to see me looking *soignée.*'

So it was that at midday, as the clock in the Campo struck – following a morning of dedicated sightseeing during which Claudia had taken notes to please her father and help her with her A level – the two split up, promising to meet at the same spot in an hour and a half. 'Go and look for your father's fresco,' advised Catherine, handing over the scribbled map. 'It's always better to have a project than to wander aimlessly.'

Claudia was surprised by how self-conscious she felt on her own, even though the city's stone-lined streets were filled with tourists and young people like herself. She began to walk quickly as if she were confident of her direction but she was soon too hot and, anyway, needed to stop and study the sketched map. It looked as if she should follow the main street above the Campo, then turn right down smaller, less-populated alleys. It was silly to be nervous, yet it felt like an adventure, setting off into the unknown. Clutching her scrap of paper and her pink-beaded purse, Claudia paused for a moment to allow her love for K to give her courage. Then she continued, happily independent.

Either her father's memory or his map or her map-reading was woefully inadequate because, after half an hour's steady walking, there was no church in sight, certainly not one with a dome as described, and she found herself in a steep-sided gully of narrow alleys and overhanging houses, decorated often by overflowing boxes of geraniums and yellow daisies. It was picturesque but not what she was looking for.

At that moment when she most wanted to sit down and regroup, she spotted a sign for what looked like a café. There were tables and chairs outside but no one sitting on them. Just her luck if it was closed. She approached hopefully and peered inside. To her surprise, the place was not only open but jammed with people, all young, chattering away at top volume. It was then she noticed the name on the sign. Caffe Svengali. Instinctively, she turned to run. Too late.

A voice cried, '*Ciao! Bella* Claudia!'

'Cloudia' again. Claudia still tried to escape but Raffaello was far too quick, dashing out and dragging her inside. In a moment she was surrounded by animated faces, welcoming her in a mixture of Italian and English. One or two she recognised from the orchestra, a strikingly fair girl, the lead violinist. They were mostly drinking Coke, although one or two had a glass of red wine and they were eating slices of pizza.

'OK! You tell us. We were good last night? *È vero?*'

That was it, she saw. They wanted to be told how well they had played. It was easy and, as they all talked at once, she hardly felt at all self-conscious. It was a little disconcerting that Raffaello kept hold of her arm but even that seemed a sign of conviviality rather than anything more intimate.

Somehow she was drinking Coke and eating pizza and laughing at their absurd English and her absurd attempts at describing her school orchestra in Italian and time was whizzing along.

'So you study here in Siena?' cried Raffaello. 'We make music. We make friends. We make good tunes.' He put his face close to hers so she could see his beautiful eyes, his smooth olive skin. 'So? Yes? *Va bene?*' He seemed suddenly quite serious.

Claudia looked back at him, also serious. It seemed that he and his friends had the power to offer her a future different from anything she'd ever imagined. She felt again as if she were outside, looking in.

'I wish–' She stopped, laughed nervously.

'*Allora*! You come. We plan duets. This year. Next year. We plan it all. Here. At the Caffe Svengali. You know who Svengali was? Yes? An English story too ...'

He rattled on, telling some story she couldn't understand. She darted a look at her watch and saw she was due in the Campo in five minutes.

'I have to go. I'm late.' It was a fight to get out, Raffaello determined to walk with her, the others wanting to know where she was staying and for how long. At least, that was what she thought they were saying. In the end she let Raffaello lead her and they went so directly that the first alley dropping into the Campo appeared in less than ten minutes. Here Raffaello paused. '*Ciao*!' he said. He waved cheerfully. He was already going back the way he'd come.

Claudia had a second of sharp regret. Doubtless she could find him any time in the Caffe Svengali but she knew in her heart of hearts that she'd never see him again.

'Darling. You look hot. Did you find it?' Catherine sat at a table with a Campari soda in front of her.

Claudia, who had forgotten about the church and its fresco, sat down and began to tell her story.

'What fun!' said Catherine, as if she could easily picture the scene. 'Maybe we'll ask some of them to the villa.'

'Oh, no,' replied Claudia, shaking her head.

On Thursday evening K and Fiona watched the Proms on television. Fiona sat with her legs up on the sofa. She said she felt a little 'iffy', nothing to worry about, just a bit 'iffy'.

K thought it an odd word but didn't worry. He trusted Fiona to speak the truth. He connected it only vaguely with her pregnancy but when she said she might take the next day off work, he became more concerned. Tomorrow Claudia would be back, on her own, at the house.

'Would you like me to stay at home and look after you?' The offer made him feel worthy, even though he knew she wouldn't say yes. A small part of him noted that if she accepted, it would make life less torturous. He would be forced to love Claudia for another day without seeing her, without holding her.

'No. No. Of course you must go.' So, he had her permission. Her encouragement.

'We should go to some live concerts,' he commented, returning his attention to the screen where an exquisite Japanese girl was hurling herself at the piano. 'I haven't heard live music for years.'

CHAPTER TWENTY-THREE

1990

K and Claudia were making love in Claudia's bedroom. The almost nursery surrounds excited K. Brightly coloured animals jumped across the curtains and when he opened his eyes he saw two stuffed toys crouched under a chair. Claudia's compliance was almost a surprise, as if she should have been shocked and screaming.

But she had led him upstairs, taken his hand as if he were the child, not her. She had seemed utterly assured, although her flushed cheeks and trembling fingers told another story. He hadn't allowed himself to predict that this would happen but he had brought a packet of condoms with him. He'd looked them out from a drawer in the middle of the night when Fiona was sleeping, after waking abruptly with the terrifying realisation that they'd already made love with no protection. He and Fiona had striven fifteen years for a baby so it had not been at the forefront in his mind. He just hoped the ancient packet he'd found would do the job.

Of course he didn't think such things as he made love with Claudia. But he managed to fit on the condom all the same, explaining tenderly to Claudia that this, too, was about his love for her.

Claudia was certain that the most important thing in her life was her love for K and its expression as they wound their bodies together. Everything she'd ever read had taught her that. Her attitude to love came directly from nineteenth-century romantic literature. And yet she was a product of her own age too. She was too shy to ask, but she wanted him to teach her how to do things better. She didn't want her inexperience to disappoint him. She almost wished she'd joined in with whispered discussions at school between girls describing what they'd got up to, or read the kind of books that made Bella flush and giggle. But she had stuck with *Anna Karenina* and *Madame Bovary*. On the other hand, she assumed K was the perfect lover – or, at least, she didn't objectify his performance in that way. *She* could fail but never him.

'Thank you.' He'd said it again. A heartfelt mumble. Claudia thought she must accept that it gave him pleasure to thank her. She opened her eyes. It was a moment of great peace, their naked bodies still gleaming with sweat, heavy with exhaustion. His, anyway. Hers was not so much tired as quietened.

'It's raining.' She could see the silvery rain against the dark trees at the end of the garden. 'I wish we could stay here for ever.'

'For ever and ever.' K put out his hand and found hers but he didn't open his eyes. Although this was only the second time they had made love Claudia recognised that his comatose state was part of a pattern. It pleased her and made her feel closer to him that she could read his behaviour. Making love to her (she didn't consider anyone else) knocked him out. She felt sure that, as before, he would rise with extra special energy.

Nearly an hour went by. K, wearied by his interrupted night, slept deeply. When he woke, he was disoriented. The rain, slipping down the windows on two sides, toned down the colours on the curtains and walls, giving a misty, almost ghostly atmosphere. Beside one of the windows he saw the pale naked figure of a young girl. Just for a second he admired the slender curves without realising this was the woman he loved, the woman to whom he'd just made love. The jerk of reality came with no time to detach the other strings of his life. As he stared at Claudia, Fiona was in his heart and mind.

Then he was out of bed, bounding across to Claudia with all the energy she had predicted.

'Where do we eat?' he cried. 'My darling! My *inamorata*! My Sugar Plum Fairy!' His love was extravagant, ridiculous. He put one arm round her waist and drew her to him, running a hand over her buttocks.

'You're tickling me. Stop it.'

He might have drawn her back into bed but he was genuinely

hungry. More importantly, he wanted to sit with her talk to her, and find out who she was all over again.

'There's almost nothing in the fridge. I only got back last night.'

He knew that. Today was Friday. She'd raced back to him. For today she was his. Live in the present! 'We'll picnic. We'll share my picnic. Wait!' Making her laugh, he grabbed her skirt, held it round his middle and capered like a jester. He wanted to make her laugh. At this precise moment he felt younger than her.

By the time he'd dashed to the car and back he was soaking wet. '*Voilà*!' He held up his package of sandwiches, letting go of the skirt round his waist. He loved the light-heartedness of it, her attempt to disguise her embarrassment at his nakedness. He was glad he hadn't fattened up in all those years in the office. 'So, where do we eat?'

'The kitchen's cosiest,' suggested Claudia. The doubt in her voice suggested that the kitchen was so very *family*. In his absence she had put on a sundress he hadn't seen before. Perhaps she'd bought it in Italy. Vaguely, he imagined hot blue skies, madonnas in dark churches. 'Here, then.' He pulled a cover over the bed and sat on it, patting a place beside him. This was their territory. It was better not to venture out.

As they ate, the rain continued to sluice around them, giving a delightful feeling of being imprisoned together. Claudia told enthusiastic stories of her trip. Everything it seemed, had been 'brilliant', 'fantastic', 'amazing'.

'And always with your mother?' asked K, trying not to sound surprised that this could be such fun.

'Mostly.' Claudia seemed wary. 'Catherine's very good company.'

'I'm sure.' K had no wish to pursue the subject. 'Look. It's stopped raining.'

'There was too much sun in Italy. Even my legs went red, although I used loads of cream.' She held up her leg for inspection.

K stared at her youthful perfection. The silver bracelet dangled round the ankle, emphasising its slimness. Claudia turned it this way and that. It was an irresistible invitation. He leant forward and kissed the soft place under her knee. He thought, there'll never be another day like this. Never.

*

At the end of the day there had to be a parting. Neither K nor Claudia made any reference to the weekend ahead. They behaved as if it didn't exist, as if K would not go to his wife, leaving Claudia alone in the house. He didn't ask how she planned to spend the time and, of course, she didn't ask him.

They said goodbye in the driveway. The rain had started again, which gave K an excuse to send Claudia back into the house and get into his car. In fact he wanted to drive around for a while so that there would be an interval between leaving Claudia and returning to Fiona. He didn't examine his motives but they were more about propriety than morals. He needed time to bury the lover and rediscover the husband.

It was several blissfully contented hours before Claudia faced the fact that she had the weekend alone, without K. Then there would be Monday. On Tuesday her parents would be back, although not till the evening, and at the end of the week she would go back to school.

Restlessly, she wandered through the empty house. She knew she couldn't play her viola so she tried to eat but that didn't work. She tried to watch television but there were only thrillers showing, which she couldn't understand. She tried to read but her bedroom, where she usually curled up, was far too filled with K. So she took her book, *Nineteen Eighty-four*, an A-level set text, down to the drawing-room in a valiant attempt to feel adult and calm. But her body got in the way. The parts K had touched seemed to be buzzingly alive and asking for attention. Even her toes, spread bare on the carpet, wouldn't keep still. She tried to make herself smile at the idea that she was a robot with all her lights turned on and flashing. But alone. On her own. Deserted. Flashing in the dark. Even then she couldn't smile.

She went out into the hall where the telephone, in an old-fashioned way, sat on a small table. She had never imagined she would be calling Bella.

'Hi, Claudia. Where've you *been*? You absolutely vanished.'

'My parents whisked me off to Italy. History of art. You know.'

'All on your *own*?'

'More like work, really.' As Claudia spoke, she had a sudden image of Raffaello and his merry companions. To her surprise, she found tears starting in her eyes. 'Well, actually, I did meet one stunning Italian ...'

'Go on! Tell.'

'He was called Raffaello. He ...' But she couldn't go on. She was fighting the desire to tell Bella about K. The tears were now running down her cheeks.

'What's the matter? Nothing happened, did it? Nothing bad?'

Bella was astute about people's moods or perhaps her crying wasn't so silent. Claudia tried to pull herself together. 'Oh, no. We just met a couple of times. He was a viola player.'

'Oh, a musician.'

Claudia heard Bella's interest drop off, just as she'd intended. Anyone who spent hours practising on his own had to be boring, as far as Bella was concerned.

'We met at a concert,' persevered Claudia, her energies diverted now to disguising from Bella her present misery. But the misery was only part of the happiness and Bella couldn't know about that either. Luckily, her friend had begun to talk about herself, this eighteen-year-old boy she'd met who was about to go travelling in India. They'd snogged for hours – her chin had gone bright red – and only stopped because he had to go and collect a car his dad had bought him. 'Only a banger but think of the freedom!'

This came to Claudia quite remotely. She was used to only half listening to Bella's sexual adventures and in her own present circumstances they seemed almost unbelievable. What was the point of snogging some boy for hours? Maybe, contrary to the accepted wisdom of Bella and her circle, Claudia was the sophisticated, mature one, and they were the silly children.

The idea restored some of her self-respect and she found, to her relief, that the tears had stopped. By the time Bella had finished talking and expressed surprise that Claudia had been allowed to stay at home on her own for five nights, Claudia felt almost confident. Compared to Bella, her life seemed so serious, so directed.

'Shit! I'm tired.' Bella yawned audibly. 'You should thank your stars your parents don't expect you to work. I was stacking shelves at five a.m. this morning.'

'Yes. I'm lucky,' agreed Claudia, not referring to stacking shelves. She put down the receiver and went up calmly to her bedroom.

Fiona spent most of the weekend either in bed or in a deck-chair in the garden. She didn't want to eat. She didn't want to talk. She wanted to be on her own. K was ashamed at the relief he felt. Friday with Claudia had been so extraordinary that he didn't think he could have kept up the pretence that everything was normal. However, Fiona scarcely looked at him. It became obvious that she was afraid for her pregnancy, that she was trying to cocoon the tiny burst of new life within her body by staying absolutely still and quiet. On Sunday, when she remained uninterested in any activity and certainly didn't plan to leave the house, K seriously thought about going to find Claudia at Meadowlands. This raised the level of his guilt but it was not guilt that stopped him. It was the fear that he would not be able to conceal his feelings on returning home and the knowledge that he would see Claudia the following day. He scarcely attempted to imagine Claudia's weekend but it crossed his mind that she might invite a friend over.

Instead K went for a walk. He didn't go the way he and Claudia had. He went towards the cricket pitch where he found a match in progress with thirty or forty spectators. Craig, whom he knew a little from the pub he and Fiona drank in sometimes, welcomed him. 'Take a pew, why don't you? Join the supporters' club.'

K saw that his left arm was in a cast. 'What did you do?'

'Fell over my golf club – no, seriously, I did.'

K took the chair indicated. There were a couple of other men and a wife in the group, whose faces were familiar. They were a relaxed, chatty lot, a crate of lager at their feet.

'Good shot!' shouted one.

'Silly bugger,' commented another, as the ball flew into the hands of a fielder. They all laughed.

K remembered that sometimes it had been like this in his office, a communal mateyness that meant nothing but took you one remove from any personal *angst*. No one without personal experience, he decided, could understand the pressures, even the torture, of working constantly alone. He would sit here for a while, unwind, drink a beer or two, watch the game and make a few bad jokes. Men, he decided, not too precisely, are much simpler than women. Thinking of his book, he added to himself, That's why they need to turn women into victims.

'Howzat!' shouted Craig.

'You're way off,' objected his neighbour.

'Weak eyes?'

'Weak head, I'd say.'

K laughed contentedly at the childishness of it all.

CHAPTER TWENTY-FOUR

1990

On Monday Fiona stayed at home again but encouraged K to go to Meadowlands and get on with his work. 'There's no point in both of us sitting around doing nothing,' she said, in her most practical tone.

Although K would have found a way of going to Claudia even without Fiona's permission, he found himself resenting her lack of emotion, her wish not to confide her dark fear. It was her natural stance: unwillingness to share weakness. On the other hand, the last thing he wanted to hear about was her dark fear. Maybe then he'd be forced to stay.

'Shouldn't you see the doctor?' he suggested, in what he trusted was a kindly manner. He was reminded, to use in his novel, that the guilty often appear to behave better than the virtuous. Yet his guilt had a notional tinge, overwhelmed by his certainty in the importance of his feelings for Claudia.

'Yes. Although I don't think there's anything to be done.'

This was the nearest Fiona had come to talking about her situation and K hovered. But what could he do? He had, after all, brought her breakfast in bed. 'I'll come back early.' She couldn't know the depth of that concession.

'No. No.'

' I'll keep my mobile turned on.'

'Yes. Don't worry.'

He saw that she truly wanted him to go. She was used to dealing on her own with the difficulties of her life. He was an encumbrance.

K walked out of the house to his car with a spring of happiness. He'd never felt more alive. He would take Claudia to her bedroom immediately, he thought, start the day afresh by making love to her. Contrary to Claudia's fears, it never occurred to him to judge her sexual performance. She was his love object. He was the dominant male. When he saw her, he was filled with romantic longings, and then he wanted to fuck her, which he did. He had forgotten or disowned the time, only a few weeks ago, when he believed that true love should resist sexuality, that it would be greater and stronger without physical expression.

'Oh, my darling! My darling!' Claudia ran out to K. She found she was crying and laughing at the same time. It had been so long, so long.

They hugged, standing for long minutes in the driveway. Claudia felt dizzy when K eventually broke away and took her hand.

'Upstairs,' he said.

Their love-making was such a mixture of the languid and the intense that Claudia felt the other times had been only preparation. 'I am all, all yours,' she whispered, without feeling the slightest bit self-conscious. Instead of falling asleep, K got out of bed and crouched by her. He pushed her damp hair off her face and kissed her dangling hand. 'Now, my dearest, most delightful queen of my heart, we'll make the perfect day.'

'It is already,' murmured Claudia, drowsily. 'Listen, I can hear that song-thrush.' She didn't quite say 'our' song-thrush. 'Do you remember when you told me about birds?'

But K had no time for birds. 'I may have to do some shopping for our lunch. While I'm gone, you can choose some poems for us to read to each other. You must play to me at some point so that means practice, too, I suppose. I'd like to read you some of my novel but I'm struggling at the moment. While you were away ...' He tailed off.

'While I was away ...' She wanted to say, 'You fell apart.' It would be a badge of honour. He couldn't write so well when she was away. Perhaps she was his muse, his inspiration.

'Come on! We've swimming and tennis to fit in too. And maybe a walk.'

'But you don't play tennis.' Claudia smiled indulgently.
'Today I can do anything.'

Although the sun shone intermittently, it was warm enough to swim and the clouds were too thin, high and stretched like gauze, to suggest rain. Claudia watched them move slowly from west to east, as soon as one passed, another forming behind. She and K were lying on their backs beside the pool. K had several times mentioned his determination to do a little work, but each time sank back, giving Claudia a sidelong smile. 'You're a strumpet, a siren, with your red lips and sapphire eyes. There's no leaving you.'

'Well, I'm going to practise.' She liked the idea of being the strong-minded one.

'No. Play to me. That's part of the plan. Remember?'

Claudia had always previously played in her room, guarding her music for herself. But, as she set up her stand on the lawn, she felt filled with boundless confidence.

She didn't tell K when she was starting, liking the idea of the notes wafting to him out of the air. A line from *The Tempest* came into her head: '*Where should this music be? I' the air? Or the earth? It sounds no more: and sure it waits on the god of the island.*'

But then she was concentrating on her playing. For the first time the piece came together so that her fingers executed what was in her head. Although she kept the music in front of her still, she barely glanced at it. It was all there, without thinking, the summary of all her hard work, an expression of her love.

K, still lying by the pool, pinioned by the weight of physical satisfaction and romantic dreams, listened to the music as carefully as he could. He couldn't tell how expertly she played, but that allowed him to react all the more emotionally. He felt her love for him in every pure note, in every vibrating chord, in every delicate quaver. He understood why the song-thrush had touched her and why she was less talkative than most girls of her age. She had this music playing inside her head. He felt humbled, protective and proud.

When she finished, he went to her and gave her a hug and commanded her to start all over again. 'It was much too short,' he said.

'It's nearly nine minutes long,' objected Claudia, 'longer when I play it. In fact, it's an unusually long movement.'

'It's still too short and, anyway, I want to watch you this time.'

After a moment's hesitation, Claudia began once more. K could hardly appreciate that this handing over of herself without disguise was perhaps an even greater gift to him than when they'd first made love. Now she was holding back nothing that mattered to her. She played slower this time, eyes half closed, head tipped sideways, listening to each vibrating note.

K stood a few yards from her, arms folded. This time he was more able to appreciate the journey on which the music took him.

Claudia took her viola from under her chin and let it hang loosely in her hand. The bow and a piece of blue silk she sometimes placed against her chin dangled from the other. She was silent, and so was K. The music still filled the air around them.

Eventually Claudia sighed and smiled. 'I'll go and put it away.' She gestured with the viola.

'I'll bring the stand.'

So they processed into the house together, one behind the other, up to Claudia's bedroom, and there they made love once more, a solemn plighting, it seemed to them both, although they said nothing.

CHAPTER TWENTY-FIVE

1990

K drove home slowly, putting off the moment when he'd see Fiona. Instead he found a note on the kitchen table.

'I've gone to hospital. Your mobile was off so I left a message.'

K read it again, then looked at his watch. It was six thirty. Not late. He sat down on a chair to try to understand better but his whole body ached with love for Claudia. What did Fiona mean, she'd gone to hospital? Eventually he remembered saying that he'd be back early and that he'd leave his mobile on. He realised he hadn't thought about Fiona since he'd left the house. He went to the fridge and poured himself a beer. He stood at the window gazing out at the dreary little garden.

Whatever had happened, he couldn't regret the day he'd just spent with Claudia. He and Fiona had met so very long ago. They had both been alone in a bar. At lunchtime. She had picked him up but it was their aloneness that had drawn them to each other. Just for a second he contemplated ending their life together. Then he grabbed his keys from where he'd thrown them beside the note and hurried back to his car.

Claudia, blithely eating corn flakes in the kitchen – even the milk seemed to taste especially delicious – suddenly realised, although she hadn't been thinking consciously about such things, that her period was five days late. Her heart, which had been so unusually active over the last few weeks, gave a breathtaking lurch. Her spoon, which had been in mid-air, loaded for another mouthful, mirrored the lurch so that milk and cereal tipped on to the table. Her heart and her hand were in league against her. She was often late. For the first time she remembered that she was sixteen and a schoolgirl. It was impossible she was pregnant. A little spurt of pride flared, then the sick terror began.

CHAPTER TWENTY-SIX

2004

All through supper I thought about the man or beast in the changing-hut. I was often silent so no one commented. Besides, Catherine was particularly animated, as was James. My aunt was more restrained and once I caught her directing a disapproving look at my mother.

By the end of the meal, I'd decided to return to the hut. If the visitor was still there, which, of course, was unlikely, I would face him out. The idea was terrifying but also exhilarating. It was with some difficulty that I preserved a veneer of calm.

'Claudie, can I have a word, please, darling?'

I looked at my mother with surprise. There was a strange note of supplication in her voice. We had finished clearing up, and my aunt and James had said goodbye and were in the act of shutting the front door. Even from the kitchen I heard the latch click. I was free to go secretly, as I'd planned, into the summer darkness. But my mother had hold of my arm.

'Now, you mean?'

'Yes, now. I want to tell you something, explain something, before Louise arrives tomorrow. You may know already. Children are so mysterious ...' She talked nervously, even timorously until we reached the drawing room when she sat down and abruptly fell silent.

In the silence I heard a heavy fluttering. Looking round, I saw a butterfly battling inside the only lamp that was lit.

'Oh, look! Poor thing.' The bulb was hot and the space between it and the shade only just wide enough for my hands. Every time I came near, it flew out, circling hysterically before returning to the light. 'It's a peacock,' I told Catherine, who was showing no interest in the challenge but sat in a rather stunned way. Once more I tried to cup my hands round the delicate wings with their round, baleful eyes. 'I'm only trying to help,' I told it, and suddenly the butterfly was still, quivering on the outside of the shade, and I had it in my palms, feeling the tickle of its antennae against my skin.

'There!' I took it to an open window and let it out into the cool night air. I stood there for a minute.

Then there was no avoiding what my mother had to say. She sat down, but not too close. 'I don't know where to begin,' she said. 'Perhaps at the end. James and I are going to get married.'

'I thought you would.'

'You did?' Catherine seemed more hopeful. 'You mean you *did* know?'

'Know what?'

'Oh dear.' She frowned and rubbed her face with a hand. 'It does seem wrong to be talking like this on the day of your father's death, but I wanted things to be clear. No more hypocrisy. No more lying.'

'I'm sorry. I don't understand.'

'Oh, I see.' Catherine paused as if trying to find a new start. 'Do you remember that holiday we took in Italy? Years ago. The same summer...' She let the words trail away but I knew what she meant.

'I remember.' In a sudden flash, I pictured those chattering Italian students. In a café whose name I'd forgotten. One had been beautiful. Raffaello!

'I told you the reason we were going so suddenly was that Douglas was unwell. That was true, but not the whole truth.' Catherine put her head down and spoke softer, faster. 'You see, I'd just told him I'd been having an affair with James. After that drinks party. I planned the whole thing. I gave James a letter saying it was all over and that evening I told Douglas. It was a dreadfully managing thing to do. Of course, he tried to get out of the holiday. But he also said he'd guessed something was going on. So he saw it gave us a chance. He told me then that he had been seeing doctors in London.'

I found myself not so much shocked as buzzing with questions. Or perhaps the questions were a way of blocking the shock.

'Why ever did you take me to Italy with you?'

'We could hardly leave you behind. I wanted you there, anyway.' My mother sounded more like her practical self. 'Since I'm being honest, I might as well admit that you acted as a buffer between us.

Douglas adored you, of course, and was so proud of you. By the time you left, we were ready to talk to each other, to work out if we could continue. Being married, I mean. It was good luck that you insisted on coming back early.'

I thought about that. I had come back to K. It struck me as a strange coincidence that Catherine should be recalling that time on the evening that a man, probably a man of the road but just possibly K himself, was holed up in our garden.

'You didn't have to tell me,' I said. I didn't feel strong enough to take on her private life.

'No. But I thought you might have guessed. I want things to be straight between us.' She looked at me questioningly, but I had nothing to say. So she continued. 'There's another reason. I know it's still painful for you.'

'Please ...' I said, meaning, 'please stop', but she seemed to take it the other way.

'Yes. I thought you'd guessed so when what happened on that dreadful morning happened, I thought I should take some of the blame. You were upset, perhaps angry. At least muddled. I was so taken up with my own emotional problems that I hadn't noticed what was going on in your life. I failed you as a mother.' She hesitated, then added, 'I'm so terribly sorry. More than anything I'm sorry for what happened to you.'

I had to answer her now. It was an appeal. I could see she was crying a little. But I was still reluctant. 'Why didn't you say anything before, if you felt so guilty?'

'I promised your father I wouldn't.'

Now it was the day of his death. Poor Father, to be cast aside so quickly. 'I never guessed,' I tried to strengthen my voice. 'So you needn't worry about that. I suppose I was much too self-centred to notice anything. You were my mother, that was all.'

I didn't mean to be cruel. Yet now I looked back, with this new knowledge, there had been something febrile about her that summer. Too much smiling. Too wide a smile. I recalled that unbearable lunch. And a visit to church with her the evening before. No, it wasn't a lunch. A drinks party, as she'd said. She'd been so excited, pulling heavy plant pots around at dawn. I, of course, had been thinking about only of K. She, presumably, had been thinking only of James. What an extraordinary parallel. The sixteen-year-old daughter and the mother obsessing over their forbidden lovers.

Perhaps she was right. Perhaps there had been something in the air, in her aura, which had affected us all.

Mark, for example. I suddenly remembered Mark, James's son. I had snatched him away from the drinks party, sat with him under the chestnut trees, getting drunk on a bottle of white wine, and he'd fallen in love with me. He'd sent me letters declaring himself, but his timing was just about as bad as it could have been. The first arrived on the day my world crashed in. The others were forwarded to me in hospital. Perhaps my mother thought they'd bring me out of myself. Of course, I never even read them.

'Why don't we hear about Mark any more?' I asked carelessly. He had had such a minor role in my life that I'd forgotten him until now. I supposed that when Catherine and James married he'd become a kind of brother. I noticed Catherine was looking shocked, more so, in fact, than at any point in our conversation.

'What is it? What's wrong?'

'You *know* what happened to Mark.'

A disquieting memory stirred. 'Do I?'

'He committed suicide a year or so after ...' She didn't finish her sentence. 'He was always very intense. He'd just started university. You knew all about it. I told you myself.'

She was right. She had told me but I was crazy at the time. Crazy people living through their own tragedy have no room in their heads for the author of other's.

'That's terrible.' The words sounded feeble. Had it been partly my fault? Leading him on under the chestnut trees – we had even played viola and piano together, I remembered, Mark sight-reading remarkably well, me bowing remarkably badly - and then I'd ignored his letters, his declarations of eternal love. I must have read one because I knew about the eternal love. I could even recall that he'd once sent me a rose by Interflora, which I'd immediately thrown into a bin. 'Poor Mark. Poor James.'

'It was a bad time for everyone.'

I was feeling restless, trapped, even. Even now I was not strong enough to deal with other people's nightmares. But I knew I owed my mother a proper hearing. She had done so much for me, never losing faith in a happier future for us all. Perhaps she could now be happy with James. I remembered that we had gone on holiday, our two families together. Perhaps that was where it had started. 'Do you remember that holiday we took in Cornwall?'

'Do you mean was the affair going on then? Well, it wasn't. But I guess that was when we fell in love.' She sounded tougher now, less apologetic.

'So you've waited seventeen years. Even after James divorced, you waited.'

'How could I leave your father after I promised him.' She paused. 'Or you?'

This was a heavy weight to carry. Another. Yet my mother must think me recovered enough for her to start a new life. Or perhaps it was the presence of Oliver. But he was absent.

'I'm sorry.' I got up and went over to Catherine. I laid my hand on her shoulder. Standing so close, I could see tears on her cheeks. I realised I had never before said sorry to her. It had all seemed too huge for apologies but now it felt right.

'I've never thanked you,' I continued. I was filled with amazement at my selfishness, which had continued to this day. I'd even cast a bad light on her wish for me to have a big wedding. But she'd been willing to sacrifice her own happiness for mine. I hoped she realised the depth of my apology. Her weeping had increased. In fact, I felt my own eyes prickling with tears. 'I'm sorry,' I repeated, and added, so there should be no doubt, 'for all the misery I've caused you.'

She paid attention then, although a little distracted by her own thoughts. 'No, darling. Don't apologise. You shouldn't blame yourself. You were a child. I should have seen.'

But I wasn't having this any more. Not with him (or someone else) literally outside our window. I stood a bit away from her. 'I was sixteen,' I said. 'Old enough to choose. I chose to fall in love. I wanted it. It was my responsibility. You have to allow me that or I'm nothing. A pawn. A child, like you say. But I wasn't. I chose my life.'

I didn't say anything else because I had only got so far. I couldn't say it was true love, or something even grander, because I couldn't be certain of that. Not yet. Perhaps never.

Catherine stood up. She seemed harassed. I remembered that this conversation was supposed to be about her and, as usual, it had turned to me. *I* had turned it to me.

'The thing is,' I began again, 'I'm really pleased about you and James.'

'Oh, darling.'

She got out a handkerchief from the sleeve of her cardigan and blew her nose. We hugged then without another word. It felt good, the best hug we'd ever had. But, like so many best moments, it brought with it a counteracting pain – the pain of what might have been.

As if reading my mind, Catherine said comfortingly, 'When you and Oliver have children you'll understand what it's like to be a mother. Mothers never need apologies or thanks but I'm glad you spoke all the same.' On this note we left the room, arm in arm, and I went up to my room, as she thought, to sleep.

My shrink is right about secrecy. After Catherine's openness and our loving hug, it was an act of gross disloyalty not to tell her about the man in the hut. In fact I would have gone out there straight away but I wanted to throw her off the scent – and then I began to consider Mark. It seemed ironic that I, who had had every reason to commit suicide, had been persuaded (not quite the right word) by the care and attention of family and professionals not to do so while Mark, a blameless, innocent soul as far as I knew, had terminated his life forthwith. Of course, I couldn't be self-centred enough to blame myself. It seemed likely that some weakness, instability or even madness in him had led him to take his own life and this trait was not in my character. It was the guilt that had made me seem mad, and I had real reason to feel it. I was guilty. As the years rolled by only one question remained: were there any mitigating circumstances?

Having rejected 'youth', I was left with 'great love'. I could discuss this with no one. Not with my mother and certainly not with Oliver. I had been over the ground with my shrink but she so clearly judged my love by its disastrous consequences that there had never seemed any purpose in confiding.

Now I was prepared to go out and confront K, if it was him, and if he'd not fled. But I decided to wait until I heard Catherine safely shut into her bedroom. In the meantime I lay down on my bed.

It was not surprising that I fell asleep. The day had been long and the night before I'd sat beside my dying father.

I slept soundly, perhaps for an hour, and when I opened my eyes the house was utterly still and dark. I felt wide awake, as alert as someone about to do a nefarious deed. I took off the clothes I had been wearing, a skirt and cotton top, and put on black trousers and a sweater.

I felt my way down to the kitchen where I picked up a torch. But when I got outside, the sky was filled with stars and, although there was no moon, it was bright enough for me to find my way around a place I knew so well. In case he was a marauder, I'd also brought with me a kitchen knife, nothing too large or threatening, merely a defensive object.

CHAPTER TWENTY-SEVEN

2004

I wanted to run the moment she turned her back on me. I felt humiliated, ashamed and ridiculous – nothing to what I'd suffered in the past but enough, you'd think, to jolt me into a different line of action. But I allowed myself a few minutes to get over the shock of seeing her so close with only a sheet of glass between us and, in that time, I lost the ability to move. I sank further back into the corner, shrugging down into the tendrils of ivy as if they would make me invisible like magic cloaks in fairy stories.

Some time passed. By the light I guessed it was an hour or more. I realised I had been asleep or unconscious, even. Something had happened not only to my mind but to my body. I tried to stand but the weight of the past had joined with the present to pinion me to the floor. My legs had literally become useless. They had carried me here and would go no further. Tears trickled out of my eyes and down my face. I didn't try to see if I could wipe them away. I was like some crumbling stone fountain, lichen-covered and derelict.

The light faded completely. Never for one second did I consider she might return. I felt so abandoned to despair that when I discovered, presumably during my blackout, I'd wet myself, I wasn't particularly bothered.

It was in this strange state that I heard the door of the hut open and felt a presence in the darkness.

'Who are you?'

The words were clear cut, sharp, even in my dreamy state. For some reason, perhaps to soften them, I translated them into Spanish: '*¿Quién eres?*' But what a question. Should I say my name to her, after all these years? That summer she had called me K. I had given it fancifully when she first asked me, thinking of Graham Greene's novel, *The End of the Affair*. It had been an odd decision, faced with an unknown sixteen-year-old girl. But it had stuck. If she called me anything, she called me K, one letter, nothing to do with my own name, the name Fiona used. Had I been trying to separate the two women even then?

I decided not to answer. So she moved a step or two nearer and asked a different question but it was no easier to answer.

'Are you dangerous?'

Well, the answer of course, was 'Yes'.

'No.' My voice was hardly more than a mumble.

'What? I can't hear you.' She sounded suddenly angry. 'I'm armed, you know.'

I wanted to say her name but the presumption seemed too great.

'Yes. I could do you damage!'

Her violence was not quite convincing but it was hurtful all the same.

Maybe she really didn't know who was huddled in the corner.

'Please.' My voice was a little stronger.

'So you're not dangerous.' She sounded less ferocious. 'I'll keep my mobile turned on just in case.'

Vaguely, I recognised her dialogue was not rational. If she'd suspected I was threatening, she had had plenty of time to fetch the police. She was just playing for time, play-acting to delay reality a little longer. She knew who I was. She had known all along and now she had come back to me. A tiny flicker of hope was kindled.

'Why are you here?' she asked now, without anger but with a hint of impatience. She had been such a dreamy girl, so accepting, unquestioning.

'I'm sorry.' I managed these words, the most important ones – save for the three I didn't dare pronounce now and perhaps never would again – with reasonable clarity. 'I'm sorry,' I repeated, when she made no response. This time the words sounded so feeble that I almost regretted them. Had I come all this way only to say sorry? The priest would have approved, but I knew it was a lie.

'Yes. Yes.'

I wasn't sure that that was in response to my apology. If so, it seemed to suggest a quick acceptance and even a need to move on, which was hardly appropriate. I knew I should move, force myself out into the open while I had her in front of me, but I couldn't.

'Yesterday I was to be married. Today my father died. This evening my mother told me she was having an affair. And now you're here.' Her tone was accusatory, but only mildly so, as if she knew I couldn't be expected to solve or explain these extraordinary events in her life.

My eyes had got used to the darkness and I could see her silhouette outlined against the relative lightness of the garden. It must be a very starry night, I thought, or the moon was hidden behind us. She was shuffling towards me, one arm outstretched.

'How are you armed?' I asked.

She started, as if she'd forgotten her earlier mention of a weapon.

'A knife. I have a knife.' This conversation was not good for us. It was violence that had torn us apart. I could hardly believe, nevertheless, that she planned to stab me. It was impossible that her nature had changed so completely. Yet she had every reason to hate me.

The hand was still approaching. I imagined the force of steel through my skin – I hoped not my face. I was tempted to shield myself with an arm and, while shifting my position, was unpleasantly reminded of my wet state. I probably smelt like an incontinent tramp on a street corner. I was disgusting.

'Don't touch me,' I said. But she didn't seem to hear me. I could see her fingers now – no knife – as white and wavering as underwater plants. The fingertips touched my face.

'Is it you, K?'

I began to cry. It was too much for me, the sudden childlike innocence in her voice. After all the agony I had caused her and others, she could still ask me that, in those tones.

'Yes, it is me.'

'I thought so.' She sounded simply satisfied and withdrew her fingers. I waited, but instead of saying more, she lowered herself to the floor, not very close to me, and crossed her legs.

We stayed silent for a long time. Who knows how long? She was so still I even wondered if she'd fallen asleep. But she hadn't for when I finally spoke, 'I came because you were getting married,' she answered quickly, 'But I didn't.'

The words hung between us.

'He's called Oliver,' she said eventually. 'He's good for me.'

183

She didn't say she loved him.

'I live in Valparaiso,' I said. I wanted her to know this.

'Valparaiso,' she repeated the word in a way more wondering than curious. 'It sounds like something out of a story book.'

'It's in South America,' I said, 'in Chile, on the coast, the other side of the Andes.' I began to tell her more, about the purple ocean, the many-coloured houses clinging to the *cerros*. My tongue, which had seemed as pinioned as my body, loosened as I told her about Captain Cochrane, the British hero who had liberated the Chileans from the Spanish conquerors. I described the strangely English Hotel Weymouth where I had stayed at first, the steep street where I lived and down which an old man had once rolled to the sea. I told her about the earthquakes that made my tin roof clang like cymbals, and about transvestites who grew beards to plait with their hair. I suppose I wanted to be a small-time Othello who made Desdemona forget his Moorish blackness by the pictures of great victories, of far-off adventures. I couldn't bear her to see me as I was. Yet I had no victories to tell her, only a story of survival and of the city that had helped me. Words could never be enough.

'I was ill for so long,' she said, when I had finished, in the same wondering intonation, almost as if she were talking about someone else – or expected me to contradict her.

The words, although not spoken as a reproach, were dreadful to me. I had caused her illness. I searched hopelessly for something to say. I almost wished I could slide back into unconsciousness. I remembered how, at such sensitive moments in our past, I had always repeated the only words that mattered, as if it were an incantation to solve all problems. Now I could say nothing. But there had been no expectation in her voice of a response. As I had told her I lived in Valparaiso, she had told me she had been ill. It was an exchange of information.

'But you're better now.' How ever did I make such a crass statement? As if she could ever be better. A 'better' person would hardly have come out at night to pass the time with the man who had ruined her life. 'I'm sorry. I didn't mean that.'

'I *am* better now.' She seemed surprised. 'I'm glad you came back. For so long I imagined you would. I imagined how it would be. Finally I gave up hope.'

'And that's when you got better.'

'No! No!' For the first time she was agitated, although she didn't move towards me, remaining just a dark mass. 'I don't know why I got better. A lot of people were trying to help me, of course.'

A fierce spasm of jealousy twisted my gut. Oliver. 'I'm glad you had that,' I said humbly.

'I work. I have a job.' The note of pride was unmistakable.

More information. Were these the rules of engagement? She told me about her job in London with an NGO. I told her I passed my time painting. Like casual acquaintances, we swapped the basic facts of our new lives, then parted. Was that how it would be? But I refused to play that game. It was absurd in our situation.

'I peed myself earlier.' I had raised my voice as if it were a boast. 'After I saw your face at the door, I lost all self-control. Or, rather, when you left. I cried. I was unable to move. I had some kind of blackout. I'm still unable to move. That's the effect you've had on me. I find it hard to care about your job. I know I should but I don't. Of course I'm glad you're better, if you say so, but I can never be better. Never.' I stopped abruptly. Was this true? I had always believed I was as good as dead. Yet I had travelled all the way from Valpo for this conversation. Dead people don't book flights on aeroplanes or become stalkers in the suburban English countryside.

Now I needed a reaction from her, but she said nothing. Her silence pressed so heavily on me that I began to believe I could move. Anything to escape the grip of her lack of response. I tested an arm, lifted it. Then a leg. 'I'm going for a swim.'

She didn't move or speak. I stumbled past her through the door and out to the pool, which, luckily, was uncovered. I paused long enough to take off my shoes, then I toppled, fully dressed, into the water. My body hitting the surface made a huge noise in the silent darkness. Around my head bubbles exploded like gun-fire.

I heard him fall into the pool as if from a long distance. He left behind him the whiff of urine.

I knew his last speech had been an appeal but I couldn't answer it. I don't expect he believed I would. And now he'd thrown himself into the pool, although not, I guessed, with a view to drowning. Of all that he'd said, the word 'Valparaiso' stuck in my head. Whether because he'd pronounced it in a special way – something intense, almost loving, in the intonation – or whether because the word itself held the ring of romance, I didn't know.

'Valparaiso.' I tried it aloud. It sounded good, round, positive, exciting. 'Valparaiso.' The second time my voice sounded a little mad. So I got up and went outside.

I watched him wallowing in the pool. The undone sleeves of his white shirt flapped about separately, giving him four arms. I wished I could smile. But I was too stunned by his presence. He had said much the same about the effect on him of seeing me.

'Come out,' I said, too softly for him to hear. 'Come out before you sink.' But I said it just as softly, so I sat on the steps in front of the hut and waited. I could hear his crazed exertion, heightened by the absolute quiet all around. Perhaps he would drown – have a heart-attack first, then drown.

I don't how long I sat waiting before the splashing slowed, then stopped. Probably it was only a minute or two. The stars seemed brighter than ever as he hauled himself out and stood in a shapeless mass, water sluicing off him. In a gasping, lumbering way, he took off his trousers and shirt. Then he looked round and saw me.

'You're still here.' He swayed forward, obviously trying to make out my features. 'I thought you would have gone.'

'No. I'm here.'

He walked over to me, ridiculous, I suppose, in his underpants and dark socks. He sat on the steps, not very close, still panting, and tried to smooth back his wet hair. Then he took off his socks. I looked at him sideways but he put his head into his hands. I could tell that he was gearing himself up for a statement, and felt a greater sense of dread than I had since he'd appeared.

'I shall go back to Valpo immediately.'

I clocked the affectionate diminutive with curiosity. This was his life.

'I was crazy to come. Wrong. A priest told me so but I didn't want to listen.'

His humility was painful but I was too out of it to react.

'I needed to see you just once more. I thought it would be at your wedding. I was all prepared for that. You in white satin, on another man's arm. When that didn't happen, I lost my bearings. I only thought of my need to see you. I should never have come. I'm so sorry. Please forgive me.'

So he wanted forgiveness. That was why he'd come. Desolation made me almost incapable of speech. It seemed that he, too, like all the others, blamed only himself for what had happened. 'It's easy to forgive others,' I said, pleased to have exposed a coherent thought. Inwardly, I begged him not to tell me he had ruined my life. Surely he, at least, would allow me to have played a real part in the tragedy.

'I have to go.' He stood up in front of me.

'Like that!'

He looked down at himself.'

'I'll get you some dry clothes.' I stood up, too, and crossed the lawn towards the dark house.

It was unnerving to enter my father's bedroom on the day of his death – although I suppose by now it was the day after. I went to the heavy wardrobe, relic of another age – the age when he'd been young – and fumbled the door open. It was a terrible thing to do, to pillage his clothes for a man who had destroyed the tranquillity of his family. I recoiled from the clothes, with the lingering smell of his aftershave, and went to sit on his bed. Perhaps I couldn't do it. Then I remembered that the tragedy of my life had not been the only tragedy in his. My mother had abandoned him – or, rather, had wanted to abandon him. I did not deserve all of the blame for his unhappiness.

I stood up again and went purposefully to the wardrobe. I found a pair of trousers, which I pulled off the hanger, then went to the chest of drawers. The stacks of neatly ironed shirts stopped me short once more. When he was working, he'd been meticulous about a clean shirt every day. When his life and health had unwound, he'd worn without comment whatever my mother or, later, a nurse had decided.

I snatched a shirt and left the room, forgetting, in my haste, to switch off the light. I saw its brightness as I recrossed the lawn. It cast a sharp beam through the undrawn curtains, a watchful light in the soft darkness. Nevertheless I didn't turn back.

'Are you there?' The pool area seemed very dark and silent. Maybe he'd gone. I imagined him creeping through the night-time fields.

'I'm in here.'

I could hear him shivering as soon as I got into the hut. I hadn't even brought a towel, let alone a sweater. I took off my own.

'Dry yourself with this.' He took it from me and, without seeming to realise what it was, began to rub himself vigorously. I hadn't brought him any underpants either.

'I've brought you trousers and a shirt. I'll go outside and wait for you.' It was brighter again outside, as if a cloud had passed. The bare skin of my arms shone with a corpse-like pallor. My bra was white too, lacy, bought new for my wedding. Soon the chill air made my skin pucker. I wrapped my arms round myself and walked up and down.

'What do you want me to do with my wet things?' He spoke from behind me.

'Just leave them. I'll deal with them.' So he was really going. Still hugging myself, I turned to him and watched as he dropped his clothes on to the ground. 'Are you warmer now?' His skin, usually dark, wore the same icy pallor as mine. He bent and put on his shoes. His feet seemed unnaturally long, rising to his naked ankles. He straightened.

'Yes. Thank you. Much better now.'

I could feel him trying to leave.

I told myself I would never see her again. There should be words for such a parting but I could think of nothing that would express my feelings, except the forbidden ones. 'I want you to be happy,' I faltered eventually.

'Happy!'

She was so startled that I took a step back. Did she mean that I had taken away the possibility for ever? I wanted to tell her that all sorts of people endured all kinds of agony and still found it possible to be happy later. The trouble was, I didn't believe it. I could never be happy.

'Goodbye, Claudia.' I walked away as quickly as I could before my tears returned.

He had gone without touching me. I had touched him with my fingertips – I could feel his skin still - but he hadn't touched me. All I had was a bundle of wet clothes, making a puddle now at my feet. He hadn't even commented that I was topless, except for my bra. He had thrown my sweater on top of his clothes, I saw, his clothes and mine massed together in a wet lump. It was not much consolation.

But what had I expected to happen? The question was too difficult. Bending shakily, I picked up the clothes and walked towards the house. The front of my body was soaked at once. But I liked clasping them to me. I had no idea what to do with them so when I saw the dustbin at the kitchen door, I lifted the lid and dumped them in it. Then I began to cry.

CHAPTER TWENTY-EIGHT

1990

Fiona had been told to stay in hospital overnight. K wanted to ask, 'Why is it this serious? You were hardly pregnant at all.' But Fiona was so silent and miserable that he didn't dare. Besides, she'd coped alone with whatever had happened – he hadn't dared ask about that either. It seemed that something had gone wrong enough for her to be taken into the operating theatre and given a general anaesthetic. There was no doctor to ask, although he'd tried to find one.

There were five other patients in the ward, two cheerful, propped high against pillows, three comatose, in much the same state as Fiona. One had a visitor who sat, like K, looking bewildered, even guilty. Did men always feel guilty when their women were laid low? K wondered, then reminded himself that he had reason. He looked at the other man again, noting his thick neck, shaved head and elaborate tattoo – possibly of Neptune. To his embarrassment, their eyes locked.

'Not too hot, is it? Just sitting doing nothing. I can't even feel glad to be a man. Not with her in the state she's in.'

Glad to be a man. K nodded in agreement. Not so long ago he'd been extremely glad to be a man. 'You've hit the nail on the head. It feels like it's my fault.'

'Had it terminated, did she?' The man's tone was sympathetic, bonding as males, but K saw that there was a misunderstanding. Yet to say Fiona's problem was a miscarriage, the hand of God rather than man, might sound like a reproof. After all, their situations were different.

He was saved the need to answer by Fiona opening her eyes and whispering his name. 'I still can't believe it,' she said. 'It's too cruel.'

'Yes. I'm so very very sorry.' He sat closer and put out a hand.

Ignoring it, Fiona pulled herself into a sitting position. 'I saw the doctor. Afterwards, I mean. I was still woozy. But I think what he said was really bad news.' Her voice rose. 'Will you find him, darling? Ask him what he meant. Maybe it was just a nightmare.'

'Of course. You should rest.' K tried to soothe her but she became more excited, extraordinarily unlike her usual self. She pressed him in a hoarse voice to go now and find the doctor, question him about what he had seen, her womb, the state of her womb. She said these words quite loudly and K felt the man at the next bed gazing at him understandingly, although he avoided his eye this time.

'Don't worry. I'll go straight away.'

He was glad to get away from her, and the moment he reached the corridor, he paused to take deep breaths and recover a little. Although Fiona's sufferings gave him a sick, unsteady feeling, he wouldn't let go of the happiness of his day with Claudia. He would do everything he could for Fiona, except regret Claudia.

'Can I help you?' A nurse approached. He noticed that her eyes were red, as if she'd been crying. He explained the situation and his wish to see his wife's doctor.

'Mr Blick won't be in till eight tomorrow morning.'

K felt a rush of anger. Tomorrow was the last day he could see Claudia alone before her parents returned later in the day. He understood that whatever had happened was not containable. Fiona had never had any problem with which she needed his help. She had always been the helper, he the helped. How ironic that at this one moment of delirious joy her need must spoil it! Again he felt a shameful spurt of anger. 'So, can I see him?'

'Not in the morning. Oh, no. But your wife will be more herself then.'

Pity, anger, and now a flicker of hope. Was he not needed in the morning, after all?

'Of course it depends on when your wife's leaving. He might still be here when you pick her up. If she leaves tomorrow. Mr Blick will see her first and decide.'

K went back to Fiona and explained how difficult it was for him to see the consultant but that she would get the chance in the morning. She seemed to have sunk back into apathy. 'Can I get you anything?'

She turned so that her face was half hidden in the pillow.

K turned too, and inevitably caught his neighbour's eye. 'Just the same as mine. Might as well go and get a beer as hang around unwanted.'

It seemed to be an invitation but the probable truth of the remark only irritated K. 'I'll stay a bit longer.'

'Cheers, mate.' He left, after patting his partner's wall-like hip, and K took up position on the chair beside Fiona's bed.

After a while, he became calmer and, reflecting that it was the right place to be, decided to stay there as long as he was allowed to.

Claudia had remembered that when Lucy (a not very good friend from school) had thought herself pregnant, she'd gone to the chemist and bought a kit to prove it one way or the other. But, of course, the chemist would be closed now. Wild ideas of jumping off tables, drinking gin in a hot bath flitted unnervingly through her mind. Instead she went and found her viola.

The music, more luxuriant than ever, filled her bedroom. K had no children, she knew that. Could it be that this was destiny, that he had come to her so that their love should make him a child? One part of her recognised these thoughts were madness, but as the music swelled and dipped, she was filled with a glorious sense of rightness and hope. How could anything be compared to the creation of new life? How could anything be bad between K and herself?

For nearly three hours Claudia played, moving from the Brahms to pieces she had learnt as a young child. Eventually, the room was completely dark and, without undressing or putting away her viola, she fell, exhausted, onto the bed.

Early the next morning K, who had stayed at the hospital till nine the night before, was called back. It seemed that the consultant, Mr Blick, wanted to see him after all. He took K into a side room and indicated that he should sit in a blue plastic chair. Immediately K felt helpless in the hands of a stronger power, although the doctor was younger than him, with wavy fair hair and pink cheeks. Despite everything, K had slept reasonably. His anxiety about Fiona stayed separate from his dreams about Claudia.

'Is there a problem?' he asked, almost cheerily.

'I'm afraid so. I wanted to have a word with you before I talk to your wife. She's very upset.'

'Yes. She's been trying for a baby for years.'

'I understand. So, bad news first? Or good?'

'Oh, good.' K was surprised at the question. Surely everyone wanted something good first as a bolster against the bad. Fiona was the most positive person he knew.

'So. We can deal with your wife's condition with little danger to her now or in the future.'

'Condition?' It seemed an odd word in the circumstances.

'I might as well get to the point straight away. Yesterday when we gave your wife a scrape, we discovered evidence of changes in the lining of the uterus. I've already taken a biopsy. I don't want you to jump to the wrong conclusion. Your wife does not have cancer at this moment. But the proper clinical procedure for a woman in her condition is a hysterectomy. We would try to retain the ovaries but at this stage I can't promise anything.'

As the doctor's voice, rather high-pitched and professionally uninflected, continued, K had the curious sensation that his body was turning from solid flesh to transparent ghostliness. Fiona had cancer. Whatever the doctor said, the cancer had started inside her. The rock on which he'd based his life was splintering.

'I want to reiterate,' continued the doctor, perhaps unnerved by K's silence, 'that your wife is in no immediate danger but an operation is indicated in the near future. A hysterectomy carries with it negligible risk to the patient's life. It is, however, a psychological hurdle, particularly for a woman who has not yet had children.'

The doctor stopped and waited for K to speak. His look was patiently enquiring but K felt that now he had given the information, the clock had begun to tick. Soon Mr Blick would rush off to deal with other situations, other 'conditions'. He struggled to get over his panic and find a sensible voice. 'She'll be heartbroken,' he said, 'heartbroken.' And suddenly they were not just words but the absolute truth.

'It won't be easy, I know.' The doctor paused, then asked, with a deferential air, 'I'm quite prepared to tell her myself – in fact, I did hint at something not quite right yesterday – but maybe you would prefer ...'

Why would it make any difference who told her? K frowned at his knees. Fiona would find no mitigation for such a disaster.

'Or perhaps you'd like to come with me.'

Later K was to wonder whether the pathetic ghostliness that had overtaken him during this interview had caused him to make a seriously wrong decision. Would the news have been better coming from him? Would Fiona have felt less isolated? If he had told her with her hand in his and words of love on his lips, she might have been comforted a little, stronger to face the future.

He had not been able to do it. On two counts it would have been hypocrisy: he did not mourn the loss of fatherhood as she had motherhood; he did not love her enough. This stark reality undermined the affection and sorrow he felt, turning him into a wordless zombie.

K stood beside Mr Blick as he told Fiona the news. They were very close together because a nurse had drawn the curtains round them, three floating walls of purple pansies. Fiona had been prepared by the nurses for his visit and sat up with a well-washed face and smooth hair. K could hardly bear to look at her expression, hopeful for a second or two. He'd brought her some dark pink chrysanthemums, bought in the hospital foyer. Now they seemed the colour of dried blood.

When Fiona understood what she was being told, she uttered one small cry. Even then K, tears in his eyes, found himself unable to touch her. He watched her sink down into the bed, turn away from them.

The doctor was just preparing to leave when Fiona jerked round and cried, 'I won't let it happen, you know! I don't care about the risk. The risk is nothing compared to having a baby. It's my body. You can't chop things out unless I say so. And I don't say so!'

Mr Blick, unfazed, took a step closer. He glanced at K, then leant close to take Fiona's untended hand. 'You're quite right. Nothing will happen unless you say so. Go home. Think about it. It's not so much of an emergency that it won't wait. I'll have the results of the biopsy then, although I don't doubt what they'll tell me. But I can't change my advice to you. Without a hysterectomy, you put yourself at high risk of developing cancer.'

Fiona snatched away her hand. Red spots glowed in her cheeks. 'High risk, is it now? That wasn't the message when—' She burst into tears.

At last K found the strength to comfort her. He took her in his arms and let her sob against his chest. Beyond her, Mr Blick gave a little flip of his wrist, as if to say, 'I'll leave you to manage this', and ducked out between the curtains.

'It'll be all right,' said K, who didn't believe this. 'It's the shock.' That was true for both of them. He noticed how hot they were, cheeks and hands slick with sweat. 'We'll take it slower. We'll talk.'

Fiona stopped crying and pushed him away firmly. 'I'm going home. And I'm not having a hysterectomy. There's nothing wrong with me. You'll see.'

'Yes,' said K, weakly. Exhaustion overwhelmed him. He put his head into his hands. This was what real life was like, he thought. This was marriage. A course was set and nothing could change. Claudia had been a mirage that he'd been fool enough to take seriously. Reality was a small house, a sick wife determined to have a baby and/or die, a weak-willed man who kidded himself he was something special. He wouldn't write his novel. That was a dream too, a self-indulgence Fiona had allowed him. He'd start searching for a job at once.

'Let's go now,' said Fiona, putting a foot out of bed.

'I'll look for a nurse.'

As K walked away, he pictured his mother bent over his father's corpse. She'd insisted on flying to Ireland where he'd been living or, as it turned out, dying, with one of the women who, for inexplicable reasons, had insisted on looking after him. Despite all the misery he had made for his wife, she'd wept in mourning. Later, over Guinness in a nearby pub, K had asked his mother why she'd paid him so much respect. 'He was my husband,' she'd said, uninterested in her son's lack of understanding.

Claudia knew K wouldn't be with her until the usual time on Tuesday but she was ready for him by seven thirty in case he managed to arrive early, keen to stretch out their last unattended time together. When he hadn't come by nine, she decided to walk to the shops and buy the pregnancy-testing kit. In fact, the long night had induced lack of belief. They had only once made love without protection, that first afternoon in the hotel. Nevertheless she would go to prove the situation beyond doubt. Besides, she was restless. She needed an occupation to stop her thinking too much.

The day was warm but unsettled. Bright spells alternated with dark clouds that dropped a few spots of rain, then moved briskly on. The wind was variable too, tugging at her loose hair one moment, then dropping away altogether, making her sweater uncomfortably hot. She felt as if summer was trying to hang on in there but was being ousted by a more random and powerful force.

She walked on the pavement, although there were mostly fields on either side. Her feet in their trainers made hardly any sound but the cars, mostly heading the same way as her, passed with noisy regularity. K would be coming from the station, the other way. She decided not to cross the road in case he suspected she was out looking for him.

After about ten minutes she stopped abruptly. It had struck her that the chemist in the small parade of shops knew her well. Mrs Newcombe was her name, a pretty, friendly woman with intelligent blue eyes. Claudia would never dare ask her for a pregnancy-testing kit. It was out of the question.

Claudia turned and, in a slightly heavier swirl of rain, began to walk resolutely homeward. She was not really worried anyway, she told herself, and, with a rising blush of happiness, *he* will be there by now. I will see *him* in a few minutes.

So convinced was she of this (he must have come from another direction, she told herself) that when she arrived at Meadowlands and heard sounds coming from the lawn, she ran in the direction, crying joyfully, 'Oh, darling K!'

Alan looked up from the tractor mower. 'Just hope the rain gets no heavier or I'll never get this grass cut.'

Of course Alan, whom she had not seen since her parents' departure, would come back on the day of their return.

'I've been for a walk,' she said. She bent down and untied one of her trainers. There was something in it, snagging at her sole. It had probably been there when she'd first set out, but she'd only noticed it now. She shook the shoe and a piece of grit fell out. She thought how minuscule it was, yet so sharp.

She turned to watch as Alan started the tractor. Something lay beside him on the seat.

'What's that?' she shouted, and then again, as he pretended not to hear. She could see it was a gun.

He drove over to her until he was very close. 'It's a gun, like, to clear those effing pigeons. I had a go this morning when you were out but they're clever, those birds.'

'You mustn't do that!' shouted Claudia, as the engine was still running. 'I don't want killing here.'

'If you say so, Miss.' He began to move away, giving a backward wave. Claudia didn't wave back.

Where was K? That was the only thing that mattered. She looked up at the sky, which had entered a blue period. A suffocating sense of impatience made her clench her teeth and roll her eyes. It seemed she had to live through all the emotional clichés. Had K had an accident? Nothing was impossible. Whatever had happened to him, she could do nothing, know nothing.

Stumbling at speed with one shoe on and the other in her hand, Claudia made her way to her bedroom where she got out her viola.

The tractor was near her window when she began to play. Its ugly roar came straight through to her, infuriating and galvanising. She wielded her bow with none of her usual sensitivity. She just wanted to make her own noise, as loud and intemperate as possible. Eventually, she flung the instrument on to the bed and covered her ears with her fists. Everything was spoilt. Everything. Like a much smaller child, she abandoned herself to the bed, narrowly avoiding the viola, and began to kick and hammer hysterically. This behaviour was so out of character that she could only sustain it for a short time, but long enough to frighten herself. She had been near to losing control like unhinged girls who cut themselves to release the pressure in their heads. There'd been one at school. She had never understood that sort of behaviour before but suddenly she did. She could have broken her precious viola without even noticing.

Claudia sat up shakily, and then with extra care, returned her viola to its case. It had been a ridiculous tantrum, that was all. If she went downstairs, she might easily find that K had arrived.

K was driving Fiona home from the hospital very carefully. He applied only the gentlest pressure to the brake and never exceeded forty miles an hour. He felt that they were both at an equally low point. They were both denied their greatest desire: she couldn't have a baby, he couldn't have Claudia. Since Fiona was showing no wish for conversation, he had time to meditate on this a little more. Of course, he'd had all night to think about it, but it seemed different with her sitting so close to him, in his protective care, as he had so often, although for less straightforward reasons, been in hers. During the dark hours, Claudia had been most vivid to him, his passion flaring so high that he had been tempted to get out of bed and find her in that large, empty house. He wasn't even clear what had held him back – they were both alone, which they might never be again. He was worried, perhaps, about frightening her. In the brightness of morning – the sun shone, cancelled out intermittently by squally showers – he was strongly aware of his fifteen years' partnership with Fiona that could never be disowned or discarded. In fact, the only mitigation to his one hundred per cent unhappiness was the sense that, at this precise moment, he was behaving well. Fiona needed him more than Claudia did. There would be time, he tried to console himself, to put things right with Claudia. They loved each other, that was what mattered. With this strange combination of good behaviour and selfish romanticism, K didn't consider contacting Claudia.

At nine thirty in the evening Catherine and Douglas arrived back at Meadowlands. Claudia was deeply relieved to hear the car and ran downstairs to greet them. She wanted to be a child again and obliterate the terrible day. She'd forgotten that Bella was supposed to be keeping her company and was surprised therefore by her mother's question: 'Bella gone already?'

'Yes,' she lied easily. It seemed so unimportant. She did notice, however, that despite the long journey her parents seemed more relaxed than usual, Douglas giving her an unclouded smile. Perhaps it was their suntans, she thought, without much interest.

'I've been playing a lot.' She returned his smile, although hers felt more like a rictus. She and Catherine hugged.

'Tea and bed,' said Catherine.

'I'm so glad you're back.' Claudia hugged her again, surprising both of them.

CHAPTER TWENTY-NINE

1990

A whole day passed without Fiona mentioning the doctor's advice. She informed K that she wouldn't be going to work that week, then reverted to her usual practical self, as if they were on an extended weekend. Although she allowed K to do the shopping, she cooked as usual, and when K dared to ask how she was, she answered, 'Fine,' briskly.

On Wednesday morning, she got out of bed, admittedly a little later than usual, and, over toast and tea, said to K quite casually, 'Just because I'm staying at home, it doesn't mean you have to. Don't writers lose touch with their books if they leave them alone too long?'

K put down his mug carefully. He'd believed that his life was to be with Fiona. She was ill – even if not apparently so – a huge, unresolved dilemma was facing them, and here she was, trying to pack him off to work like a schoolboy. It made a mockery of his self-sacrifice. 'Fiona, we have to discuss things.'

She looked at her plate. K couldn't read her expression. Maybe he'd never tried before. 'Yes, we do. But you might as well know that I've made up my mind.'

K thought about this. Presumably she meant that she would refuse the operation in order to try for a baby. In which case, she needed his co-operation. Of course she couldn't know about his sacrifice but, even so, her approach seemed graceless to say the least.

'I assume you're not planning on AID.' He heard the angry bitterness in his voice. Fiona must have too, but she didn't look up, or respond in any way. 'What I mean is,' he tried to sound gentler in accordance with yesterday's resolutions, 'that I presume I have a place in your plans and therefore we need to discuss things.'

'Yes. Yes.' At last she looked up and K saw the tears in her eyes. 'I'm sorry. I'm upset. I wanted you to understand how strongly I feel. That was all. Of course it's your baby I want. Not just any baby. I love you so much. I thought you knew that. It was selfish...'

'Oh, Fiona!' K's surge of pity and affection took him to her side. This was the scenario for which he had schooled himself. Now he had his place back again. 'You're the least selfish person in the world. I'm the selfish one. But I *am* worried for you. We do need to discuss it calmly. It's still so new ... Look, I won't go in today. The book can wait another day or two. I'll stay here with you until we've worked things out.'

As K said this, his arms round Fiona's bowed shoulders, he felt a lightness in himself, more pronounced than his sense of virtue the day before. If he could give up Claudia, the person he loved most in the world, surely he deserved this little recompense.

So keen was Claudia to become a child again that on Wednesday, over lunch, she was tempted to tell her mother everything: her love for K, their time together, the possibility that she was pregnant. Douglas had returned to work so mother and daughter sat together in the kitchen. The weather had changed; an autumnal cool wasn't even dispelled by the brightest sun. Today it was dull anyway.

'You look sad, darling.' Catherine's voice was tender.

It was almost too much for Claudia. 'It's nothing. I'm fine. Honestly.'

'It's school, I suppose. Such a long term. At least you have your music. Your father and I feel guilty that we haven't taken it seriously enough. We wondered if you'd like your last night at the Proms. Yours, not theirs, that is.' She laughed.

Claudia was touched but at the same time she couldn't help noting the irony that her parents had chosen to recognise her music just when her passions had taken a new, even more overwhelming direction. 'That would be nice,' she said. By Friday, surely something would have happened. K would have reappeared or got in touch with an explanation. This pregnancy business would have been decided one way or the other.

'Are you going to town later?'

'I need to do some shopping.'

'Can I come?'

'Of course, darling. Oh, Claudie, do you wish you hadn't been almost an only child?'

But Claudia couldn't start on this. 'I like being alone,' she said. 'What time are we leaving?'

'I know you've never wanted a child as much as I have.'

So, the discussion moment had arrived. It was supper-time. Fiona and K sat at either side of the kitchen table. While Fiona rested, K had spent the afternoon alternately reading the newspaper and wrestling with his longing to go to Claudia at Meadowlands. At three o'clock he had got into his car and started in her direction but, half-way there, he'd seen as if an apparition from his heated imagination, Claudia and her mother driving towards him.

The sight made him tremble so much that he had had to pull over and wait for five minutes before he returned home when he resorted, thoroughly unnerved, to his newspaper. At five o'clock, he took a cup of tea to Fiona and felt his resolve strengthened by her sweetness. 'I won't be like this for long.' She stroked his hand. 'It's the shock, I suppose. I'm fine, really.'

'Of course you are.' K went downstairs and reminded himself that every moment he was away from Claudia increased his strength to stay away for another. And yet if he were truly honest he would have admitted that this was still partly a game because he couldn't conceive of never seeing Claudia again. His behaviour was for *now*. Who could tell how the stars would dance in the firmament, altering his fate?

'If you've finished eating, let's go next door.' K couldn't sit so close to Fiona's pale face and dark, understanding eyes. The sitting room was not much larger than the kitchen but it gave him a lit-tle more space for disguise. 'You can put your feet up.' It was all lying now. He wondered whether that was always the case with good behaviour. They'd called it 'hypocrisy' in the sixties, fought the good fight so that his generation could be 'free'.

'I don't need to put my feet up.' Fiona walked ahead of him. Her posture was good, straight and true, unlike his mother who had been hunched long before osteoporosis had got her. He'd assumed it was a stance she had adopted to protect herself against his father's drunken belligerence.

Fiona sat on a chair and K took the small sofa beside it. 'I do believe you'd love a child as much as I will once he or she's here. Men are often like that. If I didn't think so, I'd never have tried for a baby.'

'I've never stopped you,' pointed out K. Her face was so serious that he didn't dare add, perhaps boastfully, that he'd always successfully answered her call for sex. 'But now we're talking about your health.'

'My health is my business.'

'Not exactly.' K paused. How cruel was a loving husband in this situation? What would earn Mr Blick's approval? 'If you have a baby, get cancer and die, the baby will be my responsibility.' He noticed that Fiona seemed to be looking at him with astonishment. And yet surely this was what they must discuss: life, death, the future. 'I'm sorry to sound so harsh but it's the reality.'

'Yes. Yes.' She was still gaping at him. Was it possible she had not fully understood her position or had she read something in his face that made her afraid? There was fear as well as surprise in her expression.

'We have to think it through. Doctors don't advise hysterectomies without good reason.'

'But they can.' She was trying to control her feelings and marshal an argument. It was painful to watch and K looked away. The evenings were getting dark quite early now. It depressed him as if it marked too much time passing and a dreary future. Just for a second he allowed himself to picture Claudia as she'd lain by the swimming-pool in her bikini. Even that second, really no more than a particle of a second, flooded him with excitement. He was glad Fiona wasn't paying him attention.

'You think I'm being irrational,' she said.

'I think you're the most rational woman I know.'

'Not about this. You think my need is unbalanced and is about putting right my childhood. Yet it's well known that doctors like doing hysterectomies. It's the easiest way of dealing with any problems, even at the "potential" stage. You heard him say that I haven't got cancer, that I might never get it.'

'I'm not sure he said exactly that.' Suddenly this discussion didn't seem such a good idea after all. 'I'm not trying to persuade you either way. You know that.'

'No.' He could see she wasn't convinced. Perhaps a loving husband would try to persuade her.

'Would you hate being left with our baby?'

'What an extraordinary question!' He was truly shocked.

'You raised it.' She was quite right. But when he'd said it, it hadn't sounded so bad.

'This is horrible.'

'I know.' Fiona began to cry.

Which ended the discussion to the relief of both of them.

Fiona went up for a bath and K watched the news, wondering how other people managed to make world affairs important in their lives. It shamed him to think how self-centred his was, and yet at the moment he was more trapped in his personal affairs than ever before. With his book at a standstill, he was about as worthless a human being as it was possible to be, short of someone who had committed a crime. Two things sustained him: his love for Claudia and his sense of doing right by Fiona. It was unfortunate that they were in contradiction.

Nevertheless he *was* sustained, and by the time the weather woman (in cheery red) had confirmed the unsettled lows and highs, isobars and isotherms, he could hardly qualify his unhappiness as deep suffering. There was comfort in domestic routine, in pressing the button to switch off the television, in checking the doors, in hearing Fiona pad across from bathroom to kitchen, in remembering to take her a drink.

'I had an idea in my bath.' Fiona sat up in bed, hair still swept back in a clip. She looked very young. 'Why don't we take the rest of the week and go and do that coastal walk you've often talked about? Stay in pubs like you used to in the early good days with your father.'

At once K's relative tranquillity was blown apart. He admitted finally that he hadn't given up hope of seeing Claudia before she returned to school.

'The weather forecast was pretty dire.' It was an unconvincing mumble. 'And are you really strong enough?' He knew they would go. This was the way the stars had danced about the firmament.

*

Claudia was desperate to speak to someone. On Wednesday she had managed to buy a pregnancy-testing kit without Catherine knowing. But being hopeless and ham-fisted, she had messed up the procedure and was no nearer knowing whether or not she were pregnant. She tried to psych herself up to ring Bella. Still, she didn't consider trying to contact K. She had schooled herself to disbelieve in his life outside their meetings, a life that, of course, contained his wife. Despite her misery and bewilderment at his absence, she could not call on him for help. It was the unwritten code of their love affair. Bella would have to take his place. But when she finally telephoned on Thursday afternoon, while Catherine was out, Bella was in London with a friend. Another long afternoon passed. She was supposed to be preparing her things for school but found herself incapable of doing anything. By now she didn't know whether it was K's unexplained absence or her possible pregnancy that distressed her most.

At supper-time her inwardly catatonic state – outwardly she appeared little different from normal – was broken by her father asking Catherine quite casually, 'So, has our writer-in-residence given back the keys?'

'Heavens! You're quite right. I've been so busy I hadn't taken it in properly. I don't think he's been here at all. Did he say anything to you, Claudie?'

Both parents looked at their daughter.

As she didn't answer immediately, Douglas added, with unusual good humour, 'Don't tell me he's pinched the silver and run.'

Claudia had time to recover. K had been with her on Monday, the happiest day of her life, and that was only three days ago. It felt an age but it was only three days. She cleared her throat. 'He was here on Monday.'

'But did he say anything?'

'Not to me.'

'How odd. Well, the simplest thing is to give him a ring. Perhaps he's ill.'

'And I'll check the silver.' Douglas laughed heartily, and Claudia saw that he had never liked K. Or his idea of K. It struck her, too, that she had been a fool not to have pointed out K's absence to her mother earlier. Now she might learn something.

Catherine made the call in the hallway, an old-fashioned and public situation for the telephone favoured by Douglas because no one would be tempted to enjoy an expensively long conversation. Claudia stationed herself in the drawing room with the door open. She was extremely nervous and sat on the sofa with her legs tucked so far under her that it seemed a kind of self-torture although, since her hands were pressed tightly together, perhaps it was more of a prayer.

After a few moments' silence, Catherine looked round the door. 'No reply, not even the answering-machine. They must have gone away. Very strange. I would have thought at least Fiona would let me know.'

'Yes,' murmured Claudia, as her mother seemed to need a response. Gone away? Her mind was incapable of dealing with the idea. Could this 'going away' have something to do with her?

'Of course, I don't really know much about them.' Catherine came into the room and sat next to her daughter. 'I met Fiona at that charity thing and when she mentioned that her husband was looking for a place to write, it seemed perfect. Well, it has been perfect all summer. No trouble at all.'

'No,' said Claudia. She felt as if various parts of her body had swollen as if she'd swallowed an *Alice in Wonderland* potion: her eyes felt like golfballs, just about ready to pop out of her head. 'I'm going to bed.' She managed to stand up, although her legs seemed inordinately stretched.

'Good idea. And tomorrow we'll go through your trunk. I don't believe you've unpacked half your stuff all holiday.'

As Claudia went upstairs she knew she couldn't go back to school on Saturday. She remembered, as if about another person, that she'd looked forward to these last two years, with time to concentrate on music and English. But there was no way she could leave Meadowlands without seeing K. She would have felt the same even without the pregnancy business – which still hovered on the edge of reality. For the first time, she considered the possibility of contacting K – a letter, perhaps, nothing dramatic. She sat down on her bed. This was where they'd made love. She pulled back the covers and curled into the sheets, holding herself with her arms. She was sure it wasn't over.

'And don't forget the Proms tomorrow,' called Catherine, from the bottom of the stairs. 'Brahms, Beethoven and Rattle. We had to pay a fortune for black-market tickets.'

CHAPTER THIRTY

2004

The men came early to take down the marquee. I had finally got to sleep at dawn and now stared blearily as the white wall was removed from my bedroom window. Curious, I got out of bed and watched four men dismantle the future that had been planned for me. Cheerful and disciplined, they detached canvas sheets, until the skeleton was laid bare. Everything was orderly, the poles laid in alignment on the ground, the iron bolts and screws piled ready to be loaded on to a hand truck. Last, they would roll up the flooring.

Not waiting any longer, I grabbed a bathrobe and went out of a side door to the swimming-pool. I suppose I wanted to see some evidence of my nocturnal visitor and at first there seemed to be nothing. Then I went into the changing-hut and at once saw the kitchen knife lying on the floor. How would I have explained that to my mother? And why had I taken it with me anyway? It was absurd, laughable. I bent to pick it up and, instead of laughing, began to cry. It was the tension, I told myself, and ran the knife's edge along the back of my hand. K had big hands, big, gentle hands, but last night I thought they had seemed thinner, the fingers aetiolated.

I half hid the knife under my arm and walked back to the house. I could have swum, as he had, but it was a dull white day and the water, left uncovered, would be cold.

All the time I could hear vaguely the clang of iron poles and men's shouts. Then I saw that the light in my father's bedroom was still on. My mother must have received the men, then gone back to her room for she was nowhere to be seen. I should switch it off and close the wardrobe door, which I had almost certainly left open. But the memory of my night raid jogged another memory and I hurried round to the dustbins. Suddenly I was terrified they had been emptied earlier that morning.

I laid the knife on the ground and lifted off the dustbin lid. I needed those clothes and, to my relief, they were still there, a dank cluster of trousers, shirt, socks and my sweater.

Frenziedly – my mother might appear at any moment – I took them to the kitchen sink and poured washing-up liquid over them. I relaxed a little. I returned the knife to a drawer, and now I could pretend that these were my own clothes. Sluicing water continuously, I began to swirl them around. The shirt was white and elegant, a dress shirt with proper turn-back cuffs and holes for cuff-links, although there were none. He couldn't have been wearing any. The trousers were heavy. It was amazing that he'd been able to swim in them. There was something silky down the sides, a stripe. They were dress trousers. He had kitted himself out to come to my wedding.

How unnerving to think that, if my father hadn't died, he would have watched me walk up the aisle to be joined to Oliver till death do us part. It was a scenario that seemed to come from another world.

I had squeezed out my sweater, his shirt and trousers and laid them on the draining-board when my mother appeared. She was dressed, but seemed dazed, hardly awake. 'Ah, washing.'

'Yes.' I pushed the clothes together.

'The men have come. I should get them coffee.' She brushed her thick hair off her face. 'I don't know how I'll get through this week.'

I felt sorry for her. Obviously she could hardly have James around when friends and relatives gathered for the funeral. 'Louise will be here soon,' I said. Louise, although so seldom with us, had a reputation for good sense and strength. 'I'll meet her at the station,' I added. 'Just let me dress and I'll make the men coffee.'

'They're so quick.'

She seemed to be complaining. It was her exhaustion, I thought, that was making other people's energy so abrasive. I remembered the feeling well.

She sat down. 'Did you go into Douglas's bedroom? The light was on.'

I thought of lying but I could see it hardly mattered to her. 'Yes,' I admitted, without enlarging.

'I took two sleeping pills at midnight. Then the men woke me with their lorry. I feel terrible.'

I put my arm round her. 'It'll be all right,' I said, not lying. It would be all right for her. She had a future to look forward to.

'Yes. Once we get rid of this house. I hate it.' She had found enough energy to sound fierce.

I didn't respond. I, too, had been looking forward to the house going, or so I'd assumed, the end of an era and the opportunity for a fresh start, but since last night it had come to seem an important link with the past. After all, K had come here to find me. We'd been happy here.

I lifted the heavy kettle on to the Aga.

Louise had always seemed more than ten years older than me. Now she seemed older than my mother. Once fair and willowy, she was now quite stocky and her hair had darkened enough that she seemed to be carrying our father's genes. I took her bag from her as she came out of the station. It was small, of course. She was good at all things organisational. She was also kind and conscientious. 'I'm so sorry you've had to bear everything.'

'How's poor Reggie?' I asked.

'Better, or I wouldn't have come.'

'You must be exhausted.'

'Nineteen and a half hours, door to door. What day is the funeral?'

By now we were in my car. I thought, quite sadly as I always did when I saw her, that we were strangers, despite all our efforts. We had our mother's welfare in common, though. I wondered if she knew about James. Probably not.

I drove slowly. Despite our strangeness, it was comforting to have her there. I had never been good at making friends and, after that summer, it was impossible. Bella might have played a role in my life, but she emigrated to Australia. She didn't even stay for university. Her parents were very cut up, so Catherine informed me. Maybe they believed that my unfortunate story had contributed to Bella leaving. She never contacted me after I returned, roughly speaking, to the world of the living.

'How's Oliver taking everything?' Although I was driving, looking straight ahead, I could sense she was staring at me. It occurred to me that she had never truly believed in my marriage plan.

'He's OK about it. We'll get married later, quietly.'

'Is he coming to the funeral?'

'Of course.' She was testing. 'He got on with Douglas – while he was still compos.'

'It's funny the way you call our parents by their Christian names.'

'Catherine encouraged it. I suppose she wanted to feel like something more than "Mummy". Daddy was never keen. Perhaps she did it to irritate him.'

'They were very different. Sometimes I wonder why they married.'

'I know.' I still didn't tell her about James. Louise, it seemed, really had achieved a successful marriage. Tom, who was clever and charming, adored her and she treated him with the same caring tenderness as she did their three children. Perhaps I would visit them in Hong Kong and take lessons in happiness.

'How do you do it?' I asked impulsively.

'Whatever do you mean?'

'Run your life – live it so well.' I stumbled over appropriate words.

Louise laughed. 'Thank you, darling. It doesn't always feel like that. Yesterday, for example, when I was up at five and the helper didn't turn up and Reggie was refusing to take his pills, the older two had a row and Tom told me I was going to make him late for his breakfast meeting.'

Louise grimaced but I thought that was all part of running a life well. I did get satisfaction from my job with the opening of some project we'd backed – perhaps a community-based brick-making centre or a women's self-help medical centre. But it was not personal happiness.

'You had such an unfortunate start.' Louise stretched out her hand to pat my knee.

It was supposed to be a kind remark but, of course, the exact opposite was true: those summer days with K had been too *good* a start. Even if I could get over the tragedy that had followed, nothing would ever live up to the intensity of our time together, short as it was. 'Poor Oliver.'

'Why poor Oliver?'

I hadn't meant to speak aloud. 'Oh, a million reasons.' But the one I'd meant was that I could never love him. Once I'd even told him so, baldly, but he'd stroked my shoulder – we were in bed after making love – and said that there were many kinds of love and sometimes we didn't know our own feelings. Most probably, Oliver's first love is medicine, the capability to cure. Maybe I shouldn't be sorry for him.

I allowed myself to remember that K was out there somewhere, perhaps not very far away. I shivered. But he had said he was leaving immediately. Perhaps he was already far away. His clothes, however, were now dry and neatly folded in my chest of drawers.

'Sad to think it's the last time I'll see Meadowlands.'

I was irritated by Louise's sentimentality as we approached the house. 'Catherine's counting the days.'

'I suppose you are too?'

'Oh, yes!' My eagerness sounded remarkably convincing.

Skulking back to the Fresh Ponds Hotel in Douglas Lacey's clothes had not been my finest hour. I tried to take a short-cut, got lost and extended the walk considerably. By the time I arrived it was getting light. The hotel was still locked but a sleepy girl let me in after I'd rung several times. I was about to request a cup of tea when I remembered the kettle in my room and hurried upstairs.

The tea, gulped as I sat on the edge of the bed, helped me review the evening and night's events.

I had met Claudia! This was the most important reality. Later I would think of what had happened to my body. We had talked. Well, exchanged a few words. I must assume, therefore, that I had achieved my aim in coming to England. Indeed, I had told her that I would now be returning to Chile. I'd spoken a little of Valparaiso, lovingly, as if it were my home. Which it is. She'd repeated its name with apparent understanding. So this was it, mission accomplished. I'd seen her. I'd recognised the existence of a man called Oliver who, but for an odd chance, would already have been her husband. I'd apologised. More than once. I had been abject, prostrate, ridiculous. My role in her life story was over, done, finished.

I put the empty cup on the floor and went to the tawdry bit of furniture that pretended to be a dressing-table. This was not the sort of smart hotel that provided writing-paper but I went through the drawers all the same. Eventually I was rewarded with a postcard. But my message was only for one person's eyes. I needed an envelope. Impatient, I rang the front desk. It was still too early.

I must wait. Try to sleep for an hour or two. This was my last chance to get things right.

Louise brought me the envelope. It was extraordinary but I had never seen his handwriting before. Yet I recognised it at once. The word 'Claudia', sharp-angled on the white envelope, was like his physical presence. I imagined his mouth pressed to the paper.

I resisted the temptation to snatch it and run. 'Must be a note of condolence,' I said brightly.

'Someone dropped it through the letterbox.' Louise was casual enough. 'I opened the door but whoever it was had vanished.'

'Thanks.'

I took the letter out to the garden but didn't open it immediately. I walked around with it for half an hour, then I decided not read it till after my father's funeral. It was right to pay Douglas proper respect. His funeral was on Friday. I was accustomed to waiting. Fourteen years plus four days. I understood waiting.

Once I'd written the letter and dropped it through the letterbox, I felt much calmer. At least, after I'd scuttled away through the shrubbery I did. A woman, probably Claudia's sister from her looks, had opened the door so quickly that I was nearly caught.

I had already checked out of the hotel so now it was a question of heading back to London, dealing with a few financial affairs, including putting the flat on the market. I would also go to a hospital and pay for a check-up. But nothing would stop me setting off at the first opportunity for Chile. This time certainly for good.

I was calmer because I'd written to Claudia what I'd wanted to say. She would read it and the thought of her reading calmed me. It wasn't my last will and testament but it was the last word I would ever say about that summer.

CHAPTER THIRTY-ONE

1990

Walking was something K and Fiona used to do well together. It was an area in which he knew more than she did. She was a city person, but he could tell her the history of the pathways they followed, about villages or pubs, highwaymen and smugglers, the names and habits of birds, the right places to look for a rare wild orchid. Before they'd married, Fiona had once asked him why he hadn't trained as a naturalist. That was when he'd told her about his father. Too much love and sadness were entangled there to make it the stuff of his day-to-day life.

They drove to Lyme Regis, arriving on Thursday morning. Their plan was to leave the car and set out at once along the coastal path via Charmouth, West Bexington, Abbotsbury and Studland, then return by bus on Sunday and drive home. The weather had become autumnal, cool gusts blowing from the sea and flanking up the cliffs. At first they were at sea level, clambering over rocks, slippery with seaweed, wading through shifting shingle and occasionally joining smooth stretches of sand.

K had picked up a tide timetable and knew that, fairly soon, the rising water would force them up to the cliffs but he put it off for as long as possible, revelling in the salty smells, the feeling of having entered the domain of the sea. As Fiona lagged behind, he could imagine himself alone and think about Claudia, or even imagine that she was following him. With the swirling wind in his face and his feet on the shifting seabed, it was easy to forget reality and enter a dreamer's fancy.

Fiona was not so content. The early miscarriage could not have weakened her physically, she told herself. The walk had been her idea. But the pressure of the last days and the knowledge that she could still hardly bear to face, that her womb was diseased, painted with a doctor's black cross for removal, preyed on her mind. She wished she could walk beside K, hold his hand and gain strength from his vitality. But the terrain made that mostly impossible and, besides, there was something unapproachable about his back view, the spring in his stride, the jaunty posture of his head above the furled hood of his anorak.

Fiona slowed: the rocks seemed more unstable, the sea, moving ever closer, threatening rather than exhilarating. Eventually she stopped altogether. She stood, lips compressed, gazing at the presently greenish-black sea that turned paler at the edges or yellowish where it crossed sand. She put her hands together in an unconscious attitude of prayer.

It was several minutes before K turned. Fiona had become a small, doleful figure at the edge of the sea. For a second he was filled with fierce rage. Her small loneliness felt like blackmail, the worst sort because unacknowledged. Was he not giving her himself every minute of the day? Had she not demanded this outing? What right did she have to take up a reproachful pose? K took a step towards her and recognised that the viciousness of his feelings stemmed entirely from his own guilt. Fiona had no idea of his suffering, of what he was giving up for her. His pace quickened. As if he could be himself from the outside, he tried to judge how he appeared to her. He must be affectionate and concerned, not dutiful.

'Aren't you feeling too good?' He had done it successfully. His voice was natural. He smiled and put his arm round her. And now, as a reward for the effort he'd made, his anger was replaced by loving kindness. He knew he could never imagine the depth of her unhappiness.

'I'm just pausing.'

'We'll need to get off the beach at the next track up or we'll be swimming to Charmouth.' He even laughed.

'Yes. Perhaps I'm nervous. Let's go up as soon as we can.'

They both knew this wasn't the problem, but it gave them roles, the fearful and the comforter.

'We'll have our picnic at the top. You may be hungry too.'

'Yes. That could be it.'

From this point on, K tried to be more attentive to her. The coastal path was too narrow for them to walk side by side, but he stopped to help her over tricky patches, where the path crumbled into a cliff-edge of disguising brambles, or on the steepest slopes where stones rolled from under their feet.

'This is too much for you,' he said, at one point.

'No. It takes my mind off things.'

They ate their picnic by a stile, which gave Fiona a seat and K something to lean against. K drank a beer and looked out to sea. There were a few small boats following the line of the coast. He thought they must be holidaymakers because the fishermen would be long home, and he wondered if life would ever again be as simple as the word 'holidaymaker'. But he reminded himself that self-pity was the greatest and most destructive form of self-indulgence. His mother had never felt self-pity and, in her own way, she'd survived.

'On we go?'

'Yes, sir.' Fiona smiled at him. Together they packed away the picnic in his rucksack – neither of them had eaten much – climbed the stile and resumed walking. K was leading again and, as the track was very close to the cliff edge, he went slowly and carefully.

It had just begun to spatter with rain when they reached a barrier. They saw that, some metres on, the path had disappeared to the beach below. Gulls swirled round the spot as if marking the dislocation.

Fiona shivered. 'I wonder when it happened.'

'These falls always happen at night. It's a bore, though. We'll have to go inland.'

But Fiona continued to stare, her face pale and pinched. A portion of cliff about fifty metres long had fallen, like a bite out of a sandwich, spat out on to the shingle below. The sea was coming in strongly now, churning round the rocks. Among them tufts of grass were visible, disconcerting, almost sinister because out of place. The seagulls were noisy, although far below them.

'Just imagine if you'd been walking and the ground dissolved under your feet.'

'No thank you.' K took her arm.

'A friend once said to me that living in this world is like walking on the crust of a volcano.'

'What sort of friend was that?' The rain was falling harder. He could see it stabbing at the sea below. This new fearful Fiona unnerved him enough to try to avoid taking her seriously. He wondered whether to suggest that her sensitivity was due to the miscarriage, but remembered the awful decision-making that still lay ahead and felt it kinder not to. It was odd, nevertheless, that her character should seem so changed.

At last Fiona turned away and they climbed another stile into a field behind them. But her mood remained. 'My friend meant that we mustn't be surprised by tragedy and disaster. We must be aware and learn to live with it.'

'I don't see how that helps.' He thought, however, that she was telling him nothing he hadn't known since boyhood. The thing was that she had made herself his ladder over the abyss.

'I don't know.'

They were walking together across a wide field, with surprisingly long green grass for the time of year, which was dispersing wet drops above their walking-boots.

'I'd better look at my map. Maybe we should stop before Charmouth.'

'You've always loved maps, haven't you?' Fiona watched as K pulled it out.

'We men like to know where we are and even where we're going whenever possible.' K said this before he realised how untrue this had become in the weeks since he'd met Claudia. His happiness had made him fearless. It was when he was with Fiona that he needed a map.

'There was a small pub with a couple of rooms on this road here.' He pointed at the place. 'It's two or three hours' walking instead of five or six. In fact, with this diversion, I've no idea how long it will take to get to Charmouth.'

'The pub sounds good to me.' She didn't sound particularly interested either way.

By the time they reached the pub, plodding the last three-quarters of a mile along a surprisingly busy road, they were both soaking, despite their anoraks and hoods. They hadn't talked for some time. Over the last ten years, they'd hardly taken any serious walks, too busy or too tired. A couple of hours over the weekend was about all they had managed so their exhaustion was unsurprising.

'Let's hope they have hot water.' Fiona pushed her hood back.

'Surely everyone does now.' K thought of similar arrivals with his father. Sometimes there hadn't been hot water, and after a quick wash in the basin, they'd gone down to the bar for his father's beer and his orange squash.

The room they entered was dark, but thankfully warm, and empty. K pressed a bell on the counter and a large man, with the bright blue eyes K remembered from this part of the world, came out. His shirt-sleeves were rolled up to display an intricate tattoo of a schooner. 'We're not serving yet,' he offered, in a not unfriendly voice.

K explained they wanted a room and was immediately shown upstairs to a square room with two single beds and nothing much else. It was spotlessly clean and overlooked a backyard and a rather unkempt garden leading directly into a field.

'Perfect,' said Fiona.

'The bathroom's along the corridor.'

The moment their host had gone, Fiona took off her jacket, boots, wet socks and trousers, and got into bed under the coverlet.

'I thought you wanted a bath?'

'Not yet. I need to rest.'

'You'll make the pillow wet.'

'It'll dry. You go downstairs.'

'Shall I draw the curtains?'

Fiona had already shut her eyes and made no answer, so K drew them anyway and, after changing out of his own wet clothes as quietly as he could, went down to the bar. It was impossible to avoid a sense of release.

'What'll it be?'

There were already three or four people drinking. Obviously regulars, they exchanged comments in a comfortable way. K glanced at his watch and was surprised to see it was still only six. 'I'll have a double whisky.'

'Quickest way to get rid of the aches.'

Clearly the barman knew they were walkers. K took a sip of the whisky and felt an immediate glow of satisfaction. 'We're out of practice.'

'Coming from Lyme, were you?' An older man in a bulky green sweater had joined in.

'Yes. We might have got to Charmouth without that cliff fall.'

'Had a few come in because of that. Shocking, it was.' There were various noddings and sounds of agreement.

'When did it happen?' K didn't really want to know but Fiona's gloomy words had stayed with him, making him curious.

'Weeks past. But then, under the circumstances, they'd be sure to let time pass before they sort it out.'

K became aware that all the faces round him had now changed from comfortable to grim. He was spared asking, 'What circumstances?' by the barman leaning closer and saying, in a voice hardly above a whisper, 'He always walked there with his dog, day in, day out, and that day he didn't come back. The dog survived, though, tumbling all the way down too and still barking fit to bust when they found him.'

'A miracle, the papers called it.' The green-sweatered man had used his normal voice. It seemed that they had moved seamlessly from the tragedy of a man's sudden death to the wonders of a dog's survival.

'He must have ridden the earth and stones like a slide. On top all the way.'

As the conversation moved on to more animal survival stories – a terrier recently had tumbled into the sea and swum four miles before being rescued – K decided he wouldn't tell Fiona what he'd learnt. A man had been carried to his death on the path he had walked on confidently, 'day in, day out', as they'd said. It would only confirm her crust-of-the-volcano theory. His job, he reminded himself, was to keep her happy and stable.

K and Fiona lay in their twin beds under flower-patterned duvets. It was only when K put his head on the pillow that he took in how drunk he was. They'd eaten sausages and chips in a side room and K had gone on from what had become two double whiskies (which Fiona didn't know about) to several pints of beer. It was good strong ale, brewed locally, the owner had said. It was the sort of beer his father had searched for and usually found. As K lay awake, heart pounding too fast, head swollen and hot, he recalled, with dread, that this pub had been the scene of one of his father's worst drunken excesses. It had finished with him being thrown out into the night, everybody having forgotten, including his father – particularly him

– that a ten-year-old boy was hanging around somewhere. Of course he'd overheard everything in an agony of shame and anxiety. All night he'd hidden behind some barrels in the yard and when it was light he'd gone to the front of the pub and waited for his father, who had duly turned up and taken him off for a big breakfast in a café, more a stall, really, that he'd found further down the road. Presumably he'd spent the night there too.

Restlessly, K turned from side to side. Whatever had made him come to this of all pubs? And then to drink himself into such a state that he couldn't sleep and would have a rotten hangover the next day.

'I'm sorry, darling, about all this.' Fiona's voice was so clear that K guessed she hadn't been asleep either.

'What do you mean?'

'Dragging you away from your book. The baby or rather the non-baby. My ill-health.'

As she spoke, in matter-of-fact tones, K was overwhelmed by pity. It caught him unawares, making him shiver with emotion. He jumped out of bed and pushed himself in with her, cradling her closely in the narrow space. 'You mustn't be sorry. It's not your fault. I'm your husband. I'd do anything for you.'

In a small part of his brain he knew that this fever of kindness, this declaration of caring, was fuelled by alcohol, coupled with unhappy memories of his father, but he held her lovingly all the same, and if his words were a little slurred, his spirit was firm. 'I'll never let you down, my darling. You've done far more for me than I can ever repay. Without you, I'd be sunk, washed up, not worth anything, nothing.'

He murmured this in her ear and more, believing every word, as far from the man who had told Claudia he loved her as it was possible to be.

Fiona had begun to cry softly. She wore pyjamas and the silky material was cool to K's touch. He promised her other things, eternal love, gratitude, as many babies as she wanted. He told her, with tears in his own eyes, that she had saved him from his father's fate and his mother's and, as he talked about his parents, his speech became muddled and almost incoherent so Fiona stopped crying and stroked his face. Still clinging to her, he fell into a heavy sleep.

*

The following morning K woke early with a colossal headache and was disconcerted to see that he and Fiona had swapped beds. Then he remembered that he had gone to her but what he'd said had vanished, apart from an idea that it had been full of untrammelled emotion. She was still quietly asleep in what had been his bed originally. She must have left him during the night.

K got up, went to the window, and drew back the curtains a little. It was a glorious day. The sun slanted from the left, lighting up the dew on the grass and the tall yellow daisies in a ragged bed, which were just starting to open. Below, a tangle of Michaelmas daisies fell across jagged roses whose blooms were turning to red hips. As he watched, two robins began a fight above the fruit, whirling round and round like tiny feathered dervishes.

K smiled to himself and said aloud, 'If you haven't sorted out your territory by now, it's far too late.' At his voice, or perhaps he'd flapped the curtain, both birds whisked away. K watched still and saw the shadow from an old apple tree at the end of the garden darken as the sun rose and brightened. Despite the continued pain in his head, he felt surprisingly full of optimism. He pictured Claudia listening to poetry under the chestnut trees, Claudia lying by the pool when the sun had been so hot, Claudia playing her viola on the lawn, Claudia naked in his arms. She would wait for him.

Careful not to wake Fiona, he dressed and went downstairs. There was no sign of anyone so he got himself a pint of water from the bar and went out into the cool sunshine. There were a few tables in front of the pub, which was well set back from the road. Anyway, only an occasional car passed. On the other side of the road, the land swept up to a steep, grassy bank, which carried on to the horizon. It was soothing to K's eye and to his head.

An hour or so later Fiona found him there. She kissed him fondly. 'They're serving breakfast – same as supper, I think.' She laughed.

K saw that she, too, was starting the day in a happy frame of mind. He was relieved and a little bewildered.

He learnt the reason after they'd been walking for several hours. They were once more on the coastal walk, near the edge of a jutting headland. Below, the sea sucked at the cliff's crumbling edges and he was glad he hadn't told her about the dog-walker's fall. She took a bottle of water from her rucksack and stood drinking and looking out to sea. She turned to him: 'I can never thank you enough for what you said last night. I want you to know it makes all the difference. We don't have to talk more. I shall always remember every word.'

K looked at Fiona's exalted face and wished he could remember as well as her. Whatever he'd said, the change in her was striking. Perhaps it was a good thing he'd forgotten. A vague sense of emotional falsehood began a wormy trail of unease. Was it dangerous for her to base happiness on such shifting sands? But, then, surely this weekend break was all about reassurance so why should he worry if he had succeeded beyond his expectations?

'Onward and upward!' His cheery voice, rather absurd, sailed out over the regurgitating sea.

CHAPTER THIRTY-TWO

1990

Claudia sat between her parents in the Albert Hall. Their seats were on the first tier and fairly far back. It was very hot. She thought that the passion of the music was steaming through the audience, filling them, like a pressure cooker, with emotion. She rubbed her damp hands together and leant further forward so that she could see the orchestra better. They were playing Beethoven's Pastoral, a huge, unified sound but, as usual, her ears strained to hear the first viola. Even though she knew it was impossible, she still imagined the notes, deeper and more resonant than the violins', less throbbing but more intense than the cello's. She hadn't picked up her own viola since the first morning of K's disappearance but now, fortified and inspired in this great hall, she thought she would turn to it again.

In the interval Douglas and Catherine plied themselves with champagne and Claudia with Coca-Cola. They had fought determinedly through the crowds and, with flushed animation, told each other how excited they were by the music. It was touching how pleased they were by their own reaction, Claudia thought, rather patronisingly. But their removal from home to this unknown venue made them more sympathetic to her, as they had seemed in Italy.

Yet the difference between her situation then and now was too ghastly to contemplate. She must encourage the music to ring in her ears and blot out the misery. One thing remained certain: she would not return to school, not tomorrow, not ever. That schoolgirl era was over. Whatever happened now, it was over. The immediate difficulty was that she'd still not informed her parents, who presumed they were taking her for a last-night treat. Claudia was glad when the end of the interval allowed them to join the overheated masses and push back into the hall.

They'd arrived too late to buy a programme but she knew there was a Brahms concerto for violin and cello to come. Catherine had said, 'I know it's not a viola, darling, but it's the next best thing, I suppose.' Claudia had consoled her by explaining that there were very few concertos written for viola. 'It doesn't matter at all,' she'd said, thinking dismally that, just at the moment, it was a ludicrous understatement.

This piece lasted twenty minutes, which seemed an eternity to Claudia. At first concentrating on the music, she soon allowed her thoughts to overwhelm it until the sounds coming from the stage were mere background to an unstoppable anguish. It was now Friday evening. She had not seen K since Monday. For all she knew, he might have left the country. Yet it was still impossible to believe he was doing this to her without good reason. Clinging tenaciously to her faith in his enduring love, she tortured herself with possibilities. Perhaps he was seriously ill, rushed to hospital, even dead.

As the music rose to a crescendo of emotion it penetrated Claudia's obsessional barricade, joining her own floodwater of passion. Tears rolled from her eyes.

It's all too much for me, she thought, doing her best to control her shoulders, which longed to heave and shake. 'I can't go on like this.' And it was then, as the music reached a still plateau, that she decided she must write to K.

At once she was filled with a glorious release of tension. She would write to K, tell him that maybe she was pregnant, and then he would come to her. Her resolution was confirmed and strengthened by the final delicate chords.

CHAPTER THIRTY-THREE

2004

Once I'd read K's letter I felt as if I had only one option. I called Oliver, who'd left for London immediately after my father's funeral, and arranged to meet him in his lunch break. We were always rather formal in our planning, partly because of the constant demands of his job and partly because I liked to guard my privacy.

Two Christmases ago I'd given him membership of the Chelsea Physic Garden. It had seemed an appropriate present for a doctor and it was not far from the hospital where he was a consultant. Yet he went there seldom and it was I who yearned for its healing beds of sweet-smelling herbs, the eucalyptus trees, the shrubs bearing pungent pods or curiously shaped flowers. Maybe his medical *amour-propre* felt threatened by its witch-like properties, now merging with New Age rediscovery. Maybe, considering what I had to say, it was unfair of me to arrange a meeting there. But I wanted to stage-manage it so that the emotion would be limited.

I had bought sandwiches and water from a nearby shop and was leaning against the outside wall when Oliver arrived. He walked quickly, as he did through long hospital corridors, white coat flapping in the time-honoured way. My pleasure in his directness and energy made me doubt my resolve for a second – but only for a second.

I swung my plastic bag at him, calling cheerfully, 'Disgusting ham or revolting cheese?' He was always rather faddish in his eating. Or perhaps I should say sensible. It was wrong of me, too, perhaps, to give him no clue as to the reason for our meeting.

'I've only got half an hour but you said it was urgent.'

'It is.' I fell more sober.

We walked through the little green door, through a hallway, past a conservatory and out into the secret, ordered world of the garden. Behind us the elegant red-brick apartment blocks, typically Chelsea in their steep roofs and decorations, rose above the wall, while in front the sky was blank, apart from the tops of trees marking the route Battersea Park took beside the river. Whenever I entered this garden, which was some distance from my own tiny flat in north London, I felt a contradictory mix of security and excitement.

'Can we sit down?' He looked tired and wanted to eat.

'Let's walk a little longer.' I loved to follow the grassy paths that bisected the four areas of the garden. My favourite was the water garden, where massive bunches of heavy-headed reeds and pungent borage almost overwhelmed the water's gleam.

'Then pass me a sandwich.' He was brusque, not rudely so, but in the way busy people are. Already he'd given a day out of his working week for my father's funeral. I handed him a sandwich. His face was set but not unkind. If my father hadn't died we'd be in Sicily now, on our honeymoon. I pictured us reclining, like any happy lovers, side by side on the beach. It was an unconvincing image.

'Let's visit the greenhouse,' I said. Of course I was trying to delay the moment of telling – how much explanation did I owe him? How much would he demand? – but I loved the greenhouse, with its steamy greenery and unknown tropical plants, one a carnivore whose plump lips closed greedily on unwary flies.

Today the weather was humid and it seemed hotter than ever. From somewhere a cloying scent swirled above the odours of dank vegetation.

'Christ!' exclaimed Oliver. 'They've forgotten the air-con.'

Before he could run out, I seized his arm. 'We can't go on.' It was a pathetic mew. And what was this 'we'? It was I who couldn't go on.

He stared at me, his clever pale eyes assessing the situation. He took my hand off his arm as if to think more clearly. 'A week ago it would have been our wedding day.'

'Yes.' I looked down.

'If this was a week *before* the wedding, I'd call it nerves.'

I said nothing.

'What's changed, Claudia?' His face was flushed now. Absently, he put down the remains of his sandwich on a plant with open, horn-shaped leaves where it swayed for a bit, then toppled inward. Were they sandwich-eating plants? I felt myself becoming a little crazy. Was it so easy to throw away three years?

'My father died.' Would he accept that as an answer? 'I'm suffocating.' Now I was the one who needed the air, the medicinal comforts of the garden.

He followed me out. 'Why would your father's death change anything?'

'I'm going to sit down.'.

We found a bench between two flowerbeds filled with low-growing herbs. Each bunch was meticulously labelled. From where I was sitting I could read *Perovskia* and *Abrotanoides*, plants from Afghanistan.

'It just made me understand that it wouldn't work,' I said.

'Something's happened.' He took my hand and, as his cuff revealed his watch, I saw him unable to resist a glance. 'Tell me.' His eyes returned to me. His voice was quiet and reasonable, as if I were a patient.

I could see he had no time for a serious conversation. But that had been my intention. 'I don't want to be a patient any more.'

'I thought we were lovers.'

None of it was Oliver's fault. He had helped me so much but I didn't owe him my life. Perhaps he could only understand if I told him everything. But he wouldn't believe that my decision was about the future just as much or even more than it was about the past. Oliver was already my past.

'He came back.'

At first he didn't take in the sense of my words. Then whatever was in my face — excitement, fear, determination? — impressed on him my meaning.

I could see that he was nonplussed. It would be an understatement to say that he hadn't shared my certainty that K would return, however long it took.

'I can't believe this!' For a second he was exasperated in a normal way, as if I'd failed to show for an appointment. I supposed he was too shocked to be properly angry.

'It's true.' I knew how Oliver hated indecisiveness. I suppose in his profession it spelt danger. A diagnosis, the cut of a scalpel, works on the edge of danger but hesitation is the worst option. He had taught me how to take decisions and now it had turned against him. What could he do or say?

'You're throwing up your whole life because a man who did his best to ruin it has returned? Is that what you're saying?' His voice was bitter now but still disbelieving.

I could hardly blame him. I was sweating and took off the light sweater I was wearing. 'Nothing is so simple,' I said.

'Yes, it is!' Suddenly he was almost shouting. 'I thought you'd grown up, Claudia. I thought you'd left behind the sixteen-year-old girl who allowed herself to be used, who—'

'Not *used*!' I interrupted. 'I chose to be with K.' I was angry now. It was an old argument but I'd fought it more in my head than in words. I wondered if he would remind me of the state I'd been in when we'd first met – in hospital, more often than not, although he was never my doctor. I wouldn't have blamed him for employing any means. But he had calmed down already, had even peered once more at his watch. I guessed that he'd decided it was all emotional rubbish but that he needed more time to deal with it.

'I have to go. We'll talk more this evening. His coming back has no meaning. Your life has changed. We have a life together. My darling.' He leant forward and kissed me.

I decided I preferred the anger but I sat on the bench quietly and watched him walk away. I would have to talk to him that evening but it would make no difference. For me, this was the ending. I had to deal with K's re-emergence on my own, with the freedom to approach it in any way I decided.

At this point, sitting in that secret garden, I had thought of no practicalities. Indeed, I had no idea how I could find K again, or even if I wanted to. I just knew that the lunatic hours with him had wiped out everything else. Even my job, at which I was expected back the following day, hardly seemed real. Reality only existed in his presence. All the rest felt like play-acting. Perhaps Oliver was right and I had reverted to the tunnel vision of a sixteen-year old. As I thought this, an unusual sense of hope propelled me to my feet. I looked around again, this time noting the dignified founder of the garden, Sir Hans Sloane. The stone statue was weathered but that didn't disguise his air of satisfied prosperity. He had brought chocolate to England, I remembered.

I remembered the way K had talked to me about his home, Valparaiso, Chile, then called it 'Valpo'. Was he in England? Or had he returned to Valpo? There was no urgency. I had taken the only immediately necessary step by releasing myself from Oliver.

CHAPTER THIRTY-FOUR

1990

On Saturday morning, Claudia told her parents she was ill and would have to put off going back to school. She didn't say until when. She spent the day in bed, trying to write the letter to K. The last post was collected at four thirty so she assured herself she had plenty of time. But soon she really did feel ill, her head aching, her hands clammy and her feet ice-cold. The additional tasks of locating K's address in the phone book and taking the letter to the postbox a hundred yards down the road seemed almost as difficult as finding words for what she had to say. Above all, she didn't want to appear dependent or pathetic. She was determined he would see her in the brightest light of love, although her thoughts were darkly miserable.

Time after time she took up the pad of A4 paper that had been bought for her perceptive thoughts on manners and morals in the nineteenth century. Her scribbles made her despair. Where was the inspiration she'd felt when the music had filled her soul in the Albert Hall? Then she had been longing to communicate with K; now it seemed almost impossible.

Eventually, she wrote only two sentences, before folding the paper into the envelope. Although she still called him and thought of him as K, she had known his real name for some time. Nevertheless, in a spirit of rebellion, she put 'K' on the envelope instead of his real initial. Sweating with fever and nerves, she sneaked to the postbox when her parents were out.

She returned to bed thankfully and fell into a restless doze. She woke to find Catherine standing over her with a thermometer. Mother and daughter were equally disconcerted to discover that the mercury rose to 102°F.

'You're really sick,' exclaimed Catherine.

I'm really sick, thought Claudia, with relief.

It was hard to re-enter their house with its few small rooms, its square box of a garden. K looked round with a dismal sense of entrapment. While Fiona bustled about putting away the groceries they'd bought on the way, satisfaction to be home and with him in every line of her body, K went up to their bedroom and stared moodily out of the window.

It was four o'clock on Sunday, never a good moment to survey the future. This new (or renewed), confident Fiona, had announced her decision to take one more day off work to straighten the house, then return to the office the following morning, on Tuesday. However much he'd been unnerved by her falling-apart, this was worse. She obviously presumed that he, too, would return, to the great work of fiction he'd been creating over the summer. K's inward irony, how-ever harsh, was little defence against her patronage. He reminded himself of his resolution to abandon the charade that he could be a writer, and take up a proper job once more.

But everything he had done since Fiona had been in hospital had been in instinctive reaction to her pain and misery. Without him being aware of having taken the decision, they seemed set on a course where they would go ahead together, hand in hand, heart to heart, chins up, as if the threat of cancer and death didn't exist. Finally, unwillingly, he faced the fact that whatever drunken promises he'd made to her in that Dorset pub had become the bedrock of her trust in him. She felt he had given his support and he felt utterly miserable. But what option had he? The huge deception of his love for Claudia must remain as his burden. By now she would be back at school, unhappy, of course – she would be unhappy – but freed by him to take up her life again.

K moved closer to the window that overlooked their patch of grass with its two narrow borders. He had first seen Claudia through the window of his room at Meadowlands. The evening light had given a theatrical glow to the square of lawn where she'd stood. He'd been a voyeur in the shadows of the auditorium. When he'd stepped on to the stage the drama had unfolded inevitably. Now he had no choice but to make do with the empty square of his own garden.

K became aware that Fiona was calling him. There was tea in the kitchen. Should he tell her at once that he was giving up his book, that it was bilge, filth — worse than that, nothing? A mere vacuum. Just like he was. Suddenly violent, K picked up a pile of books from a table and flung them to the floor. He would have liked to hurl them through the window-panes.

CHAPTER THIRTY-FIVE

2004

I opened my little house in Valparaiso with an immense surge of relief. I was home. The shutters were still closed but by the glimmering morning light that pierced the cracks I could see the canvases stacked round the walls. Not knowing when or if I would return, I had turned their faces away from prying eyes. You never knew in this lawless part of the city who would decide to enter and perhaps stay.

But the room – the whole house consisted of this one room and a small kitchen and shower area – was undisturbed. The only intruders were thin arms of vegetation that had pierced the crumbling masonry in several places and either splayed their outstretched fingers on the floor or pointed spiky question marks into the air. I had been away such a short time, but it was the rainy season in Chile now, when even the driest land turns green. In the same month two years ago, and other years before that, my *cerro* had lost a dozen or so houses, shacks, really, washed down to the gully below. So far this year the rain had not been so heavy.

Sighing, I set down my bag and sat on the one comfortable chair. I'd found it thrown out on to the road outside the Hotel Weymouth. I discovered a guest had complained that it was inhabited by a family of mice and flung it out of a window. But if there had been mice, their airborne trajectory had encouraged an early departure. It was a good, well-padded chair, upholstered in an elegant mauve and gold stripe, a little faded.

I sank back into it heavily, and felt all the experiences of my English trip receive a consoling welcome. Everything had changed. Nothing had changed. Until this moment, I'd had no idea of how tired I was. I would sleep now, where I was, without opening the shutters or moving to my divan in the corner.

So I shut my eyes. Immediately, the noises around seemed to double in volume. A dozen or more dogs, kept in small enclosures to safeguard their owner's property, competed for the loudest, harshest bark. Three or four birds, probably attracted by berries on a creeper over one of the windows, descended to the corrugated-iron roof and began a hysterical scrabbling and squawking. The bell of the Catholic church rang the midday Angelus. Two men passed down the road, arguing violently, followed by a wild squall of rain that swept over my head like gunfire. Clearly this was no time to rest.

I got up and opened the shutters. I had made them myself and they moved creakily but I liked them; their crude solidity was reassuring at my weaker moments. The rain had become heavier. Perhaps I had been premature in congratulating myself on no flooding or landslides. It had emptied the street of people and quietened the dogs. The church bells had stopped ringing.

For some time I stood looking out. Even through the vegetation that enclosed my little home and the sluicing silvery rain, I could still make out the vibrant colours of the city. On the wall opposite me a splendid new graffiti had appeared: a woman, bold enough for a cartoon, in pink dress and purple shoes waved a handkerchief at a man opposite, formally dressed in suit and tie. I guessed that their feet, which I couldn't see were raised in dance. This was a depiction of the *cueca*, the Chilean wedding dance. It made me smile wryly to see how much larger the bride was than her groom – a reflection of their relative importance?

Further down the street I glimpsed the corner store where I bought my milk, wine and groceries. In fact, it was hard to avoid its battered rainbow clothing of orange, yellow and blue paint. I would visit it later and, over my modest purchases, exchange a few words with Maria de la Luz, whom I'd watched change from carefree young woman to overworked shopkeeper, housewife and mother of five. She seemed happy, though, a silver medallion of the Virgin swinging against her ample bosom. Could it be she had certainty?

I continued to watch from the window, allowing the so unEnglish sights to remind me of what I did when I was there. The idea that I was a painter could still surprise me, like a child who suddenly discovers he's grown up and is both excited and nervous. Surely I didn't have the boldness to put paint on canvas and call it a picture. Yet I had, and over the last two years I had sold a number of paintings – not for much money, certainly, but the buyers had presumably wanted to hang them on their walls. In the summer – the Chilean summer, that is, in November – I'd been offered the chance of an exhibition by a Chilean entrepreneur called Pablo. I would try to put it off until January to give myself more time to prepare. For some time I'd been working towards a new project, painting the *ascensores*, the dilapidated late-nineteenth- and early twentieth-century cable-cars that linked the lower town round the bay with the heady excitements of the *cerros*.

The possibility of amassing a proper body of work had never seemed quite real to me but my trip to England had given me permission for a future. I had seen Claudia. I had apologised. I had sent my final word in a letter. There was nothing more I could do. At the hospital, the doctor had suggested I must use time as if it were precious. This itself was a new idea.

I turned away from the window because I was shaking with cold. The Chilean winter was not as harsh as that in the northern hemisphere but my house had no heating and the damp soaked into the walls. It was lucky that oil paintings didn't suffer in such conditions. I went into the kitchen, turned on the overhead light, the electric ring and the ancient English Baby Belling. The light flickered, there was a pop and all three went off.

It had been absurd to turn them on together. I smiled to myself. Life was back to normal. I went to the drawer and took out pliers, screwdriver and wire. Then, at another thought, I put them into my pocket and went to the door. Best to start life afresh with a glass of red wine and a hunk of bread. With an old canvas as umbrella, I hurried out, avoiding puddles that soon combined into a rushing river, and headed for the grocery.

The day after my meeting with Oliver in the Physic Garden, I returned to my job. I felt more focused and energetic than ever before and when, after a month, I was offered a working trip to India, I took the opportunity eagerly.

I telephoned Oliver to tell him. 'That's good,' he said, without much warmth or apparent interest.

I understood then that my policy of keeping in touch, to show him that he was still important to me and my affection undimmed if changed, had become an anachronism. Oliver was cutting free. His clear, unsentimental approach was what had attracted me in the first place. I should have realised sooner that he would not allow himself to remain in an ambiguous situation for long. He had a perfect right to be angry.

'Yes. I'm very excited.' I would have to let him go entirely, although a little part of me was still hanging on to the life raft he'd provided.

'You must send me a postcard.'

'I'll do that.'

I was calling Oliver in the evening from my first-floor flat. It was already dark outside but I hadn't drawn the curtains and a street-lamp was bright enough to cast a tall shadow on my wall. After I'd said my final goodbye to him, I tried to tell myself that being alone was not so bad. For many years to be alone was to be tortured by doubts and remorse, to relive endlessly the events of that gruesome morning. But now I was stronger. After all, the guilt (which no one had wanted me to feel) had not lasted a lifetime, and the life I had disclaimed in my madness was still patiently awaiting me. I was young – thirty wasn't old. And when I'd been very young, before all this had happened, I'd enjoyed solitude. It had been a trademark of my character. I had made music and walked alone. Even Bella, my closest friend, had been kept far from my inner life. This was the nature I'd been born with and surely it hadn't changed. Solitude was a pleasure. How relieved I felt to have escaped marriage with Oliver!

Moving purposefully, I went to the kitchen and took two eggs and a tomato from the fridge. After I'd eaten, I'd settle down with the files about the project in Tamil Nadu that I was to monitor. Later still, I'd have a bath, then go to bed with *The Pickwick Papers*. I'd never previously been drawn to Dickens.

Only at night when the light was off, would I allow myself to dwell on K's re-entry into my life. He was going back to his chosen city, Valparaiso. The oddness of our meeting hardly bothered me, or his assumption that we couldn't or wouldn't meet again. It was my choice now. He had come to me and I could go to him. Thus, in a way, my solitude was false because while he existed I could never be alone.

CHAPTER THIRTY-SIX

2004

I had never admitted I was ill before I left for England. I blamed my occasional sickness and headaches on the dank winter months and the lack of heating in my house. Now that my visit to the hospital in London had forced the truth upon me I didn't allow it to affect my behaviour. The tin roof leaked and I pulled my bed away from the walls, taking care to avoid the drips, but it didn't seem to make much difference. Eventually I bought an electric heater but it blew the electricity more often than it warmed the room.

Of course, I recognised the situation was ridiculous. Having sold the flat in London, I had plenty of money to rent or even buy a modern flat downtown in the *Plan*, where I would be secure and comfortable. There were even a few apartment blocks fairly high up in the *cerros* where I would still have my view of the bay and the multi-coloured buildings that tumbled down towards it.

On the other hand, I'd already told the local priest that some money would be coming his way to help finance his home for waifs and strays. He would be amazed when he discovered how much. Over fourteen years Fiona's flat had become valuable.

But the reasons for my staying put were even more complicated. One afternoon Maria de la Luz brought up my shopping to me. She was shocked by my surroundings and I felt the need to mount a defence. 'It's my home,' I said, speaking in Spanish. 'My refuge.'

'It's wet,' she insisted, 'unhealthy, unhygienic – maybe even dangerous.' She crossed herself. 'Four bad men built this place. Their spirit has not left. I understand now why you're not well.'

This mixture of practicality and superstition galvanised me. 'It's my inspiration.' I waved at the canvases and easel. 'Without this place I couldn't paint. I've lived here through twelve winters. I can't abandon it.'

She didn't try to convince me – her pursed lips suggested that you couldn't convince a madman – but went into my kitchen where she heated some soup for me. I was sitting in my chair wearing a coat but shivering. What a miserable specimen I must have presented.

'You're sick,' she announced, as I tried to swallow the soup – which was much too hot, and filled with sugar, like all food in Chile.

'Just cold.'

'You go to hospital and have the doctors look.' It was a womanly command, the sort that reminds a man of his mother and when someone else had taken responsibility for his life.

'Yes,' I said. 'It's all under control.' Which was one way of putting it.

She left me soon after, promising to return with another blanket for my bed. She was a good woman. With her five children, one of whom was disabled in some way, a less than positive husband – just lazy, I think – and the shop to run, she certainly didn't need a hopeless foreigner to add to her burden. I should have discouraged her ministrations but, for the time being, I enjoyed the sensation of someone caring for me.

In a moment I would get up and begin to paint before the light went. The rainy days had streaked my windows, and creepers still twirled around, growing too fast for my scissors to keep up with them. But today the sun was out, a humid sun, its aureole misty with rain, but there was more light than there had been for weeks.

Perhaps in contradiction to Maria de la Luz's pronouncement, I decided to broach a new canvas. I usually had three or four on the go but the weather had slowed my progress and many dated to before I'd left for England. It would do me good to start something fresh.

I usually worked from sketches done on the spot, sometimes immediately in oils, more often in pencil with the colour indicated. (In the summer it was too hot to sit outside for any length of time – except perhaps in the evenings.) I wanted to develop my *ascensores* paintings for which I had taken photographs and bought postcards earlier in the year. I was not happy with those I'd already painted. I needed to do some sketches, visualising, thinking, but I already felt the impatient beat of anticipation, which overrode the sickness.

Stumbling a little, more from eagerness than frailty, I chose a small canvas, about eighteen inches square. I'd stretched it years ago to paint a two-tone orange and yellow doorway I'd admired but then it had been repainted an ugly green. Eighteen inches was perhaps an odd size to catch the impression of a cable-car line that stretched hundreds of metres up the hillside but I had found that compression often threw up an interesting composition.

The canvas was ready primed and I'd painted in it a Chilean undercoat of a musky red-brown, which would do well. As I reviewed my palette, with its parade of soft yellows, ochres, saffrons, reds, browns to garish lime, turquoise, purple and orange, I felt a burst of gratitude that I should have been allowed this true pleasure in colour. I recalled, as I had often before, Matisse's comment that 'Colour is the poor man's gold.' Despite the endless difficulties of producing a painting with which I was half-way satisfied, hardly surprising since I was entirely self-taught, this joy in my palette – my choice of colours had been the same for years – never left me and gave me the incentive to try again and again.

I propped up a couple of photos taken half-way up the Ascensor Espiritu Sancto and picked up my brush, hesitating at the hardest and most exciting moment. Since my drawing skills remained shamingly limited, the structure of my picture often defeated me for days, weeks even. That half-sunny early afternoon, with no preliminary sketch to work from, I was being more daring than usual. Probably it was desperation. My heart pumped louder and harder, and my outstretched hand with the brush, and its load of brownish-purple, shook.

I dabbed modestly at the canvas. I had taken my photographs standing at the back of the descending cable-car so that I recorded the rising car approaching the station at the top. Both were painted a luxuriant earth red, trimmed with a glowing yellow. The sun had been brilliant that afternoon, several months ago, the shrubs had sprouted a rich green on either side of the cable and my camera had caught a glimpse of the run-down but brightly coloured buildings to its right. Boldly I slid two lines down the canvas, a scrub of vegetation, the box-like car, the bigger box of the station. I thought of that inevitable hair-raising second when the car teeters on the edge of the entrance and feels, just for a moment, as if it will hurtle backwards into the abyss instead of achieving the womb-like security of its destination. Even after years of travelling on the *ascensores*, some much steeper than the Espiritu Sancto – one takes you through a solid rockface as if you were in an up-ended tube train – I still recognised that fearful moment. Would the great fall be avoided one more time?

Sometimes I watched my companions, usually sturdy, black-coated women from the *cerros*, travelling back from menial jobs in the *Plan*, the city below. Did they harbour such terror? Did Maria de la Luz? I suspected not: their life was too hard for imagined tragedy.

And yet that was what my series of *ascensor* paintings was about: the danger of the cliff edge. They were, in truth, about Claudia and me, Fiona and me.

I stood back to look at the canvas. The few daubs and dashes I'd made over the last hour would mean nothing to an outsider; to me, it was a good start. But I couldn't continue. My hand was shaking and a pounding headache knocked at my skull. Maybe a walk would help, some fresh air. I'd been cooped up far too long. Although I was almost entirely reclusive, I occasionally went out for a drink or a meal at one of the local bars. Now and again I visited the slightly more upmarket Hotel Weymouth. It had been smartened up since my stay, painted a good strong yellow with emerald-blue roofs, and the clientele included more foreigners and visitors from the *Plan*, but I was fond of the terrace, with its views down to O'Higgins Square and beyond it to the wide sweep of the bay. From it, I could also survey the tracks of several *ascensores*.

I wound round my throat a scarf I'd picked up from the flat in London (mine? Fiona's?), went outside and, turned briefly to lock the door. I hadn't bothered for many years but now I would be sorry to lose my paintings to an intruder.

I started to walk. The rough streets were drying quickly but many were streaked with mud and rubble washed down by the rain. I took the route away from the corner shop, wanting to avoid Maria de la Luz's disapproval as her patient made his escape. My spirits were high. I should have been daunted by the work ahead – I planned twenty pictures in the series and I had finished none that satisfied me – but I was only thinking of the conception and more excited than I'd ever expected to feel again.

Besides, the sun was out and warming my shoulders. My headache took the rhythm of my tread and became less painful. Certainly it was hard work climbing – I had to go up and round a ravine before descending a little – but it was good to exercise my muscles, good to feel summer coming closer. By early October the middle of the day would be hot and the warm dark evenings back.

I circled past the tall trees and formidable whitewashed walls of the old prison. When I had first arrived, during the Pinochet years, it was still functioning as a jail, the politicos overfilling the cells, which were divided horizontally so that six could sleep where before there had been two. Five years ago, it had become a so-called arts centre, run by an enterprising ex-inmate. He'd spent twenty-five years behind the walls and now lived and worked in two rooms by the entrance that had been occupied by the prison staff. Now and again I had a drink with him and we talked about holding an exhibition there. I thought it only too ironically appropriate, given my past, but he was more interested in walking, talking art, and insisted on showing me a long, dark video of prostitutes and pimps, reading his poetry as they paraded round the prison's grim corridors, cells and punishment boxes. He strutted at their head, Pied Piper to men in drag with sequins and furs, women scarved in black hair, bewildered students dragged in to make up the numbers.

Unusually, Ernesto was standing by the great gates as I passed. '*Hola!*'

We exchanged greetings. I asked him what he was waiting for.

'A whole coachful of tourists,' he told me proudly. His Spanish was thick with the smoke of a million cigarettes. Yet he was still a handsome man, even charismatic.

I congratulated him on his tourists – he showed them round the prison, telling lurid tales of the horrors that had been perpetrated against Pinochet's enemies – and declined his invitation to join them.

'You are too solitary, Señor.' He came closer until he could put an arm round my shoulders. 'In prison solitude is the worst punishment. Yet you choose it freely.'

'I'm on my way for a drink at the Weymouth.' I had no intention of entering a quasi-philosophical discussion with this born-again showman. Besides, now I'd stopped walking my headache was surging.

But Ernesto was looking beyond me. The coach was approaching, a Nirvana for him of the rich and gullible. I extricated myself from his grip and walked on.

At first glance the hotel seemed empty. Few tourists came to Valparaiso, and from overseas almost none. I had thought – worried – that, with various grants available to renovate the older buildings and those strong enough to withstand earthquakes, this would change. But Chile was still too remote, the Andes and the ocean a double barrier. Ernesto's prized coachload were probably from Santiago, or perhaps Argentina, or another South American country.

I walked through the bar, rang a bell and, when no one appeared, continued through to the terrace.

A man sat with his back to me at the far end. On the table in front of him was a bottle of beer, a glass and a basket of bread. I found a table as far from him as possible. He was, however, still in my eyeline and, as I looked beyond him to the view, I recognised the wide set of his shoulders, the well-brushed but slightly too long, greying curls.

I would let him find me, as he usually did.

Soon a young man came and took my order. Although I addressed him in the peremptory tones used by all true Chileans to waiters, I saw Craig's shoulders twitch, as if he recognised my voice. But he didn't turn round.

Perhaps he wanted a moment on his own too. I had last seen him when he'd told me of Claudia's imminent wedding. It was surprising that he should still be here two months later. I drank some wine, which immediately made the thumping in my head spin into over-drive.

Since my return to Chile I'd allowed my trip to England to find a calm place in my mind. The burden I'd carried for so long had lifted, or at least lightened, so it had become bearable. I didn't want to think about it. But there was Craig, his hunched shoulders so English in his well-cut jacket. He would ask me all kinds of questions. I drank some more wine. This time it hit my stomach, warming and consoling. I lifted my eyes to the nearest *ascensor*, the Artilleria, and watched the two cable-cars – as small as toys at this distance and painted a nursery yellow – cross each other and continue on their perilous journey.

Craig stood up. To leave the terrace, he would have to pass close by me. I lifted my glass again.

'I thought I recognised your voice.' He stood in front of me with all the solidity of business success. But his expression was concerned, even shocked.

'What is it?' I asked, the wine churning inside me. 'I'm not a ghost.'

'No. You've lost a lot of weight, haven't you?'

So that was it. Something as mundane as food, or lack of it. Since I never saw myself in a mirror and certainly never weighed myself, my appearance was of no importance to me. 'The rain must have washed some away, just as it does with the mountainside.' I was pleased with the image.

Without being invited, he sat down and fiddled with my bread. 'You know I told you about Claudia's wedding?'

'Yes.' I felt my face flush like a child's.

'It was cancelled. That is, postponed.'

'I know.'

'What?'

Suddenly I was filled with anger. 'Look,' I said – or shouted, 'It's over fourteen years since that summer. The fun is over. No more macabre imaginings, no more mileage out of horror and disaster. I don't know where you get this idea that you're my personal messenger angel. It's just prurient gossip – and I don't need it. How I don't need it!' I stopped. My head felt too befuddled to create coherence out of the tumble.

'I'm sorry. I'll go away.'

'No ... no.' I put my hand on his arm. My anger had evaporated into a feeling of acute illness. 'Forgive me. I think I've got a fever.'

'Eat something. Why don't you eat something?'

I picked up a piece of bread and put it down again. It would stick in my gullet. That had been the problem recently. 'I know about the cancellation of Claudia's wedding because I went to England.' It felt extraordinary to say her name openly.

'I see.'

I knew what he wanted to ask. 'Yes. I went and found Claudia. As you know, the wedding was put off because of her father's death. It was nothing to do with her. It was merely a postponement. I hadn't seen her since that morning fourteen years ago. I'd thought I was going to witness her future, her marriage.'

'You wanted closure.'

'Closure?' What an idiotic concept. 'I wanted peace. I wanted to understand.' I poured some more wine into my glass. I was not telling him the whole truth.

'And did you find what you wanted?'

The six o'clock darkness, so beautiful and so regular in Chile, was closing round us. He was warm enough in well-fleshed body and tweed coat but I had begun to shiver, despite my fever. The sights and sounds of the city, which had receded during our conversation, came back pell-mell, with a bus crunching its gears round the road twisting past the hotel, dogs howling at dusky delights, women shouting, seagulls twirling harshly above, bells tolling the passing of day and, far below, the humming base of a big ship signalling its entry into the bay.

'What did you say? Did you ask me something?' He seemed unwilling to repeat his question so I hurried on, 'I'm painting for an exhibition, you know. It's never too late to succeed.' I heard myself give a wild laugh. 'My life is here now, in Valpo. At night I dream of the city. Do you know what Neruda wrote about it?' Suddenly I wanted to share my love for this city, heartless and over-vigorous as it often seemed. 'Listen.' I began to gabble some lines: '"*Valparaiso es un montón, un racimo/de casas locas…*"'

After a while I couldn't continue. I found a handkerchief in my pocket and wiped my eyes.

Craig leant forward. 'I do understand a little. I've bought a house, not here but along the coast. I came here to grow vines but the country took hold of me.'

I tried to recover myself. The walk, the wine, saying Claudia's name aloud had been too much for me. I was sick.

'Let me drive you home.' His voice was gentle.

He paid then and led me to his car. In itself this was an odd experience. While I had been living in Valparaiso, I had behaved as the poorest inhabitant, walking mostly or, if I had something heavy to carry, taking the bus. His car was seductively warm and comfortable. He asked me for directions but I was almost asleep, hardly coherent, so it took us a long time, circling the head of the *cerros* before descending in the wrong direction and being forced to drive up again. At length, we passed the brightly lit corner store, and I called, 'Here! Just up here.'

He stopped the car – very thankfully, I'm sure. As we got out, I saw him assessing the area with surprise. But he said nothing. I knew, of course, that the obvious signs of poverty, the tin roofs garlanded with electrical wires, television aerials and grubby washing, the wildly overgrown patches of what might have been gardens, the dirt and rubbish in the street, the endlessly barking dogs and the people, much darker-skinned than in the *Plan* below, would not appeal to him. He would see it as a sign of breakdown.

I found my key and let us into the house. At least the dry day meant that I couldn't hear dripping. I put on the overhead light. The journey had calmed my mental state but my head still pounded and my body was still weak and chilled, despite the strong red wine.

'Where's your bed?'

I pointed to the corner. I didn't blame him if he was in a hurry to get out. Through his eyes I saw only too clearly the desolation of our surroundings.

But he didn't leave. While I prepared for bed, pushing a pile of art books under it as a hint to the mice to stay away, he looked through my paintings. I didn't have the energy to stop him and perhaps I wanted it anyway.

When I was under the blankets, he pulled up the big chair and sat by me.

'Haven't you something more entertaining to do?'

'I'm amazed by your paintings. You've progressed so much.'

I remembered he'd seen a couple I'd shown in a mixed exhibition. Three or four years ago. 'You like them?'

'Oh, yes!'

I decided to believe him. He was a businessman. There was no need for him to lie.

'I have a one-man show in January. Perhaps February.' I hesitated whether to tell him about my theme. It was still too early.

'With these pictures?'

'No. Well, maybe some. I must paint hard.'

He didn't say anything to this. There was quite a long silence during which I drifted near sleep.

'How long did you stay in England?'

It was an abrupt return. ' Not long. Longer than I'd intended.' There was another pause. Once more I drifted.

'You didn't hear, then, that Claudia has broken off her engagement. Finally. No postponement.'

He was looking intently at me, his bullish red face steady in the wavering light. I shut my eyes. Why had he told me this? It was easier to contemplate his motives than Claudia's. I wouldn't even start on that. Besides, I didn't necessarily believe him.

'Why have you told me this?'

'I don't know.' When I opened my eyes and peered at him through the gloom, he seemed confused. 'It's just, whenever I see you—' He broke off. 'I don't think you've lost all rights.'

He was sorry for me. Was that it? It was impossible to believe that such a man could be a romantic. Probably he was just a meddler, as I'd suggested earlier.

'It doesn't mean anything to me any more.' An obvious lie, of course, since I'd flown to England on the basis of his wedding information. Yet there was a certain truth in it now. I suspected that at some time I would tell him my situation.

'I should leave you to sleep.' He stood up.

I was relieved but also, after the news he'd brought me, wakeful again. I thanked him for the lift, his concern, and watched him go through the door. He made no mention of returning and I found myself curiously bereft. Too late, I recalled he'd mentioned buying a house up the coast. I would have liked his address, the first time I'd wanted to continue a personal relationship since I'd been in Chile. Perhaps it was a sign of weakness – or increasing strength.

I tossed and turned. Finally I gave up trying to sleep and sat up. The overhead light threw weird shadows on to my paintings, which Craig had left in disorder. When I shut my eyes, they spun on my inner eye. The effect of the wine was receding and I felt ravenously hungry but couldn't make the effort. Instead I feasted on my meeting with Claudia beside the pool. Its nightmare-like quality, my blackout and subsequent incoherence, her suspicion and silence, all this had mellowed in my memory. After my plunge into the pool, cleansing, revitalising, she had brought the clothes that had belonged to her father. It had been, at the very least, a peace-offering. I had them still, in a chest of drawers, although I hadn't worn them again.

Could our meeting have influenced Claudia against her fiancé, her intended, this Oliver? It seemed impossible that the human wreck I had presented could have affected her in any way, except, possibly, with pity, and I didn't want that.

I opened my eyes again and watched my canvases jitterbug round the walls. If I'd had proper lighting, I'd have got up there and then and picked up a brush. Instead I lay back and consoled myself with images of the dawn. First there would be the birds, sparrows mostly, rattling the creepers against the tin roof, twittering noisily in a subtly different accent from those I knew in England, or so I liked to think. Then the light, infiltrating my shutters, of pearly white changing, if it was to be a sunny day, to lines of concentrated rainbow. Summer was on the way, I convinced myself, so it would be a sunny day. The raucous energy of children dashing to school would be joined by screeching scooters and some cars. I would stay awake till this cacophony of sound came to support my solitude. But gradually I became aware of another thin humming in my ears. I listened for it, trying to recognise the notes. It was the melody that had once meant more to me than any other sound in the world. I sank down into my pillow and let the viola float me off to sleep.

The following day, I got up early and walked, head down, arms swinging, to a second-hand shop three streets away. As I passed the grocery, Maria de la Luz waved and shook her finger at me. I smiled brazenly. The sun was shining, as I'd predicted, and although I felt weak and a little strange, I was filled with energy. Today I would paint to music.

For several years, I had owned a radio. In the morning I listened to a station called, rather romantically, Universidad Santa Maria. They played a fairly mixed bag of music for a couple of hours and I'd catch some Mozart or Haydn mostly. I'd tried, but not too hard, to tune in to the BBC World Service but never succeeded so gave up with some relief. The odd newspaper kept me as much in touch with English affairs as I wanted. Without trying I learnt Spanish from the local radio announcers and commentators. Then my radio had given up the ghost.

Now it was only music I wanted. The man behind the counter was grotesquely fat and very short, almost a dwarf. I knew he was standing on a box. His shop was crammed with so much junk, that it seemed a waste of time to ask for a particular item. But I had furnished my room (such as its furnishings were) mostly with his offerings and knew his particular genius.

'*Hola*, Rinaldo!'

'*Señor Inglés.*'

I explained what I wanted: a CD player and a dozen classical CDs. It hardly mattered what. I didn't even consider asking him for the music I'd heard in bed last night. His boxes of CDs were collected randomly, from passing travellers, women who liked to clear out, or the dead. There were plenty of the last category round here.

'*Al tiro,* Señor.' It used to shock me, that particularly Chilean expression, which translated as 'at the draw of a gun'. Now I accepted it without thinking as 'Right away, sir.' With one chubby hand, he picked up a mechanical claw attached to a long pole and extended it far to his right. Within a second or two he had the handle of a portable CD player in its grip, which he let down gently at my feet. It was a faultlessly executed manoeuvre.

'*Bravo!*' I clapped. 'It has batteries?' I knew it wouldn't but I liked to tease him. He believed batteries were the work of the devil. He would say, 'Why did God give us electricity if he wanted us to waste our money on batteries?' We had had all kinds of skirmishes over my soon-to-be defunct radio.

'No batteries.' He turned his back firmly, apparently in no mood to play the game. So I bent to the box of CDs and picked out a selection, ranging from Mozart to Schumann, Brahms and Britten. All my purchases came to less than three pounds, in English money.

As I walked back, this time past the grocery store, Maria de la Luz ran out. 'I saw you yesterday!' she cried, in Spanish, of course. She clasped her hands together. 'You walk out as if you are well. But I see you in the morning.'

'Oh, Maria, Maria.' I tried to placate her. 'Don't be so anxious. A friend brought me home in a car.'

'A car! As if a car saves a man who wants to kill himself.'

This stopped me in my tracks, it had been delivered with such vehemence and conviction. As she turned away, I followed her into the shop. Another customer came in behind me, an old man for bottles of gas and olive oil. I watched him stow them away in a bag and hoped he would remember which was which.

'I don't want to kill myself.' I was earnest, like a schoolboy trying to persuade his teacher. Maria was cutting open a large bag of potatoes behind the counter. 'I have my paintings,' I said, 'an exhibition.' Now I was showing off.

Yet it was ironic that the first time anyone should tell me I was trying to kill myself was the first time that I had no desire to die. Not yet.

'Six cans of soup,' I muttered, almost breathless with this realisation, 'and four batteries.'

She handed them over without comment. 'All right, Señora, I will tell you what no one else knows. I have been to hospital in London already.' I tapped my head. 'It is inside here. They can do nothing. *Nada.*' Then I repeated the word forcefully. '*Nada.*' Which was near enough the truth. 'But just for you,' I smiled winningly, 'after my exhibition is over I will chase after the best doctors in Chile.' I persevered – she was still disapproving: 'Look, I'm fine today. I've been shopping. Next time you come we'll have music. Perhaps we'll dance like that couple painted on the wall.'

'Huh!' But she smiled at my reference to the *cueca* graffiti and we parted amicably.

I returned to my house, had some soup and started to work on my *ascensor* painting. I would set up my music when I needed a break. Almost idly, I wondered what Claudia was doing at that moment. Most of my attention was for my painting but a little part of me worked out the time in England – five hours ahead, four o'clock in the afternoon. She had a job, she had told me, so she would be in her office, looking at her computer screen, perhaps, or talking to a colleague. Maybe she was explaining that she was not to be married. It was so long since I'd worked in an office that I could hardly remember the level of personal communication. It was better to work on your own, I told myself, and turned all my concentration to mixing a favourite colour, a combination of alizarin crimson, phthalo green and ultramarine, with a dash of black and white which, if I pulled it off, made a rich brownish-purple, the kind of colour that drew you into the centre of the earth.

CHAPTER THIRTY-SEVEN

2004

At the beginning of October I flew to India. My life had been so circumscribed by tragedy and illness that, apart from the odd weekend trip with Oliver, I hadn't left England for years – in fact, not since the visit to Italy with my parents.

I found it absurdly liberating to show my passport (new) and pass through into the departure lounge where I would join other (normal) passengers and get on to an aeroplane. Some psychologically tortured part of me half expected a fierce individual to bar my way and direct me to a holding pen for traveller rejects.

I was also ordinarily nervous about the job ahead, which gave my excitement an edge of fear. I was glad I had been allocated a window seat where I could hide from my fellow passengers or, indeed, let my heightened imagination soar out into the wide sky.

It was impossible, under such circumstances, to avoid thinking about K. He lived at an even greater distance from England than India, over wider seas, higher mountains, or so I imagined. I leant forward to the pocket in front of me and pulled out the in-flight magazine. I turned to the map and looked for South America. It was amazing that I'd never done this before, I thought, then reminded myself that I hadn't known before where he was or whether he was alive or dead.

'Planning your next trip, are you?'

I had hardly noticed the man seated beside me except that he wore tracksuit bottoms. 'Not really.' I hesitated. 'You don't happen to know where Valparaiso is?' The map only showed Santiago. 'I know it's in Chile,' I added, feeling foolish.

'Head west from Santiago till you hit the coast.' I moved my finger obediently. 'Down a bit. Yes, that's it.'

I kept my finger on the spot, tied there with my imagination.

'It used to be an important port before they built the Panama Canal. Once I thought I'd found a new tourist destination. Sadly, I was wrong.'

'You travel a lot, then?' I looked at him more carefully and saw a pale face with pouchy eyes.

'I run a travel business, Faraway Places, but good old Valpo turned out to be a step too far.'

His 'good old Valpo' grated on my ears. 'Thank you for your help,' I said primly, and bent to get papers out of my briefcase, as if I was keen to work.

The tactic failed to deflect him. After he had ordered champagne from the stewardess – I declined – he began to reel off everything he knew about Valparaiso, the lower city or *Plan*, built in a narrow strip round the harbour and bay, the upper, which straggled higgledy-piggledy over the hillside '... so that you felt if one building fell from the bottom, the whole lot would collapse like a pack of cards. The two parts of the city are connected by century-old cable cars.' Eventually I realised that his 'good old Valpo' disguised an admiration of the city that stretched his imagination alarmingly. All the same I was pleased when, after another quarter-bottle of champagne, he fell asleep abruptly, leaving me once more to concentrate on my freedom.

I really did need to read through several new papers about what awaited me in Tamil Nadu (I was flying to Chennai, once Madras) but my neighbour's words echoed distractingly in my head. As he'd talked, I'd noticed he wasn't English as I'd first assumed, but from Australia or perhaps New Zealand. His accent was faint, as if he'd been away from his own country for a long time. I thought of these millions of people who are displaced from their home countries or take themselves off. This was what K had done, fleeing from something so terrible that he couldn't even remain on the same continent.

Yet I had remained. I had been too frail to run, too young. My survival had depended on those closest to me, who gave me constant love and attention. Eventually their efforts had succeeded and I had tottered on to my legs. But he had gone where there was nothing, no one. I paused and, this time, accepted a small bottle of wine from the stewardess. Why did I believe he had had no one? He might have a wife and children in Valparaiso, going up and down in the cable-cars in a happy little group.

An image of the man in the changing-hut dispelled the idea. He had been like an animal, as he'd described himself (I thought, but wasn't sure). I tried again. He had been like a hermit, with matted hair and unwashed skin. He was an unsociable animal, not a family man with a couple of children skipping at his side. I was the one who had found a partner, if only to discard him.

Outside the window the sky was clear blue with a bright layer of gold as if the unseen sun spread a protective varnish. With nose almost pressed to the window, I thought that K, too, had once chosen a partner. I felt a long sigh make its way through my body. During our weeks of loving, neither of us had admitted the presence of his wife. I had not even when she stood in front of me at my mother's drinks party. I had made her a non-person, and then she had entered the frame to burst everything apart. She had exerted her will in such a way that she would never be forgotten and nothing could ever be the same again.

Yet I had still refused to recognise her. Even in my mind, I had declined to pronounce her name or status: K's wife. They had been married for fifteen years, longer than we had been separated. We had been together hardly more days than they had years. If I was serious about K, I had to recognise this. He was not only my lover but a widower.

I blinked away a well of tears. The wide, heartless sky gazed at me without a flicker. But he had come back to me, I told myself, and then he had written.

When our meal came, my neighbour woke, ordered wine and began to talk again, this time about India. His agency promoted a trip from Chennai along the coast to the south, taking in the old French colonial city of Pondicherry. He passed me a business card over our chicken tikka – we were travelling Air India – then began to describe the Madras beach (as he called it) in the evening. 'A smooth purple sea, thousands of people out for a cooling walk, balloons, babies, grilled sweetcorn, children flinging themselves through the waves, saris the colours of the sunset, like flags in the breeze, a skewbald pony, men blowing into shells at the edge of the sea, a shooting range with dolls as prizes ... As the sky loses its brightness, a long string of moon globes illuminate the beach.' From Madras he moved on to Tirukalikundram, or something like that, where tame vultures swooped down to be fed by priests. He wrote the name of the next place on my napkin – 'Mamallapuram' – and described 'the most fabulous early stone carving in the world…' He was simply rehearsing his travel brochure, but my earlier feelings of freedom and exhilaration returned. I could visit the places he was talking about. After I had spent time with my Indian colleagues, assessing the success of their work, I had five days to do as I liked.

After we'd finished eating, my companion slept again, the ability, perhaps, of a man who travelled constantly through different time zones. I was solidly based in English time so it was still afternoon for me and I concentrated more seriously on my brief. The names and places I was studying seemed more real the closer the plane brought me to them.

I was met at the airport by Hedghe, a driver employed by our office. He came from Bangalore and spoke five languages, which he assured me was necessary in the south.

It was two or three in the morning Chennai time, so he dropped me at my hotel, an efficient characterless place on a busy road, and told me he would return at nine.

Of course I couldn't sleep, but not in the dazed, useless way of the past. Once more I went through my information. We partnered an organisation run in India by Indians. We had an input into various projects but fund-raising was our major role. I had to find a photographer to accompany me to their newest project, an orphanage. If all went well, I would return home with enough material to compose an illustrated report that would wring the hearts of private donors and perhaps even the Treasury. Although we were a smallish set-up, we were ambitious and linked to two other NGOs in Holland and Italy, so we weren't afraid to hold out a begging bowl to the highest in the land.

As I struggled to read in the dim light, I felt proud that I had been chosen for this task. There were no pictures yet of the orphanages so I imagined rows of big dark eyes in half-starved faces. It was needed because of the rise in AIDS – that part made miserable reading.

By seven thirty I was downstairs, breakfasting on toast and

pineapple juice with groups of young businessmen and air steward-esses.

At nine I stood outside, watching the flood of life that I'd heard passing by my window since dawn and I could now see for myself. The noise, the smells, exhaust fumes cancelling the bright sunshine, should have been overwhelming, but I liked it. I waved energetically as Hedghe drew up at the kerb. I liked it all: the skinny boys with old-fashioned ghetto-blasters on their shoulders, the motor scooters puffing out smoke like rockets, the ox-cart negotiating the six lines of honking traffic with stolid imperturbability.

'I'm so glad to be here,' I announced to the gathered staff when we reached the office. 'It is an honour to meet those who do the real work.'

Apart from two formidable sari-clad matrons, most of the team were my age or younger. As far as I could make out they were up at five and didn't go to bed till midnight. Mira became my special friend. She was very slim, wore pencil-tight jeans and a T-shirt. A camera dangled round her neck. 'When I've stopped being good, I shall be a photographer,' she explained seriously. Then she smiled. She didn't think she was being good. And I had found my photographer.

On the fourth day of my trip, we went to the orphanage together. We drove off early but it was already hot, the sun shafting off the brand new coastal road. Every now and again our wheels crunched over rice laid to dry on its oven-hot surface, to be winnowed for free by passing traffic. Sometimes we had to avoid piles of peanuts or sweetcorn.

After an hour or two Mira turned right and the jeep bumped over a dusty, uneven track. The contrast was so great that I must have looked foolishly shocked.

'In a country the size of ours you can't expect all the roads to be tarmacked.'

We made our way slowly through one village, then another. One had a high gate gorgeously painted, another a vast wooden horse with fierce-looking rider guarding the entrance. The houses had mud-baked walls with palm-leaf roofs. Beyond the open struts of a half-built one, I saw rows of children sitting on the sandy floor. Their shirts shone white against their dark skin. The girls wore red ribbons in their hair. 'Every village has a school?' I asked.

'Certainly. Perhaps not every.'

We arrived in a flourish of dust in front of the orphanage. It, too, seemed only half built but someone had set a painted tin barrel filled with orange marigolds at either side of the doorway.

'The older children will be at school,' explained Mira, as I unstuck my shirt and cotton trousers from my sweating skin. I wiped my face on the scarf round my neck. 'But we'll meet the staff,' she continued, 'the small children and babies. Good photo opportunities.' She smiled a little wickedly.

We were there for nearly three hours, during which, apart from a couple of breaks for sweet tea, I took notes and Mira photographs.

I was staggered by the needs of the orphanage. Already four hundred children lived there, and the numbers rose daily, yet the water supply ran only twice a day, if they were lucky, and the sanitary facilities would have been considered barely adequate for a B-and-B in England.

'What can we do?' said the director, a frail-looking man with a slight cast in his eye. 'Turn away the helpless?'

During all this time, I'd hardly been able to take in the children's individual faces, except now and again to point Mira in a particular direction. Eventually we were taken outside to the shade of a large banyan tree, with benches arranged round it.

'Sit,' offered the director.

I have never sat down more thankfully. I accepted slices of coconut and a sickly sherbet drink. On my lap, my pad bulged with information. Momentarily, I closed my eyes. I opened them again to see a group of about fifty children, aged no more than four or five, being led into the dusty space in front of us.

'One, two, three,' intoned their leader in English, and they began to sing, their piping voices as high as birds'.

It took me a minute to realise they were singing English words. Mira nudged me. 'You hear.'

I listened more closely and gradually, through the stunning heat and my exhaustion, I made out the song: '. . . for she's a jolly good fellow, For she's a jolly good fellow, And so say all of us.'

I'm not ashamed of what happened next: I burst into tears. It was all too much, the desperate poverty, the unforced hopefulness, the real beauty of the scene. And they were singing for me. I knew I was just the representative of my agency but I was sitting there, mopping away tears with my scarf as I had my sweat earlier.

When they stopped singing, the director and everyone else stared at me in some consternation, I stood up and forced myself to smile, at which everyone else smiled too.

'I am so happy,' I said, 'and I always cry when I'm happy. I am so happy that we may be able to help you a little. Your singing is beautiful, but I deserve no praise. You deserve all the praise. Thank you.'

Then I walked among the children and helpers and soon a child was clinging to each of my hands and a cluster of others were holding on to my clothing; the naughty ones pulled at my shirt, then ran away giggling. It felt all the more astonishing, because I'd had almost nothing to do with children.

'Shall I rescue you?' Mira ceased snapping for a moment and took my arm.

The high-pitched flutter of children's voices, 'Miss, Miss,' ceased and they regarded her with solemn eyes. They knew she was taking away this unusual entertainment.

'Yes,' I said, sighing. 'I'd hate to keel over and die in front of them.'

'A tiring day,' agreed Mira. 'But I've an idea.'

She drove us back to the smart new road, turned off to the left and bumped down a different track until we reached a small beach hotel, fronted by a palm-covered veranda. It was mid-afternoon and no one was around. Far away, over acres of pale sand, the sea mirrored the white glare of the sky.

As I sat down at a wooden table, Mira sprang towards a drinks machine with shouts of glee. 'Iced Coke, Claudia?' Sometimes she made me feel old.

The Coke turned out to be at boiling point since there was no power to the machine but the peace was incredible, the only sound a rustling as a light breeze caught the palms above our heads.

'You don't have children?'

What was it about Mira and that hot still afternoon that made me recount my story? Even my shrink had been forced to drag out every word. But now I told it willingly, somehow feeling that Mira needed to know everything about me for a proper answer to her question. The orphanage had set me off, I supposed, the hordes of parentless children who had so little when I had had so much, yet seemed so prepared to enjoy themselves. I was shamed. Yet again.

Mira was an inspired listener. Perhaps it was part of her job. She appeared to be interested, but never shocked.

She had not been to England so it might have seemed like a fairy-tale to her, however unpleasant the climax. When I drew to a close, telling her about K's reappearance in my life, she listened especially attentively, watching my face. She didn't seem to know where Valparaiso was but, like me, she rolled the syllables appreciatively before she asked, with a blithe expression, a series of unanswerable questions 'You will visit him? He is single? You love him still?'

I found myself laughing, a little hysterically. 'What do you think?'

'Plenty of time for children.'

Since I had told her everything, she knew about that early pregnancy. 'With him, you mean? He's old now. Fifty-five.'

'That *is* old.' Her face fell.

'I know nothing about his situation.'

She leant back in her chair with a wise expression. 'You will go to Valparaiso because you're curious.'

'That's not a very good reason.'

'But it's true. People do many important things out of curiosity.'

I thought that, after all, she was very young. As we'd been talking, the sun had lowered and moved to the west. Several groups of guests from the hotel had passed us and settled on the sand. Their figures cast long shadows that had turned from white to yellow. Some children splashed at the edge of the sea.

'It's not so hot any more,' I said. 'Shall we walk a little.' I needed to move now, shift the weight of memories from both of us.

More people were coming on to the beach. A woman draped with brilliantly coloured sari lengths came towards us. She displayed them one at a time, letting the breeze fly them out from her shoulder as if they were pennants.

'I'm going to buy one,' I insisted, although Mira told me that they were of the lowest quality of silk and dye, not even a full sari length.

I chose an unusual white one, printed with silver butterflies. It seemed the most beautiful thing in the world to me but Mira remained unconvinced. 'You should go to the silk factory and buy properly.' She didn't understand that I wanted something to remind me of this afternoon when I had revealed secrets and the sky hadn't fallen in to crush me. I looked at the sea, its brightness turning to mauve and dull pink as the sun's last rays dipped below the horizon.

We walked further and other hopeful beach-sellers came to us with sweetened nuts, sticks of sugar cane and more slices of coconut, even orange juice on chunks of ice.

'Be it on your head – or, rather, your stomach,' warned Mira, ominously.

Our roles were reversed: she was the sensible, older woman and I was the headstrong child. 'I'm starving.' That afternoon nothing could have killed me: I was inviolable – although I drew the line when three small boys came up with a skewered terrapin.

Before I was ready, Mira turned back. I was still unused to the speed at which night descended. She explained that the great black road became even more dangerous after dark, when the marker rocks for the drying rice or peanuts became a real hazard, as did all the other unlit carts and tractors, and the murderous buses.

'Just drive slowly,' I advised.

'Not possible.'

I soon saw what she meant. Everybody moved at their utmost speed. If a car had slowed to the speed of a bicycle, then the hair's breadth estimations made by other methods of transport would have been thrown out of kilter, resulting in even greater chaos.

It was at the moment when our headlamps lit a troupe of dancers and musicians, in full dancing regalia, and even Mira slammed on her brakes, that I thought I'd left one thing out of my story: music.

'Please, stop.' For once she obeyed me – or perhaps she was intrigued. A full-scale performance in the middle of hectic traffic might have been a first for her too. But soon enough cars, trucks and people had gathered to make an auditorium for the players, our headlights putting them on the stage. There were six or seven dancers, all elaborately costumed in red, blue and gold, four musicians, one with a tambourine, one with a guitar-like instrument, a drummer and a trumpeter.

They couldn't have been further from a privileged girl in England's home counties who thought she could play the viola – an instrument best known for its appearance in the esoteric string quartet. I had questioned everything about myself for so long, always coming in with the lowest estimation, but I had cut off my music without question. My shrink hadn't asked about it either. My music had disappeared as completely as K.

'They're travelling players.' Mira looked at me. 'You like it?'

'Very much. I used to play a lot. Before the time I told you about.'

Mira laughed, shocking me rather. I tried to believe it meant that she believed in my happy future. But maybe she hadn't taken too seriously what I'd told her. Fourteen years must have seemed a long time. 'I played also. But so badly. I thought I was Ravi Shankar.' She laughed again. So her laughter had been at herself.

We drove on again and arrived back in time for a huge curry with the other staff. When I lay in bed that night, I thought of the orphanage but I also heard music in my head. Not that piece from the summer, but the cacophonous sound of the road mixing with what we had been taught to call 'Western Art Music'. It seeped through me to join the voice of the director with a cast in his eye, 'At least we must care properly for their bodies,' and with the children themselves, the high sweetness of their voices, 'For she's a jolly good fellow. And so say all of us.'

Eventually they sang me to sleep.

CHAPTER THIRTY-EIGHT

2004

At Christmas I went out to Hong Kong. It was a further freedom.

Louise's husband, Tom, picked me up from the airport. We hadn't met for a couple of years and I could see he was surprised by me. I was wearing a red jacket and pulled an efficient black case. I think he'd been expecting a wreck. Perhaps Louise hadn't kept him up to speed.

His expression was a present that I held close to me during the following ten days. The children, the two eldest on holiday from university in England, were lovely too, accepting me easily as their aunt, pleased that my arrival meant treats, boat trips, meals in restaurants.

One scorching blue day we hired a launch out to an island called Coluane. Louise suggested a hat as my skin was white from an English winter but I chose factor twenty-five instead and let the sun and wind flow across my cheeks. Behind were the turrets and spires of modern Hong Kong, ahead the green mountains on the small islands that attended China's shores.

'We'll have lunch in a piece of old Portugal,' shouted Louise.

Reggie stood beside his father. It was his illness that had stopped Louise coming over in the summer at the time of my father's death. He was ten, an afterthought in their family, and seemed perfectly fit now.

'Twenty-eight degrees celsius and rising!' He had turned to shout at me. I waved back. His siblings hadn't come on the expedition, preferring the air-conditioned cool of a cinema visit with friends, so it was just the four of us. We tied up under the lee of a large black barge that had brought over a crowd from the mainland. We could see them ahead, all of the women and some of the men carrying umbrellas against the sun.

'They've come to buy dried fish from the villagers,' explained Tom.

It was strange to wander through a traditional fishing village, which would have looked the same hundreds of years ago, with its wooden shacks and rows of drying fish, such a short distance from one of the most modern cities in the world.

'Enjoy it while we can,' said Louise. 'The next two islands, Taipa and particularly Macau, are gradually being overrun by high-rises. Macau's got more casinos than Las Vegas.'

In my avidity for new places I felt like a gap-year student. Everything delighted me. When Tom and Reggie went off to look for a swimming-pool, Louise and I settled in an elegant Portuguese-designed square. At the far end, facing the sea, was a small but decorative rococo church, on either side restaurants and cafés, fronted by pillared and porticoed arcades.

I had been in Hong Kong for three days now but Louise and I hadn't spoken about anything important, – except my trip to India. Perhaps it was enough for her to know that I was operational, planning a positive future.

'Wine?' she asked.

'Oh, definitely.' I was happy enough to sit there silently enjoying the warmth and light-hearted atmosphere, but Louise had always had an open face and I guessed suddenly she had sent Tom and Reggie off so that she could talk to me in private. My face reddened in a preparatory panic. I couldn't remember whether I'd told her at our father's funeral that K had returned, that I had seen him again.

'I know about James,' Louise was blushing. 'Mother wrote. She said you knew already.'

What shaming self-absorption! She wanted to talk about our mother's lover, not mine. Until she'd said 'Mother', the name 'James' hadn't meant anything to me. 'Yes. It's good. Have they decided when to marry?'

'It was a dreadful shock to me.'

'I'm sorry,' I had jumped ahead too quickly. Quite possibly, Louise still didn't know about the early love affair. If I'd been Catherine, I wouldn't have told her. There was an innocence about her – I'd be kind enough not to call it narrowness – which made her the more easily shocked of us. I hoped she wouldn't question me too closely. Of course I hadn't told her about K's return. 'The house is sold,'

I added. 'Did she tell you that too?'

'Yes. That's why she told me about James. She's moving in with him.'

'I see. That's news to me.' I was glad she'd found out something before I had. It made me less responsible.

'I gather they've known each other for years.'

'Oh, really?' I was not to be drawn. But I thought, with one of those little flashes of memory not recorded at the time, that quite possibly the Save the Children afternoons had been cover for more exciting assignations. It struck me, with ridiculous post-dated jealousy, that on the uncomfortable occasion when K had come to lunch on the terrace and I had gone for a swim she had been flirting with him. As if one lover wasn't enough.

'I guess Douglas was a dour kind of husband,' I said. It seemed safe enough ground, but Louise picked it up at once.

'Marriage isn't about whether your husband's a ball of fire.'

'No,' I agreed hastily. We drank our wine. Too much, if my next remark was anything to go by. 'I might be travelling to Chile in the new year.'

Yet Louise, who had no idea of K's continuing existence and certainly not of his present home, could receive this information casually. 'I didn't know your agency had projects in South America.' She'd assumed it was a working trip and I had another chance to keep quiet.

'They don't. K lives there. In Valparaiso. On the coast.'

It was funny, really. Or cruel. I could see I had ruined her day. It was bad enough when I'd broken off with Oliver. She'd pinned on him all her hopes for my happy future. She'd never been able to cope with K. She had never met him. He was the wicked bogeyman who had ruined her little sister's life. Now she didn't want to believe in his existence. It was cruel of me, not funny at all.

'Forget I spoke,' I said loudly, and smiled. 'It's all fantasy. A touch of the sun.' We were strangers, really. Mira had understood. 'Look, here come Tom and Reggie.' They were swaggering happily across the square, just a hint of damp in their similarly blond hair. 'You found a pool, then,' I called, determined to erase my words from Louise's consciousness. Yet at exactly the same moment my determination to go to Valparaiso in the next couple of months became irrevocable. The leap in my heart was a mixture of terror and delight.

'So, is it grilled fish all round?' said Tom, resting his hand on Louise's shoulder.

Who can know what is in the heart of another?

CHAPTER THIRTY-NINE

2004–5

Craig came back to Valpo on New Year's Eve. He drove me up to a friend's apartment so that we could watch the firework display in the bay. He made no comment that I was still living in what he called my 'shack' and I didn't invite him to look at my new paintings. It was the wrong moment. Tonight I would take a few hours off from the feverish schedule of work I had set myself.

The apartment, although modern, stood very high in the *cerro*. It was filled with the Chilean rich, with their seamless golden skin and pale linen suits and dresses. They were welcoming to me, the eccentric English painter who chose to live among the poor. I accepted a goblet of wine – from the region behind the coastal town of Zapallar, I was informed, for many of Craig's guests were wine-growers. There were children, too, and babies, although it was already late. Despite the crowd – the room was almost overfull – everyone seemed related to everyone else: mothers, fathers, cousins, aunts and uncles. It was like a family party, but they were kind, found me a chair by the wide windows, told me about their visits to London, assured me that the date of my exhibition was in their diary.

That was why Craig had brought me. He was a good friend. He'd even presented me with a 'Christmas present' of a soft blue shirt – my first present for many years - which I was wearing.

At midnight the black sea so far below was lit by a wild upward rush of colour and sound. The fireworks were placed on the vast battleships that normally sat in the harbour with the gloomy air of anachronism.

Now they were the launch-pad to a sky world of Miró and Chagall, peacock tails and autumn leaves. The noise was less graceful, warlike explosions echoing through banshee screams as the rockets tore upwards, but even in the clear night air they were muted by distance, and my eyes gloried in the vast moving canvas, from east to west, reaching, it seemed, to a limitless horizon.

I had watched the celebration before, of course, but never with the same concentration or the same depth of emotion.

'Glad I brought you?' Craig appeared, to pour me another drink. I was sitting so far forward to the windows that I had become unaware of the party behind me.

I didn't answer him – he would know by my stance what I was feeling, my spirit reaching far out beyond us perched so precariously atop the *cerro*. Then it flashed into my head that this would be my last new year, that I was anticipating my own death, a great colourful journey into the unknown.

I turned to him quickly, 'Thank you. It's fantastic.' I had my paintings to finish.

'You could say it's a come-down for the Chileans, once the proud possessors of a great navy, that is now the setting for the third largest fireworks extravaganza in the world.'

I let him talk. After all his care, I mustn't rush away. I concentrated now on the double image of the fireworks, mirrored in the glassy waters of the bay. Although the ocean was still, captured below the mountains in a wide natural harbour, the spinning whorls, fountains and flowing cascades of colour and light shimmered mysteriously on the watery stage. I half closed my eyes so that the rockets seemed to stream both up and down in impossible projection.

'Of course, it wasn't really a Chilean navy.' Craig was still holding forth. 'The great admiral was British, Admiral Cochrane rescued them from the Spanish. Even Neruda wrote a poem about him as the country's hero. But, no doubt, having lived here so long, you know the history better than I do. . .'

After a while he went away and I was alone again. This time my attention was drawn to other parts of the city below me. Along every *mirador*, where the steep sides flattened for a place to stand and stare, there was a shifting crowd of black figures, silhouetted against moving lights, below the globes strung between a line of trees. I could imagine the celebrations, the singing, the dancing, the music. This might not be Copacabana beach but the Chileans knew how to enjoy themselves. In an hour or two they'd start eating, a feast of meat and fruit, washed down with beer or, for the sophisticated, *pisco* sours, sweet and strong. They wouldn't even think of bed till dawn. For a second, I yearned to be out there with them. How foolish! I was already at a party, with friends.

I brought myself back into the room, held out my glass for more wine and found myself facing Pablo, the owner of the gallery where I would exhibit my paintings. Valparaiso is a small world.

'You are painting well, eh?' He spoke in Spanish, although I knew his English was good. This was a Chilean night.

'I'm painting hard every day. Not just during the day.'

'I heard you were unwell.' He was a thick-set man, with a great head of thick black hair.

'I'm well enough to paint.' I lifted my glass. 'And to celebrate.' He needn't know anything more.

'I'm glad. People are excited. Valparaiso hasn't had a good painter for many years.' He was very serious, staring hard into my face. 'Soon we must talk prices. Soon I must visit your studio. We must go as high as we dare. People here respect what is costly.'

'It's the same everywhere.' The prices were of little importance to me. I had never regretted my decision to give the local priest my blood money – the proceeds from Fiona's flat. I had told him I chose to live like a poor man and he had decided I was a kind of saint. Ironic, really. I was never tempted to tell him the truth. But I allowed him to say prayers for my soul – not that I could have stopped him.

Pablo had frightened me, though. It was true that I would have to submit to his visit, to his estimating my work. 'Give me a couple more weeks,' I said. 'Or perhaps three.'

'Of course.' He turned away, then back. 'You should eat and sleep as well as work.' He spoke in English this time, as if to make certain I understood.

'Thanks.' I smiled at him, trying to instil confidence. In fact, the amount of wine I'd drunk on an empty stomach had swept away earlier intimations of mortality. My reclusive existence hadn't prepared me for the loss of inhibition, the sudden rush of energy, artificial or not.

A very beautiful woman was standing at my elbow. She wore a sleeveless black dress, and her skin and her hair were the colour of Aztec gold. She was obviously curious about me. Her wide almond-coloured eyes stared at me as she answered my questions in perfect English, with only the slightest (charming) accent.

She was separated from her husband, she told me. She had four children, all boys. They were grown-up now, and she had two grandchildren.

'I am a grandma!' she exclaimed. '*Abuela.*' She used the Spanish word as if to rub it in. Maybe she was testing me, but I knew Chilean women married young and had large families. Besides, her fecundity excited me.

Now she asked me questions. What did I paint? She wanted to know 'exactly'.

'I paint your *ascensores.*' I laughed at her expression. 'Not one naked lady on a velvet *chaise-longue.*'

'Ah, no, no.' I had embarrassed her.

Around us the air of carnival was rising. Only the smallest children had dropped off to sleep, finding comfortable corners on the floor or on the laps of the silver-haired matriarchs who sat benignly upright.

'What is your name?' I asked.

'Maria Eugenia.'

'You are very beautiful, Maria Eugenia.'

From the kitchen there came smells of barbecuing fish and meat, accompanied by cries of sudden panic or delight at which one person or even two would fly out with tales of charred fish or succulent meat. It was theatre, a celebration of living that I had long thought behind me.

I couldn't share in the food with much gusto, but as the night progressed, the fireworks a thing of the past, I stayed as close as possible to Maria Eugenia. I was determined to end the evening with her, imagining her, in a hazy, drunken way, naked on that velvet couch.

But she had many relatives and friends there and it was only by an amazing stroke of good luck that, as the dawn reached over the hills behind us, I found myself seated next to her in a car, headed in the direction of Vina del Mar.

'Ah, Maria Eugenia,' I whispered in her ear, 'don't go down with them. Follow me and we will continue our celebrations at the Hotel Weymouth.'

So it was that we found ourselves 'breakfasting' on its terrace, accompanied by dozens of late-night or, rather, early-morning revellers. It was surprisingly easy to persuade her from there to one of the bedrooms – next door, as it happened, to the room I'd stayed in fourteen years ago.

It was a miracle that I could make love in my condition, but I did, and as I came I thought of Claudia, her yellow hair streaming like a comet in the sky. But there was no anguish, only wistful nostalgia.

Maria Eugenia was a kind, attentive lover. One of those flashing ideas that this might be the last time I made love came into my head and I was glad that it was with her and not with a passing lady of the night in whose services I had occasionally invested.

After we had slept for a while, and with the drink still taking us from a too hard reality, we smiled, almost laughed at each other. I wanted to ask why she had got out of the car with me. Instead, I said, 'So you will go back to your husband, your marriage?'

'Perhaps.' We were whispering in Spanish. The walls were thin, the hotel filled with the fallen. 'He must need me. He must beg me.'

'Yes. He should beg you. A woman of your gifts.'

She squeezed my hand. 'And I shall come to your exhibition.'

'Yes.' She had meant that we would not meet again like this. I began to think of my paintings. An abstract version of the *ascensor* Cerra Monjas, looking down from the top, was giving me particular trouble. I could not achieve, however hard I tried, the impression of a breathtaking drop, almost as if the brightly painted little car would fall into the ocean below. Suddenly I saw that that was the answer: a splash of deep blue-green at the base of the painting.

'You're so thin. Like a boy.' Maria Eugenia put two fingers on my hip. But they fell away as I sprang out of bed.

'We must go!'

'In such a hurry?' She grumbled a bit, but good-temperedly. I wondered briefly to what elegant flat or house in Vina or up the coast she'd return, but only briefly because I was impatient to get to my painting before the flood of energy left me.

Fittingly, we parted at the entrance to the *ascensor* Concepción. As so often on a day that was to be hot, a thick mist or *neblina* clung to the *cerros*, disguising the harbour and the city below to which Maria Eugenia was about to descend – and disappear.

I waited long enough to watch her wave amid the crowds of post-party revellers. Then I began to walk back to my paintings. I didn't plan to leave them again until it was time for my exhibition.

CHAPTER FORTY

1990

Early on Monday morning K crept from Fiona's side – she was still sleeping comfortably – and went out to the garden. His legs were stiff from the long walk and his head was heavy – although it was probably his heart.

The soft, damp air revived him a little and he gave a few desultory stretches. Then it struck him that there was no reason why he shouldn't go to Meadowlands that morning. Claudia would have returned to school on Saturday. He could go back. He *must* go back to explain to Catherine the reason for his sudden departure. Amid the lies and secrecy, there remained the truth that he had stayed away to look after his wife. Catherine would understand that and, for some reason, he wanted her to think well of him. Because she was Claudia's mother? He would confess that his novel was not working out, another truth, and that he was planning to return to a normal working life. (Whatever that might be.) He would gather up his belongings, his laptop, his pads, white and yellow, his reference books – all useless, all lies.

While K made these plans, he walked round the garden, rather like a man in a cell, making at intervals, and unconsciously, grimaces and grunts. It was as if he was trying to persuade his body of the new (or old) path it was to tread. But Brother Ass was not so easily convinced. The deadness of his designated future broke out in rebellion, in small but anguished yearnings for Claudia.

He fought on, however, and eventually went inside to make two cups of tea. A streak of sun had edged through one of the windows and he noted the tiny lift of spirits it brought him. I may not be a writer, he told himself, but I am sensitive to the world around me.

Slowly, with a cup of tea in either hand, he walked up the stairs to Fiona. She was sitting up in bed, waiting for him.

'I feel a fraud not going to work.' She looked delighted with herself and him, as if the canker in her womb meant nothing.

K reproved himself for any bitterness in his thoughts. He sat on her bed. 'I'd better go and sort things out at Meadowlands this morning.'

He'd told her of his decision to give up writing and had been considerably surprised at how little she'd resisted or even shown interest. 'You must do what you think best,' was all she'd said. It struck him now that she'd been humouring him all along and never truly believed he'd be a writer. Perhaps she'd only given him those months of freedom as a *quid pro quo* for her right to have a baby.

It was just after eight thirty when K left the house. He noticed the postman's van, rather later than usual, coming down the road. He thought vaguely that there was unlikely to be anything interesting for him and carried on.

Despite a still-high temperature, Claudia insisted on dressing and coming downstairs. Her restless wanderings and shining dark-circled eyes worried Catherine. 'If you won't stay in bed, at least settle somewhere warm and comfortable.'

'Can't you see I'm hot?' Claudia hurried away into the large, chintz-filled drawing-room where she stood at the window playing with the ties that held back the curtains. The piano irritated her with its absurd load of photographs and shut keyboard. Music, too, had let her down, she thought irrationally. It was now a whole miserable week since she had last seen K, and her panic and despair made her quake both inwardly and outwardly. Then she reminded herself, as she had since about five that morning, that today her letter would arrive. Today K would know the situation and he would come to her. So beleaguered was her mind and so great her need that she had given up worrying that he might be away from home. She felt certain that he would read the letter – was even now reading it – and that he would drive up at any time, very soon, otherwise ... But there was no place for 'otherwise'. He would surely come.

So Claudia continued her feverish perambulations. Her ears, quickened by anticipation, noted and placed the others in the house: her mother in the kitchen talking to the recently arrived cleaner, her father, who had been persuaded to take more time off work, fiddling in the cupboard under the stairs.

Yet when K's car did come down the drive, more hesitantly than usual, she missed its arrival. She was in the bathroom, and by the time she emerged, he had driven past his usual parking place to a corner beyond the entrance to his workroom.

She hadn't heard him coming and she couldn't see his car. She decided to return to her bedroom, away from her mother's attentions. Then, perhaps, she'd go to the pool. Then he would certainly have come.

K felt as if he were returning to Meadowlands in another age. The pain of his love for Claudia remained but felt like a past tragedy. He sat at his desk with the stage of green lawn beyond the window and remembered the evening she'd first entered his view, the damp smell of newly mown grass, the murmuring of sleepy birds and the bright slenderness of her body.

He'd brought two bags in which he began to pack his things. Afterwards he would go and find Catherine, an interview to which he was not looking forward. He had behaved irresponsibly, the sin disguised at first by Fiona's emergency, and then the far greater sin towards Claudia. He put his elbows on the desk, his head in his hands, and allowed himself to picture, as well as his imagination would allow him, Claudia in her school surroundings. At ten thirty on a Monday she was sure to be in class – studying Shakespeare, he decided. '"Shall I compare thee to a summer's day ..."' he recited romantically. That was what she had been to him. But it was over now, love affair and summer, just as Shakespeare had predicted: '...but summer's lease hath all too short a date...' His room, which had been pleasantly cool, was cold now, draughts sneaking through the window-frames and even the walls. There was no 'eternal' summer for Claudia and him.

K looked up again and noted the changing colours of the chestnuts at the end of the lawn. They were still green, but the green had a dry, russet edge to it. Even on this light September morning, the leaves were crinkling towards death.

The best thing, K told himself bracingly, was to forget what could not be. Claudia was young, a *schoolgirl,* he repeated to himself, and would get over him soon enough. He must clear out as quickly as possible. With this in mind, he began to work much more hurriedly and soon had his two bags and the laptop lined up by the door. He turned back to check the room once more, and perhaps to say farewell, and his eye was caught by a figure disappearing behind the left frame of the window. His eye had seen more but his mind informed him of nothing but an anonymous outline that had crossed his view in the direction of the swimming-pool.

Turning his back on such mirages, he picked up his bags and went downstairs to his car, then returned for the laptop and a few other loose items. He was tempted, when everything was neatly stowed in the boot, to mount the stairs once more, allow himself a little journey into what might have been. On the other hand he hardly wished to put off his interview with Catherine any longer. He could always take one last look later.

Feeling that the situation demanded formality, he stood at the front door and rang the bell. As he waited, he smelt a faint, agreeably medical aroma from the great cedar tree on the other side of the drive. It was impossible not to recall his picnics on the bench, the strains of Claudia's viola. A sickening feeling of loss made him clasp the doorknob for strength.

The door opened inwards and Catherine confronted him. He had staggered forward a step, but recovered himself. 'Oh,' she said, not unfriendly. 'The bad penny.'

'I'm so sorry. I ...'

'Come in. I was just going to make some coffee.'

He followed her down the passageway into the kitchen, which smelt of fresh-roasted coffee and toast.

'Take a seat.'

K sat down. He identified a desire to burst into tears and confess everything. The cosy room was giving him a false sense of comfort and security.

There was a banging at the door. 'Ah, you're back. Good morning.'

It was Douglas. He was carrying a shotgun and a bag slung over his shoulder. Dressed in a checked Viyella shirt and corduroy trousers, he looked more relaxed than K had ever seen him. Despite this he felt uneasy. His interview was with Catherine, not her husband.

Catherine turned from the stove. 'You're not going to clean that in here, are you, darling?'

'I was, actually.' He smiled at her. 'But I don't have to.'

'How about the garden?' Catherine explained to K: 'Douglas hasn't been out shooting for years and years. But I've persuaded him to take a bit of time off and forget his cares with a few days of mindless killing.'

'My brother has a shoot in Northumberland,' added Douglas.

'I see.' K knew nothing about such grandeur.

'I'll shift to the garden, then, as long as I get a cup of coffee at some point.'

'You're an angel.'

K was struck by the unusual warmth between them. But when the door was shut behind her husband, Catherine sighed and smiled at him, 'Now we can talk in peace.'

Were all marriages a mix of affection and deception? K wondered, as he accepted his coffee and prepared to begin his speech. 'Unfortunately my wife was rushed to hospital. She's fine now but it put everything out of my mind. In fact, it's changed a lot of things.'

As K spoke, he was amazed by how true it sounded although it left out the most important part of the story, which affected Catherine. 'I'm sorry,' he said. 'It was irresponsible.' During his telling, he was determined not to mention Claudia's name, which he knew he couldn't pronounce without emotion. He slid quickly on to his need for a paid job while Fiona was unwell, leaving out, to salvage a bit of pride, his failure as a novelist and Fiona's planned return to work. 'It's been such a wonderful summer,' he said, trying to keep his voice level. 'You've been so kind.'

What could Catherine say? She was sorry about Fiona. It had been a pleasure having him. She was sorry about the novel. Perhaps another time? She, too, didn't mention Claudia's name, which, contradictorily, he regretted. 'Well, I'd better take Douglas his coffee before it's cold.' She stood.

'I should say goodbye then.'

She seemed surprised. 'You mean you're going now? This instant?'

'Yes. I'm all packed.' He tried to sound cheerful, matter-of-fact. 'I left the keys on the desk.'

'I see.' She paused, frowned. 'You'd better come and say goodbye to Douglas, then.'

'OK.'

They walked out of the door and across the lawn together, not talking. K felt exhausted, as if he'd run a race. He quelled an insane desire to flee for his car and head home.

Claudia's presence, now that he was really leaving, was everywhere, in the grass trodden so often by her long, narrow feet, in the trees where they'd listened to birdsong together.

'There he is.' Catherine pointed to the gardener's shed not far from the tennis court, although the nets, he noticed, were no longer up. They walked over briskly. Douglas had one gun leaning against the shed and was cleaning another, pulling a long rag through the barrel.

'Our writer-in-residence has come to say goodbye,' explained Catherine. 'He's hanging up his pen for the time being.'

Douglas looked pleased rather than otherwise, K thought. 'Time to move on, eh?' He hardly took his attention from his gun, his thick greying hair half hiding his heavy face. As always, it was hard to believe he could be Claudia's father.

Claudia had wandered miserably to the pool and, wrapped in a red towel, sat down in a deck-chair. Finally exhausted by her vigil, she fell into a superficial sleep. She woke to the sound of voices not far away. She lay still, trying to distinguish them, although her heart had already told her one was K's. So he had come to her, as she'd expected. Now he was here, she felt gloriously languid and unhurried. Even the hot beat in her head seemed a positive force now, not an illness. Perhaps she would let him find her here.

But in another moment she had changed her mind. How could she delay a second? She sprang to her feet and, still clutching the towel round her, hastened away from the pool to the lawn. There, she hesitated. K and her parents were hidden by the garden shed but she could still hear their voices. Any second, she knew, K would come round the corner towards his office, towards her, and she would run towards him.

K felt an increased eagerness to leave – even a sense of panic, as if something dreadful would happen if he stayed. But Catherine stood close to him and Douglas continued to grumble about his guns. Apparently he'd found an unknown one in the shed. 'Quite illegal. You have to lock them up, you know.'

K didn't know and didn't want to know.

'It's probably Alan banging away at the pigeons. Really, the man's quite irresponsible. He's half gypsy, you know.'

'Is that so?' said K who didn't know again. He decided to take his chance. 'I'll say goodbye then.'

He started walking away at once, across the lawn, away from the shed and the house. For some reason his heart was pounding.

He saw Claudia before she saw him. It was only for a particle of second, but long enough for him to register a vast surge of love that winded him and stopped him in his tracks.

Then she was running towards him, the red towel she'd been wrapped in dropping to the grass. She was wearing a light blue swim suit and her long legs flashed like blades in the light. As she ran, she held out her arms to him and uttered little mews of joy.

What could K do but stretch wide his own arms and welcome her into a tight embrace?

They were clasped together, Claudia's head draped over his shoulder, when a noise made K turn, Claudia still in his arms. Over her shoulders he saw Fiona. She was shouting, then screaming, her mouth wide in anguish.

At the same time, Catherine and Douglas emerged from behind the shed, Douglas carrying a gun in his left hand. They looked uncomprehending. Fiona was screaming accusations.

K tried to let go of Claudia but she clung to him with all her strength. She was whispering in his ear, about love and something else, but he was too shocked to hear it.

He had no choice but to take her with him. From the three points of a triangle, they all converged, no one quite hearing what anyone said, everyone understanding something different from the scene.

K tried again to extricate himself from Claudia, to hand her over to her parents. He needed to calm Fiona, find out why she had suddenly burst on them like this (she must have walked, he thought, since he had the car). But she had taken Catherine's arm and was shaking her, outrage in her face and voice. When Douglas intervened, she berated him too.

'Let go of me, Claudia. Please!' K was desperate.

'No! I won't. I won't!' He had never heard her voice so childish.

Then Fiona was beating K, determined to reach Claudia whom he tried to protect. Her naked skin was so vulnerable, so soft as she clung to him, and he could hardly recognise Fiona. Her face seemed more animal than human, her mouth in a wide grimace, lips drawn so far back that her gums showed. Everything became very quick, a kaleidoscope shaken by an angry hand. Over it ran a disjointed soundtrack, filled with ugly snarls and grunts, cries and commands. K became aware that Fiona was saying the same words over and over again, as she whirled round them, fists flying. 'Love' was one word, 'hate' another, 'baby' a third. He also thought he heard Catherine telling her husband to put down the gun.

But then something even worse happened. Abruptly Claudia let go of him and began to fight with Fiona. They were snatching at each other's hair, trying to bite each other's fingers, gouge out an eye, yapping shrilly like angry dogs. Like dogs, too, they whirled round so fast that K found it hard to know where to dash in and grab. 'She's mad! She's mad!' he panted, meaning his sensible, good-hearted, practical wife.

There was blood on Claudia's shoulders, on Fiona's animal face. 'Get them apart!' screamed Catherine.

K half noticed that Douglas was bent over, unmoving, as if in pain. He knew he had to act. But why did he choose to lunge at Claudia, to pinion her hot, bloody, sweating body in his arms? As he did so, his face came very near to Fiona's. Her eyes, dark and swollen, locked on his. She asked him a question. Afterwards he wasn't even sure that she'd used words but the meaning was clear: Do you want her? And his eyes must have given an answer for he was sure he hadn't spoken.

In a flash the kaleidoscope was shaken again and she'd darted to the shed. Of course, K followed her and Claudia him and Catherine both of them, so when Fiona picked up the gun that was leaning against the shed, only Douglas, still struggling with his personal demon, wasn't close. In fact Claudia, as if planning to attack again, was closest of all, sobbing hysterically.

K imagined the danger. Catherine imagined the danger. A gun, even unloaded, as this must be, sounded warning bells of danger. Both of them lunged to pull back Claudia.

CHAPTER FORTY-ONE

2005

I didn't let K know I was coming out to Chile. Of course I had no address for him but doubtless I could have discovered it easily enough if I'd tried – through the British consul or someone.

I wanted to arrive independently, suss out the ground and even leave open the option that I would not make contact. That might seem odd behaviour but, after all, he had done the same, travelling to England to see me, then leaving again after one brief and weird meeting. There was the letter, certainly. Without it I would never have taken the long journey towards him.

The power of a letter is enormous, inestimable. Without my letter to K on that summer morning fourteen and a half years ago, the greatest evil would have been avoided. Fiona had opened it inadvertently, mistaking my defiant 'K' for 'F'. Easily done. My girlish handwriting also helped her to assume that the letter was for her. My baby – the baby I had written about in that letter to K – did not survive that morning. One might say Fiona killed it, although at the time my miscarriage hardly rated on the scale of tragedy. I guess those few people who knew assumed it was a positive side-effect.

Strangely, although I'd been so frightened to find myself pregnant and, after that horrifying morning, lost my wits for months, if not years – truly, years - the loss of the baby joined every other loss to make an even bigger black hole for me to fall into. The baby, if it had existed, would have proved the reality of our love affair. So much destruction as the result of one letter.

Or is this to simplify a situation that would have headed for tragedy inevitably, a naïve schoolgirl in love with a much older married man?

Was there any chance of this turning out well? Nevertheless there was no reason for such a cataclysmic horror.

I took K's letter with me to Valparaiso. After my stint in India, I wasn't afraid of finding my way round a foreign country. When I arrived at Santiago airport, I quickly discovered that a constant stream of buses headed for the west coast, for Vina del Mar, Zapallar or Valparaiso. The air journey had taken nearly twenty-four hours but I felt fresh and filled with energy as I left the airport. It was about ten thirty in the morning, a glorious day in high summer, as hot as it had been in India but without that particularly Indian smell, which Mira had at first told me laughingly was 'people, masses and masses of them', then added, still smiling, 'Or cow dung. Take your pick.'

The countryside around the road seemed almost uninhabited by people or animals. The lower ranges of the Andes carried on for miles with a few vineyards covering the foothills. The coach was full and well air-conditioned, but soon all the passengers on the sunny side, where I was sitting, had pulled down their blinds. My neighbour leant across to do it for me and I wanted to object, 'But what about the view? What about the rich red earth, the groves of silver eucalyptus, the rocky river gullies, the far-away mountains, the turquoise blue sky?' Instead I turned to my guidebook and tried, once again, to understand the layout of the strange city to which I was travelling.

We had just passed through a deep cut when I noticed that the atmosphere outside had totally changed. My neighbours let up the blinds. We were enveloped in a deep mist, probably a sea mist as we couldn't have been far from the Pacific. But that was little consolation.

I turned to my neighbour, an elderly woman with whom I'd already exchanged a few words in my GCSE Spanish. I gestured outside, '*Lluvia*? Rain?'

'No. No.' She shook her head emphatically, '*Neblina*.'

'*Neblina*.' It was my first word from the area. Perhaps it was appropriate: a murky softness overtaking the previous sharp brightness. I hoped not. I had come here for clarity not murk. The lowering of my spirits was natural tiredness, I told myself, after such a long journey. Grey skies were unimportant.

We were on the outskirts of Vina del Mar – an old church, a few houses, roadside stalls selling fruit and eggs – when the bus took a left-hand fork. The sign reading 'Valparaiso' made my face flush ridiculously, as if I were a child about to win a board game: 'Valparaiso. Journey's end.'

The woman beside me pointed outside and told me (I think) that these were new roads, *'las nuevas carreteras'*. I looked at her proud face more closely. She had Indian blood: her weathered skin was dark and her cheekbones high.

She began to speak to me again but too quickly for me to pick up even a word. I wondered if she could tell me how to find the Hotel Weymouth, then decided I would rather take every step of discovery on my own.

The bus entered a city but this wasn't the Valpo of K's description. There were apartment blocks, offices, arcades of shops, modern, shabby, uninteresting. We continued to descend and there, ahead, was the ocean, a vast expanse of green, muffled in the dour *neblina*. Yet it seemed to me that occasionally I caught the glint of a curling ripple as if the low cloud and mist were preparing to lift.

For a while we drove beside the sea and then, without warning, we were inside a modern bus station. All the passengers descended very fast, then dispersed even more quickly so that I found myself alone with my bag. Spotting a bar selling coffee, I went over and ordered myself a double espresso. I needed strength.

That was all it was, a temporary physical weakness. When I came out of the station into the hot, busy street, I was fired up again with my sense of mission. I stood for a moment and watched a bicycle pedal past, laden with a calor gas drum. Every now and again the rider paused and beat out a tune on his drum to attract customers. Further up the pavement a little boy with dark curly hair broke free of his mother's hand and began to dance, his face filled with merriment.

I walked until I came to a wide road, with a large cream-painted church and a rather ugly modern building, besides shops and cafés. I was becoming impatient: I recognised this as the *Plan*, not my destination. I decided to pick up a taxi and go straight to the Hotel Weymouth.

As we drove upwards at what seemed an almost vertical angle, while the car groaned and the driver told me things I couldn't understand, the focus outside changed from blurred to sharp. The sun had broken through. It shone on colours such as I'd never seen in any city before. They seemed randomly placed, a turquoise door with a yellow lintel, a burnt-orange wall with crimson bricks crumbling out of it, whitewash spattered with black graffiti, whole explosive sentences, topped in purple-framed windows, protected by straw matting. Washing hung across rooftops like a string of flags.

I watched all this from behind a swinging parade of embroidered Virgins, crosses, toys and beads, which were taped or tacked along the top of the taxi's windscreen. They tilted towards the driver and me, the road was so steep, sometimes even touching his forehead as he leant forward either to will the car on or to engage in further enthusiastic but incomprehensible explanations.

'Weymouth!' He pointed, using an accent so far from the English that I didn't understand for a moment. It hadn't taken as long as I'd expected and cost much less. I fumbled for a small note. Then the car was gone and I was standing in the road beside ornate green-painted railings. Behind them was a deep yellow building with steep turquoise-blue roofs and a porthole window above the front door. It was ribbed all over as if it were made of corrugated iron, although I supposed it was more likely to be narrow slats, and it was attached to a mass of taut wires like a tethered balloon.

I stood for a long while studying the building because I was nervous. It was very hot and sweat prickled inside my clothes. It didn't strike me that I might not find K, but it was perfectly possible that he would be embarrassed by my tracking him to his new home, his place of refuge. He might be angry. Perhaps his letter to me was the end of the affair, as far as he was concerned. It was rather late to consider such a possibility.

The hotel door opened and an old woman came out and passed me. She was dressed all in black with a black cape, her grey hair in a tight bun. I hoped she wasn't an omen.

She glanced at me curiously without smiling. It was time I plunged into the future. But even as I pushed open the door, a niggling voice wondered whether it wasn't really the past.

I slept that afternoon, until darkness shrouded the window of my small room. The Hotel Weymouth was much less grand than its name, more of a B-and-B. The owners were English, of course, I had known that. They told me I was lucky to get a room: this was high season. And I thought it was high season for me too. My sleep had refreshed me and the warm night gave me a sense of security.

When I said I was going out for a walk, the owner insisted on marking my map with safe areas. We stood in the foyer, decorated with grainy thirties photographs of Weymouth's esplanade. I told him (not quite truthfully) that I was an experienced world traveller and he mustn't worry. He gave me an ironic once-over. I suppose his expression reflected my Englishness, my fair hair, pale skin and height.

'Stay in the *cerro* Concepción or Allegre and you'll see everything you want: great vistas, beautiful old houses and museums, restaurants serving terrific fish, bars with the best red wine, tree-lined terraces, market stalls, shops and galleries, even an ex-prison.'

'I'm exhausted already,' I said, smiling, but I was examining the word 'gallery', turning it over in my mind. K was a painter now, he'd said.

'Are there many galleries?' I asked.

'Not really. We're not grand enough for too much art. There are some local painters, however.'

My face grew hot. I both wanted and was afraid to hear K's name. To avoid the possibility, I said goodbye hurriedly and set off in the direction my host had indicated.

At first I was climbing steeply up carved stone steps, past a ramshackle mix of buildings, and then the road turned sharply right and I found myself on a pedestrian walkway, circling the hillside with occasional viewing points to the sparkling city below, the fathomless sea and sky beyond. It was clearly a popular place for a stroll and soon I was one of a crowd, old, young, whole families including babies in slings or toddlers in push-chairs.

I came to a wider section, where there were small ornamental trees, benches and some stalls, selling leather purses or necklaces made of bean pods. A group of young women, not far away, were singing. They were crouched in a circle and in the middle a man played a guitar. Behind us a splendid white building stood in its own garden. I could smell mimosa and eucalyptus.

I sat on one of the benches. A stall selling popcorn set up nearby and soon the sweet, sugary smell overwhelmed every other.

I was stuffing myself with popcorn and sugar-coated nuts when a little girl in a tasselled crimson cardigan, stood in front of me, her black eyes staring unblinkingly. I held out the paper bag with popcorn but as soon as she took a step forward her mama caught her up and swept her away. That made me feel lonely or, at least, too obviously on my own, so I studied my map – pointless as I liked being aimless – and set off again.

This time I found my way to a shabbier neighbourhood, no big buildings, a few small bars, a lot of dogs barking. Some of the houses were only one floor high, pressed closely to their neighbours. Often one dwelling leap-frogged on top of another and occasionally the windows were overhung with oleander or bougainvillaea. Sometimes the plants were like cords winding in and out of the bricks and indistinguishable from the wires and cables that tied up the buildings like parcels. The area was so poorly lit that I could hardly make out the colours except that occasionally the gleam of pink or yellow would strike out from the gloom.

On one street corner, where there was a lamp, I was surprised by two huge figures painted on a wall, a woman in a purple mini-dress, stepping up to a man with a smart suit and slicked-back hair. In his hand he flourished a handkerchief. As I stood trying to guess at its significance, a man passed rather too close to me and stopped. I pretended not to notice. I had no idea whether I was still in the 'safe' area, but there was no one else around and men don't stop without reason. I commended myself for not having brought my handbag. On the other hand, I thought, with the absurd calm one sometimes finds at such moments, it would be ironic to come so far to find K and be thwarted at the final stage by some untoward adventure.

I looked at the man out of the corner of my eye. He was small, young, hardly more than a boy. I took heart. We eyed each other.

'*Estas perdida?*'

I could understand that. No, I wasn't lost. 'No.'

'*Te llevo.*'

The sweep of his hand made it clear he wanted to be my guide. We were still several paces apart and there was something humble and unthreatening about his stance.

'*Galería?*' I asked impulsively. 'Pictures?' I outlined a frame with my hand.

'*Bien. Te llevo,*' he repeated, and began to walk away, looking over his shoulder to see if I was following. Again, he was giving me freedom and I felt reassured.

We proceeded in this way, him a few steps ahead, me following not too closely, over a considerable distance, long enough for me to wonder at the oddity of our situation and recall the story of Orpheus, in which he must not look round to his wife or she would be cast back to the Underworld.

My confidence in my guide was justified because he brought me out of the darkness into a wide, steep street where there was a church, a fine blue-painted villa, lights and people.

'*Aquí lo tiene. La Galería esta allí,*' he said, pointing at a narrow street opposite the villa. I could see an open door filled with brightness.

'*Gracias. Muchas gracias.*' I found money from the pouch at my waist and handed it to him. He was gone in a moment.

I hesitated. No one was going in or out of the bright door but the blue villa contained several loud-talking people of about my age. I went in and found myself in a modern cultural centre with an arcade of small shops, including a large bookshop and a dazzling array of lapis-lazuli and silver jewellery. The skeleton of the old building was still there, ribs of heavy wood, a grand old staircase and wide, bow-fronted windows. I could see a terrace, suspended invitingly over the same spacious sea and sky, the same spangled city as I'd seen from my earlier *mirador*.

I made my way to it and captured the last free table. A waiter brought me wine and olives. No one else took any notice of me. They drank beer and talked excitedly. I noticed when they ordered more that they didn't look at the waiter but barked out their commands. Clearly I was among Valparaiso's rich, even though, by English standards, everything was extremely cheap.

But even as I relaxed, I knew this was only a preparation for crossing the threshold of that bright doorway, its image, as in a fairy-tale, beckoning me onward.

The paintings swirled about me in a dizzying pattern of colour. So strong was the impact in that not very big room, entirely empty apart from me, that I looked for a chair to sit down. There was none. So I started along the walls, trying to separate one picture from another and understand what the painter intended. This cooler approach was contradicted by a wild question that beat up my emotions all over again: could K be the painter? It would be a crazy coincidence, of course, that I should be led to his exhibition, even that he would have one to coincide with my visit. Yet the fantastic nature of our intertwined lives made anything seem possible while, more prosaically, they had told me at the Hotel Weymouth, there were few painters round here. More important, I remembered how K had described the city on that dark night at Meadowlands. These were the paintings of a man who felt the same way.

Looking around, I could see no catalogue, nor could I decipher the signature on the canvases. After all, I didn't even know what initial or name he would use to sign them. I returned to the paintings. Although I hadn't yet experienced the *ascensores*, I had read about them in the guidebook and quickly recognised the dangerous elevations and breathtaking falls. The technique verged on abstract but the painter had managed to convey a physical reality so that the drama of the little cars, suspended in transit, gripped the viewer.

I studied each picture carefully. There were fifteen, not many for a show, each one about three feet by five, some horizontal, others vertical.

'*Demasiado tarde*, Señora.'

I had looked at the whole exhibition twice, when a loud male voice made me jump. I turned round and saw him standing in the doorway, a burly figure with curly black hair and an open-necked green shirt.

'I'm sorry?'

'You are English?'

'Yes.'

'Too late. I said it was too late, Señora. Today is the last day. Everything is sold.' He smiled cheerfully. His English was very good, although he spoke with Spanish cadences and accent.

'I'm lucky to have seen them, then. Even if I can't buy.' In fact I'd never considered a purchase so had scarcely noticed the red dots.

'You like them?' He came in further.

'Very much indeed. Do you have a catalogue? A list.'

'Alas, no. We did but they ran out, as you say, just like the paintings ran out to all the admirers. It is a big triumph for the painter.' He looked at me questioningly. 'Perhaps you're a friend of his. Perhaps that is why you visit so late.'

'No. Yes.' I became very flustered. 'The truth is, I don't know who the painter is.'

At this he laughed heartily. 'And I was imagining you as a long-lost daughter. He's a bit of a mystery, our painter. A ... How do you call it? A *hermitano*, no family, just a few friends. His success is all the more great for that. It is a true artistic success for your compatriot.'

I couldn't let him continue any longer. The clues seemed too apposite, the tension, as I waited for his name, almost unbearable.

'I'm sorry. I need ...' The blood had suddenly drained from my head, as if I might faint.

He was immediately concerned. 'You are unwell? Wait. Take my arm.'

To save myself from falling, I did take it. 'I'm sorry. I only arrived from England today. It's four in the morning my time. I ...'

Still he hadn't said the name and, now, deflected by my weakness, he hurried outside and returned in a second with a wooden chair, which he insisted I sat on. 'There, Señora, you will recover immediately. It is hot here. Shall I put it outside?'

I sat quietly for a moment while he hovered.

'No. Thank you. What's your name?' I asked eventually, cowardly or perverse. 'I am called Claudia. I'm staying at the Hotel Weymouth.'

'Claudia, that is Chilean. He pronounced it 'Cloudia'. I heard a distant echo from long ago but didn't try to identify it. 'You prefer B-and-B to the smart hotels at Vina, Claudia?'

'Yes. It is more sympathetic. And now I feel better, as you said, and must go back. You have been so kind.' I stood up. After all, it was enough. I had seen the paintings, I had given my name. If K was the artist, he would find me.

'Yes. No time for a beer? No. I am Pablo – after the poet. There are many of us. Tomorrow I shall be taking down the paintings. A sad task. They go where I may not see them.'

'I'm so glad I didn't come tomorrow.' I paused. I was already at the doorway. 'Will the painter, the artist, come tomorrow to help you?'

He looked surprised. 'No. Certainly not.' He put his hand on my shoulder. In England it would have been an intrusion: here, it was merely friendly. 'You want to meet him?'

'No!' I reacted sharply and then felt foolish. 'Maybe.'

'That is difficult. Not impossible. Or perhaps impossible. Come tomorrow. We will see.'

'Thank you.' I left then, almost laughing at myself in having made a sort of date to meet a man who might not be K. But I was quite certain that K was the painter, just as six months earlier I had known he was the man in the changing-hut.

I don't know how I got back to the hotel. It took a long time and I had to study my map several times but somehow I made it. Maybe it was the steep green roofs I saw gleaming by the light of a newly emerged moon.

I fell into bed and slept as if unconscious.

'Señora! Señora!' I was woken by someone calling and banging on my door. I looked at my watch. It was eleven o'clock in the morning. Still half asleep I got out of bed and opened the door.

'A letter.' The young man pronounced the word very carefully with a huge roll of the R.

I took the envelope. 'Thank you.'

'I wait.' Again the two words were given serious production, as if he'd just been taught them.

I shut the door and went back to the bed. Although it was so late in the morning little light came through the blind and I guessed the *neblina* was here again.

My room was painted white but beside the bed there was a small woven rug. Its strips of bright colour reminded me of last night's pictures. I sat and stared at it, long enough for one colour to bleed it another, while I found the courage to open the letter.

It was from Pablo. I should have known it was not from K because the 'Claudia' on the envelope wasn't in his handwriting.

'Senorita Claudia ...' So I was no longer 'Señora'. '... the painter would like to make your acquaintance. He will not be at my *galeria* but he invites you to visit him at ...' There followed an address, with no telephone number. 'The boy who have brought this letter will lead you there. He is Miguel.

With respectful greetings and good wishes, Pablo de Unamuno Gimenez.'

I reread the letter. The 'make your acquaintance' struck a surprising note if K was the painter, but could be explained by Pablo's written English, which echoed the formality of Spanish, or perhaps K had not wanted to reveal too much. It was strange, I thought, reading the letter once again, how he had been the impersonal 'K' during that summer and now he was 'the painter', an even more anonymous term.

I chose to wear a yellow dress with a pattern of crimson roses. I wore black hoop earrings and black sandals. At the last minute I wound about me the length of pale sari silk I'd bought on the beach in India. I smiled as I thought it was like a bridal veil. Miguel sprang to his feet when I emerged. He had been sitting on the steps outside the hotel. He was short and stocky, no more than twelve or thirteen.

'Coffee?' I asked, when we'd gone a few yards down the road. He looked at the hotel but I didn't want to go back so I shook my head. Clearly he had used up all his English. It was no good asking him how far we had to go or anything else, although I guessed it couldn't be a long walk or we'd be mounting one of the buses that hurtled past us as we turned a corner.

I had been right about the *neblina*. It covered the whole area in a great grey cloud of dank mist, which, perhaps luckily because the boy walked fast, brought down the temperature considerably.

We were moving upwards almost continually, often up flights of steep steps, but at the same time veering west, although it was hard to tell with all the twists and turns and I'd left behind the guidebook. My leg muscles, sore from the previous evening's climbing, began to ache continuously.

'Coffee?' Miguel pointed to a narrow entrance, set three steps below road level. I found myself in something more like a cave than a room but beyond was a small wooden deck. I stood outside, expecting the breathtaking view over the city and out to the bay, but the *neblina* made everything indistinct. A loud rumbling, seemingly under our feet, surprised me and for a moment I thought I was experiencing one of the city's famous earthquakes. Then a cable-car emerged hardly more than twenty yards away and rattled off down a track, hidden by overhanging buildings, wild grasses and shrubs.

I drank my coffee and tried to eat a sweet pink cake. I also tried, and failed, to pinpoint our position. Once again, I was in the hands of an unknown guide. I thought that truly I had travelled to the ends of the earth and, not just because of the coffee, my heart began to beat painfully hard.

CHAPTER FORTY-TWO

2005

I lay waiting for her arrival. I could have got up and dressed but I wanted her to see the worst. Besides, just as when I'd visited her in England, her imminent presence unmanned me. It was strange, perhaps, when you consider the opposite effect she'd had on me during that summer. She had turned me into a god. True or a retrospective exaggeration, I liked the idea. Love turns us as nearly into gods as is humanly possible.

Pablo had come to see me at nine, very early for him. All the time he was with me, a bird on or near my roof cawed repetitiously. Eventually, I said irritably, 'Send off that bird, would you?'

He looked surprised. Perhaps he thought I hadn't been giving enough attention to his unusual woman visitor. 'Like an archangel,' he told me, speaking in Spanish. 'So tall and straight, with flowing yellow hair and red cheeks, until she became overcome by fatigue when she had the sheen of mother-of-pearl.' Pablo was always a romantic, and over-excited by the success of my show in contrast to my gloomy situation. He wanted me to be rescued by a beautiful maiden, a modern reverse of the damsel-in-distress story.

Outside he beat off the cawing bird so energetically that a whole flock rose up. They shrieked and tittered before flying away.

'So, you want to see this Claudia.' His bulk filled the doorway. Her name was real enough, except that he pronounced it like a cloud. Around him the *neblina* swirled mysteriously.

I sighed to disguise my emotion. 'I don't need your help, Pablo.'

He didn't answer this. Ever since my exhibition had been in the planning, he had taken responsibility for my welfare. 'You are responsible for my paintings, not for me,' I had told him, to which he'd answered with a flourish, 'You are your paintings.' I hadn't told him about my illness but perhaps Craig did or Maria de la Luz. He had a nosy nature, but a kind one.

'So. Again. You see her. I will write. Miguel can take the letter. You agree, eh?'

I had agreed. Before I'd even had time to think what it meant, I'd agreed. So Pablo left me in peace, although not before assuring me that 'Your Claudia is *in love* with your paintings. It is a fine start.'

I knew there was no point in saying, 'She is *not* my Claudia.'

While I was waiting, I put on music. The rich strains of Brahms's third symphony compensated for the lack of paintings on my walls. Over the last months before my show, I had taken them from the floor and hung them round me, partly to see if I needed to make changes and partly as encouragement to my failing energies. Now I was back in my previous twilight world, proud, I must assume, at my sales success, but also bereft.

Music was some compensation. Craig had insisted on getting me a better machine and more CDs. When I had pointed out that, without batteries, it would blow my fragile electrical system in a matter of minutes, he'd brought over a dour character who'd pulled various wires out of the window and connected them into some unidentified source. Now I could listen to music day and night.

Between them, Pablo and Craig would have taken over my life. Craig had offered to whip me away to his vineyard behind Zapallar where I could be looked after by his housekeeper and maid. But I was forceful in defence of my independence. The only change I allowed was a daily visit from Maria de la Luz's eldest daughter, Rosa, who ran errands and brought food that, much to her distress, I usually failed to eat.

The waiting for Claudia lasted several hours. These days, I was used to inaction. At first I listened to the music. More often than not I played this third symphony, even though I risked crying during the third movement. Although it had been written a decade earlier, the wonderful melody reminded me, unmusical as I am, of the Brahms viola sonata that Claudia had practised over and over again.

When the CD finished, I got up – more like, staggered up – drank a glass of water, wrapped myself in a blanket and sat in my chair. Even in these hot summer days – the temperature regularly in the nineties – the morning *neblina* seeped its vaporous cool into my room. Soon it would dissolve and a shaft of hard brightness would thrust through the little window.

I wanted to speculate on why Claudia had come to Valpo and yet I knew it would be a mistake. Let her come. Let her see what I had become.

I began to picture the visitors this city had seen over the several hundred years of its existence. Until recently they had arrived by sea, sailing-ships before steam, those from Europe rounding the terrifying Cape Horn where icebergs float like maritime bulldozers. Valparaiso was the Promised Land, the deep harbour, the high protective mountains. For rank men who had spent months on board ship, crusted with sweat or frozen with chilblains and worse, used to the darkness of the hold or the glare of the deck, Valparaiso was a paradise of fresh water, fruit trees, cool glades, warm rich earth. No wonder earthquakes hadn't frightened them off and that they had thrown up a crazy town on an almost vertical slope. They were sailors, seafarers, come to rest, but not too securely. I remember visiting Neruda's home, more as if a ship had been flung up onto a rocky crag than a house, its five floors jutting out over the city, the top one where he worked like an eagle's nest.

Valpo would always carry the imprint of the brave, I thought, even if it had fallen on seedier, lacklustre days. When the *ascensores* were first built, they had carried a different clientele, people from around the world, from Britain, Germany, the Americas. I was just one in a long train of adventurers. Even the magnificent Admiral Cochrane had fled an England that had imprisoned him and denied him his rightful place in the navy. He had become an admiral in the Chilean, not the English navy.

But what about Claudia? She was coming to visit a man who was no more than a letter to her. K. I remembered that English summer's day when she'd asked for my name and I answered her: 'K'. Even then I'd known I wanted her to think me special. What conceit! After all, what is so wrong with plain 'Jack Smith'? If I'd had more energy I would have laughed. Maybe if I'd called myself by my real name she'd never have fallen in love with me. But, of course, I didn't believe that.

This waiting for Claudia was not such a bad experience, I decided. I got up and put on a different CD – this time Tchaikovsky's Pathétique, whose tone is set by the opening viola. I had played it through many times before I recognised the instrument and now I put it on in deference to Claudia.

During our stilted and bizarre exchange of information in England, she hadn't mentioned music. She was in charity work, overseas aid, she'd implied. Perhaps that was why she was here. Perhaps I shouldn't assume I was the sole reason. Would this upset me?

But this was the path of speculation I had decided not to tread.

The sun was right through my window when I heard steps approach my door. It might have been Maria de la Luz or her daughter, but I knew it was not.

I had got into bed again, and as I heard the knock, I felt, crazily, like the wolf being visited by Little Red Riding Hood. 'What big teeth you have, Grandma!' But it was only a moment of hysteria, and I calmed myself by looking at my dim, empty room. The music was no longer playing and the single shaft of sun lit only one corner. Sometimes when I was painting I'd lifted off sections of the corrugated-iron roof.

'Come in.'

Claudia stood nervously in the doorway. Backlit, her hair glowed like a halo. As she came in further, I saw she was wearing a yellow dress with crimson flowers. This was not a woman come with weeping or gnashing of teeth. Around her shoulders was a gleaming white shawl.

'You're in bed.'

I suppose I should have been more prepared for her surprise. 'Yes. I'm tired today.'

'Oh.' She stayed where she was, peering, blinking a little. My room must have seemed dark after the glare outside.

'Pull up that chair.' I didn't offer her a drink. I needed her to sit down, gather herself. She sat down, crossed her legs, uncrossed them. Her legs were very pale and she wore black sandals with an elaborate criss-cross of straps. With a sharp stab, I remembered how her long, slim feet had caught at my heart. I looked away.

'I'm tired,' she said. 'Miguel walked so fast and there are so many steps. Can I get a drink of water?'

'There's a bottle in the fridge. Through there.' I pointed.

She was up immediately. When she returned with the bottle and two glasses I saw that her hands were shaking. I declined a drink and she only sipped.

'I hope you don't mind me coming like this?' Her blue eyes gazed appealingly.

I was unused to blue eyes. I thought about the answer. I wanted to be truthful. 'You got my letter?' I asked.

'Oh, yes.' She paused. She had begun to twist her fingers in the shawl held now in her lap. She saw where I was looking. 'It was cool at first. With the *neblina*.'

The world '*neblina*' on her lips gave me another stab. She had crossed over into my world.

'Not any more.'

'No.' She hung the shawl on the back of the chair and leant forward intensely. 'I came because of your letter. But maybe I was wrong?'

Here she was asking again. So quickly we had reached the heart of the matter. But I was not ready. 'I'm glad you saw my paintings,' I said.

'Oh, yes!' She was fervent in her admiration. As she described what she'd understood by them, I watched her flushed cheeks and sincere eyes with increasing awe. How could she have so much generosity of spirit after all that had happened? I had come to her in England as a crazed beggar, an appellant, a penitent, but she was elevating me beyond any dream.

'I'm just a painter,' I said.

She was immediately subdued. 'Was I gushing?'

'I'm grateful for your praise. Success is new to me.' I considered telling her the important role she had played in my paintings. But it was so complicated and led to such tumbrils of despair. Perhaps later, or another time.

For a few minutes of silence we were stiff, almost strangers. 'I'll have some water now,' I said, to break the mood. She stood up and handed me a glass, and as she bent forward, I imagined her hair brushing my face. But it didn't, and she withdrew to the chair.

She was looking round the room. 'Have you lived here long?'

'Since the beginning, except for a little while at the Hotel Weymouth.'

'I'm staying there.' She seemed embarrassed by this, saying it as if it were a confession.

'That's all right by me.' I smiled. 'It's a friendly place. I still go there for a drink now and again.' I remembered the circumstances of the last time I'd been there, with Maria Eugenia. It seemed an age away.

'I only arrived yesterday and I went out wandering in the evening.'

'You've seen a bit of Valpo, then?'

'Yes. It's a bewildering place.'

We had become strangers again, tourists exchanging reactions. I lay back in the bed as she talked. That way I could watch her less obviously.

'Are you ill?' It was an abrupt question.

I could see she didn't want this to be the case. She had asked the question with a frown, not only of sympathy, I thought. I felt sorry for her. 'I have good days.'

'Yes. Or how could you have painted so many pictures?'

'I wanted to finish five more.' But she didn't take the hint. I began to tire of lying in bed, of putting a dampener on her hopefulness. It could be better than this. 'If I have a good day tomorrow, we could take a boat out into the bay.'

'I'd love that!'

Her enthusiasm was catching. I pictured us side by side in a motor-boat, with the great South Pacific surging under us and all around the huge grey battleships like moored whales. 'Are your family well?'

Her expression changed to that of a child contemplating the right answer to an examination question. 'Yes. Well, you know my father died.'

I was feeling more daring. I felt sure now that she had not come on a whim or for work. She had not even mentioned work. 'And Oliver? Your fiancé, is he well?'

She blushed deeply. The colour moved from her cheeks to her neck, then gradually faded. She put up a hand as if to shield herself from my gaze. 'We're not engaged any more. It wouldn't have worked.'

I relented. Why should I pretend? 'I know.'

'You know!'

I liked her capacity for astonishment. It was so youthful. But it made me feel old and mean. 'I have a spy here. Craig. He owns a wine business and travels often between Chile and England. He brings me gossip.'

'Gossip!'

'News, then. He was the reason I knew about your marriage. The reason I came to England last summer.'

She looked down, twisting her fingers now that the shawl was gone. 'It was like a dream. When you came. My father's death. My marriage. My non-marriage. I couldn't take everything in. It was too unexpected. Too sudden. I couldn't think properly. Then you wrote.'

'Yes.' The letter that had given me calm. 'I'd wanted to tell you that for fourteen years.'

'But you left.'

'Oh, yes. I left.' What did she mean? Of course I left. She had made a new life for herself. She had her fiancé, Oliver. I was merely putting the record straight, not intervening in her life. I am not a monster! We were both silent, turned away from each other by our separate thoughts.

'I suppose I shouldn't stay too long.'

I assumed it wasn't a question. She was going to walk away. With sudden greed, I checked out every part of her, her gentle expression, which couldn't hide the complicated pain of her thoughts, the long pale limbs, the cheery yellow and red of her dress. 'Will you come back?' It was an impulsive cry.

'Oh, yes.' She leant back in the chair and smiled in a much more relaxed manner. 'I don't have to go.'

'Go! Go! But come back tomorrow. At the same time. I'll be here.'

'Perhaps you'll have a good day and we'll take the boat.'

'Yes. Exactly!' I couldn't understand the impatience that had overtaken me. It might have been her beauty. I was resisting its spell. Beauty has such magic. Or perhaps it was my illness. I needed to shut my eyes – take my pills first, then shut my eyes. What did she want of me? What more could I give her that I hadn't written in my letter? Couldn't she understand that it was too late?

I must have shut my eyes for a moment because she was standing over me. An edge of sunlight flared down one side of her face and body. She bent to kiss my cheek. I held my breath and her hair stroked my skin. Neither of us spoke. I watched as she left.

Later, Rosa came and laid her hand on my forehead, fussing and clucking. She said she would get the doctor but I told her there was no point. She knew that well enough.

After I left K, I walked until I found the entrance to an *ascensor*. The car rattled downwards and I felt as if I were going through one of his paintings. Everything I did related to him, his presence so near, our date the next morning gearing me to a painful level of expectancy. And yet I was young, only thirty years old, with suddenly unfettered freedom ahead of me. I was thousands of miles from my home. I was both drawn tightly to K and vibrating with the thrill of new adventures. I felt as if there could not be one without the other. I had twenty hours ahead before I could see him again.

Food was number-one priority so I found an outside café in O'Higgins Square, not far from the harbour, and ordered tortilla. Everybody round me seemed to be eating ice-cream, glass bowls filled with blobs of strawberry, orange, lime and vanilla. The colours reminded me of the houses up the *cerros*, and at the same time I pictured the dim pallor of K's room in such contrast to everything else, including his own paintings. One side of me wanted to mull over our meeting, try to understand the nuance of his remarks or even the general thrust, if there had been one. Instead I allowed myself to live in the moment. When the tortilla came, I ate with gusto, then set off to walk round the harbour.

I stood on the quayside and stared out to sea. Far off on the horizon, hazy with heat, a white ship passed from north to south. I thought, We could be on that ship.

The moment she had gone, I began to look forward to her return. While Rosa bathed my face (quite unnecessary as I could do it myself but apparently 'Mamita' had insisted), I pictured Claudia's re-entry at the doorway, her position in the chair, the dress she might wear, her mouth, a little pinched as she thought of what to say.

All the self-control I had drawn on during her actual presence, leading even to a kind of sharpness and impatience, now fell away. In my reflections I could be as emotional as I liked.

'Go away,' I commanded Rosa. 'I need nothing. Nothing. You understand.'

'I know.' Of course she knew. Maria de la Luz knew. It was extraordinary that I had found such a group of good people to look after me or, rather, that they had found me. I was looking for nothing. I deserved nothing.

Much later that day Pablo came with Craig and the doctor. The two large men filled my room, their voices rustling like English autumn leaves.

The doctor was small and crouched over me with his fingers on my wrist. '*Me siento bien*,' I told him. It was true. I did feel good. But I could hear the weakness in my voice.

The doctor spoke softly to me in Spanish. 'Do not be rough. Pretend your head is a priceless vase on your shoulders.' He checked my tablets and left.

When Craig and Pablo followed, I noticed that both men were carrying packages under either arm. 'What have you there?' I asked. Even in the dusky light, I could see the guilt on their faces.

Pablo spoke in Spanish. 'It is your paintings. For safe-keeping.'

I felt confused. 'I sold my paintings.'

'Not these.' Craig spoke in English. 'The canvases you put in the kitchen cupboard.'

'Ah, those.' I lost interest then, except to think that the rustling had not been their voices but the paper as they bound them up.

'Are you asleep?' It was Pablo by the door.

'Not yet.' I could hear the curiosity in his voice. It made me smile. 'She came, Pablo, and she comes again tomorrow.'

'Good.' This was Craig, I thought, who knew the whole story, and yet he said 'good', '*bien*'. Sometimes now I didn't notice whether we spoke Spanish or English.

I had supper on the terrace at the Hotel Weymouth. I was tired after my long afternoon of walking round the city and beginning to be nervous about my meeting the next morning. When I saw Pablo's tall figure coming towards me, I felt grateful, almost ready to fall into his arms.

I had already finished my meal, but he said it was still too early for him and would only accept a beer. 'I wanted to see you were all right.'

'Oh, yes. I've had a fascinating day.'

He let me tell him about the naval museum, the Cochrane museum, the Anglican church, the *miradors* and *ascensores*, and everything else I'd seen to fill in the time, and then he asked, 'You saw the painter?'

'Oh, yes!' I couldn't tell him about that. 'Thank you. You were so kind. I'd never have found my way there without Miguel.'

'He's a good *chico*. You'd like him tomorrow?'

'Could he?' I realised that, absurdly, I'd been expecting Miguel's knock at my door.

'I will arrange it.' He looked at me – with expectation, I thought – but there was nothing more to say. 'Now I must leave you in peace.' He stood up and went quickly.

I sat on by myself. I preferred it outside to my stuffy room and I knew I wouldn't sleep anyway. The sky was dazzling with stars, and every few minutes, as if there were too many for it to contain, one broke away and flew down to where the ocean mirrored a second firmament.

Later again, I opened my eyes and saw Maria de la Luz sitting in my chair. Her short brown fingers made complicated patterns with a piece of crochet in her lap. I watched until she looked up. Tomorrow Claudia would sit there. Her fingers were long and white.

'Why are you here so late, Maria de la Luz?'

She got up and came close as if I wouldn't hear her from so far away. 'I like the peace. The night is clear. Tomorrow there will be no *neblina*.'

At dawn, she left, blessing herself or me. Perhaps she felt she'd defeated the demons of the night.

CHAPTER FORTY-THREE

2005

Rosa came, her fingers modest and gentle.

'Put on the music, Rosita,' I asked her. 'Today I'm going to have a good day.'

The sun had not yet come through the window, but I determined to dress myself and be prepared. Rosa helped me. In fact, it would be truer to say that I helped her. I held her arm and went across to my chair. My breathing rasped in my chest.

'I'll be back later,' she told me.

'You're a fine girl.' It struck me that she was probably just the age Claudia had been when I'd first met her. 'I'm going on the ocean today.'

'You've chosen a beautiful day. But the sun will be hot.'

I sat in my chair and waited.

He was playing music when I came in. I knew the piece, the Brahms third symphony. The beautiful third movement had just begun. He was sitting in the chair and the room seemed brighter than it had been the day before. Somehow the music, his being in the chair, the sunshine, made me realise how ill he was.

'Claudia! Come in. You see? I'm up and waiting for you.'

As I approached, I was acutely aware of the angular shape of his skull, the narrowness of his shoulders, the prominent bones of his back. He looked seventy or even eighty years old, his skin paper thin, beads of sweat on his forehead. I couldn't understand why I hadn't noticed it yesterday. I kissed his cheek. I wanted his music to stop. I had brought him a present of music. I put down a case

I carried with me.

'Where shall I sit?'

'Oh, anywhere!' He flapped his hand at non-existent chairs. So I sat on the bed, glad to be a little way distant while I digested my impressions. The room was much hotter than it had been the day before. He was excited, even a little feverish, judging by the red points on his cheeks, and the music was a distraction.

'I play this music for you,' he said. 'But perhaps music is no longer important in your life.' I saw how even talking was an effort for him.

I wanted to cry but my corner was not dark enough for that. 'I gave it up after that summer.' It came out more baldly than I'd intended. 'But I've brought you a present.'

Ignoring this, he exclaimed, 'You gave up your viola? Altogether?' He was shocked, and I guessed it would be another mark to chalk against himself. I had travelled to Chile with the intention of talking about everything that had happened since that summer morning fourteen years ago. Yet I was silent. I guessed why Pablo had come to me the evening before: he had wanted to gauge my reaction to K's condition but I hadn't noticed it – or, at least, not taken it in.

I wanted to know what was wrong but I couldn't make myself ask him.

'It's much hotter today,' I said.

'So they say.' He was having difficulty seeing me in my grey corner. 'You shouldn't have given up playing. A talent is important.'

'Maybe I'll start again.' I took a cushion from the bed and came and sat on the floor near to him. Maybe we would talk after all. 'So much has changed recently. Is still changing.'

'I can't believe how young you are.' He leant forward and reached out a hand to me. It was so thin that I could see the veins shine blue-red. 'I didn't love you because you were young, you know, but because you were you.'

'You told me that in your letter.' I was keen to calm his agitation. I crouched there at his feet, I did feel very young, an acolyte to the decrepitude of his age. I was wearing the same dress as the day before – nothing else had seemed so sun-filled and appropriate – but now the yellow and red struck me as garish, almost a mockery.

Above my head, K was talking urgently. His breathing was nearly as loud as the words. Occasionally he broke into Spanish. I had shifted to an angle so that I saw his face only with difficulty. My sense of the true nature of the situation was growing.

'Surely you have another chair!' I burst out. I would never give him my present now.

He blinked as I stood up. I was hot and my dress clung to me at the back.

'A chair? I'm so sorry.' He pushed himself up with difficulty, holding on to the arms of the chair. 'You sit here. I'll lie on the bed.'

As he walked, or rather hobbled, head down across the room, I remembered, ironically, yesterday's suggestion of 'a good day' and a joyful boat trip on the ocean waves. Yesterday afternoon, after I'd seen him, I'd stood on the edge of the harbour and watched other couples embarking and imagined how it would be for us, arm in arm, under the blue sky.

Overcome by anger, I jerked the chair forward with savage violence so that it screeched along the bare boards. K turned in the process of lowering himself onto the bed and the expression on his face, humble, but also hopeful and loving, enraged me further. How dare he? How dare he be ill? I could have stamped my feet like a child. Had it all come to this?

He must have seen my expression – I was certainly in no mood to hide it – but he said nothing and got on with the arduous process of arranging his long bones on the bed. I could see he needed the cushion that I'd put on the floor for behind his head, so I spitefully put it on the chair and sat down.

There was a silence. The music must have stopped earlier, although I hadn't been aware of it. I laced my hot fingers together and felt the engine of fury heat me even more.

'You're angry.'

I refused to look at him. From his voice I knew the sadness I would see in his face. But what else had he expected? Was I supposed to fall to my knees and pray for his soul? Or maybe turn myself into a nurse and wring out cool cloths for his fevered brow? 'Of course I'm angry! I'm angry with you for being ill, with me for expecting happiness, with Pablo for leading me to you, with Valparaiso for taking you from me, with the *neblina* for not being here to disguise my humiliation–' I stopped abruptly. Why should I feel humiliated?

'I see.' K leant forward just a little. 'If I were you, I'd go, walk out now, while you're strong and angry. There's nothing to keep you here, no future, just a tragic past. I won't blame you or even be particularly unhappy. Please go, I beg you.'

He was calm, his voice quite firm, even though hoarse. But I was in raging confusion. I jumped off the chair and began to harangue him, my own voice shrill and ugly, sweat pouring off my face. I wagged my finger and tore my hair and tears of self-pity joined the sweat. I would have shaken him if I hadn't felt disgusted by his lack of flesh.

'Do you need help?' I became aware of another presence, the room lighter with the door open.

'No! No! I'm leaving!' I swung my bag onto my shoulder and ran past a tall man, not Pablo, barging into him in my clumsy fury. Then I was outside in the noise and heat and glare.

Craig sat where Claudia had been a moment before. I hid my shaking hands under the coverlet. I felt my mouth, fish-like, gasping for air.

'I guess she didn't like what she saw,' I whispered, trying to smile.

'No.' Craig frowned. 'It must have been a shock.'

'So I would assume.' But, of course, I hadn't assumed it.

'Not good.'

'No. Would you get me water?' I needed a moment on my own. I had told her to go while she had the strength. Now I needed to find some. I closed my eyes.

Craig came back with a glass. He picked up the cushion and put it behind my head. 'Has she gone for good, do you think?'

'There's nothing to keep her here. I told her that.' I managed to keep my voice steady, although it was hardly more than a whisper. I remembered that she had mentioned a present and wondered for a moment.

'I see.' Craig shifted uncomfortably. 'I can't stay. I've a lunchtime meeting with the chairman of a consortium of Californian wine-growers.'

'You certainly can't stay.' I forced my lips into another smile. It would do no good for Craig to understand my feelings. 'Rosa will be in soon.'

'Good. Good.' He stood up but still hovered uneasily. 'Americans eat lunch before Chileans have finished breakfast.'

I gave him a task to help him on his way. 'Put on the Brahms, would you?'

He turned up the music higher than I usually played it. The still room swelled with rich chords and innocent melodies. Gradually they drowned the sounds of Claudia's fury. How extraordinary it was that she had carried such powerful seeds of expectation all these years – after what had happened. Perhaps that was a sign of her youth, with youth's greater powers of recovery. She was still young. She still loved me. Oh, how she loved me. Now she thought she hated me.

Yesterday I had tried to believe we could talk finally. But I understood now that our situations were too unequal. It was love or nothing. With the help of the music, I would replace today's screaming prosecutor with yesterday's gentle visitor, sitting demurely in her pretty flower-patterned dress. I closed my eyes.

But instead of an image of loving constancy, the black heat of my mind's eye watched the crimson flowers leak outwards and turn into bloodstains. The blood had run everywhere, like a terrible growth across her pale skin and blue swimsuit. Desperate to banish this spectre and the even more terrible one that lay on the stained grass under the red drape, I pulled myself out of bed and stood, trembling, in the middle of the room. Cymbals clanged inside my head. I raised my hands pleadingly.

Rosa came later and found me fallen on the floor. She put me back into bed and told me I was not to stir again. There was no possibility of that. Darkness came. The blood filled my head now. I knew that. I listened with resignation to the barking of dogs, the other night sounds, and gradually my exhausted mind rewarded me with an image of Claudia wandering barefoot under the chestnuts at Meadowlands.

I did something I'd never even dreamt of before: I picked up a young man and invited him back to the Hotel Weymouth. I offered him a glass of wine but I meant something else. I was crazy with disappointment, hatred and self-loathing.

Alberto, as he was called, was hardly more than a boy and very nervous. He kept glancing over his shoulder as we walked. Once he put his arm round my waist, and a moment or two later dropped it again. Neither of us tried to speak.

Despite the scorching heat – it must have been early afternoon – I walked very fast, climbing long runs of steps so that my thigh muscles cramped painfully. By the time, we reached the hotel, I was soaking wet and the thought of lying with another hot, sweaty body was unbearable. I gave him money and sent him away. But even that felt like failure. Exhausted, I dropped on to my bed. I was still too angry to cry.

Maria de la Luz was sitting in the chair when I next surfaced. I wondered if I should regret writing that letter to Claudia. It was what had brought her to me. But I hadn't written it with that aim. Not at all. What if I'd written 'I am dying…?'

'*Qué*, Senor?'

I must have spoken aloud. '*Nada*, Maria.'

'*Sopa*, Senor?' She stood up and bent over me, straightening the pillows.

'*Más tarde*, Maria.'

She went back to her seat again. Some time later, the doctor came. He talked to me of the likely effect of my fall, of hospital, oxygen masks, drips and intensive care. Of alleviating the pain. But that was impossible. I turned my face to the wall. I'd lived long enough.

CHAPTER FORTY-FOUR

2005

The dawn was soft.

The dawn was soft.

I was glad of the *neblina*.

I reached out my hands to the *neblina*. A stranger bent over me and, murmuring words I couldn't understand, rubbed oil on my forehead and on my chest. I guessed there were more people in the room – I thought I heard Claudia's voice – but the *neblina* dimmed my sight.

I reached out my hands to the *neblina*.

I knew the way now. In the grey light I went slowly, hardly daring to arrive, knowing I would have to say goodbye. I had showered and dressed in a daze, putting on that same yellow and crimson dress even though it was soiled. I don't know why I did that.

There were a lot of people on the streets, although it was so early, but they might as well have been ghosts.

I paused for a moment at the wall painting showing the woman in a purple mini-dress and the man with a white handkerchief. Now its meaning seemed clear to me. He was waving goodbye.

As I neared his door, a woman came out and a man, a priest. The woman stopped and said something in Spanish to the priest. He approached me with his hand raised. He was several inches smaller than me, quite young and stocky. I understood he wanted to give me a blessing so I bent down. He laid his hand on my head and said a few words, then they stood aside to let me through.

I never did say goodbye, or tell him I loved him. He was still lying in the bed when I entered the room but I could see he had gone. I went and crouched beside him. I took the hand nearest to me. It was not quite cool yet, and still supple. I held it to my cheek. Then I laid it down gently and pressed my lips against his forehead.

The shame of my behaviour last time I had been with him burnt briefly. But only briefly. At last I was able to cry. I had lost him once before for fourteen years but this was for ever. I had been right to be angry. He would have understood that. We had waited so long for each other but in the end he had given up.

I stayed beside K until the *neblina* had dispersed and the room was illuminated by a wide sunbeam. I had been aware at various times of people behind me but no one had disturbed me.

When I eventually stood up, I was so stiff that I would have fallen if Pablo hadn't taken my arm. The second time he'd supported me. The first time K had been still alive. The tall Englishman I'd knocked out of my way the previous morning was also there.

'Thank you.' My face was stiff, too, with dried tears. I went to the kitchen and sluiced water over my face and neck.

There were more people in the room when I returned. Two women bent over the bed with white cloths and a bowl. I knew what I had to do. Nothing is ever too late, I told myself.

I found my bag and took out my viola case. This was the present I had brought for him the day before. Now I played for his soul, the Brahms melody I had practised every day of our summer together. The people in the dark room carried on with what they were doing as if a strange Englishwoman playing a viola in the presence of a dead man was the most natural thing in the world.

I had been practising and I could hear the notes as smooth and beautiful as they had ever been. The sound was loud in the confined space but I liked that. The air of sadness was replaced for a time with the warmth of music. When I had finished I put away the viola carefully and turned to find the faces looking at me now. I tried to smile but that was a foolish idea.

'I think I'll go.' I put my hand to my head and then to my heart. 'I wanted. I wanted.'

The Englishman stepped forward. 'I'm Craig, a friend of Jack's. Would you like me to come with you?'

I stared at his sympathetic face. 'Jack?' Although I knew it was K's name, I'd never heard anyone use it. 'I'll be all right.'

'No. Please.'

So he walked beside me and I thought that if I'd addressed that fatal letter to Mr Jack Smith instead of to 'K', Fiona would never have opened it and maybe, things would have been less terrible.

But it was only a passing thought.

'He found success here?' I wanted to hear it confirmed

'Oh, yes. Sadly, only near the end.'

'You heard me screaming at him yesterday?'

'Yes.'

'You must have been very shocked. Someone screaming at a dying man.'

'Perhaps you didn't know.'

'It was the reason I was screaming.'

'Ah, well, then.'

'I had planned to play for him.'

He said nothing to that. We stood outside the gates of the Hotel Weymouth.

'I loved him so much.' We stared at each other. 'He didn't have to die.'

'He thought he did.'

'Even when I came to him.'

'It was too late. Sorry.' He put out a hand to me. 'I don't mean you failed. It was too late for him.'

I became aware of the sun beating hard on my face and head. 'Yes. We both waited too long.'

He didn't say anything and in his silence I read the knowledge of the horror that had kept us apart. And I thought that perhaps fourteen years was not too long after all.

CHAPTER FORTY-FIVE

1990

They were all so close: K holding Claudia, Catherine just behind
and Fiona facing them with the gun. Her wild eyes were half closed,
the barrel of the gun awkwardly held and flailing in the air. K leant
forward to snatch it, to grab the butt and pull it away, but Claudia
hampered him, still trying to dash at Fiona. The noise in K's ears
was terrifying: Claudia's screaming shrill and continuous, Catherine
shouting and sobbing, Fiona grimly determined, hissing and growl-
ing.

Suddenly Fiona had more control of the gun and was lunging
forward as if she planned to use it on Claudia like a bayonet. 'Get
her away!' screamed Catherine.

Still clinging to the struggling Claudia, K managed to reach round
her with one arm and push away the muzzle of the gun. In that split
second he had a premonition of a far worse disaster about to take
place for which he would be responsible. But it was too late. He had
made his choice.

The explosion silenced everything, even the echoing after-waves
flew silently to the sky. K that he had let go of Claudia after all
because he saw her staggering backwards. She had turned into a
fountain of blood. Blood ran from her face, poured down her bare
chest, over her neck and shoulders, painted red her torso and arms.

Catherine sank down to the grass. Her mouth gaped and her
hands flapped. With a supreme effort of will, K managed to move
just enough to catch Claudia as she fell. Her weight caused him to
reel and nearly fall with her. He saw that he, too, was covered with
blood. Gently, he laid Claudia on the grass. Then he looked and saw
what lay beyond.

With Catherine and Claudia strewn across the grass and Douglas still crouched in his own private pain, it was K alone who understood what had happened. Fiona, or the part that remained of Fiona, stained the grass far redder than Claudia. Claudia was uninjured. It was Fiona's spurting blood that covered her.

Leaving Claudia, K dared to approach his wife. The sight was so macabre and ghastly that his one wish was to hide it from the world. Forcing his trembling legs into action, he ran to where Claudia had dropped the red towel, and brought it over to Fiona. He laid it over her carefully but it was impossible to hide all the horror because the towel wouldn't spread far enough.

'She did it to herself?' Catherine had recovered and was standing above him. 'I thought ...'

'Yes.' K stood up. They both looked over to where Claudia lay quite still on the grass.

'I think she's fainted.'

'It's better like that.'

Catherine went to her daughter.

K sat where he was. He waited for the police to come, for ambulances, for retribution. He thought of shooting himself but didn't know how. Fiona's death was entirely due to his behaviour and nothing could ever change that. She had trusted him with her happiness. She had believed in him and his promises. She had loved him and he had destroyed her.

But even this was cast into shadow by the worst guilt of all. In the split second he had turned the muzzle from Claudia to Fiona, he had *felt* the cartridge in the gun. Yet he could not regret his action. Claudia lived. There was nothing for him now but to sit there, waiting.

Waiting.

AFTERWORD

2005

Jack, my friend, was buried on a steep hillside, following a Catholic mass. The sky was clear blue and the sun blazed down. There was a surprising number of people, considering, as Pablo often said, that Jack had lived almost as a *hermitano*. They were an unhomogeneous crowd, worn-looking women in black mantillas, perhaps parishioners who liked a good funeral, including, of course, the good Maria de la Luz, and her daughter Rosa, who'd cared for him. There was a tall man with the bruised face of a criminal who, I think, had come from the prison on the hill, plus a fearsome-looking hunchback and a couple of transvestites. Pablo, who'd done most of the organising, was there with his son, Miguel. Gill and Chris, the English owners of the Hotel Weymouth, hovered on the outskirts. There were others, well-dressed men and women in suits and ties or black linen dresses, whom I had seen at Pablo's gallery, presumably those new admirers who'd bought Jack's paintings. Among them was the elegant Maria Eugenia with whom Pablo swore Jack had had some sort of last fling.

The sun was so hot that some of the mourners carried black umbrellas over their heads, a picturesque parade across the *cerro*.

After we had dispersed, I offered to drive Claudia back to the hotel. I couldn't help feeling protective of her as I had of Jack. I expect I was curious, too. It was a sudden ending for someone who had travelled so far. She thanked me gratefully, and as soon as we got into my car, I guessed she had questions too. 'Why the mass, Craig?'

I understood that she was asking the easy things first. And it was easy to answer. 'He was a benefactor of the local church.'

'I like that. A man who does good. Bene-factor.' She pronounced the word slowly with a break in the middle. 'That's a fine epitaph.'

I told her that the priest couldn't believe his luck. From a non-Catholic. A non-believer. 'I think he decided Jack was a closet Catholic. Hence the mass.'

'But he wasn't?' It was a humble question, admitting how little she knew about him.

The car was air-conditioned and draughts of ice-cold air dried the sweat on our faces. 'Not as far as I knew. He just wanted to give his money away. It was after he came back from visiting you in England.'

I waited for another question but she fell silent then until we arrived at the hotel.

I suggested we order a sandwich and a drink on the terrace, and she accepted quickly. It was quite full, but we found a table in the far corner so that instead of seeing our neighbours we looked down on to O'Higgins Square and the broad blue ocean beyond. The she asked another question: 'Did K know he was dying when he came to England?'

I looked at her carefully. 'He had tests in London. Obviously he'd suspected something was wrong. They found he had a brain tumour.'

'A brain tumour!' Shocked, she repeated the words as if trying to understand their importance. 'Could he have been saved? I mean if he'd had treatment.'

'He didn't want it. We tried. The doctor tried. He wouldn't even go to hospital. He said he'd been told it was inoperable. But none of us knew the truth.' I saw no reason to add that the immediate cause of his death had been internal bleeding from the fall he'd had after her visit.

'I see.' Our sandwiches came. Heavy bread filled with spicy sausage. I could see her distaste. She pushed away her plate. Sweat was glistening on her face again. She was dressed in black, heavy clothes, possibly worn on her journey from an English winter. Her long pale hair was drawn back tightly from her face. She wore no makeup. It's funny how one imagines that the heroine of a great tragic love story should be beautiful. She was nice-looking, nothing more. The sort of middle-class young woman you could meet all over the English home counties.

I asked if she wanted to go inside out of the sun.

'No. I'd rather be too hot.' She found a tissue in her bag and wiped her forehead. I guessed she preferred to talk out here in the open.

There was no way she could know how I had been affected by their story. From the first reports of Fiona's macabre death, I had followed the case in the papers and when, by sheer chance, I had come across Jack's place of refuge, I had felt linked to him by a deep sympathy. I suppose it was because, all those years ago in England when we had met occasionally in a pub or at a party, I had noticed how mismatched they were. Fiona had tried to confine him – that was the crux of it, I think. She wanted him too much.

Claudia began to speak again, her eyes fixed on the horizon: 'K sent me a letter when he was in England. He told me he had always loved me, that he had thought of me every day for fourteen years but that he had done something unforgivable that put him beyond human reach.'

I put down my sandwich. 'I don't quite understand. Of course he blamed himself for his wife's suicide. That was a dreadful weight to bear. But I can still remember reports of the inquest. Her action was blamed on a hormonal imbalance or something similar, following her miscarriage, and she'd just been told that she had cancer and shouldn't risk children. There were plenty of reasons for her to commit suicide. There was never the slightest question of anything else. Even the cruellest reports didn't insinuate anything more.'

As I spoke I regretted this mention of 'cruellest reports'. The viciousness of the newspapers, with photographs of Jack looking like a salacious old Lothario and Claudia about ten, had helped to put me on their side.

She brushed aside my remark: 'Yes. I was hardly sane at the time,' she leant forward and fixed me with her intensely blue eyes. They were her best feature. 'K wrote something else in his letter.' She paused.

I had got over the strangeness of her referring to Jack as K. She always pronounced it quite naturally as if that really were his name. 'What did he write?'

'He wrote that he had turned the gun towards his wife so that I should be safe. He wrote that he suddenly sensed there was a cartridge in it. He believed he'd murdered her.'

I could hear her voice trembling at these terrible words. I wanted to cry, 'No! No! Enough! The man is dead now.

But she was remorseless. 'When I first read the letter, I took it as proof of the depth of his love for me and avoided considering his feelings beyond that. Now I understand the effect the conviction of his guilt had on him.' She looked at me expectantly.

Jack had condemned himself but that didn't mean he was right to do so. I wanted to defend him. 'She pulled the trigger, didn't she?' I said confidently, as if it were a simple matter. I wanted to say, 'None of this is important. You loved each other. Let that be enough.

'I don't know. He didn't say. I expect so.'

'Then either she wanted to kill you or she wanted to kill herself.'

'Or it went off accidentally. Or he pulled the trigger. But I'll never believe that.'

What pointless dialogue. Like a mockery of a court case. I thought of telling her why I had never married. Each new girlfriend had had to inspire the kind of love Jack had felt for Claudia. None of them did. None came near it.

'There should never have been a cartridge in the gun,' I said. 'If anyone was guilty of murder, it was your gardener.' I even knew his name: Alan. I didn't call him that, though, not wanting her to know how closely I'd followed the case. She didn't know either that it was I who had sent Jack back to her. It was I who had brought them together again.

'What will you do now?' I asked gently.

'Stay here for a bit.' She stared down at the table, quite calm again. 'I need a little peace.' She looked up at me. 'I'd like to tidy up his things, if I may.'

'Of course.'

'Spend time where he lived for so many years. Where he learnt to love this city. Where he learnt to paint. I used to wonder where he was so very often…' She didn't finish the sentence.

There was a long pause before she spoke again, this time with more passion: 'He wanted to die, didn't he? That's the truth.'

'Yes. I believe he did.' I looked at her questioningly.

'I understand now that it didn't mean he'd stopped loving me. I regret my outburst in his room, of course, but he would have known it was a declaration of love. I regret that we never talked seriously. But we never had, so why should we start now? We just fell in love.'

She stopped and I saw, to my surprise, that she was smiling slightly.

After another brief pause while the waiter took away our uneaten sandwiches, crisped and sweating with the sun, I couldn't resist a further question: 'What about the future? You'll go back to your fiancé?'

'Oh, no!' She stared at me as if suddenly doubting my intelligence. 'Oliver and I were passing boats in the night.' Perhaps I was looking anxious because she added, 'Don't worry, Craig. I do have a future.'

'I'm glad. You deserve it.' She had served a long sentence, yet she was still young. 'Jack wouldn't have wanted you to despair.'

'No. I won't do that.' She smiled again, this time with a breathtaking transparency as if she looked back to past love and forward to future hope. I had been wrong. She was beautiful.

ACKNOWLEDGEMENTS

With thanks to Sebastián Gaete, my son-in-law, and to his Chilean family, for introducing me to their country. To Bruce Hunter, my agent, for keeping faith as always. To my editor, Jane Wood, without whom this book wouldn't exist. To Hazel Orme, my beady-eyed sub-editor, to Belinda Wingfield Digby who nobly typed the manuscript from my hand-writing, and to Sara O'Keeffe who untangled endless annotated drafts. To Dr Simon Cave for more advice on medical matters. To Charlotte Johnson Wahl, an encouraging and discriminating early reader. To all my family, particularly Rose and Chloe, also highly-tuned early readers. And finally, to my husband, Kevin, who has seen me through seventeen novels since I read aloud the first as we sat under a tree in Dorset.

October 2005